CONTRIBUTE

First Edition
First Printing, 2017

Book design by Christopher Loke
Cover design by Christopher Loke
Cover images by DezzShah/Pixabay; Foundry/Pixabay; Unsplash/Pixabay

Jolly Fish Press, an imprint of North Star Editions, Inc.

Library of Congress Cataloging-in-Publication Data (Pending)
ISBN 978-1-63163-098-9

Jolly Fish Press
North Star Editions, Inc.
2297 Waters Drive
Mendota Heights, MN 55120
www.jollyfishpress.com

Printed in the United States of America

For the fans of CONSIDER

CONTRIBUTE

THE HOLO SERIES
Book Two

KRISTY ACEVEDO

JOLLY
FiSH
PRESS
Mendota Heights, Minnesota

PART 1

"If you want to find the secrets of the universe,
think in terms of energy, frequency
and vibration."
—*Nikola Tesla*

CHAPTER 1
DAY 1

THE HOLOGRAMS SHOULD'VE warned us to take a deep breath. Close our eyes. Then again, the holograms should've done a lot of things. Like told the truth.

Traveling through a vertex is like being dragged underwater through blinding ice. The mask of the universe suffocates me, ignoring that I'm a human being who needs oxygen and heat to survive.

I have one thought as I'm pulled through a blanket of frozen light:

This. Is. Death.

My body fights with my mind as my muscles and lungs scream, *Go back. Please, please go back.*

But I can't go back. I made my choice.

I chose friends.

I chose truth.

I chose death.

BEFORE MY CHEST explodes, before my anxiety has time to kick into overdrive, I am pushed through the vertex onto my hands and knees. Blinded by harsh magenta light, I gasp for air, my chest filling and collapsing with each deep breath.

I am still alive.

I am still alive.

My heartbeat pounds behind my eardrums, reverberating inside my skull and blocking out all other sound. Despite the utter disorientation, my mind dizzy with the lack of oxygen, I scan the surroundings for any sign of attack as the purple-pink glow around me fades in intensity.

I am in a huge, windowless space that resembles a concrete warehouse the size of Dad's grocery store before the looters on Earth burnt it down. Before my world fell apart. Up ahead, hordes of people from Earth who made it through before the comet disintegrated wait in lines for their turn to enter through unmarked passageways. Holograms identical to the ones that betrayed us stand guard. It reminds me of a massive airport security checkpoint. Destination unknown.

I glance behind me at the empty white space. The metallic blue vertex I traveled through from Massachusetts disappears in the fading magenta light. I have no passage back to my world. *To my parents.*

I gulp air, slowly grasping what I have done, what I have lost. The room spins as my body begins to sweat. *No, no, don't think about it now. Don't fall apart. You can't fall apart. Stay pissed off. Think about the others. They need to know the truth. They need to know it was a colossal trap.*

One of the androgynous holograms steps forward and hovers over me. I squint as ambient light filters through its gray uniform.

"Hello. Please state your full name and age."

If only the hologram had balls, I'd punch them into its throat. I find my footing and stand. I open my mouth ready to answer, *Alexandra Lucas, age eighteen.* On second thought, if they can lie, so can I. The less I reveal, the better. Knowledge is power, after all. The first two names that come to mind are from *Doctor Who* and *Star Trek.*

"River . . . er . . . River Picard. Eighteen."

The hologram gestures forward with its arm. "Welcome to 2359, River Picard. Please wait in line to join our world." It bows and adds, "May your contribution lead to freedom."

More politeness. A cover for world domination.

As I join the last of the people in line, I watch families and friends hug, relief and gratitude spilling from their naive, worried faces. All oblivious, scared, grateful victims. I bite my tongue to keep from screaming, *Run! Fight! It's all a cosmic scam!* Looking at the holographic guards, I know it's not the time. I need to pretend that I don't know the comet was a fake until I uncover why humans from the future sent holograms to trap us here. I need to understand their motive to know my next move. I need to wait. I need to find my friends first.

Waiting is the absolute worst.

Standing last in a crowd of loud lines, I examine myself to see if my clothes are ruined, my skin shrunken or decayed, my hair burnt off. Same fleece-lined hooded coat, short black boots, jeans. My curly, long hair not singed away. The silver heart ring from Dominick and the charm bracelet from Rita, reminders of my 18th birthday only months ago. My fingernails painted with the color Meet Me on the Star Ferry, chipped by me peeling them as usual. When I chose that color, I imagined reuniting with Dominick on another planet, that it would be romantic even if the Earth had been destroyed in an apocalypse. How sick is that?

My backpack still sits on my shoulders, heavy but intact. The only pieces of my life on Earth carried on my back. Everything I've ever known feels deleted. I'm a conch without a real shell. Vulnerable to the elements. Vulnerable to everything.

Focus. Embrace the rage. I blink away the gathering tears and wear anger as armor. A reminder. An ally. If I survived the vertex, then the others probably did, too. Dominick. Rita. My brother,

Benji, and his new husband, Marcus. Penelope, my grandmother. And everyone else who left before me. I need to find them. They don't know what really happened, and I need to warn them before it's too late.

A sinking feeling in my gut tells me it already is.

At the front of each line, a hologram waves the next person forward into a tall, enclosed rectangular black structure. After a few seconds, the person exits in a daze and enters an adjacent room. I stuff my hands in my pockets like Dominick does when he's nervous, hoping to stop the shaking. *That's where the cloning happens, I bet.*

A white-haired woman wearing purple glasses and a teenager with acne scars and slight facial hair on his chin abandon their spot in line and walk toward me.

"Excuse me, young lady," the older woman says. "Were you the last one through the vertex in Quincy, Massachusetts?"

The noise around us dims. All heads turn from the back of the lines, waiting for my response as if I hold the secret to Area 51.

My voice sticks in my throat. "I think so."

Faces contort with mixed emotions. People cover their mouths in a collective gasp, and the echoing word "no" floats through the room.

I change my answer. "Maybe not."

"We're looking for my daughter." The older woman's voice wavers, and her hands begin to shake. "She's a police officer. Said she'd be right behind us."

The teen turns his back on us, but I see his shoulders tremble with grief. I think I just inadvertently delivered the news that his mother is dead, lost in the catastrophic comet collision with Earth. The one that never happened.

Before I respond, another woman around my mother's age with an infant balanced on her hip steps forward, full panic in her bulging eyes. "Did you see my husband? Tall, dark hair, chubby, with a big tattoo of an owl on his neck?"

They look to me for answers. I should tell them they're all okay. The Earth is fine. We're the ones who are screwed. But I don't know what's really going on, and letting out the truth too soon might give these future humans ammunition. *What if they kill us all here and now, and the rest of the population stays trapped in ignorance?*

"I'm not sure," I stall. The truth bubbles and burns inside of me like lava in a volcano that's not allowed to erupt.

"Thank you," says the older woman with the purple glasses, tearing up at the last moment. She turns to her grandson. "We'll be okay, Nolan. We have each other."

He throws a black hood over his head to hide his face.

The wife with the missing tattooed husband hugs her baby to her shoulder, caressing its wobbly head. Her chin trembles uncontrollably. She returns to her spot in line but keeps staring back at the area where the vertex disappeared, probably hoping by some miracle another one opens and her husband runs to find her.

I clamp an invisible vice on my tongue while my heart screams to tell them. Staying silent transforms the truth into something far worse. Like the enemy has inserted its secret inside of me, and I am forced to carry it for them.

Time passes as people grieve the loss of loved ones who didn't make it through a vertex. I was the proverbial nail in the coffin, the period on the sentence. I witness and absorb their pain. This is what the future humans did to us. *I need to remember. Always remember.*

A hologram waves Nolan and his grandmother forward one at a time into the rectangular black box. I see him pull his hand away from his grandmother, and she covers her mouth and finally breaks down.

One by one they disappear into the next room after they leave the box. If I could plug my body into a socket, the energy running through my veins could probably light New York City.

Soon, all that's left in line is me and one bald, bearded man with dark skin and a nice suit. The last two people waiting for the universe to chew them up and spit them out.

He glances over his shoulder at me. "Tough situation in line. Being the last one saved. You handled it well."

That's the most ironic statement a stranger has ever said to me. *I don't handle anything well.*

"Whole thing is surreal, isn't it?" he says.

I nod. Holding up a heavy lie makes small talk impossible. I'm like Atlas from the Greek myth, carrying the fate of people on my shoulders. Except I'm only a mortal, liable to meltdown and collapse.

He sticks out his right hand and loosens his tie with his left. "Dr. Aiyegbeni, Boston Children's Hospital. My patients call me Doctor A."

I shake his hand. "River Picard. High school senior."

"Waited until the last minute, too, huh? Thank god we got through. Shows something about us. We don't give up easily."

I pick at my nail polish and shrug.

"Or we were in complete denial about leaving." He strokes his salt-and-pepper beard and laughs with a deep chuckle that shakes his upper body. "Are you meeting family here?"

"Yeah." Hot regret builds with each ticking moment. "You?"

"No, I dedicated my life to medicine instead." His shoulders shift in his suit, and I sense regret. "Thank god we made it through."

I rip off a chunk of polish from my thumbnail.

The hologram at the front of our line waves Doctor A. forward. "Say *PSF OPEN*," it commands.

Doctor A. straightens his suit. "Nice to meet you, River. Good luck here."

"Same to you."

He picks up a duffle bag from the stone floor and marches past the hologram. He even nods politely to it as if it cares. *Oh, Doctor A., how far we've fallen. Already treating our captors with respect. Inadvertent Stockholm syndrome.*

"PSF OPEN."

One side of the encasement clicks open, and he enters. *I imagine an alien crawling underneath his skin to set up shop, his face twisting in agony when it burrows into his spinal column.*

After several seconds, Doctor A. steps back out looking dumbfounded, then shuffles into the next room. He doesn't make eye contact.

The hologram waves me forward.

"What does this thing do?" I ask.

"The PSF is used for decontamination. You must be processed. Decontamination, Evaluation, Integration."

Decontamination. That word pulls me out of one worry and into another. Memories of HAZMAT suits and a stinging shower flood my brain. I hug myself for support.

"Do you require assistance?"

"No, I'm fine. I just need a second."

My nostrils burn with the ghost scent of the chemical soap used at the hospital after the first vertex sightings. *Deep breath, hold it, release.* Out of habit I spin my backpack around to get my medication, but the hologram is staring at me. Instead, I strip my coat off my arms to escape the heat. *More deep breaths, in and out. Focus.*

"It has been approximately eighteen point six-one seconds. Do you require more time?"

My hatred for holograms grows deeper as my anxiety fades. "No, I'm fine." Maybe if I keep saying that to myself, I'll believe it.

"Do I have to go through decontamination?"

"Yes. You cannot integrate with our environment carrying malignant bacteria and harmful viruses from the past. The PSF will scan through your clothing and supplies and eradicate any problematic findings."

PSF. Eradicate. Sounds painful. I exhale. "What's a PSF? Will it hurt?"

"A PSF is a photosonic filter. There is no pain involved. Your body temperature may rise slightly. It is temporary. The sonic vibrations also help relax the somatic system."

It points its translucent arm to guide me into the black box. *Sonic vibrations. Somatic system.* My brain is teeming with questions, but I approach the structure anyway. It reminds me of a stand-up tanning booth. Or a black TARDIS. I'll go with that.

"Say *PSF OPEN.*"

I have no choice. It's the only way to find the others and tell them the truth. "PSF OPEN."

One side of the encasement clicks open. I walk inside the tall rectangle with my backpack on my shoulders and my coat twisted in my hands. As soon as the door clicks shut, my heart flickers into mini-spasms. It's not like a tanning booth or a TARDIS. It's like an upright coffin. *Is there enough air in here to breathe? What if this is part of the future humans' evil plan? I'm a freaking idiot—I walked right into another trap. Some futurized gas chamber. What if it's not gas? What if they fill it with water and I drown? Or even worse, what if it's a giant microwave, and I'm dinner?*

I bang on the blackened walls and scream, "Open it! Let me out!"

It's too late. A soft hum fills the machine. White light floods under my boots. The light and sound waves penetrate through my clothing, traveling from the soles of my feet, up my ankles, over my calves, to my knees, waist, arms, shoulders, and scalp and then back down again. It repeats the process, and I stop fighting it. The steady hum and gentle vibrations massage my skin, and the light radiates heat to my nervous heart.

It ends too soon. I could live in here.

The door clicks open.

"Say *PSF EXIT*, not *OPEN* to leave a photosonic filter mid-process."

"I'll remember that," I say, too exhausted and relaxed to argue. *I'm an idiot; the PSF didn't hurt anyone else—why did I think it was a trap?* So glad I was last in line so no one witnessed my freak-out. Public humiliation is my fastest path to a panic attack.

As I move into the next room to join the others, I notice that my fingernails have been stripped of all Star Ferry nail polish. Cleaned. Convenient. Creepy. *I never even knew it was happening.*

In the next area, the chaos starts slowly, like water coming to a boil on a low flame. It takes a few minutes for the panic to spread. Body language shifts. Faces drop, and the respectful attitudes morph into loud, open questions and outrage.

Doctor A. spots me. "What's going on?"

I shrug. "Can't see over the crowd."

On tiptoe, I strain to get a better view. Even though there's nowhere to go, my mind starts mapping imaginary escape routes. I've had my share of angry crowds to last several lifetimes. Along the far wall, people are being scanned by a color-changing light coming from the walls, floor, and ceiling—without a black box this time. Looks harmless enough. After the people are scanned, they are led to the right side of the room to wait for the rest.

The woman who asked about her missing tattooed husband is scanned next, along with her baby. Right when I think she's passed the exam, a nearby gray hologram snatches her baby from the light scan.

Are they selecting us one person at a time for experimentation? Human guinea pigs? I'll unleash the truth before I let them take me.

"Give me my baby!" the mother screams. She attempts to punch at the chest of the nearby hologram, her fist passing through its translucent body. Like trying to fight with sunlight.

Another hologram holds her back as the others carry her baby away.

They can touch us, and we can't touch them.

How is this possible? And how will we ever rebel against the untouchable?

I rush over to the nearest hologram.

"What does that light do? Where are they taking that baby?"

"It is an HME. Holographic medical evaluation. The child must require further medical assistance. It will receive specialized care and will be integrated when the system releases it."

"So you just take a baby away from its mother?"

"Family interferes with proper treatment. The child will be released once he or she is deemed healthy."

I consider this. "So what if I have some crazy disease or something? Do I not get to join your world?" *Do they incinerate me with the trash? Do they toss me down a garbage chute vertex and spit me out into space?*

"You will receive the proper treatment for your medical needs before integration into our world."

You will. No choice.

I watch as the mother screams and pleads and kicks to change the situation. The holograms don't flinch. Instead, blue electric currents swell up from the floor and zap her legs to silence her. Her body collapses and convulses in spasms.

"The BME has been automatically activated," nearby holograms announce in unison. "Please remain calm and orderly as we deal with the infraction."

A clear, crystalline structure encases her body, subduing her in place on the ground.

Everyone backs away. Self-preservation.

This is no utopia. It never was.

The holograms signal for us to continue processing as if nothing happened. We must walk past the frozen mother to face the medical evaluation. I walk with my eyes to the ground, waiting for a random bout of lightning to zap me. Even though my hands are shaking and all I want to do is run screaming, I continue forward. I have to.

I watch as more people are selected and collected by the holograms, leaving their families and friends behind to worry. *I remember Dad and Mom, left screaming for me in the middle of a winter street. I abandoned them.* An unnatural pulling and pounding gathers in my chest, the familiar, false heart attack symptoms that come when I'm at my worst. Heat radiates from every pore on my back, and the crowd blurs as I try to escape my own existence. It's time for a pill before I lose it. I spin my backpack around and scour through the bottom of my bag for the bottle.

The crowd moves forward, more people scanned with the medical light and passing. Some fail the scan and refuse to leave with the holograms, only to be carried away unconscious for further treatment. *Or possible incineration—who knows at this point.*

Only two pills left. Even though the hospital refilled my prescription of Ativan after the riot, I popped a lot of them in the days leading up to the comet. I swallow one, leaving the other lonely pill in the bottle, my breath shallower with each second. *I'm stuck on another planet, in another time, without my parents, with conniving holograms, and only one more pill? I'm going to die.*

The HME light evaluation looms ahead. *Will I pass or be admitted against my will?* Hives form on my arms, and an avalanche cascades inside my chest. I can't give in. I must find my friends, spread the truth, and return to Earth.

The crowd slowly enters the light for judgment. We have no choice. *Decontamination, Evaluation, Integration. No escape.*

I watch the grandmother with the purple glasses and Nolan, her teenage grandson, face the light. They both pass; the woman removes her glasses looking bemused and discards them, and the teen's acne clears up instantly. *I wonder if Dominick no longer has glasses after he went through the procedure. But I liked his glasses.*

Doctor A. faces the light and passes without a problem.

As I pass the frozen mother for my medical light scan, I check to see if she's alive. Her breath hits the surface of the clear structure and fogs the inside. Reminds me of an action figure trapped inside clamshell packaging. She can't seem to speak or blink, but her eyeballs shift and she glares at me with brown, terrified eyes. There's nothing I can do to help her, and it kills me.

Before I know it, I face the HME light. My body senses the imminent danger and reacts, flight response activated, but the light cements me in place. The color-changing medical scan washes over my body, and all I can think about is how it's going to annihilate me after everything I've been through, everything I've seen, before I get to tell anyone.

"Someone help! It's going to kill me! They're all liars!"

Gray holograms surround me. One holds a small, cold device to my forehead, and in a flash, all goes dark.

WHEN I WAKE, I find myself on a table, unable to move. It's like a classic alien abduction, and I'm the next victim. My clothes have been removed, and I'm draped in an oversized, iridescent uniform and matching boots. My ring and bracelet are missing. They might as well have removed my heart from my chest.

A low, disembodied voice fills the room. "One moment. HME ready. Please state your name and age if your condition allows."

"River Picard. 18," I say aloud to the empty room. "Where are my clothes? My jewelry?"

"Your clothing has been upgraded. Earth clothing and jewelry have been repurposed. Primitive jewelry may interfere with bandwidth technology."

My throat closes. "But those were sentimental to me."

"Sentimental. We do not recognize that word in our database."

The coldness in its response threatens everything human inside me. None of us belong here.

After a short pause, a beam of color-alternating light starts at my head and runs down my body. *Not this again.* Other than a slight warm feeling, there is no sound or physical discomfort.

The bodiless voice states, "According to your earlier body scan, you had an elevated heart rate and tachypnea; overactive adrenal glands causing high levels of epinephrine, norepinephrine, and cortisol; a hyperactive amygdala with lower prefrontal activity; lower than average hippocampal volume; low serotonin; high dopamine. We have temporarily treated your symptoms. To stabilize levels, you should return for daily treatment over a seven day period."

Something releases, and I am able to sit up. My mind feels so clear it's like I've been asleep for a week. "So am I sick? I don't feel sick. Wait." I look around, talking to the air. "Is all this connected to my anxiety? You can get rid of it?"

"Checking database. Symptoms will diminish over time with scheduled treatments."

"What are the treatments?"

"Special auditory and photonic treatments. Visual cortex

imagery will be provided for enjoyment and to help recondition neural and behavioral pathways."

I imagine the future humans probing me while I was unconscious. Or a holographic doctor like on *Star Trek Voyager.* Except he was cool, and that was fiction. *What if they brainwash me into submission? What if they condition my brain to stop questioning in general? What if I end up happy and oblivious to whatever they are planning? What if this freaking HME thing can read my mind right now?*

I can't do it. But with only one pill left, I don't know how I will cope.

Oh, god, I'm actually having anxiety about alien holograms taking away my anxiety. It's like a freaking anxiety paradox.

"The HME will exit program automatically. Please see the table in the next room for Integration."

A pleasant beep marks the end of the voice transmission. My backpack's on the floor, but my coat is missing. I walk to the next room wearing the hideous, shiny uniform. A clear glass table and chair sit in the center. Nothing else. Blank walls. No attendant. I'm not sure what to do. The glass chair seems too brittle to sit on, but I try.

Another monotone voice announces, "Please place one hand on the surface and do not move."

I wonder if they are about to slice off my hand as a punishment. I choose my left hand, the one missing Rita's bracelet and Dominick's ring.

It takes a second for something to happen. Then a beam of violet light envelops my hand. I flinch as warm liquid surrounds and hardens into a clear, two-inch band around my wrist. When the light disappears, I snatch my hand back from the table to check for possible skin damage. The band feels like it's made of thick glass, loose enough on my wrist not to hurt, tight enough not to be removed. There doesn't seem to be a clasp or seam. Like a flat, glass handcuff. Suitable for invisible captivity. *I want it off.*

"Hologuide ready. Double-tap your bandwidth on your wrist to begin. Your hologuide will be your personal assistant to integrate you into our world and answer your questions. We want you to feel comfortable with your choice, so you may modify specs at any time. May your contribution lead to freedom."

Contribution? You mean kidnapping. Freedom? Real freedom doesn't pretend to give people choices. I double-tap the glass cuff bandwidth, and a life-sized, androgynous hologram appears at my side wearing a gray uniform.

"Welcome, River Picard. We are here to guide you through your integration into our world. Please follow."

Despite every bone in my body swarming with suspicion, I find myself following my hologuide down a rounded white hall-way, a rabbit hole into Wonderland. At least for Alice it was only a nightmare. She could wake up.

"Where're we going?" I spin the bandwidth around my wrist, trying to stretch it forward off my hand. *I want it off.*

"Integration." My hologuide walks over to the far wall. As it moves farther away, its physical form changes from transparent to a more solid-looking form. If I didn't know better, I'd mistake it for human. Except that its fake skin and cropped hair look flawless.

It reaches the blank, solid wall with no door or window and says, "Say *EXIT*."

It must have a glitch in its protocols, but I'll play along.

I take a deep breath and squeeze my backpack strap. "EXIT," I say to a wall.

The surface shifts and wavers like a mirage over a hot highway.

"What the—?"

CONTRIBUTE

The molecules of the wall scatter like electronic tadpoles and vanish, exposing us to the outside world.

"Welcome to Solbiluna-8, River Picard."

CHAPTER 2

DAY 2

THE NIGHT SKY is like nothing on Earth. Two brilliant moons, one half the size of the other. A blanket of moving stars like cell phone lights at a sold-out concert dance through the dark atmosphere. Movement like one of Van Gogh's paintings. Surreal. Dangerously romantic.

I take in a deep breath to test out the oxygen levels. The air is crisp with a strange, pleasant aftertaste like mint and vanilla. My New England winter clothing would be completely wrong for the weather. It's a perfect sixty-five degree night.

Around me there are other people talking to their hologuides. I search for my friends and family, for Doctor A., Nolan and his grandmother, or the grieving mother hopefully reunited with her baby, but they are nowhere in sight. I just want to see something, anything, familiar.

God, what has happened to us? Why are we here?

"Welcome to our planet," my hologuide repeats. "Please follow."

We travel together down a gray walkway that glimmers like diamonds are embedded in the asphalt. *If that substance is asphalt.*

"What's that shiny stuff?"

"We embed all pathways with nanoholocoms, computers the size of a grain of rice. They collect light and vibrations as energy sources. We depend on them to carry out designated holographic programming throughout our world. Your bandwidth allows you to navigate the nanoholocom network."

I spin the bandwidth on my wrist and nod like a dog waiting for a treat. Must not fall for a scientific siren singing a tale of sophisticated tech. I need to remember that I am Revenge Girl, Truth Bringer, on an away mission.

The sinking feeling returns. I am on an away mission. *Away from my parents. Away from my home. Away from my planet. I'm not even in my own timeline.* I must always remember what they did to us.

The hologuide follows a path lined with built-in, lit panels toward a beautiful, glasslike, circular building glowing in the darkness. Through the transparent exterior, I can see people walking inside on several floors.

"Where are we going?"

"You have been assigned to solitary LU, or Living Unit, QN25-50-1-9-100."

Sounds like solitary confinement. "So it's where I'll live?"

"Yes, it is your temporary home during the initial integration."

I tap my hands back and forth on each thigh as I walk to calm myself like Arianna, my most recent therapist, taught me. It helps me concentrate on my physical body and not on my racing fear. Sometimes it works if I can focus. I wonder if my counselor ever made it here with her baby. I wonder if they took her baby away for medical issues like what happened to the other mother during the medical examinations. I wonder if she brought any pills with her.

"What else do we have to do for the integration process?"

"You must learn our customs and decide how you would like to contribute in order to fully integrate into our world."

Something in its language terrifies me. The word "integrate" reminds me of the word "assimilate," which reminds me of the Borg from *Star Trek* and being forced into sameness. Losing one's culture to merge with another, like it or not.

"How do I find people?" I ask as my fingertips tap my legs.

"You will be able to search for them using your bandwidth once you are granted full bandwidth access and planetary travel rights. You are not allowed to leave your assigned LU community until the travel ban is lifted."

I never even considered not finding Dominick and Rita. That was an absolute. Never mind Benji, Marcus, and Penelope.

"When is that?"

"When step one of integration is complete."

"How long will that take?"

"Indefinable."

I take a deep breath to ward off the negative energy. "I'll just have to find them the old-fashioned way."

"Old-fashioned way. We do not recognize that phrase in our database."

I roll my eyes and follow the hologuide into the glasslike building. The structure has QN25-50-1 on a holographic digital display near the front entrance. We pass through an archway and a short, clear corridor to another outdoor space.

"This is the Hub, your LU community space," my hologuide says.

The shape of the building reminds me of a poster my English teacher had in her classroom of Shakespeare's Globe Theatre, but stacked three times higher, with a circular arrangement of floors and hallways surrounding an outdoor area. Like a large glass and metal donut with the center carved out. It's as if we're squirrels living in a giant, hollowed-out glass tree stump.

Children chase an oversized bubble floating and darting above them in the lush grass. Each time one of them manages to hit it, it changes color. Adults nearby keep lookout. None of them are wearing the ridiculous uniform I'm swimming in. They have on fitted uniforms in various colors and patterns, some patterns even moving within the fabric.

"Can I get different clothes?" I ask my hologuide.

"You can modify your uniform per your specifications. Hold the fabric and say *MODIFY CLOTHING.*"

"Hold the fabric?"

"Yes."

I follow its directions. "MODIFY CLOTHING."

Above the sleeve, in midair, a holographic screen appears with tons of digital options.

"The holigraphy system adapts to your finger movements. Swipe and tap the holoscreen on instinct."

I touch a uniform shirt and pants option, and my basic uniform instantly forms around my body type. The iridescent fabric can be changed to any print I can imagine. Rita must love the fashion here. I choose all black.

Off to the side, I spot Nolan and his grandmother, who still think their relative died because she didn't make it through a vertex, arguing with a hologuide. I can't quite make out the conversation, but I recognize an argument from a distance by their facial expressions. Their hologuide doesn't show any sign of stress, of course, and keeps responding with the same neutral stance.

Huge, lush bushes and tropical flowers fill the area with a sweet, warm smell that reminds me of when we went to visit my grandmother, Penelope, in Florida when I was little. A large stone surface with a glass circular center and hovering metal cap sits in the middle of the Hub. A few people are gathered around it. I wonder what the platform is for. *Virginal sacrifices?* At least I'm safe from that.

The Hub is lit from the ground and above with tiny lights in the surface of the building and the walkways. Like fireflies frozen in glass. People sit at multicolored tables with attached benches in a seamless swirl design. Even though there's no visible kitchen area, a savory aroma mixes with the florals in the air.

"Holocom food is created at the HDP." My hologuide points to the stone platform. "It is third ration time."

Third ration? My stomach gnaws at me, and I try to remember the last time I ate. Days ago? Can't be. No wonder my head feels woozy. My sore shoulders serve as a steady reminder of pushing Dad's wheelchair through a slushy, crowded highway for miles. *Of abandoning my parents to run through the fading vertex.*

"Good," I say. "I'm starving."

"Starving. We do not recognize that word in our database."

We approach the altar, and I look around for a potential trap, like my hologuide tossing me up and serving me for dinner.

"The HDP creates the food designed by the nanoholocom network based on dietary needs and stored ingredient levels."

More acronyms. "Don't tell me the food is holographic," I mumble.

I hear a chuckle that I already recognize. Doctor A. stands next to me.

"The food has to be real," he says. "Can't eat light after all. Think of it more like a 3D printer. We started using them at the hospital. Nothing on this scale, though."

"So basically a computer creates and cooks the food? Like a 3D printer and a microwave put together? Or like a *Star Trek* replicator?"

"Sounds about right," Doctor A. says.

My hologuide explains further. "The nanoholocom network sets the meal based on needs and supplies. You cannot order specific food. Rations are based on your personal caloric and nutritional needs." It points at the platform. "Place your hand on the surface so it can read you. It provides three food rations per person per day."

"What if someone has an allergy?" I ask.

"Allergies have been eliminated," it replies.

"Seriously?" Doctor A. sounds impressed by the information, but his eyebrows furrow and he goes quiet.

A young girl with pigtails places her palm on the platform. She doesn't have a hologuide with her, but she seems to know what she's doing. The surface under her hand illuminates in orange, and a beige plate and fork materialize. Slowly, layer by layer, what looks like shiny, dark green noodles gather on top.

My hologuide continues. "The food is safe, nutritious, and made with attention to human taste, texture, and aesthetic design."

Doctor A. places his hand on the surface. I wait my turn.

"You do not have to wait for each serving to finish," my hologuide says. "The scale of the HDP is designed to serve approximately fifty people at a time."

It doesn't have to tell me more than once. I place my hand on the platform, and orange light outlines my hand. Soon a plate of noodles materializes next to it. The cold stone surface reminds me of the kitchen countertop at home. Mom prepping food that Dad gathered from the grocery storage at his work. My grandmother, Penelope, telling her how to cook Thanksgiving dinner. Late at night watching Mom drink tea, Dad making sandwiches. These are my last good memories of them. I lift my plate of printed food, and it feels like a betrayal.

I wonder what my parents are eating on Earth. There was hardly any food left in stock. *Empty store shelves. Chaos. Abandoning them, stranded in the middle of nowhere, with no food or heat or transportation or electricity* . . . If I keep worrying about them, I'll go mad. My lone pill already calls to me, and I ignore the urge. I need to save it for an emergency.

I search the Hub for future humans, but everyone looks like they're from Earth. Only a few have their hologuides near them. I spot the mother who was electrocuted and frozen in punishment after her baby was taken during the medical evaluation. Still no baby in her arms. She stares off into the night sky the way Dad used to during his Zombie Nights with PTSD. Only this is fresh trauma. Witnessed trauma. I want to go over and whisper the truth in her ear. *Would it make her feel better to know we are all victims?*

"River, do you want to eat together?" Doctor A. asks. "Or did you find your family?"

A lump rises in my throat. I really don't have the energy for small talk, but I need a safe, familiar face. Time to blend in with the crowd to avoid outcast status. "Sure. I haven't seen my family yet. I just got here."

Doctor A. nods, and together we walk to a table and bench.

"Do you require our assistance while eating?" my hologuide asks.

"I don't think so," I say, imagining it trying to spoon-feed me.

"We will deactivate, then. When you require more assistance, please double-tap your bandwidth." It bows. "May your contribution lead to freedom."

How freaking annoying. What does that even mean? Are we supposed to feel free now that we've joined their world?

"So, decontamination and evaluation," Doctor A. says, swirling a curl of dark green noodles onto his fork. "That was an experience."

"I kept thinking it was like an alien abduction." *There's no place to wash my hands before eating. Great. I imagine all the tiny germs crawling across my palms.* "How long was I gone?"

He laughs longer than necessary. "You were gone for a day. Give or take. If that's how time works here."

I was unconscious with an alien doctor for a full day, with no recollection of the events? I wonder where they put the probe . . .

"Where are you from?" he asks.

I pick up one noodle and pray that it's not a futuristic worm. I bite the end, chew, and with one taste I realize how hungry I am. Screw the germs; I can't eat fast enough and start shoveling noodles into my mouth.

"Sorry," I apologize with a mouthful of food.

"Not necessary. Didn't realize traveling through a vertex would leave me so famished, either." He waits a minute, then asks again, "So, where are you from?"

"Massachusetts."

"Well, yes, according to my hologuide, everyone in this community came through the Quincy vertex in Massachusetts during the last phase, probably in the last two weeks or so."

I look around. "We're organized by vertex location and time left the planet?" *Only the last couple weeks? So that would mean Dominick and Rita aren't here?*

A weight presses on my chest. My hologuide said we can't leave our LU community. *I can't do this alone. I need to find my friends.*

"Do you know how long until we can travel?"

"They haven't said."

I'm never going to survive without them.

"Makes sense to organize people this way when you think of it. Helps us integrate with another world if we have people around us from our regions on Earth. Alleviates language barriers and naturally allows for family and friends to stay together."

I hadn't thought of that. Can't say the future humans aren't logical. *Of course it only works when you leave a planet with family or friends.* "Which ones are the future humans who sent the holograms? I don't see anyone who looks different."

"I asked the same question. We aren't allowed to mingle with the vances during the first steps of integration. Too much for our little brains to handle. We aren't culturally aware enough. Presumptuous."

"The vances?"

"Short for advanced humans. That's what everyone's been calling them."

I nod and examine the people around us for signs that they are vances in disguise. Other than the odd uniforms, everyone appears to be part of a typical, random sample of humans from Massachusetts. I watch Nolan and his grandmother approach the food platform. She places her hand on the platform for food, but Nolan keeps his hands crossed. I think the grandmother is trying to convince him to eat. He doesn't respond, and I don't blame him. I can't imagine how hard it is to actually lose a parent. I feel sick just going through the mental motions of what it would be like to lose Dad all the time.

And now both my parents are lost in another time. Three hundred years ago. Dust by now.

Don't go there. Don't get destroyed by a thought.

"So, Doctor A., what's your specialty?" I say to distract myself.

"I'm a prenatal surgeon."

"You do surgeries on babies?"

"Yes, even still in the womb."

"That must be stressful." I search the grass for the mother missing her baby and husband. She's still staring off into space. People nearby look on with sympathy, but no one says anything to her.

"You get used to it," Doctor A. says. "The stress actually makes it exciting."

Stress doesn't make anything exciting in my world. Stress is gasoline to a dancing flame.

I take another bite of noodles and chew as I scan the faces

in the Hub area. So many families, all strangers. Until I lock eyes on a familiar face.

The noodles twist in my stomach. It takes me a moment to recognize her since her hair's brushed back and she's wearing a clean, fitted sky blue uniform.

It's the crazy lady.

The crazy lady.

She looks much healthier than the last time I saw her. Then again, the last time I saw her, she was foaming at the mouth near the vertex site before the ambulance arrived.

And she gave me the note.

Before she died.

On Earth.

When the truth is shrouded in fear and clouded by dreams,
when fact and fantasy become deviant lovers,
maybe there are no real heroes anymore.
Or maybe that's when heroes are born.

I was right. How can this be possible? How can she be here, alive?

Crazy lady leans against a wall. She's quiet. Calm. Nothing like I remember. I try not to stare. When I sneak another peek, I watch her avoid the noodles on her plate and instead bite into her actual fork and eat the prongs.

"Are the utensils edible?" I ask, startled.

Doctor A. studies the fork, breaks part of the handle off, and chews. "Remarkable. It tastes like a thin, slightly sweet cookie. Or bread. I wonder . . ." He moves his noodles aside and breaks off a chunk of his plate and puts in his mouth. "Remarkable. No waste or cleanup."

My stomach lurches in queasiness, wondering if I should try it. I watch crazy lady avoid the noodles and continue eating her fork instead, eventually tossing most of her noodles and plate back on the platform. *What does she know that I don't know? Maybe the green noodles are like Soylent Green, from that old sci-fi movie that Dominick made me watch. Maybe that's why the vances kidnapped us. For protein.*

I puke in a patch of perfect, glowing bushes.

DOCTOR A. CHECKS my pulse and feels my forehead like Mom used to do. She was right about fevers 99.9% of the time based on her palm reading.

"I'm fine," I say. "I just ate too fast."

He guides me over to a glass water fountain. A holoscreen on the side reads:

`For personal hydration only. Storing or cleaning with water is forbidden.`

I wonder what the penalty is for filling up a bottle. If I had a bottle. Beheading?

The fountain registers my hand with an orange glow before working. As I inhale large gulps of water, I search for crazy lady out of the corner of my eye. She's nowhere in sight. *Was she just a projection from my imagination? Am I hallucinating?* The fountain shuts off automatically before I'm done. I press my hand against the side again, but it won't turn back on.

"I can walk you to your LU," Doctor A. offers. "You'll miss the Skylucent, though. Fantastic display. I saw it last night."

I visually sweep the Hub area for crazy lady and find her lying in the grass. "I think I'll stay. What's the Skylucent? Is it like fireworks?"

"You'll see," Doctor A. says, then smiles and wipes his salt-and-pepper beard with his hand.

Lovely. More mysteries to worry about.

A huge flash of light appears and repeats over the night sky in the Hub. I wonder if it's their version of a thunderstorm, created by them since they said they can control the weather on the hologram Q&A website back on Earth.

"Looks like it's about to start," Doctor A. says. "Best spot is in the grass. Shall we?"

Other people are slowly gathering and lying on the dark grass. Doctor A. crouches down and waves me to the ground.

Smoke fills the upper atmosphere, blocking out the stars. I swear I sense less oxygen already. *Take a deep breath, look around. No one else is concerned.* A hush comes over the crowd. *How can everyone be smiling when they are about to kill us with toxic fumes?*

A holographic 3D film in the heavens begins over our heads. The smoke works like a massive screen in the night sky, the holographic images projected and illuminated in front of it. And what did the vances pick for us to watch to make us feel at home? *Finding Nemo.* The ground even seems to vibrate at the right times, the sound bouncing off the inner walls of the Hub. I swear I can smell the scent of seawater from the film as a tropical fish swims near me. With this technology, it's no wonder they could create a massive holographic comet to trick us to come here. The question is why. I steal glimpses at crazy lady. I think she fell asleep in the grass.

Even though I've seen *Finding Nemo* a million times, it's nothing like this experience. I *am* Nemo, touching that boat and getting pulled into another world while Dad is desperate to bring me home. That parent-child tug pulls at my heart stronger than ever, like I'm the one trapped in a glass fish tank. *How will we ever find each other again? Did my parents survive?*

Thinking about my parents unleashes pent up tears for all I've lost. I don't bother wiping. I need to let it out. I need to remember. Grieving is stronger than fear. Grief is my worst fear realized and digested and coming back out of me in a new form. *I am more than three hundred years into the future, which means my parents are long dead and their remains have been reduced to dust particles. For all I know, they might have been recycled into the air I'm breathing now.*

Sometimes we are trapped by truth. Sometimes we are trapped by lies. I'm not sure what's worse.

When the movie ends, and the last of the Skylucent effects fade into the night sky, people stand up and brush off their individually holofied uniforms.

"Simply spectacular," Doctor A. says and reaches out a hand to help me to my feet.

"Amazing," I admit.

A melodic sequence of beeps fills the air and interrupts us. A huge holoscreen appears and hovers over the crowd. People around us chatter excitedly and stare up at the screen, unconcerned.

"Is this part of the Skylucent?" I ask.

"Didn't happen yesterday," Doctor A. says, scratching his beard.

On the screen, a man my father's age with shoulder-length, graying hair and a smooth face holds his arms out wide from beneath a white robe. He wears a long, metallic necklace ending with an intricate, glowing amber gemstone. Like a vertex caught behind glass. Behind him, a crowd wearing similar clothes sits in a semicircular arena.

"Greetings. We are the meritocracy, the ruling body of Solbiluna-8. My name is Keron. I serve as the voice of the meritocracy. Welcome to our planet.

"We hope you enjoy acclimating to our world during the integration process. Our culture and science are different from what you experienced on Earth. We hope you will sample everything our world has to offer. Please sample our luxuries, such as the

Skylucent and the Holospaces for recreation and education. Soon we will allow full travel and communication. We must disclose one, final element in our social structure that we are sure you will find reasonable."

My chest hollows at his words. Something is wrong. *This is the catch. This will unite us to fight to go home, or this will destroy us.*

"Solbiluna-8 is built on the belief that humans were made to thrive, not toil away precious time. You will not be required to work on our planet, and we will supply all of your needs. As higher beings, humans are meant to think, explore, create, and enjoy. We have based our world around that ideal. By providing freedom from commerce, we provide freedom from work."

Through the darkness, I see people around me, smiling at one another like they've won the lottery.

Keron continues. "In order to continue this luxury for future generations, however, there must be a cost."

There's always a catch, always a cost.

Keron swoops his robed arms around and holds his hands over his heart. *If he has a heart.*

"We need your contribution in death."

CHAPTER 3
DAY 2

DEATH? THEY CAN'T be serious.

My arms pulse with fear and my legs go numb. I need my parents.

Several people in the Hub voice their complaints and fears simultaneously. On the holoscreen, Keron extends his open palms and continues speaking. I can't hear what he's saying through the noise. Someone shushes the crowd.

". . . want to be honest with you. Much like on Earth, where humans could donate their bodies to science upon death, we hope you will each donate your body upon death for your brain pathways to be uploaded as a biohologram. Our nanoholocom network only works with the vast pathways of the human brain. All other artificial intelligence in our history paled in comparison to the seamless integration of combining holographic light entanglements with the natural decision-making capabilities of the human brain."

I glance at the people around me, all eyes on the screen. They have to know it's a trap. No one would ever willingly agree to it.

"Rest assured only your thoughts and neural matrix will be integrated with our systems. The donation of your brain's complex synapses allows our bioholograms to function. As a biohologram, you will no longer have physical and emotional needs. In this holographic state, you will be able to work for our society, assuring that future generations of humans will enjoy the same luxury of leisure during their life span that you did. You will continue past your physical death date as a biohologram until your programming degrades, which can last up to fifty additional years.

"Contribution is not mandatory. In fairness, however, those who do not wish to become bioholograms will have to work in our world and have less time than others to enjoy all of the luxuries we have here. The choice is yours. Once you decide, please let your hologuide know. Your hologuide is also available to answer any questions. You have just over thirty more calendar days, or 722 hours, to decide. May your contribution lead to freedom."

He bows, just like the holograms, and the screen vanishes. The crowd stays silent for a minute, letting the choice sink in.

"Can you believe this?" I say to Doctor A. He has to understand that it's like making a deal with a technological devil.

"It's remarkable," he says. "That level of biological and technological integration. I'll have to look into it further."

"What?" *He can't be serious.* "You'd consider doing it?"

"Contribute your body to help the next generation? Extend your life in a new form? A way to preserve you? Perhaps. But I don't want to give up working. I love medicine. Maybe I can do both."

What happens when something goes wrong? What happens if you say yes and then change your mind? What happens if you say no and change your mind? What happens if you die quickly and they can't upload your brain? What happens if you live a life of leisure and then kill yourself? What do they do to even those odds? I'm sure it's unspeakable. What are the consequences?

The crowd grows louder and louder with questions and nervous excitement. I should tell them now. I can't let them make this decision without knowing the whole truth. It's like a repeat of the history. *Sweet talk, trick, and trap.* But I'm only one voice in the crowd. How will I ever convince them?

I spot crazy lady daydreaming among the people, her eyes still searching the air for answers. She refocuses and heads through the rowdiness for the exit.

"I'll see you tomorrow," I say to Doctor A. I don't wait for his response. Before I even know what I'm doing or why I'm doing it, I follow after crazy lady. I have to make them understand. I have to get home.

I head across the dark Hub illuminated by tiny pinpricks of light on the ground and turn a corner. Crazy lady walks down a glass and metal curved hallway, enters a transparent cube unit in the wall, and turns around. She mouths a command. Must be an elevator.

"Wait!" I yell.

She holds the door for me, and I'm in. I can't stop staring at her once the clear door closes. Bad elevator etiquette on any planet. I have so many unanswered questions.

"What's your problem?" she barks at me.

"Nothing," I mumble, looking away and trying to remain calm while my stomach and mind decide that this whole follow-the-crazy-lady plan was a bad idea. I never planned what to do once I caught up to her. As the soundless elevator travels higher and higher, my stomach dips lower and lower. I don't even know where this thing is taking us. I close my eyes to avoid the glass view. I don't want to know how high we've gone. It finally stops, shifts, and begins traveling horizontally around the large circular floor. The sensation in my stomach doesn't improve. Like being on a conveyor belt about to be turned into a manufactured object.

"This thing goes sideways?" I ask.

"Maglift. Works using magnetic suspension. Goes in any direction."

So there's no pulley system. One glitch and I plummet to my death, splattering near the Hub for all to see. The idea that technology cradles our lives in its cold, dead hands scares me. But maybe it already did in our world, and I just never thought about it. A pulley system is a mechanical form of technology. *So why is intangible technology worse?*

Crazy lady peers at me like she's trying to read my mind. "Looking at you is giving me weird déjà vu. Have we met?"

Act cool.

My face burns hot, but she doesn't seem to care. Her words make sense; they're not a jumbled mess of poetry and nonsense like in the past. She's not crazy in the future. Angry maybe. Not crazy.

"Earth to whack job?" she spouts.

I shrug my shoulders and shake my head no. I can't tell her what I'm thinking.

That we've met.

That she somehow gave me a note from my journal, which gave me the last push of courage to plunge myself into this world.

That I witnessed her death. In the past.

And now she's here. In the future.

Somehow, she's the key.

The quiet tension in the maglift grows unbearable.

"I'm River," I blurt, holding out my hand. "River Picard."

She looks at my hand and back up at my face without shaking it.

"River, huh. You don't look like a River. Rivers are peaceful, granola types. Parents usually hippies. Nah, you got way too much boiling under there to be a River."

It annoys me that she can read me so easily. "And what are you, a cop?"

She laughs dismissively. "No, definitely not a cop. Katherine Kirkwood. I was released with the last round of prisoners. Thank god for comets."

My heart freezes and falls through time. *I am trapped in a maglift on another planet with crazy lady, an ex-con I met in the past somehow. And we are surrounded by holograms who kidnapped us and want us to become bioholograms when we die.*

My mind cannot adapt to the past, present, and future. I came here following her lead, knowing there was something waiting on the other side, that the other side wasn't just immediate death. *I thought I could come here and change everything. But I'm just one girl.*

The maglift slows to a stop. My peripheral vision is the first to go before I lose hearing and then all other senses fade to nothing.

CHAPTER 4

DAY 2: 722 HOURS TO DECIDE

CRAZY LADY'S SUPPOSED to be the key, but she doesn't know anything and is, in fact, a criminal.

Maybe she's not real, and she's really a hologram.

Calm down or they'll put you in a time-out cocoon.

I wake up completely disoriented with my hologuide and Katherine, aka crazy lady, standing over me.

"You passed out," Katherine says.

I'm on the hallway floor outside the maglift. People who left the Skylucent event have stopped in the walkway to see the commotion. I'm the attraction. Me and my medical crisis. *Way to make a first impression. It's not embarrassing at all. Not one of my worst nightmares brought to fruition, people staring at me in concern for my well-being and sanity while an escaped convict looms over me.*

"No, I'm fine." I sit up, and my eyesight blurs. Maybe I'm not fine.

Doctor A. comes running. He flashes a small light into each of my eyes using his bandwidth.

An HME disembodied voice interrupts. "Please step back from the patient."

Doctor A. sighs and backs away. The HME sends a wave of colored light and vibration across my body. The dizziness doesn't subside.

"Why is my hologuide here?"

"Automatic activation when the HME is initiated," my

hologuide says, "to provide patients with a familiar face to alleviate fear and administer emergency care."

"She has regained consciousness," the HME voice says.

"No kidding," Doctor A. says. "What kind of asinine medical evaluation was that?"

The voice states, "The patient requires additional sustenance and rest. Please move her to a private location or the HME will admit her to our facility."

"No, don't admit me anywhere," I say, scrambling to my feet. "I'm fine."

Once I get to my feet, however, my vision fogs again.

"We can bring her to my LU," Katherine says to Doctor A. "It's right there."

Doctor A. nods. They each hold an arm for support.

"Can you walk?" Doctor A. asks.

"Yes, just dizzy." The hallway has a clear, railed partition. The Hub is visible far down in the center of the building. Even with the barrier, I move as far from that drop as possible.

As the two of them lead me to Katherine's LU, every time I look at Katherine, I see her as crazy lady and feel like I'm going to vomit. The two images are not blending well in my mind. Like having double vision.

What if she went to prison for murder? What if she's bringing us to her room to kill us? She could chop us up and flush our body parts down the toilet. Would the transparent emotional police box come fast enough and surround her if we scream? Maybe I should scream now. I'd be trapped, but safe from her.

I am not letting her out of my sight.

"She was sick at dinner," Doctor A. says.

"What's the matter?" Katherine asks me. "Don't trust holocom food? You just got here."

I'm not explaining myself to her.

"I'm just joshing you," she says.

Stupid move. Don't piss off the ex-con. Like poking a tiger with a sharp pencil.

"The food's fine," I mumble.

We wait outside Katherine's LU while she places her palm on the door to unlock it. Doctor A. asks me to move different parts of my body to test my reflexes.

Inside crazy lady's—I mean Katherine's—room, a tropical paradise transforms before our eyes. An oasis of comfort. I spot a hammock in a corner. I want one of those in my LU. I could read *Harry Potter* in my hammock and destress like in my visual relaxation safe place.

They place me on the bed. My hologuide joins me at my side.

The HME voice fills the space. "Volunteer to acquire additional food rations for the patient?"

"I'll go," Katherine says. "Katherine Kirkwood."

"Permission granted for Katherine Kirkwood to acquire additional food rations for River Picard."

"What would happen if she needed surgery?" Doctor A. argues with the air. "Would a light and a bunch of sound waves fix that? Would you ask for a volunteer to cut her open?"

The voice ignores Doctor A. If he's not careful, he'll end up plastic-wrapped for his behavior.

"The patient needs rest due to high levels of stress hormones. No long-term effects or other issues detected."

"I could've told you that," Doctor A. says.

"Put me in the hammock," I say.

"I don't think that's a good idea," Doctor A. says. "It's not stable."

"Please," I beg. "I think it will help."

"Listen to the patient, Doctor," Katherine adds, grinning. *Why is she grinning? Is the hammock booby-trapped?*

Katherine and Doctor A. hold the hammock still while I ma-neuver my limbs and body into the roped chair. My imagination and reality come together. Quiet minutes pass by as I enjoy the comfort. A book would complete me. I asked Dad to install a hammock on our front porch, but he never got around to it. He didn't understand that certain comforts are not luxuries; they are coping necessities.

"I'll be right back," Katherine says, and leaves to get the food.

My hologuide still stands nearby, watching me. Sometimes I wonder if it's thinking of ways to annihilate me. "HOLOGUIDE EXIT."

"We cannot exit program at present time due to HME override. HME will determine when hologuide shuts down."

"That's what I need," I say to Doctor A., "a hologram staring at me when I feel dizzy."

He laughs and whispers, "They creep me out, too. Like a ghost following you around."

"Exactly." *Part hologram, part soul of someone who contributed in the past.*

"So how are you feeling? Dizzy, hungry, tired? Any other symptoms?"

Normally, this is when I tell people I'm fine even when I'm not. Doctor A. seems like he's seen a lot, been through a lot, and come out better for it. Something in the spark in his eyes, the roundness of his laughs, the wrinkles in his forehead.

"I have generalized anxiety disorder. With panic attacks. I only have one pill left from my prescription, so I'm trying to save it. I can have racing thoughts, heart palpitations, nausea, sweating, trouble breathing. Hives when it's really bad." I pause, and add, "I think the speech about contribution freaked me out. And I didn't eat much for days before coming through the vertex."

He doesn't respond. I wonder at first if I misjudged him, and if he's one of those people, like my brother Benji, who thinks anxiety is not a real problem, just a wimpy, self-inflicted torture, and that with tough love it can just go away. I used to wonder the same thing, but my counselor, Arianna, had been working with me on accepting that it's a stress and thought processing problem that causes physical symptoms. Not a sign that I need to toughen up. A sign that my brain chemistry and processing is different.

"I'm surprised they're not pumping us all full of drugs to help us adjust," he jokes. "This level of change is bound to shock our systems."

I smile, and the room spins. "Maybe they are."

"Take deep breaths with your diaphragm and let them out slowly as I'm sure you've been trained to do. If you aren't taking your anxiety medication at the same rate as you were accustomed, you may also be experiencing withdrawal symptoms, including more anxiety and depression. That's why people can get addicted to meds. It can both help and exacerbate the problem."

"No one ever told me that." I think about how many times I took extra pills just to sleep when I technically wasn't experiencing anxiety yet. That could've been making me worse. "So I'm gonna get worse?"

"Breathe. Not necessarily. Did you ask the HME for alternative treatment?"

"It wants to give me a light lobotomy."

He belly laughs, rubbing his beard. "I take it you refused."

"Not letting those things near me if I can help it. I just don't know if I can handle this place once I run out of pills."

"You came through a vertex alone, dealt with that crowd asking you about their loved ones. You're tougher than you think. If you need more help, I'm here. As for the HME treatment, you're a smart cookie for not accepting medical treatment that you don't trust."

Just hearing his soothing voice is a comfort.

"Katherine's an ex-con, by the way," I say. "She told me in the maglift. Don't trust her."

Doctor A. doesn't show any sign of fear. They must teach that in medical school the way they teach therapists not to react to crazy talk.

He plops onto a nearby chair. "I'm not surprised."

"Why do you say that?"

"I've met many former prisoners here. Remember, we're arranged by vertex and time left the planet. They weren't allowed to leave until the final weeks."

"Oh, shit, we are surrounded." The room spins again, and I hold on to the roped hammock for support.

"They were rehabilitated during the medical screening. The worst are still being treated, locked in their LUs. I'm sure the vances know what they're doing." The furrowed lines between his eyebrows say otherwise. "If they can have us donate our brains at death to support their world, I'm sure they can handle a few convicts."

There's so much he doesn't know, and I want to tell him. The truth is on the tip of my tongue. I give him a weak smile in response as the door slides open. Katherine returns with a bowl of food from the platform.

"I couldn't bring water. Sorry. Can't carry it from the fountain."

"Even if a patient is dehydrated?" Doctor A. closes his eyes and shakes his head.

"I'm fine," I say as Katherine passes me the bowl. It's full of warm, brown nuggets. They could be futuristic fudge. *Or animal turds.*

Doctor A. turns toward Katherine and sticks out his hand. "I never introduced myself. Dr. Aiyegbeni, Boston Children's— Doctor A. for short."

"Katherine Kirkwood." She doesn't shake his hand. So I'm not the only one she snubs.

Doctor A. smiles it off. "And obviously you've met River."

"Yeah, Mississippi and I met briefly in the maglift before she crash landed."

My body shivers with a weird déjà vu that I can't place. Maybe I'm coming down with an alien fever. I take a tentative bite of the morsels and chew. It's like a mix between a Tootsie Roll and a mini-meatball. I don't want to know what it's made out of. I scarf down the food, ignoring the small talk between Doctor A. and Katherine. A few minutes after I finish, the HME releases me from its care.

"Would you like us to deactivate?" my hologuide asks. Despite the comfort of the hammock, I need time to process everything alone.

"No. Can you bring me to my LU?"

"Yes. Please follow."

"I can walk with you," Doctor A. offers.

"No, that's fine. Thank you, but you've already done enough. I'd like some time alone."

He listens to me, but his forehead wrinkles again. "I guess I better go as well. Long day. Much to think about. It was great meeting you," he says to Katherine. He doesn't try to shake her hand again. He learns quickly.

"Likewise," Katherine says with a smirk. I can read that smirk. It says, *You don't know me at all, Mr. Doctor. I'm not nice. I've done time. I kill people like you and turn them into mulch.*

"River, I'll check on you tomorrow," he says.

I nod. I'd agree to anything to get some sleep. That food did me good.

I follow my hologuide out of crazy lady's—I mean Katherine's—LU and into a maglift.

"Say *LU 9-100*," my hologuide instructs.

I follow its directions. Once the door closes, I move into the farthest corner and wait for the ride to end. Of course my LU is located on the top floor, nine stories up from the Hub.

Once the door slides back open, I cling my body to the opposite solid wall, away from the visual drop of the Hub, and follow my hologuide to a door labeled 100 on a digital screen.

"Touch your hand to the door."

"Shouldn't I say something like *DOOR OPEN*?"

"No. All LUs are locked against simple commands. You must place your hand on the door so it recognizes you."

"Recognizes me?"

"When you went through the initial evaluation process, the nanoholocom network recorded your complete body spectrum scan during your HME scan, including your fingerprints, iris patterns, genome sequence, current aura luminosity, and vibrational frequency. It knows your complete biosignature by touch."

My insides ignite. "You can just do that? Scan me for everything? Shouldn't you ask my permission or something?"

"Basic nanoholocom protocols do not need permission to function. You cannot exist and interact with the nanoholocom network without a complete biosignature scan and bandwidth."

As much as there is to admire about the technology on Solbiluna-8, they lack a basic understanding of human rights. Then again, they stole us from our world, so what did I expect?

I slap my right palm on the door.

Underneath my hand glows orange although I can't detect any change in the material of the door. A clicking sound, and the door slides open. The interior of my LU is underwhelming. Apparently the interior design of things isn't important in the future.

My LU is a single room, about the size of a small bedroom, the same size as crazy lady's and fit for a solitary like me. One wall is completely made of glass, a gorgeous view of a distant, dark mountain range and star-lit sky spread before me. Three white walls sparkle with nanoholocoms across the surface. No furniture except for a small bed. No hammock. One corner holds one of those coffin machines that disinfected me—I can't remember the name.

"Where's the rest of the furniture?" I really want a hammock.

"You haven't modified your LU yet."

I'm too tired to care. As I walk across the barely lit room, a soft light from the ceiling follows me to illuminate my path. Like being tracked by a spotlight. I crawl into bed fully clothed in my black uniform and boots and climb under the softest, most luxurious blanket I have ever felt. My hologuide stares at me.

"Do I have to shut you off?"

"We automatically shut off after five minutes of inactivity."

There's no way I'm letting that thing stare at me for five minutes while I try to sleep. Talk about feeling haunted. "HOLOGUIDE EXIT."

My hologuide bows and says, "May your contribution lead to freedom."

It dematerializes into a million particles in front of my eyes, reminding me of the fake comet that trapped us here.

Time to sleep in a world that's kidnapped us and wants to trick everyone again. And I can't talk to my friends or my family for who knows how long. And crazy lady didn't even recognize me.

Maybe she wasn't real and my mind made her up as justification for abandoning my parents for my friends.

Maybe I traveled through a vertex and aliens hooked me up to a machine that is feeding me all these thoughts and I'm actually unconscious.

Or maybe it's a terrible hallucination I cannot escape. Instead of traveling through time, I'm locked up in a psychiatric hospital.

Like that episode of Buffy *where she wonders if she's actually in an asylum and Sunnydale is really a figment of her imagination.*

I need medication before I start whacking my head against the non-padded white walls. I want to scream. *How do you express your feelings in a world that will medicate you for them?* Then again, my world was pretty fond of medicating emotions. Hell, I'm fond of it.

I grab my last pill from my backpack and hold it in my hand. *How am I going to survive without my pills? Without my friends? Without my family? I can't fucking do this. I'm not a hero.*

My body fires into hypermode. Sweat drips down my back, and I can't do anything to stop my brain from fighting a losing battle with nothing.

Twenty minutes. The most it should last is twenty minutes. I put the pill back in the bottle. I can do this. I'm safe in this room. I just have to wait it out.

Too bad I don't have a watch and my phone is dead, so there's no way to mark the endless passage of time. I rip off my clothes to escape the onslaught of heat pouring off my skin. As a last resort, I rush over to the black decontamination thingy.

I whack the side of it. "Turn on! OPEN!"

It pops open and I step inside. The warmth bothers me at first since I'm already overheated, but my body adjusts. Every time it shuts off, I turn it back on. It's temporary, but it's something.

I hope it can't overheat. What if using it too much causes a weird cancer? What if I spontaneously combust?

Despite my mind spinning, the light and sound traveling back and forth over my skin soon strips away my stress and lulls me into oblivion.

CHAPTER 5

DAY 3: 711 HOURS TO DECIDE

I WAKE UP groggy and sore at the bottom of the decontamination/glorified outhouse box. My stomach groans in rebellion. I sit up and remember where I am. The emptiness of the room matches my insides. I wish I could talk to someone I love.

My backpack sits somewhere on the floor in the blackness. I search for it, and the soft spotlight returns. I never realized how annoying conveniences can be.

Grabbing my bag, I unzip it and lay the contents across the floor. I pull out my copy of *Harry Potter and the Sorcerer's Stone*, the printouts of Rita and Dominick's online existence, my journal, a black pen, an extra elastic for my hair, a dead cell phone and plug. Obsolete relics from another lifetime. The things that were most important to me when fleeing my home planet. No picture of my parents. No pictures of my friends. I expected them to be with me. The T-shirt from Dominick that I packed has been confiscated along with my ring and bracelet. The spotlight on me and my belongings illuminates how alone I am. *This is real. We were stolen. I am trapped here without anyone I love.* My hands begin to tremble, so I shake them harder to regain control.

Outside the glass wall, a sun rises on the horizon, just like on Earth. Huge navy mountains surrounded by bright vegetation. The vibrant color looks like someone has ramped up the contrast on a TV screen. A brilliant lavender sky. A scarlet river. I wonder if it rains red here. *Blood rain, staining the beautiful surfaces with the truth.* Probably not—they have the power to control the weather. They have power over a lot of things.

A collapsible oval toilet extends from a wall with the press of my hand. At least I think it's a toilet because of the shape and height, but it doesn't have water in it. Oh, well. When you gotta go, you gotta go. I sit, pee, and reach automatically for toilet paper. There isn't any. Great. I shake and jiggle a little, which doesn't really work well in girl world, then stand. *What am I going to do when I get my period? That won't be pretty.* Before I have time to find a flush lever, an automatic white light fills the basin, evaporating all traces of urine. A strong, hot urine smell wafts up from the unit. I can only imagine the stench light-annihilated shit will leave behind. Guess not everything is as advanced in the future without water. They haven't mastered smell.

I want to splash water on my face to help wake up, but there is no water. I want to brush my teeth, but there's no sink or toothbrush or toothpaste. Instead, I wear the same black holofied uniform as yesterday and head down to breakfast in a maglift of death.

At the platform, I wait for my food to materialize. I'm afraid it's going to be green noodles again. It's not. It's a mushy, lumpy, brown and green concoction.

I notice that the top of the Hub is no longer open to the sky. A huge, domed glass ceiling, cut in segments like a huge diamond, filters in light in careful segments. Small rainbows flock the ceiling. The longer I stare at the ceiling, the more I notice the glass patterns shifting slightly over time to bring more light to different sections of nanoholocoms. Must be their way of controlling shadows so all the nanoholocoms can fully charge. Funny how we expect truth to be in light, and lies to be in shadows.

Off to the side of the Hub, Nolan and his grandmother eat

breakfast in the table area. I find a seat in the grass and scoop up warm lumps of mush with pieces of the bowl like everyone else is doing. The food resembles oatmeal, peanut butter, and honey, with slices of a sweet, pink fruit unlike anything I've ever tasted. Like a kiwi mixed with orange, ginger, and cinnamon. A bony bird with brown, downy feathers on its wings squawks in the large tree nearby. Like a tiny lizard chicken. Dominick would love it. A dinosaur in the future. The tree reminds me of an Earth red maple tree, except that when the wind blows, the leaves clink together to make a magical tinkling sound.

A chime clangs and resonates through the Hub. Everyone stops talking. People stand and automatically gather in the grass. I worry that the chime sound triggered a Pavlovian response, like trained dogs running for a treat. *Why aren't they worried that it's another catch? Another fine print in the contract with the vances?*

Above us, a glowing holographic image of Earth appears and rotates in midair. Some people look up. Some lower their heads. I stand to blend in with the gathering crowd, worrying that this is another sacrificial message, another terrible countdown, another impossible choice.

A voice echoes through the Hub. "We will now have our daily moment of silence for Earth, and for all those who could not join us." Another chime.

A blond teenage girl leans against her parents. Others around me wipe at the corners of their eyes. The woman who was missing her husband and baby when we were first processed finally has her baby back. She holds the infant over her shoulder while staring up blankly. Some clasp their hands forward in prayer. The hooded teenager and his grandmother are still sitting on a bench, not participating with the crowd.

I try to fake it, mourn for those lost, pretend I miss the existence of my not-really-destroyed planet. It's physically impossible. The anger at what the vances have done to us, how they want us to contribute ourselves to their technology, and how reverent everyone is being toward the whole thing overwhelms me. The sudden urge to scream out in the moment of silence builds inside my chest, to scream the truth, to scream that Earth is still there. Perfectly fine. We are the ones who are screwed.

Real tears find me. Tears for my parents. Tears for myself.

The blond girl taps my shoulder. "Are you okay?"

"No, I'm not okay. It's not okay."

I spot Doctor A. near the entrance. I bet he wants to take my pulse again.

I can't tell them yet. It's too soon. But I want to scream it across a loudspeaker: "NO!"

Everyone turns in my direction. *Oh, god, did I say that out loud?*

"It's not fair!" Nolan yells, jumping up from a table, his grandmother trying to grab him back.

"Nolan, please calm down," his grandmother says.

"Take him outta here," a man on my left yells. "He's being disrespectful," says the woman with him.

I lower my head and avoid eye contact, trying to seem reverent when I want to join the teen's rebellion. *No, it's not fair, Nolan. It never was.*

Nolan unleashes his own rage. He darts to the side and kicks to loosen a large, decorative stone. Heaving it to his chest, he carries it over to the food platform and slams it onto the base. No visible damage appears, but the sound of rock hitting rock vibrates through the Hub. The sound echoes in my ribcage.

His eyes grow wild. He searches for something, anything to destroy. Exactly how I'm feeling about Solbiluna-8. Poor kid. He just wants his mother back. His life on Earth back. *He's gonna get electrocuted and cocooned by the behavioral system.*

Maybe I should tell them now. It might make it better.

It might make it worse. I might get electrocuted.

Two men step closer to try to stop him.

"Get ahold of yourself," his grandmother says.

He ignores her and reaches for the heavy stone once again, bent on destruction.

Before the men reach him, Nolan's body freezes with the rock in his hands, blue electric flames surrounding his legs. He and the rock go down hard. A clear encasement washes over him, shellacking him to the ground.

His face transforms from rage to nothing. His eyes zone out the way my Dad's did during Zombie Nights.

His generic hologuide materializes next to him. "The BME has been automatically activated. Please remain calm and orderly as we deal with the infraction."

"Please, someone help my grandson!" the grandmother says. "It's hurting him."

I want to help. I do. I fight the urge to grab a rock myself and try to smash the shell pinning him down. An insidious thought stops me: *I could be next, trapped in another clear Zombie box.*

I'm not a hero; I'm a coward. Looking around, I'm not the only one.

What a dangerous and effective controlling technique. Small acts of self-preservation. *This is how genocide begins. This is how humanity ends.*

Nolan's grandmother covers her face with her hands. Doctor A. rushes over to help her. Everyone else returns to what they were doing beforehand. The children begin another color bubble game, stepping over Nolan's body to chase the bubble. The immediate apathy and casualness of everyone disturbs me even more than the incident.

What's worse—trying to fight the invisible? Or becoming the invisible?

"Kids these days. No class on any planet." The couple near me moves away, as if I have a rude disease they might catch.

No one cares except me and Doctor A. It's my job to make them care.

I need a plan. I need my friends.

I need crazy lady to change the future.

SITTING ON MY bed in my LU, the situation in the Hub still bothers me. I open my hologuide program.

It bows. "River Picard, please state your needs."

"How does the BME system work? What does it do?"

"The BME, or Behavioral Modification Emergency, immediately stops the movement of the individual or object in motion. For humans, it is followed by immediate treatment of PM and AM, or PhotoMeds and AudioMeds, until the threat level normalizes."

"So it can be activated if a person gets upset?" *Damn, I'll be next in no time.*

"No, it is activated when there is an attempt to destroy, commit violence, or break one of our laws. We must prevent problems from escalating to maintain order for the sake of society. Instant public rehabilitation."

Instant public rehabilitation for a boy grieving in anger. For a mother missing her baby. *I wonder what they do to whistle-blowers, people who tell the truth. How will I ever fight them if they trap and drug me at the first sign of mutiny?*

Crazy lady is the key. I need to find out what she knows. *Find out if she's real or just a new psychosis.*

"Your LU has not been modified yet," my hologuide says. "You may modify the room environment to meet your specifications of comfort."

I look around the blank space, reflecting the emptiness inside me. I would like a hammock. "Why, is there like a furniture storage area or something? You don't use money here, right?"

"We do not use currency on our planet. You are supplied with daily rations for all your needs that cannot be modified."

"So how do I get more furniture?"

"Hold your hand on your bandwidth and say *MODIFY LU*."

I obey, curious as to what will happen. "MODIFY LU."

Every inch of every surface of the room lights up with tiny pinpoints of light. The walls, the floors, the ceiling. Like technological glowworms.

A holoscreen appears and floats above my bandwidth.

"Holy crap." I stand automatically. "Why didn't you show me this earlier?"

"You did not ask. You exited the program. You required sleep."

"Right."

"The nanoholocoms within your LU environment will design what you need. Simply touch the specs you want to modify on the holoscreen."

On the screen is a holographic representation of the room. I touch the wall area on the display and visual options appear. I choose a specific wall, wall color, and a red option, and that entire wall in my LU immediately turns deep red, as if fairies had painted it with a magic wand. I adjust for vibrancy until I find my favorite shade of lipstick red.

I touch the furniture option and choose a chair that reminds me of my Dad's lounge chair, and then the hammock of my dreams. I choose room placement for the furniture and BAM, it forms on the spot, at first transparent, and then gradually filling in with details and depth.

"How is this even possible?"

"LU nanoholocoms are designed to create living environments. You will find that Solbiluna-8 is highly accommodating."

Accommodating. More like a kidnapper who lures children with candy and lost puppies. Like a Trojan horse that destroys a culture. Like Pan, the satyr, who played his flute and made the nymphs come under his trance to have his way with them.

"But it's holographic furniture." I walk over to the chair, which looks as real as any chair from Earth. "If I sit on it, won't I just fall through?"

"No. There are three types of holographic material: transitive, it looks transparent and things pass through it; semi-intransitive, it looks solid but things pass through it; and intransitive, it looks and acts like a solid."

"But holograms are made of light."

"Yes."

"Light is not a solid."

"No, but the nanoholocoms create the sensory experience of a solid. The bed that you slept on is an intransitive hologram created using resequenced, quantum-entangled photons."

I stare at the bed. I don't understand. I poke it with my finger, and the mattress feels like . . . a mattress. When I try to sit on the chair, however, the material bends and morphs, decomposing under my touch. My butt hits the floor.

"It takes a few minutes for new objects to completely quantum entangle. Please wait. Once established, they can reassemble in a second and retain coherence."

"You could've told me that."

"You did not ask."

For the next hour, my hologuide stands beside me as I

transform my LU into a mini-apartment, complete with blankets, pillows, rugs, and other comforts. I even add a large window with a moving, fake view of the Atlantic shore. I was wrong; the interior design of the future is amazing. It's as if I've stepped into *The Sims*. Dominick must be in love with the technology in this world.

I lose track of time in the excitement of creating things in my LU from nothing.

"Where's the sink? Can I make a sink?" I ask my hologuide.

"One moment. What files would you like to sync?"

It takes me a few seconds to understand the miscommunication. "No, *sink*. S-I-N-K."

"One moment. Sinks do not exist here. We do not use water for cleaning purposes."

"Then how do I clean things?"

"The PSF is used for disinfection." It points to the black decontamination box.

PSF. I need to remember those letters. "I guess I'm done, then."

"Hold your hand on your bandwidth and say *LU MODIFY EXIT*."

"LU MODIFY EXIT."

Modifying an environment is addicting. You can wield your power and make things submit to your whim. I stare at my hologuide in the gray uniform.

"How come sometimes you're transparent and sometimes you're not?"

"Outdoors we use more energy for greater depth perception in full light. Indoors we conserve yet maintain visual acuity. We have the ability to shift between transitive states based on need."

"Can you be modified?"

"Yes. Hold and say *HOLOGUIDE MODIFY*."

A mini-version of my hologuide emerges on a holoscreen floating over my bandwidth. I change its gender to female, its hair to a long, royal blue ponytail, and its uniform to a deep cranberry. It transforms before my eyes. Then I see the *Name* modification.

"I can give you a name?"

"Yes."

"What do you want to be called?"

"That is not a question we can answer."

I ponder names. How do you name a hologram? *Data? Seven of Nine? HAL?* No, no, something different . . .

Not a human name. That will personalize it too much and make it too familiar. It's a means to an end. It's just my—

I press the IDENTITY space and say "SIDEKICK." My hologuide repeats it aloud to confirm. At least if I have to call it, I'll never forget what it really is. Just a sidekick. Every hero needs one. Satisfied, I exit the modification panel and sit idle for a moment on my bed. It doesn't seem real that it's fake. That's a mind-bender.

No matter how cool this place is, I don't belong here. We don't belong here. I can't let myself get distracted by the technological possibilities.

I exit the hologuide program and poke the holographic lounge chair to check for readiness. It seems stable, so I slowly lower myself and rub my hands along the sides. Just like Dad's favorite seat, but without the smell. I can hear his voice yelling about privacy and human rights and communism. He would hate it here, but I still wish he was with me to help me fight. I miss his strong voice. When I left, he could barely speak.

Mom must be mourning Benji and me as if we've been taken. She will never understand that I had to do what I had to do. Dad will. At least I hope he will.

In reality, Mom probably isn't crying because she's busy putting Dad back together. Dad's in a wheelchair, getting weaker and crabbier, and possibly taking it all out on Mom since she's the only one left beside him. *Rage will slowly take over because he will feel helpless that he cannot be the hero for the family. He might become suicidal. He might kill them both to escape the misery of losing two children in a colossal, holographic kidnapping. A holonapping. A chrononapping. Hologenonapping. We don't even have language for this type of crime.*

The truth is that Dad may not have totally recovered. He may still be tethered to an oxygen tank. Schools might still be closed, so Mom may not have a job.

They might be starving to death. They may never have made it home.

A familiar stirring begins in my chest, and I almost return to the PSF to stop another anxiety attack, assuming it'll be worse than ever since Doctor A. warned me about withdrawals. It's not anxiety, though. I hug my legs, curl up in the chair, and let myself cry. Grieving is stronger than fear.

The loneliness encircles me like the cast of a dark shadow I can't escape. I need Dominick's touch on my skin again and one of Rita's famous pep talks. I need their laughter in my life. I look through my backpack and find my journal, with the printouts from their social media departure pages folded inside. We were so happy then. Young. Free. It will never be the same.

Holding my journal is like discovering a piece of my naive soul. I flip through to read the journey of the past six months, an innocent voice not knowing if she should stay or go, betray her family or her friends, or listen to the repeating voice of holograms promising salvation. I start scribbling angry comments in the margins, arguing with her, trying to change the past with a pen. But no one can do that. No one has that power.

Except crazy lady.

I flip through my journal to my entry that reads:

When the truth is shrouded in fear and clouded by dreams,

when fact and fantasy become deviant lovers,
maybe there are no real heroes anymore.

It's still there, untouched by her. I search through my belongings for her note, the one with a copy of my words with the alternative ending, *Maybe that's when heroes are born.* I had it crumpled in my hand before I ran through the vertex. It's not here. I must've dropped it when I was running through the crowd. Back on Earth.

Crazy lady affected me in the past, gave me that last incentive, and it cost her her life. I still don't understand how she did it, but I need to learn to trust her. I can't just sit here and wait, afraid to make waves and get plasticized and drugged while people start promising their contribution. I came to deliver the truth.

Who am I kidding? I also came here to see a boy. And my best friend. Instead, I have to deal with a convict.

Maybe motives matter less than we think they do. Maybe all that matters is what happens as a result of our actions.

It's time to stalk crazy lady and figure out how we're connected.

THE LIGHT OUTSIDE changes dramatically throughout the day as I wait on a bench in the Hub for Katherine to make an appearance. She has to eat sometime. I read my copy of *Harry Potter* to pass the time and wait for her to show her face. Above, a kaleidoscope of colors and patterns unfolds as sunlight reflects off each intricate facet of the dome. It's hard not to lose focus under something so beautiful. Streaks of pink, orange, and deep blue stripe the lavender sky. One sun. I guess some things don't change no matter the planet. Unless maybe if a planet had two suns. Not sure if that's possible. I wish I had paid more attention in science class.

I wonder if Dominick is looking up at the same sky. I wonder if he's thinking about me. He must be in heaven surrounded by all this technology. Wait till he finds out the truth, that it's really some hidden hell.

Rita came alone a while ago. I wonder how she and her religious runaways are doing. Maybe they can teach me the ropes. *What if she never actually made it through the vertex? What if she's still on Earth, and here I am looking for her?* No, she would have contacted me. And at least she'd be safe, I guess.

The tiny dinosaur bird is back. It squawks like a lone raven from the red wind chime tree, summoning our deaths. People in the Hub, however, seem happier than ever. They ignore the fact that Nolan, the boy who flipped out, is still stuck to the ground in the BME shell throughout lunch. Around dinnertime, the shell vanishes, and he stumbles to his feet. His grandmother runs with her food to him, scooping bits into his mouth. He doesn't fight it. The lobotomy fear zaps through my mind. *A knife scraping gray matter from beneath my skull.* The image repeats several times, getting more graphic each time. I rub the back of my neck to reassure myself that there is no wound.

No one else acknowledges Nolan's punishment and his grandmother's concern. People eat, mingle, kids play holobubble ball. The place is paradise for some, while others move invisibly through a hi-tech, holographic world. Not much different from Earth in that way. Even when the technology changes, people remarkably stay the same.

Doctor A. speaks to the grandmother, places his hand gently on her arm. They leave the Hub area together. Doctor A. is too nice to be human. He's nothing like the humans gathering in the

Hub for dinner. Like ants to a donut, here for their piece of sugar. Until they realize they are victims, too, they won't care.

Tonight's meal is a deep brown, loose liquid with soft foreign vegetation, including some purple clumps that taste like potatoes. I eat and read until I spot crazy lady walking toward the platform. I pinch myself to check that I'm not dreaming. Wonder if pinching works if she's a hallucination. Or a hologram.

Tossing my book in my backpack, I grab my journal and start recording her movements. She walks over to the platform for a food ration, then leans against the Hub wall to eat. She sips from the side of a bowl, chewing periodically. I chew, following her lead, following her movements, refusing to take my eyes off her this time.

That's when I first notice it. When a heavyset man with shaggy hair walks past her, crazy lady pushes something into his hand. They don't make eye contact or discuss anything. I bet they were prisoners together. Drug dealing prisoners. She served time. Big time. Maybe it's for dealing.

That actually reassures me. Dealing drugs is different from being a serial killer. *Unless she was a drug dealing serial killer.*

Stop it. What are the chances? As my counselor would say, there's a difference between possibility and probability. *Is it possible? Yes. Is it probable? I guess not.*

I take down descriptions of them in my journal in case someone finds my body. A list of suspects.

As Katherine eats, Doctor A. returns to the Hub, and being his polite self, joins her. *Didn't he listen to me? I told him she's a criminal. Some people are too nice for their own damn good.* I could walk over and casually join the conversation, but that would require too much emotional effort.

I add Doctor A. to my list, leaving an asterisk near his name and a note that says, "Not a suspect." I watch as she hands him something after he's finished eating. Minutes later, I see him pass the object to a teenage girl a few years younger than I am with pin-straight hair sitting in the grass.

The dinosaur chicken bird squawks from the nearby tree. It needs a friend like I do.

Doctor A. sees me, waves, and walks over. I stuff my journal into my bag.

"Are you feeling better?" he asks.

My heart climbs into my throat. "Oh, yeah. Much better."

"Great to hear. You staying for the Skylucent tonight?" He rubs his hands together, and it makes me nervous.

"Uh, not today. Heading back to my LU, actually." I sling my backpack over one shoulder.

"Have a good night, then. Glad to hear you're feeling better."

"Thanks."

People gather in the grass for the show, and I step around them in the darkness. It's too dark to see what's happening in the shadows and wherever crazy lady vanished.

I return to my LU and sit in the PSF to calm down.

Katherine was convicted for something on Earth, and she keeps handing people things. Drug dealer or murderer, she's part of my past, part of my present, part of everyone's future.

And Doctor A. is in on it. Whatever it is.

My curiosity feeds my anxiety, which in turns feeds my need to keep stalking her for more information. Information usually stops my mind from spiraling with unanswered questions and possibilities. I'm afraid this time more information might be the last thing I can handle.

I miss my friends like I miss the ocean.

CHAPTER 6
DAY 4: 686 HOURS TO DECIDE

I'M LOSING ALL concept of time other than light and dark, hunger and sleep. Maybe that's supposed to be how life works when you don't have anywhere to be. Time becomes an irrelevant measurement, each day blurring into the next, with nothing to do—other than save people from lying vances who want to force people to contribute. I add a twenty-four-hour digital clock to my bandwidth. Below it, a countdown to doom.

The muscles in my shoulders, lower back, and calves ache. I stretch and yawn automatically, pulling myself up from the bottom of the PSF in the dark. My movement makes light and objects materialize, including the bed and pillow made of light and fancy computer programming. I might as well give the holobed another shot.

Sleep and technology work magic when merged together. By the time I wake up again, I feel like days have slipped by. According to my bandwidth clock, it's 1500 hours, so midafternoon. Pulling myself up, I vow never to sleep in the bottom of a PSF again.

I am completely disoriented by my surroundings. The room is dark and empty, but as soon as I move, lights flicker on and furnishings reappear. It's like I had a bizarre dream, and instead of waking up out of it, I brought it forth and created it around me. It's unsettling.

No sink. Can't wash my face or brush my teeth. As I wait for a holographic hairbrush to quantum entangle, I create a holographic mirror on the surface of one wall, not that I really want to see what my curly hair has decided to do in these conditions. My hair has grown fluffier in all directions, the ends curled up unevenly. I attempt to smooth the dry fluff into a bun without water or gel, and a frizz halo forms.

I step back into the PSF to freshen my body, even opening my mouth during the process to see if it will clean my teeth. Running my tongue along my teeth, it feels as if the film of tartar is gone. Only the problem with the PSF is it doesn't help wake me up; it only makes me more relaxed and ready for more sleep.

I'm glad that the PSF filter cleans everything, including my black uniform—this just might be the outfit that I die in. The wound of loneliness opens from holding on to everything and trying to be strong when I don't even have a real friend.

I double-tap my bandwidth. SIDEKICK appears, still modified with a blue ponytail and red uniform.

"River Picard, please state your needs."

"I need tissues. Toilet paper. Do you have any paper products on this freaking planet?"

"You may request supply rations from the HDP. You are granted two supply rations per day for personal needs that cannot be made holographically."

It would be useless to chuck something at it. "Why didn't you tell me that before?"

"You did not ask."

Oh, how I hate artificial intelligence. *Can't it see that I'm barely holding on here? Can't it anticipate human needs and just fill me in?*

A knock on my door makes me jump. No one knows where my LU is, and holograms can't knock. Can they? A screen materializes on my wrist. *Please don't be a former prisoner come to devour me.*

A bushy salt-and-pepper beard fills the screen.

"River Picard?" Doctor A. asks through the monitor.

My heartbeat goes berserk even though it's the doctor. Since he and crazy lady might have a secret pact, I'm not sure how much I should trust him anymore.

Just ignore him and he'll go away. The guilt of being mean to him after he was nice to me wins. "Yes?"

"I'm here to check on you. Didn't see you at breakfast and lunch today."

I debate whether or not I should let him in. He was with Katherine, and she handed him something that he passed to someone else. Not exactly the worst offense. Not exactly the actions of an innocent man. *What if he's here to attack me? Lure me into trusting him, and then WHAP! Do I have something I could use to protect myself? Could I beat him with my copy of* Harry Potter?

I grab the book from my backpack for safe measure. Despite my fear, I say, "DOOR OPEN." I need some human contact before I start having conversations with SIDEKICK or the PSF.

Doctor A. looks a little younger today. Fresher. He's still bald with a beard, but there are fewer wrinkles around his eyes. Not sure how that happened.

"River, I thought I'd make sure you're feeling stronger."

"I'm okay. Getting a lot of sleep."

"Sleep is good, as long as you're not avoiding the real world through dreams."

He already knows me too well.

He continues. "If you're feeling up to it, how about some fresh air, enjoying integration? Some recreation in the Holospaces? Meet some kids your age?"

Oh, god, no. Socializing might push me over the edge. I'm doing all I can to hang on.

"It's good for solitaries like us to meet others."

Solitaries. I've already been labeled in my four days in the future.

"I'm fine, thanks." I should just come right out and ask him directly what Katherine gave him. The words sit on my tongue, cling to the back of my teeth, and refuse to be set free. I don't trust his motives. He's hiding something.

"Isolation is not good for mental health, especially in an unfamiliar place. I can come with you if that will help."

I can tell by the concern in his eyes that he's not going away unless I comply. I put down my book, and he shows me the way. Harry would have confronted him.

DOCTOR A. BRINGS me to the first floor of the LU community. I always assumed it was storage for the Hub or additional LUs, but the rounded hallway is marked by a holoscreen that reads *Holospaces,* followed by more than thirty white doors, each with another holoscreen on it. When Doctor A. touches a screen, it changes so we can see a visual feed of the people inside playing different hologames, some hi-tech, some basic sports. Some doors are visually locked when he touches them. *Don't want to know what's going on in those rooms, but I hope someone scrubs them afterward.*

He touches a screen and says, "Here she is."

Inside, the room looks like a family room, with two large leather sofas, a coffee table, lamps, a rug, and a fireplace. A teenage girl lounges on a sofa while playing a holographic card game in midair. The same girl he handed something to in the Hub, something he got from crazy lady. It's a conspiracy.

"Kendra, I brought a friend."

"Hi, Doctor A." She stops playing and drapes her straight, chestnut hair across one shoulder. "How's Nolan today?"

"Nolan is doing quite well. On the road to recovery. I'd like you to meet River."

"Nice to meet you." We shake hands awkwardly, my palms sweating, and I see her wipe her hand on her kitten print uniform. With her large, innocent blue eyes, I can tell she's the type that would rescue stray puppies and cats if she could.

"Nolan and Kendra knew each other in school," Doctor A. says. "She could use a friend while he recovers. I'll leave you two young people to have some fun."

I see what you did there, Doctor A., and I don't like it.

I wave, plotting revenge thoughts, but knowing he did it out of kindness to us both. A painful, forced socializing, pull-my-fingernails-off kind of kindness.

"So . . ." My mind goes blank. "I'm sorry, I forgot your name."

"Kendra. And you're River."

"So it seems," I mutter under my breath. "What're you playing?"

"An old card game my grandfather taught me. They have it programmed in the Holospaces. We can play something better, though. Stuff you can't even imagine. Holographic games, sports, adventures, and a ton of activities. You can even invent your own and share it or keep it private. Makes the virtual reality games with goggles from Earth look childish. Nolan came here once with me before he was zapped."

"Okay, let's try one. How does it work?"

"You search through the Holospaces with your bandwidth. I'll show you a cool one I found." She holds her bandwidth and swiftly moves through several holoscreens as if she's lived here for a thousand years.

"I like this one: 999myth."

As soon as her finger presses the holoscreen above her bandwidth, the entire room lights up with a blinding number of nanoholocoms.

"Oops, I forgot to tell you to close your eyes while it sets. You can open them."

I blink several times before my eyes readjust to the room. Except we are no longer in the room. We're in the middle of a mountain region with majestic, mythological creatures wandering past us, including a herd of winged unicorns.

I spin around. "Holy crap. Did we just transport?"

"Nope. We're still in the same room."

"Are you serious?"

"Totally. And you can interact with everything, but there are no consequences. Nothing is real. You could jump off a cliff and be perfectly fine."

I reach out and pet a small creature that looks like the off-spring of a goat and a dog. It's like being on a Holodeck from *Star Trek*. Only a real one. Thirty of them.

Why would we ever leave and live in the real world?

"Do another one."

"Okay, I like this one: 24-7HoloDay."

"Is that supposed to be a joke?"

"Yeah, it's like a vacation. Close your eyes."

When I open them, I'm surrounded by a tropical luau with draping tapestries, lanterns, coral flowers, and bamboo chairs overlooking an ocean the color of lime-green punch. I slip off my boots and move my toes in the white- and gold-flecked sand. Every soft particle warms my skin.

"Do you want to stay here and go swimming, or would you rather play a holosport program?"

"Is there a program of Earth? The Atlantic coast?"

"Probably. New programs get added like every second. When I get better at it, I'd like to design my own." She flicks her fingers, and with a few swift movements, finds one.

"Massachusetts, I assume?"

I nod, my throat constricting.

"Here goes."

And stretched out before me is the Atlantic Ocean. The familiar, salty breeze whips stray curls across my face. I kneel in the sand. It's not soft like in the HoloDay program. It's coarse and warm, just like home.

I take off running down the beach and jump into the cool ocean fully clothed in my uniform except for my boots. The only odd sensation is when I get a little water in my mouth, it instantly disappears. My muscles relax with each wave. It feels so close to the real thing, I scan the shoreline and expect to see Dominick or Rita. The thought jars me into the moment. *This isn't home. This isn't home.* I frantically swim to shore and stagger toward Kendra.

"Are you okay?" she asks.

My body shakes in the heavy, wet uniform. I grab her bandwidth.

"EXIT HOLOSPACES."

And just like that I'm back on dry land in a blank Holospace room. My uniform and hair aren't even wet.

I run out into the corridor barefoot and lean against the wall. Kendra carries my boots and socks with her. "Are you okay? What happened?"

"I never want to go back inside there."

"Why not?"

"Because . . . it's . . . something's missing. It's not right."

I don't tell her the truth. I could easily lose myself in there, holding on to what I've lost on Earth. Spend all my time in the peacefulness of fantasy instead of moving forward in the harshness of reality. If I don't let the truth out soon, people might forget what reality even looks like, might contribute themselves wholly to the false glamour of this world.

BY DINNERTIME, I am famished for whatever concoction the platform has in store for us today. Carrying my journal with me, I read a note to self to ask for toilet paper. At the platform, I make my request, and it prints what looks more like a sea sponge. Maybe I'm supposed to use it and then toss it in the PSF for next time? These vances are disgusting with hygiene.

As I wait for my food, Katherine makes eye contact and heads toward me. My insides turn against me, and I pray I don't vomit again. I'll be known as the Puking Girl.

She looks me up and down.

"Mississippi, you're a bit of a recluse."

You're a criminal. We're even. "Haven't been feeling well." I grab my food and the stupid sponge.

"Your hair . . . I had a better look in prison."

"Yeah, I know. Frizz city."

"Ask for seed oil. My hologuide recommended it."

"Thanks. I hate talking to my hologuide. It freaks me out."

"Fine, but you won't get anywhere if you don't ask the right questions."

How right you are. I place my hand on the platform and request the seed oil. It forms in a clear tube, similar to the capillary kind they use at labs after they prick your finger.

"This will last me one day."

"No, that stuff's magic. You can even use it on your skin and to brush your teeth."

"I should ask for a toothbrush."

"Pace yourself. Only two supply rations a day. If you create new programs for the Holospaces, you receive additional rations. 'Course people have been blowing their extra rations on extra Holospace time. You'd think four hours a day would be plenty."

I can still feel the fake Atlantic Ocean on my skin. I need an ally. I have to take a risk.

"I need to tell you something."

"Shoot."

"No, something important," I whisper. "I need someone I can trust. And . . ." I point around at the nanoholocoms embedded into everything, "I don't want to get zapped."

She draws me closer with her finger and whispers into my ear. "I hacked the nanoholocom controls in my LU and took the BME offline. If that's what you're worried about."

"You did?" This scares me but makes me want to be her best friend at the same time.

She smirks. "It's my specialty. Let's go."

My anxiety spikes at breaking the rules and trusting Katherine. A lump rises in my throat, and I still follow her. I really am irrational.

I KNOW I shouldn't trust Katherine alone in her LU without knowing more information about her, but I can't fight the vances and get back to Earth alone. I pick at a hangnail on my thumb.

"So Mississippi, what's eating you?"

"Nothing." *Maybe it's the fact that you could fillet me at any second, but I also need to trust you to save Earth even though I don't understand why.*

"Don't give me that bullshit. You just told me you have a secret. And you've been watching me, taking notes in that book of yours."

My stomach drops, and I try to keep my face emotionless. "No, I haven't."

She stares me down, letting me know I'm busted. "Spill it."

I can't tell her what I know. I need more information first. I climb into the hammock, leaving the sponge and journal on the floor while I eat my dinner. "Why were you in jail?"

"Why do you care?"

"I don't know," I stall. "Curious."

"You're afraid of me, aren't you?"

"No," I lie and spill crumbs on my chest.

She sits on a chair and looks at the floor.

"I was in for fraud and computer hacking mostly."

It's the last thing I expect her to say. I brush off the crumbs. "For doing what?"

"Credit card fraud. Identity theft. Hacking systems." She chuckles. "I worked for Apple for a few years when I was younger. Before my life took a turn and I moved back to the East Coast."

"So you stole people's credit cards? How'd you end up with such a long sentence?"

"It's a little more than that."

"Try me." My boldness surprises me. Her sharp responses make me defensive instead of afraid.

"You know enough. Now tell me, Mississippi, what's your story? Why are you here alone? Last minute departure without friends or family. You're the anomaly, not me."

I tell a half-truth. "My father was in the hospital. He got hurt in a riot. I waited as long as I could for him."

It's so much more than that, so much more since she even had a part in it that she doesn't know about, and I don't understand and I want to tell her everything.

Katherine continues. "My kid died. Cancer. If this whole thing had happened sooner, years ago, my daughter would have lived. The HME would've saved her with their advanced medical knowledge. What do they say, everything happens for a reason? Bullshit. Sometimes things happen for no reason at all."

"I'm sorry—"

She waves me off. "These holograms showed up, and it was a get-outta-jail-free pass for me. Except I wasn't sure I wanted it. No one is that nice. Nothing is that free. Too easy. I'm not contributing until I see every step of this integration. You shouldn't, either. Something's not right, and I know you feel it, too. I saw it in your eyes when they did the fucking Earth remembrance yesterday morning and that kid flipped out."

Her blunt truth opens up a part of me. It's easier to trust people when they break through their layers of emotional protection. She also reminds me of my dad, caring but broken and bitter about the past.

"I need to tell you something big, but I'm afraid to say it out loud."

"Like I said, I temporarily disabled the BME in here. I can't hack into a system while being monitored."

"Why did you hack into their system?"

She grins. "Your secret first."

I should be afraid of her. She could kill me now and no electric current would stop her. Instead, the truth bubbles up to the surface, and I finally let it loose.

CHAPTER 7
DAY 4: 679 HOURS TO DECIDE

KATHERINE PACES THE LU, more excited than afraid.

"Wait, so you're telling me that you ran through knowing you were safe on Earth, and having no clue what the hell was going on here? That's some brave, stupid shit. For all you knew, we were dead."

"No, I knew you were alive." I chew on a hangnail.

"What do you mean, you knew? How could you know? You mean, you hoped?"

"No, um . . ." I think of a way to break it to her gently. It's impossible. I cannot tell her she gave me a note in the past that had a message from my journal. I've watched enough sci-fi, time travel episodes to know not to set something in motion. Especially something that ends with Katherine dead. "Yeah, I guess I hoped."

A full minute ticks by as the information sinks in between us. It's a relief to have someone listen to the truth.

She crouches down near the hammock. "There's a group," she whispers. "They need to hear this."

"What group?"

"The Umbra. It's a secret organization set up by the United Nations before we left Earth. Certain government officials were given instructions. They recognized that it's never good for one side to have all the power, and with Solbiluna-8 being so advanced, we would need to catch up fast. I was invited to join when I arrived. Reputation and all."

She sits closer to me, and continues. "We've been slowly growing, working on conspiracy theories, pulling apart nanoholocom units to study them. After the meritocracy announced the contribution plan, we've been discussing our next move. Your information could move the Umbra into high tactical alert mode."

"Are you, like, terrorists here?"

She smiles at the word *terrorists,* which makes my muscles tense. "No, no, nothing like that. They want the best for Earth humans, and they believe knowledge is power and leverage here. Yet we're being kept happy and ignorant."

"Did Doctor A. join the group?"

"You are observant, aren't you? You'll fit right in. Come to the meeting tomorrow and tell them what you told me. They'll listen. Your testimony could be vital to our cause."

I take a deep breath, hold it, and let it out. I finally told someone, and she believed me.

"So, you write?" Katherine asks and picks up my journal from the floor.

"No—" I almost flip the hammock over as I snatch my journal from her hand before she manages to read anything. "Not really. A little."

"Get your panties out your ass. I won't read your little diary."

Note to self: Don't let Katherine near my journal ever again.

ACCORDING TO KATHERINE, the Umbra meeting changes location each day, and only some of the membership are invited. That way if the nanoholocom network or the BME catches them, the vances won't be able to dismantle the entire operation at once. You have to wait for someone to hand you the number of the LU to get into the meeting. They never say it aloud. She said she'll make sure that someone finds me.

I wait in the Hub the next day, exhausted after hardly sleeping throughout the night. The dinochicken squawks at random times from its safe spot in the tree. It's probably wondering what in the world we're doing here. Just like we are. I sit under the tree and lean back against its rough trunk. A gust of wind blows by and rustles the leaves, sending music into the air and flipping the colors from dark red to purple and back again. I have to admit it's kind of peaceful here. Aside from the squawking bird.

As I lean forward to read, a few strands of my curly hair get caught in the tree bark, a natural Velcro reaction.

"Ouch," I mutter and rub my head. My hair gets tangled in everything. A piece of bark hangs where I pulled forward, so I rip it loose. The dry bark in my hand seems ancient, empty, like a wooden fossil. The scratchy texture under my thumb reminds me of Dad's face when he doesn't shave. I'm surprised there are no twigs or fallen leaves under the tree. This place is as super clean as Disney World. Disturbing.

Kendra, the girl I met in the Holospaces, waves and plops down next to me under the tree. I stick the bark in my pocket since I don't know if littering is a crime.

"Do you mind if I eat with you?" she asks in a commanding voice that doesn't match her kind, round face.

"Sure," I say, annoyed. *Why ask after you sit?*

"Nice day today. Perfect weather. Then again, it's always perfect weather, so that's not very good small talk, is it?" She takes a bite of food and chews slowly.

I nod. If I don't encourage her, maybe she'll leave.

"Still avoiding the Holospaces?"

I point to my book. "I'd rather read."

"You brought a book with you? We should start a library

here of books from Earth. Although there is a Hololibrary in the Holospace, and your bandwidth can display reading material."

She's one of those do-gooder types. I need to get away from her before she makes me volunteer for something.

"I'm heading up to my LU. Nice to see you again, Kendra."

"Wait," she whispers. "Take this."

She hands me a note with 5-88 on it. I look at her face for confirmation and remember her connection with Doctor A. She doesn't show any sign of being a top secret agent. I wonder why she was recruited. My respect for her just skyrocketed.

"See you during the Skylucent," she says, and winks. My hands shake so much the numbers blur. It's now or never. This is why I came here.

Later that night, when the lights flash in the sky to mark the Skylucent event, I head to a maglift and travel to the right LU. At some point in the trip, the doors open, and Doctor A. enters along with Kendra. None of us speak in the maglift. I guess that's how spy situations work—you suddenly pretend not to know each other when shit goes down.

Once we arrive at the right floor, we step into the hallway. No one else is around. *We're going to get caught and zapped unconscious by the BME, then tortured until we confess to our treason. Public execution in 2359: Restrained in holographic stocks in the middle of the Hub, flocked with holograms. Electrocution by lightning strike from the weather-controlled atmosphere. My face frying and bubbling as I crack under the pain and spill my guts. My dead body unrecognizable from the burns.*

Doctor A. knocks on the door marked 88.

"Please wait while I visually verify your entry," someone says through the door.

I reach into my pocket for the bark from the tree, something to hold on to as I wait for what's about to happen. Of course, it's missing. I lose everything.

A minute later, the door clicks open, and we are let into the Umbra.

CHAPTER 8
DAY 5: 652 HOURS TO DECIDE

ONLY A FEW scattered halos of light illuminate the area and follow movements. My eyes can make out about thirty or so shapes of people gathered around in the dim light. The room seems much larger than any LU I've seen so far.

Katherine steps forward. "I called a special meeting to discuss new information that supports our cause. This is the girl I told you about, River." She pulls me toward her so that I'm on display. "She has important information to share about the vances."

"Don't worry," she whispers to me. "The BME is disabled in here."

I clear my throat, but before I have a chance to speak, there's commotion in the background. Someone shouts, "Alex?"

I turn in the direction of the familiar voice.

Benji.

I promised myself next time I saw my brother, I would punch him. Instead, I race toward him and hug him with all the strength I have left.

"Oh, my god, you made it," he says.

I cry. It's not about him. It's not about him.

"Where's Mom and Dad?" he asks.

Guilt floods through my veins for what I'm about to tell everyone. Even worse since Benji will hear that I abandoned our parents.

"Benji's your brother?" Katherine interrupts, nodding with approval. "Small world. So I take it your name's not River, then?"

"My real name's Alexandra Lucas. Alex." Saying my name aloud reclaims a small piece of my lost identity, a small piece of home.

"Now that's a name I believe. It's nice to finally meet the real you."

"Likewise," I say, as a former image of her demise flashes through my mind.

"What do you know about the vances?" Benji asks, pulling on the front of his navy blue uniform to straighten it. His tone implies doubt that I would ever have anything valid to say. Typical. Missed you, big bro.

I turn my back to him and focus on Doctor A., Kendra, Katherine, and the eyes of strangers in the shadows. *For all we know, they could be hologram spies.* I have to try anyway. It's do or die.

"The Earth is fine. There was no apocalypse."

Murmurs in the background. Benji crosses his arms over his chest and says nothing. Katherine nods for me to keep going.

I pick at my clean nails while my hands shake. "The comet was a hologram. It was all a hoax."

Doctor A. reasons. "Our own scientists saw it coming. Tried to stop it. If you made it through a vertex in time, you didn't see the comet crash."

I shake my head. "I didn't make it through at first. I was too far away. And there *was* a comet, and it crashed, but it turned into tiny orbs of light and just disintegrated. People cheered at first. They thought it missed. But then—" I see the horror and chaos unfold before my eyes again. "Everyone freaked and started running away in terror. I jumped through as the vertex closed. I couldn't let all of you think you'd been saved. Let you contribute. I'm telling you, the comet was a hologram."

Doctor A. reaches for a nearby holochair, clearly distraught. Kendra places her hands over her mouth.

"Why would the vances make up an apocalypse?" Kendra asks.

"I don't know. But we can't let people contribute to this world. We have to tell them and go home."

"Easier said than done," Katherine says. "If Earth still exists, it fundamentally changes our mission."

A man with so much hair on his arms and neck I could braid it steps closer. His deep voice bellows through the dim light. "Why should we trust her? She even lied about her name."

"I lied about my name because I didn't want to give the vances any information about me. I don't trust them. They already took enough from us." I pause and tuck a few stray curls behind my ears.

Katherine joins my side. "Think about it. Where are the vances? Why are they playing with us in these integration stages? Asking us to contribute? Why can't we travel? We knew something was up. We just never thought it was this big."

"I don't know," the hairy man says. "That's some weighty shit."

"So Earth is still there?" Kendra whispers.

I nod. "Yes, but who knows what happened after I left. Could be chaos. They're probably mourning us the way we're mourning them. Or turning on each other."

I left my parents in the middle of nowhere during winter with no food, shelter, or transportation. Dad in a wheelchair, Mom alone to fend for them against a fleeing, desperate mob. Visceral images of my parents being devoured by a hungry crowd, body parts being hacked and chewed. Bone marrow sucked, eyes split and shared. Brains slurped and hearts bitten.

What if just thinking these thoughts makes them true?

Don't get tricked by a thought. Don't get tricked by a thought.

"Mississippi," Katherine nudges me with her shoulder. "You with us?"

"Yeah." I wipe my eyes.

Katherine addresses the hairy man. "Beruk, you have to consider the possibilities."

"We can't refocus our energy toward returning to Earth on mere hearsay."

"But it's true!" my voice cracks, my hands trembling in front of me.

Doctor A. stands and waves me over to his holochair. I plop down from emotional lethargy as my legs give up.

The room quiets.

Benji finally speaks. "Beruk, I can vouch for her. If Alex says it happened, it happened."

I never thought Benji would be the one to believe me. He usually treats me like a psychotic wimp.

Before Beruk has a chance to respond, an older man with a leathery face chimes in. "I agree with Benji. Let's move forward on this."

Beruk approaches him. "Jackson, with all due respect—"

Jackson stands taller, chest out. "Are you questioning my authority?"

"No, sir," Beruk says, maintaining eye contact with Jackson.

Jackson turns to address the room in a commanding tone. "We need to switch gears immediately. Continue to gather evidence and information. Contact all Umbra as soon as possible. Professor Marciani, we need to move on developing holographic weaponry."

"The DQD prototype is almost ready," another man answers from the back corner of the room. He twists his hair into knobs on his head. It reminds me of when I chip my nail polish. Something to do with all that nervous energy. "Jackson, if I may add, if Earth is safe as this young lady says it is, I suggest researching vertex technology to help us get home."

"Agreed," Jackson says.

Beruk concedes. "We'll need more recruits."

"Do it. Keep this information confidential. If the vances find out we know, they might attack before we are ready. I stated this once before, but it begs repeating: I highly recommend that no one contributes to Solbiluna-8 until we have more information."

Katherine nudges me in the chair and whispers, "You did it."

Game on. They believe me, thanks to Benji.

As everyone moves into talking plans, possible motives, and actions, Benji pulls me aside.

"Are Mom and Dad in your LU?" he asks. "How's Dad?"

I thought he had understood. "They didn't make it."

"What? Why? Did Mom decide to stay with him? Did Dad . . . "

I pull at a hangnail, making it bleed. "No, they were both alive when I left. Dad was conscious and in a wheelchair. Like I said, we ran into traffic and then a crowd at the vertex and couldn't get through."

"I told you that would happen. Damn it." He runs his hand quickly through his cropped hair. "But you still made it. I didn't think you had it in you." He almost looks disappointed.

Anger merges with the guilt in my chest. "You mean to ditch them like you did?"

"Alex, it wasn't like that. You all should've left sooner with me and Marcus."

"And abandon Dad. And then what? Have Mom be a victim of the vances, too? And no one ever know it?"

Silence. Benji and I are right back where we always are, even three hundred years in a parallel future. Location doesn't change the truth.

Someone taps me on the shoulder. It's Marcus, my new brother-in-law and last math teacher before schools closed. "Alex, we've been so worried."

I give him a half hug since it's weird hugging a teacher. He smiles his gentle smile. Why can't he be my brother?

"You joined the Umbra, too?" I ask.

"I'm helping with the math involved, although sometimes it's over my head."

"I haven't seen either of you eating in the Hub."

"We've been managing the Umbra meetings from different LU rooms," Benji says. "It takes a lot to secure an LU site and then move locations. Worth it, though, to stay off the radar. We tend to get food super late and bring it with us. I can't believe you're here. I had given up hope."

He purses his lips, and his face hardens. They haven't just been worried; they've been assuming I was dead. It's nice to see him upset over me.

"So you believe me?" I ask. "About the comet?"

"I need to verify your facts. Beruk was right. We can't start a rebellion based on one witness. I know you, though. You wouldn't have left Mom and Dad to die in a comet crash. Something had to happen. Something to piss you off. It's the only explanation. When you get angry, you turn into a banshee. I can see you running toward a vertex in anger. That's not a normal person's response."

And there he is. My brother, back in my life again.

"Thanks, I think." I suck on my bleeding hangnail. "So you'll fight to get us home?"

"I'll investigate. Whether or not I alter the Umbra's mission is another story."

Oh, god, did someone put my jerky brother in charge? "Are you one of the leaders of the Umbra?"

Benji laughs at me like I'm a child. "Not the leader. The Umbra is a big group, so we're separated for now. Military carries weight, though, and there aren't many of us in this LU community." He smiles with a confidence I don't think I've ever felt in my lifetime. Even with his arrogance, I'm desperate for familiar faces to remind me of home.

Marcus says, "He's being modest. He's third in command here after Jackson and Beruk."

Beruk broods in a corner with a handful of Umbra. Jackson, Katherine, and the professor talk on the other side of the darkened LU. The obvious tension among the troops doesn't bode well.

LATE INTO THAT same night, I lie in my bed made of holographic light and allow myself to think about Dominick and Rita. Seeing Benji and Marcus today gives me hope that I'll see my friends again soon. Hope is more painful than people admit. There's a void in my universe without Dominick and Rita. Like a ghostly imprint of where my friends should be. I told Dominick I loved him, but I never told him how much being with him means to me. I know I'm not easy to love, and he stays consistent, always ready to let me back in. And Rita, like a sister, always there to make me laugh, to talk to about anything, and even when I'm going off course, helping to steer me back without pressure.

I imagine my parents back on Earth, helping to rebuild society. I see Dad strong, back in good health, managing a new grocery store for the community. I see Mom in the elementary school office, waving to me like I'm a famous movie star. My parents. That's how I want to remember them.

But the truth is, the Umbra might not be capable of fighting for our rights in an advanced world, and I may never see my friends, parents, or Earth again. They might be lost in time, dead for centuries. If that's the truth, there's a part of me that wants to die with them.

CHAPTER 9

DAY 6: 635 HOURS TO DECIDE

AFTER THE SECOND meal ration, I scribble into my journal to deal with the jitteriness growing inside of me. I sketch a picture of the dinochicken to pass the time. When someone taps me on the shoulder, I jump and slam my journal closed.

"Sorry," Kendra says. "Katherine told me to come get you."

She doesn't have to ask me twice. I crave information.

We ride in a maglift to the latest Umbra location. I clutch my journal as the maglift rises.

"I hope this doesn't sound rude," I whisper, "but how did you get recruited?"

She smiles and whispers back. "Jackson's my grandfather. My legal guardian. Likes to keep a close eye on me. It's nice, if a bit claustrophobic."

"Sounds like my dad. He's military like Benji."

"Yikes, so you have it double."

Had it double. Funny what you miss when it's gone.

As soon as we enter the LU, I'm overwhelmed by the difference from yesterday's meeting. The number of members has tripled to more than a hundred. To one side, a tactical area with handwritten charts. Jackson, Beruk, and Benji argue while two others record information. Across the room, a well-lit laboratory where clusters of people experiment on various bits of technology scattered across a glass surface. Katherine waves from that area and meets us halfway.

"Mississippi, Benji requested that I tinker with your bandwidth to scramble your biosignature name."

"Don't I need my biosignature to function?"

"You'll still have a biosignature. All I'm doing is making your name randomly fluctuate every time it's used so the system can never track the real you."

"So it's like a constantly new alibi?"

"Exactly." She grabs my wrist and starts flying through functions I've never seen on a holoscreen above my bandwidth.

"She did mine, too." Kendra says. "Jackson's orders." She rolls her eyes.

The door opens, and I worry that the vances have discovered our hideout. Doctor A. enters the LU.

"I'll be back," Kendra says, and soon she and Doctor A. are in a deep conversation across the room.

Katherine refers to a holoscreen above her own wrist, copies a bunch of holographic code, and tosses it from her screen to mine. "Almost done."

"This LU is huge," I say.

"We needed more space to fit new recruits and projects after your handiwork. LU walls are modifiable, so it's easy to link together a network of rooms and expand based on size. I assume that's how LUs adapt to families. We're meeting around the clock now. Lots of changes since yesterday."

"Looks like disagreements in some areas," I say.

"Yeah, well, change does that." She lets go of me. "All set. You're one of the elite Umbra now. Untraceable. I've only done that to top-clearance members. And their families."

"I feel safer already," I lie. If only it was that easy.

Katherine shows me around the Umbra, introducing me as "the Earth witness" to people who weren't present at yesterday's meeting. As she does, people nod at me in approval and shake my hand. I avoid eye contact.

"Jackson outranks everyone here." She points across to the tactical room at Kendra's grandfather. I remember him from the first meeting talking to the professor. "Doesn't say too much. People request permission, he says yes or no. Likes to be left alone. Beruk and Benji do most of the legwork. He steps in when there's dissension."

As she shows me around, I notice that some Umbra smile at Katherine, but scowl when they pass by the tactical area, and at Benji in particular.

"Some members seem a little angry at my brother."

"Nah, it's an ex-con thing. They don't trust authority. Nice thing about ex-cons, most of us are really good at hands-on learning, and are not afraid of taking risks or pulling things apart to learn how they work. We tend to be bored, we thrive on information, and we aren't afraid to break rules to get what we want. You gave us something real to fight for. Sometimes that helps society. Ironic, isn't it?"

More ironic that I'd be the person to join you.

"How did this group form again? It's amazing to see so many different people working together."

"The UN planned it ahead of time with special forces. They had the foresight that we would need to establish power here by collecting as much information as possible and branching out in stealth. That's how Benji was recruited back on Earth."

He was under special orders? Is that why he was so adamant about coming, even if it meant leaving us behind?

Katherine continues. "Remember George Rogers, the astronaut? He's one of us. At a different location, though, since he was one of the first to leave. Oh, let me introduce you to one of my closest associates."

She points to the professor with the knobby hair. Up close he smells terrible, like body odor and Parmesan cheese.

"Professor Marciani is one of MIT's leading experts on holography . . . well, expert based on three-hundred-year-old information. We go way back, right, Professor?"

"To California days." The professor tips an imaginary hat toward me and continues tinkering with a holographic screen.

"He's the one who got me into the Umbra. Brilliant guy. And there's Beruk."

She points to the man with the incredible arm hair who gave me a hard time yesterday—who's in an argument with Jackson and Benji. I'd take the professor's smell over Beruk's personality any day. It's like he's doing it for the anarchy. I notice that when he argues, his lip curls with a slight, sadistic edge. I trust him even less than the prisoners. At least with them I know what I'm getting.

"Your brother is great," Katherine adds. "He calls it like it is. Marcus, I don't know very well. I wouldn't trust Beruk as far as I can throw him, which isn't far."

I pick up a disabled nanoholocom unit from a table. Like a tiny pill capable of a billion calculations. *Wonder what would happen if I swallowed it*?

Dominick would love working with the Umbra. Maybe when he arrived he joined the group at a different location. I remember watching him step through a vertex, his red Converse sneaker the last image my heart memorized of him. It can't be the final one.

"What can I do to help?"

"You already did it. You brought us the truth."

"But there has to be something else I can do."

"Let me think about it. Your brother asked me to give you a low profile."

"Why?"

"Said you get stressed out easily."

Where is Benji so I can hit him? I can't sit useless while everyone else around me dismantles nanoholocoms. With time on my hands, all I'll do is think in circles and feel inept.

Then I think about Nolan, the teen who got zapped, who's mourning his mother because I didn't tell him the truth. And the mother who had the missing baby and thinks she's a widow. Because I didn't tell her the truth.

"Do you have time to help me with a quick project?" I say to Katherine.

"Depends on what it is."

"Hold that thought. I'll be right back."

I find Doctor A. and Kendra and pull them aside. There's something I need to make right.

"Doctor A., how's Nolan doing, the one who was punished by the BME?"

"Kendra and I were just talking about him. He's better. Not emotionally the same, though."

"But stable. Not flipping out on people."

"No, quite the opposite."

"Okay, then. I'd like to do something, but I need your help."

DOCTOR A. BRINGS me, Katherine, and Kendra to Nolan's LU. His grandmother answers the door. Doctor A. speaks with her while Katherine messes with the LU controls. Kendra and I walk toward Nolan, who stares at us from a small holobed without changing his expression.

I liked him better angry. At least there was spunk in him.

"Hey, Nolan," Kendra says. "How're you feeling?"

He shrugs.

"Do you remember me?" I ask.

"No," he says. His eyes flick away, and he shrugs again.

"I remember you. You lost your mom."

He stares at me from across a desert of empty emotions. I know that look. It's my dad's look.

"All set," Katherine announces. "BME disabled."

"How do you do that so fast?" Doctor A. asks.

"Even though it's a complex surveillance system, it still basically works the same way. Monitoring all areas using nanoholocoms and biosignature readings for signs of behavioral issues. I don't technically disable it; it's too big. I set up a false reading for this LU. It thinks we're sleeping."

Nolan can't stop looking at Katherine. It takes him a few minutes to respond. "It can't electrocute me?"

"Not right now."

He nods and rolls over. Maybe it's not the right time. His grandmother comes over and steps between us.

"What is this about?" she asks.

"Do you trust me?" Kendra asks, putting her hand on Nolan's shoulder.

He wipes his face. "Always."

"We're all part of a group called the Umbra. We're trying to get home to Earth."

He sits up and leans closer. "But Earth's gone."

"Earth's fine," I say. "Your mother is fine."

"Don't screw with me. That's not even funny. You said you were the last one through. You said . . ."

So he did remember me. "I know. I had to say that at the time. I didn't have the Umbra's protection. The BME would've stopped me."

Instantly, his energy changes. "Where's my mom?"

"On Earth. The Earth wasn't destroyed. Kendra will explain everything to you, and then she'll show you around the Umbra tonight. We'd like to recruit you to help us fight back."

He looks at his grandmother, and then at Doctor A., who nods in encouragement.

"I'm in. All the way."

His grandmother takes a deep breath, turns to Doctor A., and says, "Can I join, too?"

A weight disappears from behind my heart, and I breathe a little deeper. One more recruit to go.

I leave Kendra and Doctor A. with Nolan to discuss further details. Katherine and I search for the woman and the baby to tell her that her husband is alive on Earth. The nanoholocom network still won't let us search for people, but even if I could use it, I don't know the woman's name.

"Can you tap into the communication system? Unblock it early?" I ask.

"No. Don't think I haven't tried. It's not blocked; it's more like the program doesn't exist on our bandwidths yet. We'll have to ask people if they've seen her and the baby."

Great. Starting conversations with complete strangers is not my strength. "I haven't seen her in a while," I admit. "She used to come to the Hub for some meals."

"And you would notice."

"I'll take that as a compliment."

"You should. It was."

She's like Benji if he had a personality.

"Let's start knocking on doors," Katherine says. "This better be worth it, Mississippi."

When someone answers at each door, we ask if they've seen a woman with a baby around four months old. They send us to other locations. Katherine and I take the maglift to more and more LUs based on leads. A woman with fuchsia hair answers the next door, and behind her a man plays with a giggling baby. She sends us to another LU where a party is in full swing. An older woman with long, white-blond hair and gallons of makeup answers the door and invites us inside. People jam to music, some dancing, some singing karaoke, the lyrics holoprojected on a wall. Nanoholocoms glow and change color to add to the ambience.

"Special occasion?" Katherine asks, impressed.

"We just contributed," she says. "See?" She points to her bandwidth, which emits a soft golden light around her wrist. "Time to celebrate our freedom."

I look around the room at the crowd of glowing bandwidths, a sign of acceptance. Of assimilation. Their happiness and ignorance makes me feel ill. "Already?"

"Why wait?" the woman asks.

Katherine shows no reaction and changes the subject, asking her about the woman and the baby. Based on her description, the woman nods.

"I know who you're talking about. I visited her a couple times, tried to get her to join us. Can't help people who don't want it, you know what I mean?"

She gives us the LU room number. I leave the party uneasy and angry at their ignorance.

"We need to tell them," I say to Katherine.

"That's only one room of people. We need to save as many as possible. If the vances catch on before we're ready for them, we're screwed."

That's not how I do math. I focus on one person, one thing at a time. Easier to not get overwhelmed by all the possible problems. All the possible casualties.

We travel to the next LU to look for the woman and the baby. More than ever I want to help her, to let her know her husband is alive on Earth, and she can join us to fight for justice.

No one answers the LU door no matter how long I knock.

"Maybe she's not here," Katherine says. "She could be eating in the Hub."

"Have you seen her around lately? At any meals?" I ask.

A baby's cry echoes behind the door. I knock louder, and the baby's cry increases in intensity.

"Maybe she's asleep," Katherine says.

"Ma'am?" I knock even harder until my knuckles turn raw. "I'd like to talk to you about your husband. The man with the owl tattoo on his neck? I have information."

If anything were going to make her answer, it would be that. Nothing. Something doesn't feel right.

"Give me a sec," Katherine says. She messes with the nano-holocoms in the side panel. "I have to disable the BME in the corridor first before I can try to unlock the door. Keep a lookout."

I am not the person to keep a lookout. It's like asking a guppy to watch for sharks. I swear my knees actually knock into each other from my legs trembling. I thought that was only reserved for cartoon characters.

Katherine's illicit movements echo down the curved hallway as I glance left and then right and then left again.

"Can you go faster?" I ask.

"If you don't talk to me," she says.

My eyes move left, right. Left, right. Left, right. My temples hurt.

A noise. Maglift doors opening.

"Katherine," I whisper loudly.

She turns her back to the panel and leans on it to block her progress. A group exits the maglift and travels past. They are too busy chatting and laughing to notice our movements. As they walk, the golden glow from their bandwidths swings by their sides, shining against their vibrant uniforms. *I always thought fighting for freedom meant fighting for happiness. Why am I fighting so hard against something that's making people so happy?* It must be nice to go through life without a worry. I spin my clear bandwidth on my wrist.

Katherine continues working. After a few more minutes, she says, "Bingo."

The door opens.

The woman's body dangles above us from a rope, her body wrapped in a BME bubble in midair. Her baby cries from a clear, oval bassinet. I cover my face with shaking hands and run out of the room, and I don't stop until I'm in my LU.

It's all my fault. It's all my fault. I should've told her the truth when I had the chance.

CHAPTER 10

DAY 6: 630 HOURS TO DECIDE

LATER THAT NIGHT, Katherine explains to me that the mother tried to hang herself and the BME stopped her in mid-air. Guess suicide is against the rules in Solbiluna-8. They need our brains functioning for their contribution program after all.

Doctor A. tries to reassure me that it's the vances' fault this happened. Their lie made the woman believe her husband was dead, and they took her baby away for medical treatment without her consent, which made her desperate with grief. Nolan's grandmother has volunteered to watch the infant indefinitely.

I swallow my last pill.

All night I lie awake in my bed not moving. *She almost died and that baby would've had no one. I wonder who will tell that baby what almost happened to its mother when it grows up. I wonder if it will hate me.* I can hear the baby screaming for its parents in the darkness, surrounded by nothing but holographic technology.

Alone. No one hears that kind of pain.

As the sun rises outside my LU window wall, the red river in the distance welcomes me. *If I drown in it, would the water paint my insides scarlet, marking my guilt and shame like a reverse baptism?*

I try to convince myself that the woman is alive and the baby is alive and that everything will be okay. But the guilt wraps itself around my soul and squeezes like a snake devouring its prey. I remember being so desperate to find an end to the pain I contemplated swallowing my life away. It's a place I never want to revisit, yet it's always there, and a part of me hates it, a part of me is afraid of it 'cause I know how it tricks your mind into believing that oblivion and escape are better than life itself.

I stay in bed and wait to feel safe again.

The sleep-filled day turns into a sleepless night and into another day. Someone knocks on my LU door, and the nanoholocom screen lights up on my wrist. I ignore it. They'll leave eventually. The door makes a strange sound, like technology scratching a chalkboard, and it opens without my permission. As soon as I see Benji in my doorway, my muscles seize with expectation. Benji takes no prisoners. He never lets me wallow. Wallowing is a human's right.

I double-tap my bandwidth. SIDEKICK appears next to me, and before it can greet me, I scream, "Security breach. He's going to kill me." It's not true; I just want Benji out of my LU. Leave me to drown in the guilt river that I deserve.

"725 Walnut," Benji announces. My holobed evaporates, and my body hits the floor with a hard plop. SIDEKICK disappears, and my room has gone dark, the only light from the sun through the wall-length window.

"Really?!" I sit forward and run my hand over my elbow, the same elbow that has a small scar from my first run-in with a hologram on Earth. It's almost nonexistent after all my time in the PSF.

"Shut up and listen." He crouches near me. "You can't crumble."

I scoot away from him. "A woman tried to kill herself. I should've given her hope. Told her the truth from the beginning. We're taking too long. Some people are sad and desperate and need to hear the truth. Some people are happy and starting to contribute and need to hear the truth."

"Alex, you gave us the information we needed to increase our efforts and fight to get home. If you stay in hiding, it will look like you lied. It will look like I trusted you when I shouldn't have.

People are asking questions. You can't stay in this room. Do it for Mom and Dad."

Mom and Dad. I need to remember what the vances did to us. I stand up to leave, to do what's right. My mind chooses that moment to visualize my parents dead, hanging from the ceiling in our living room back on Earth.

I crawl into a ball on the empty floor of my LU and rock back and forth to get the image out of my head. I try to imagine my happy place, a hammock on an island with a book to read. The image only lasts a moment before the ropes of the hammock morph into ropes around my parents' necks.

"Alex?" Benji touches my shoulder.

I look up at him. "They're dead."

"No, the woman and her baby are okay."

"Mom and Dad," I whisper. "I bet they're dead." I rock back and forth to slow the deep, unsettled energy soaring through my system.

He crouches next to me. "You can't think like that."

I hold my head in my hands. "I can't stop it."

"Where're your pills?" he asks and glances around the room.

"Gone," I manage to say. "I took the last one."

"Shit. Do that breathing thing you're supposed to do."

"I am!" I yell.

"Good," he replies. "I can tell it's really working for you."

"Shut up. You don't get it." I breathe in deeply, hold it, and let it out.

Benji sits on the floor with me. "It's okay to be afraid. I'm afraid. I don't know how we're gonna pull this off, but listen to me. We're gonna pull this off. We're not gonna let them win. We're going home."

Silence passes between us as I tap my fingers on one thigh,

then the other, back and forth, following with my eyes to focus on movement instead of emotion.

Benji puts a hand on my knee. "I need you to stay focused so I can stay focused. Stay angry. Anger will keep you fired up. You have more empathy than most people. Hold on to that. Your protectiveness for people. Feel injustice for them. Fight for them. And let them fight for you. It's how I cope. So much easier to fight for others instead of for ourselves. Singular pain can be too personal; the pain of a multitude can be powerful."

I let his confidence seep into me, like wings to fight the wind.

Benji hugs his knees, creasing his navy blue uniform. "I worry about Mom and Dad. Mostly at night. Hey, you remember when Dad and Mom dressed like werewolves and made me piss my pants?"

"Yes!" I crack up. "Then you hid under the porch and wouldn't come out, so Dad turned the hose on you. It was hilarious."

"Good times."

"Remember when we went to Florida to visit Penelope, and you said there was a baby alligator in the toilet?" I laugh more. "I was afraid to go to the bathroom for days."

He chuckles. "I didn't think you'd take me seriously. So gullible."

"Shut up," I push his legs with my legs, and he flops over. The room echoes with our laughter. "What the heck did you do to my LU?"

"Disabled the nanoholocoms using a secret skeleton code." He puts out a hand and helps me off the floor.

"Your secret disabling code is our address?"

"Why not?" He pulls on his uniform and brushes his pants.

"I don't know. It's just not cool."

"Things don't have to be cool to work."

"Does the code work anywhere?"

"Nope. Only works in LUs in response to my voice. Short range. Fastest way to temporarily secure spaces in an emergency."

"Can I have my holofurniture back?"

"Only if you come to the meeting after breakfast."

"So I either get to live in an empty LU or come to the meeting? That's blackmail."

He grins. I want to kick him in his smug teeth.

I GRAB MY journal and go down to the Hub for breakfast. The ritual Earth-mourning ceremony has begun, so I blend in and wait. It creeps me out to watch people stand around a glowing hologram of our planet, lowering their heads in sadness and respect. More bandwidths gleam like warm sunlight on their wrists. A golden shackle that they see as freedom. I almost run forward and tell them the truth, but that would ruin the Umbra's plan. *What if the BME suddenly zaps all the Umbra dead in this LU community? Can they do that? No other communities would have our information. The truth would die with us.*

Breakfast at the platform consists of blackened mush on flat yellow bread. Looks like it could be black hummus on pita bread. Tastes like sweet, overripe bananas and burnt peanut butter on cardboard. Worst meal yet. Your appetite changes when your enemy is the one serving the food. There's a line at the fountain to get the thick substance to stay down.

The dinochicken is back in the same tree, yapping the same tune. A gust of wind blows by and the leaves on the tree lift and fall, flipping from dark red to purple and back again. Every time I see the tree with that bird in it, I have a weird sense of déjà vu. With more people around, it tends to squawk more often, like a curmudgeon agitated by our human presence. To get away from the noise, I walk around the perimeter of the LU community, as far as we are allowed to travel until they lift the ban. *If they lift the travel ban.* I can't entertain that thought. I will see Dominick and Rita again. Soon. The outer walkway where SIDEKICK brought me when I arrived is off limits. Instead, there's a locked glass gate that blocks the entrance to the LU. We are hamsters in a glass wheel.

Through the gate, I admire the scenery of Solbiluna-8. The longer I stay here, the less foreign the dark, sharp mountains, red rivers, and technology become. I've even grown to like the glow of two moons and moving stars above us at night.

I write in my journal to remember who I am.

The Umbra meeting is held at a different LU, and inside it's the biggest one yet. Nolan and his grandmother attend. The dark rings under his eyes are gone, and he's more animated as he talks to Kendra. At least I helped him in time. Like Benji said. Focus my anger and empathy on small acts of kindness.

Doctor A. waves me over to him near the front of the room.

"Something's going on," he says. "From what I gather, there's dissension with how to move forward. We're going to vote."

"What's the problem?"

"Beruk wants to plan an attack now. Tell everyone in the community, escape the LU, and mutiny. Benji wants to find evidence, gather information, and wait to tell other communities. Jackson has decided to take a vote."

Katherine comes to sit with us. "Mississippi, we missed you."

"Benji talked to me." I pick at my fingernail and peel off the tip. "And he shut down my LU nanoholocoms to force me to come."

"Yeah, your brother is something else."

"You mean a jerk?" I say, smirking.

She pulls her long hair back into a loose ponytail. "I mean a leader."

"There's a fine line between the two," Doctor A. says, "and often, unfortunately, they can go hand in hand."

Doctor A. might just be one of my favorite people.

Katherine shakes her head in disagreement. "He handles Beruk, and that's saying something."

"What's with that guy?" I ask.

"He's been pissed ever since he got here and they erased his tattoo collection. He had one for every year since he was eighteen. What's he, like, forty-five?"

"Who erased his tattoos?" Doctor A. asks.

"The PSF. Guess it restores and repairs your skin when it disinfects. Left him extra bitter."

Makes sense. It stripped away my nail polish. Tattoos are something else, though. Like stripping away art.

"He's ready to start a war," Katherine says.

"Over tattoos?" I ask.

"Whatever gets 'em here. We need his security knowledge. I heard he owned a private bodyguard service. Elite stuff. Benji's been doing a good job convincing people to keep quiet until we find evidence. I don't think we're ready. We're still doing small-scale hacks on the nanoholocoms. Nothing that could handle a massive attack. We don't even have real weapons that work yet."

The room quiets, and Beruk hacks up phlegm to clear his throat before talking. "You are all here to vote. If we agree that what Alexandra Lucas said about Earth is true, then we should be fighting immediately to return. The longer we wait, the more people will contribute. We can't let our people be tricked again. Who knows what the vances are planning? We need to spread the word and rebel. I have an escape plan."

"But that's the point," Benji begins. "We don't know the vances' motive. How can we fight without understanding who these people are? Maybe they need us to contribute to survive. Maybe their population was depleted by a war or a virus. Maybe they want slaves. We need to know their intentions."

"We know their intentions. They took us," Beruk says. "If they needed us to help them, they should've asked. We are wasting time. Our security forces cannot do our jobs locked up in here. We need to map out the region as soon as possible, join with the other Umbra forces, and form an army. Now."

"With what weapons? Professor Marciani's team still doesn't have a working DQD from the specs the United Nations provided. No other Earth weapons or explosions will work here. Are you really going to use brute force?"

Beruk gets louder. "Sometimes it's all we have. Science can't always keep up. We need numbers. We need tactical information about the landscape that we cannot get sitting here. I can get us through the glass gate and into the mountains."

"We'd be sitting ducks."

"Katherine can block our bandwidth ID signatures. It would take time before the system would notice we were missing."

"You are forgetting some people like it here," Benji adds. "They don't want to rebel. They only want information for information's sake."

Did my brother just turn Earth traitor?

"After being stolen? You can't be serious," Beruk says.

"Very. Some like life here better than on Earth, and we haven't even seen all it has to offer yet. Have you spoken to people? Like really listened? They love the idea of contributing, of not having to work, of getting to enjoy their lives more. They'll want answers, yes, but they aren't ready to rebel against Solbiluna-8."

I go numb inside. I trusted Benji.

Beruk sucks his teeth and then mutters something under his breath.

Benji ignores him and continues, addressing the room. "I know how hard it is to stay quiet. Not to tell everyone what we know and start a war. But heroes know when to fight and when to wait.

Waiting gives us time to develop weaponry to use against them. They have the BME and environmental controls that work as a holographic shielding. We need to learn more about the vances and find out their weaknesses. We need time to find evidence, integrate with other LU communities, spread the rebellion, and gather forces. We have to do this right. If we force an attack now, we will be isolated, and we won't have as many allies as you think. Then the truth about what happened on Earth dies here. We cannot let that happen. People deserve to make their own decisions based on the truth."

Benji stands with his hands across his chest. I understand why he wanted me here. Marcus stands beside him with his hand on his back. Like Mom used to do with Dad. Giving support. Taming the beast.

Jackson addresses everyone. "The voting is simple. Gather to the right if you want to fight now. Gather to the left if you want to wait."

Beruk steps to the right side of the LU and Benji steps to the left. Slowly, people move to different corners of the room. As much as my brother annoys me, as much as waiting kills me, the truth is impossible to ignore. I go to the left and join him, along with Marcus, Katherine, Doctor A., Kendra, Nolan, his grandmother, Professor Marciani, and other people I haven't gotten to know yet, including some that I didn't think liked Benji. Katherine has clout.

Surprisingly, many people also gather near Beruk. While Benji wins the majority vote, the number of people on Beruk's side shocks me. How can they be so ready to jump into an unknown battle unprepared?

Jackson speaks. "For now, we wait. Beruk, work with your special ops team on an escape plan in case the vances don't keep their word. Start training Umbra in combat, especially in using DQDs. Benji, your team should continue gathering information through the nanoholocom network. Along with the DQDs, I also want the professor's team working around the clock on reverse engineering a vertex as soon as possible. Let's get back to work."

Even though Beruk loses the vote, he has a triumphant look on his face. I know that look. If Benji's not careful, there'll be an Umbra rebellion before we come up with a unified plan.

We have to convince everyone that gathering information and spreading the word to other LUs when we can is the best tactic. Strength in numbers. Strength in knowledge. There has to be something we can do to expose the truth. Catch the vances in another lie. Somewhere. Something.

BENJI AND MARCUS show up at the platform for dinner. I down the slippery lemony cubes with nests of crunchy noodles suspended above them, like eating raw ravioli with magical chow mein. I write notes from today's meeting into my journal, coded enough to protect Umbra secrets. The dinochicken squawks from the tree, and I wonder what it's trying to tell me. When I look up, I see Benji coming to eat with me while Marcus talks with Doctor A. My journal will have to wait.

Benji and I eat under the strangest circumstances. At home in our kitchen, I always tried to avoid him at mealtimes so I could digest my food without wanting to throw up in his face. And here we are, being civilized on a high-tech, immoral planet. I never thought I'd appreciate his company.

"Can't adjust to the food here," Benji says. "Especially eating without real utensils. And I'm not ready to spend one of my supply rations on a fork."

"I know. It's barbaric."

He scoops up a slippery cube with a piece of his plate and stuffs it into his mouth. "Good, though. Chewy inside."

"Yeah, I don't want to know what's in there."

"Knowing how you think, human flesh."

I laugh, chew, and then the thought persists, my brain filling in the missing details. *Human bodies being dismembered and skinned like cattle. Baked into pies.* Maybe I should join Rita and become a vegetarian. Then I remember writing in my journal that the vances are pretty much vegetarians, and I chew tentatively.

Marcus and Doctor A. continue in a deep conversation. I worry what it's about. "How are things going with you and Marcus? Must be tough to have a honeymoon here."

"Okay, I guess. We never celebrated since we thought people were dying on Earth. When we first arrived, we spent time in the Holospaces to pretend it was our honeymoon vacation. Couldn't really relax, though."

"I can see that." I crunch on the savory topping.

"How was Dad when you left?" he asks.

I eat too quickly, a noodle sticking in my throat. "I told you. In a wheelchair. On oxygen."

"No, I mean emotionally."

I cough to dislodge the food, my eyes watering. "I don't know. Defeated, I guess. You know how stubborn and independent he is."

"He never talked to me much after I told him about Marcus. I knew things would be different afterward. I guess I was hoping for more." He looks off into the crowd gathering in the Hub. "With everything going on in the world, I thought it would help him understand what really matters. Bigger picture. Guess certain prejudices stick even then."

"That's just how he is. He was M.I.A. when I broke down after almost getting tossed into a vertex by that drunk guy. It's about him, not you."

Benji slides the food around on his plate. "I was never going to tell him."

I'm not sure how to respond. "He still loves you. You're his son. He just doesn't handle major changes well."

He rubs his chin. "You're naive if you really think that." He downs a cube the way people eat raw oysters.

"Thanks, by the way," I say.

"For what?"

"For being there. For pushing me back into counseling."

"Kicking and screaming."

"Is there any other way?"

The dinochicken bird lets out another loud yap.

"That freaking bird is back."

"What bird?"

I point to the tree. "Are you telling me you don't hear that thing? Look! I swear it's been every ten minutes tonight. It's the same thing over and over again."

"Reminds me of you," he says, grinning.

I almost dump my plate of food in his lap. But, you know, rations.

ONCE AGAIN I can't sleep. I lie awake in my restored holobed thinking about Dominick and wondering how long the first level of integration will last. He must think I didn't keep my promise. He must think I'm dead. I hope he doesn't hate me for not leaving with him. The absence of his touch each day is wearing me down.

I miss Rita's sweet singsong snarky voice, always a friend, always telling me the truth even when I don't want to hear it. Being around her makes me a better person. Being without her makes life bleak.

We have to find something, some kind of evidence to stop Beruk from trying to start a war too early. But there's nothing here. We're trapped in this stupid circle community without running water. Without our old friends or even vances to complain to. There aren't even any animals here except for the birds. Well, bird. Actually, I haven't even seen a bug. *Wait a minute, that can't be right.* I jump out of bed, run out of my LU, and look over the glass railing at the Hub. Even in the darkness, there's got to be something. Sounds of nocturnal animals, insects, anything. I hear nothing but the sound of wind in the leaves, and the few voices carried up from the center of the Hub from sleepless adults. Maybe it means nothing. Maybe. Even though it's the middle of the night, I use a maglift to travel down to the Hub. In the backlit darkness, I move near the red chime tree and wait. The bird is silent. I know this feeling. I'm onto something even if I don't know what it is. Kind of like crazy lady with the note.

That's when I get an idea. I reach over and peel another piece of bark off the trunk and hold it in my palm. Its emptiness calls to me. I walk back to the maglift with the bark in my hand, not taking my eyes off it. Sure enough, as soon as I get inside, the bark dematerializes in my hand. I race to Benji and Marcus's LU and touch the door. It beeps but doesn't open.

"It's Alex," I say.

Seconds later, Marcus opens the door, half awake.

"Alex, what's wrong?"

"The bird and the tree. They aren't real. They're holographic. Why are they holographic? They are supposed to be real. And where are the other animals? Insects?"

Benji stumbles over. "Not all of us have insomnia, Alex. Can't this wait? We can save animals in the morning."

"Remember I talked about it at dinner? It's not real. The vances are lying again about what's real and what's fake, and I don't know why."

Benji rubs his eyes, yawns. Marcus glances from him back to me, waiting for a response from either side.

"You sound paranoid."

"Stop being an ass and listen to me. Every time the exact same thing happens: the bird squawks, the leaves clink, all exactly in the same sequence and timing. It's too planned. And I haven't seen any other animals anywhere. So I ripped off some bark and I swear it disappeared in my hand by the time I got to the maglift."

Marcus steps in. "Mathematically speaking, if it's responding in that much of a pattern, then it could be programming. Although animals do follow natural patterns, so there's no guarantee."

Benji looks from him back to me, incredulous. "You are validating her insanity. She's sleep-deprived and stressed out."

"We could at least run some tests. Check it out," Marcus says.

"But why would that area be holographic?" Benji asks.

"Exactly," I say. "Why? What are the vances hiding?"

Benji yawns again. "Fine. In the morning. It doesn't seem like that big of a deal."

Marcus winks at me as I leave their LU.

I can't sleep all night even with the PSF's comfort. My gut tells me I'm right while my mind keeps repeating Benji's comment that I'm just being paranoid. I don't know which is right. My mind loops and loops on possibilities and consequences.

Anxiety is a bitch.

AS SOON AS the sun cracks the horizon between the blue mountains, I throw on my black uniform. Funny how little I care about clothes and fashion here. Wonder if Rita feels the same or if she holofies her clothing options every hour.

No one answers the door at Benji and Marcus's LU. I eat breakfast, sit through the painful Earth-mourning, hoping upon hope to see them, or another member from the Umbra start investigating. Finally, Katherine and Doctor A. show up together.

Before their food materializes at the platform, I interrupt. "Did Benji and Marcus talk to you?"

Katherine replies. "Not now, Mississippi."

"But I told them—"

She pushes me into the platform, my hip bone hitting the stone and silencing my thoughts with dull pain. When Doctor A. doesn't flinch, I know I'm in the wrong.

"Wait," she says. "Don't blow this."

I rub my side. As she backs away, she hands me a note with an LU number. It's her personal room.

ONLY JACKSON, KATHERINE, Benji, Marcus, and Professor Marciani attend the meeting. Benji asks me to tell them my observations. I bet he didn't invite that many people because he thought it'd make him look weak if he's caught taking the paranoid ideas of his freak sister seriously.

When everyone goes silent, my insecurity spikes. Maybe the bird thing is all in my head. The more time that has gone by, the stupider my idea sounds. Maybe I'm wrong.

"Alex?" Benji says.

It's too late to back out. I tell them my anxious thoughts about the bird being a hologram even though it's supposed to be part of the real living space area of the Hub, and I explain how the broken-off piece of bark disappeared.

The professor twists one of his hair knobs. "It would take a lot of energy for the nanoholocoms to track every twig, every grain of sand, never mind if those parts separate from their source . . . hmm . . . I'd like to try something."

"Shoot," Katherine says.

"The temperature may have to remain constant, or at least within an acceptable degree range, due to the method of entanglement used on the subatomic particles and photons. Perhaps one reason they need to control the weather." As he speaks, his tone and speed change. From mild and slow, to energetic and rapid. You can't hide that kind of enthusiasm. "If I heat things up in that area, it could disrupt the local entanglement, and we'll see how much of that area is holographic."

"How much of the area?" I ask. "You think there's more?"

"Possibly," Professor Marciani says.

"Wouldn't the environmental controls just compensate?" Benji asks.

"That's where I come in," Katherine says. "I've been hacking into small-scale systems. I think I can disable the environmental controls in that area, the same way I disable the BME from working in small areas, if I put up the right firewalls to mask the environmental readings. We're called the Umbra, after all."

That sounded legit. It's the first time I've been part of a real Umbra mission, and I like it. "Umbra like an umbrella?" I ask. "A shelter or something?" A line from the Rihanna song slips out of my mouth, and Benji rolls his eyes.

"The word *Umbra* means the darkest part of a shadow that is cast on a planet during a solar eclipse," the professor says. "We represent the importance of that shadow in understanding and investigating the light. Holograms are nothing but glorified light."

"Let's try it," Jackson interrupts. "Tonight. After dinner. Is that enough time?"

Both Katherine and the professor agree. Ugh. More waiting. More worrying. More overthinking. *What if I'm wrong and I'm wasting their time? What if I'm right?*

IT'S THE FIRST Umbra experiment held out in the open. The day couldn't possibility be slower. I write in my journal, memorize passages from *Harry Potter*, take a nap. I even stretch and run around my LU's circular level again to help with the anxious feeling that comes from being nervous, excited, unsure, and embarrassed all at the same time.

I head down to the Hub early to take notes. The dinochicken clamors in the same tree. I count and track its sounds, write them in my journal. It doesn't squawk by a set time, and I start to doubt myself. I watch and write everything down. It takes an hour before I see a pattern. Every time ten people walk past it, it cries out for two seconds. Then it shakes and stretches its bony wings and sits, and a small gust of wind flips the leaves of the tree around it. The exact same sequence begins again, and once the tenth person passes by, it squawks, it stretches, and the wind blows. I'm right. I know I'm right.

Dinner is a huge bowl of an odd, warm, dark green concoction with chewy black bits. Delicious in nutty flavor, disgusting in texture. I need to take small sips to get it down. Doctor A., Kendra, Nolan, and his grandmother, who's holding an infant, arrive. People naturally surround them to check out the baby. My heart hurts from too many feelings. It looks like a normal night in the Hub before the Skylucent. If I can define this as normal. Beruk comes with his own crew, a bunch of hardened misfits ready to fight whenever and wherever without thinking it through. Even in the year 2359, our ignorance rears its violent head. Funny that most of the released convicts are against Beruk and don't want to rush into war. It's reassuring, and I understand why Katherine respects them. Jackson, Benji, and Marcus arrive, followed by Katherine and the professor. They move near the dinochicken, and I join them, pointing to my findings in my journal, but saying nothing aloud. They observe, count ten people, and the bird stays silent.

"That can't be right," I say. "I just tracked it."

Benji sighs loudly. Katherine stares him down.

"Was it this crowded before?" Marcus asks, as clusters of people walk past to gather for the Skylucent.

"No," I admit, the fear rising inside at being labeled a failure in public.

"That could add a different variable," Marcus says.

Professor Marciani nods in agreement. "Perhaps there's a movement and time component."

"Explain," Jackson asks Marcus.

"Alex could be right, it could happen every ten people. However, when it's crowded, to avoid continuously singing, there could be an added timing element, say, of only reacting after so many minutes regardless of hitting the ten-person threshold."

Beruk comes over. "Is there a problem? What are we here for?"

"It's your call," Jackson whispers to Benji.

"We've come this far. You ready?" he asks Katherine and the professor.

Professor Marciani tips an imaginary hat. Katherine gives a thumbs-up.

Benji announces, "Everyone else, back to dinner."

As Umbra forces disperse in the area, I linger. Benji grabs my arm and pulls me away from the tree.

"But I want to see what happens," I argue.

"Let the experts do their work. You can watch from here. Don't call attention in case it fails. Plus, there's a chance that they'll be punished like Nolan for messing with the temperature controls."

My heart falls to my stomach. "I thought Katherine was safe-guarding the area."

"Alex, there are no absolutes with this stuff. We are flying blind."

The dinochicken squawks again. I hold my breath and watch Katherine inconspicuously prod the nanoholocoms near the area and tap on her bandwidth. After she nods at Professor Marciani, he gets to work under the tree. *Please don't let the BME get the professor for listening to my crazy idea.* The professor pours a small amount of liquid into a metallic device, adds something else, and backs away. Smoke and sparks surround the base of the tree. Flames lick the trunk, and the environmental controls don't activate.

Nothing happens.

Beruk leans closer to Benji. "Campfires? What is this, Girl Scouts?"

Anger mixes with my embarrassment. Jackson clears his throat. I open my mouth to protest, but nothing comes out. Before Benji gets a chance to respond, everything shuts down. *Everything.*

The environment dematerializes before our eyes, the small flames extinguished as the tree vanishes. Our uniforms revert to the basic iridescent design.

We are no longer standing in the Hub.

We are no longer standing on a planet.

We are standing in an open space, surrounded by metal, glittering gadgetry, darkness.

It was all an illusion.

PART 2

"How beauteous mankind is!
O brave new world
That has such people in't!"
—*William Shakespeare's* The Tempest

CHAPTER 11

DAY 9: 558 HOURS TO DECIDE

EVERYTHING WAS AN illusion.

Of course. The holograms' specialty.

A series of windows line one area, ceiling to floor. It takes me a few seconds to process. Outside the windows, a fleet of sleek ships with pointed fronts and cone-shaped bellies, fully expanded into the pale blaze of engines. Like metallic darts puncturing the darkness. Too many to count.

Doctor A., Kendra, Nolan, and his grandmother cradling the baby rush over to us.

"Good god. Why are we in space?" Doctor A. asks.

"I don't know," Katherine says. "But I don't like it."

"Look at them all," Nolan says, staring out the windows.

Jackson, Beruk, and Benji stand speechless.

"There are hundreds of them," Kendra says.

"The vertexes on Earth must've led to ships, not to a planet," Marcus says.

Reality sets in as the Umbra and non-Umbra take in the sight.

We revealed only one ship. Possibly only one deck of only one ship. There are so many more ships full of people who think they're on a safe planet. Who think Earth was destroyed.

Each truth just reveals more lies.

Dominick and Rita could be on a different deck of this ship, or on one of those other ships. So close and yet so far. I wonder if every deck can see the ships outside the windows. If they are seeing this right now.

A melodic sequence of beeps echoes through the open space. A huge, floating holoscreen appears where the Earth-mourning ceremony usually happens.

This can't be good, this can't be good. What have I done? I back up slowly and bump into Benji. He places his hand on my shoulder. It's shaking.

On the screen, Keron, the leader of the meritocracy, flocked by other members in an arena, stands with his hands clasped gracefully before him.

"Greetings from the meritocracy, the ruling body of Solbiluna-8. We are meeting again earlier than expected. We understand there is a problem with the environmental controls. We want to reassure you we have everything under control. You are on a star vessel and have not yet arrived at Solbiluna-8. We are sorry if this has caused you discomfort in anyway. Rest assured this was as we intended.

"We created the false environment to introduce you to some of our technology as you travel to our planet. We only wanted to bring you peace and acclimate you to our culture. We know how hard it is to relocate to a new world. Environmental controls will be reestablished shortly for your comfort. Thank you for your understanding and patience during this trying time. We look forward to your arrival. May your contribution lead to freedom."

He bows, and the screen flickers off and disappears.

"Bullshit," I say.

"Of course it's bullshit," Kendra says. "They never explained this in the holograms' questions and answers back home."

"Why didn't the vertexes just bring us to the planet like they said?" Nolan asks.

Marcus answers. "Perhaps it's not only about bringing people.

Perhaps they needed the ships to make the vertexes and project the holograms on Earth."

"Which would also confirm Alex's claim is possible," the professor adds. "Earth wasn't destroyed."

"How?" I ask, still transfixed on the silver ships floating in the darkness.

"In order to trick the NASA sensors and have a holographic comet approach Earth, the vances could've used spaceships in close proximity to keep a hologram of that caliber projected through space and through our atmosphere. Ships were probably hidden in our solar system the entire time."

"Like cloaked, you mean?" Katherine asks.

"Yes. It's the only way they could've pulled off such a scam. It's ingenious. I'm not sure how they shielded themselves from the nukes, but it shows what they are capable of."

Benji squeezes my shoulder, and for the first time, it almost seems like he's proud of me.

"What do we do now?" Katherine asks Jackson. "Do we tell everyone the whole truth?"

Jackson glances past the crowd of Umbra to the others. They've gathered near the huge windows with wide eyes, muttering about the possibilities, more excited than concerned. Like a true adventure has begun instead of a betrayal.

"Not yet. We still don't have evidence that the vances have done anything sinister. Just our word. The meritocracy justified a reason for the spaceships. So we wait, as decided by our vote. No one else on those other ships knows any of this. We need to build a larger network first, contact those other ships."

Beruk crosses his hairy arms over his chest. "You still aren't willing to budge. We have evidence that they lied about being on a planet."

Benji steps in. "We are outnumbered and outgunned by a

hi-tech culture that's clearly more advanced than we assumed. We are only one ship. Look out the window. None of them have a clue."

"While you're doing that," Beruk says, "I want my team working on taking over this ship if necessary. We need to figure out schematics, locate the engines, fuel, navigation, weapons, escape pods."

"Agreed," Jackson says. "Katherine, do you think there's a way to tap into the other ships' nanoholocom networks and send them coded messages?"

"There's always a way," Katherine says, grinning. "The problem is whether or not they will recognize them."

"Get to work on that immediately. Top priority. Then help Beruk and his team."

She nods, but I can feel her anger from here.

"Professor, keep your focus on using vertex technology and the DQD weapon prototype."

The professor salutes and twists his hair.

As Jackson delivers orders, from the ground to the ceiling of the spaceship, an electric bluish-green energy comes tumbling down and up to meet each other. It grows and spreads like a veil over reality, casting over all that was and showing us what isn't. Even our clothing returns to our individualized, holofied designs. It's the most beautiful and disturbing thing I've ever witnessed. It takes virtual reality and lays it across the truth. Like growing a garden on top of a graveyard.

I SPEND THE next day on the spaceship trying to pretend it's a planet. My brain can't handle it. We are trapped here against our will, like living in a snow globe, or a fish tank, or a doll house. They control our environment, food, water, and housing from wherever they are. Now that I know it isn't real, the trees seem sinister, the air seems artificial. Hell, I guess it is.

Aren't we the weak link in the fleet? The chink in the armor? Why keep us? Are they going to wipe our memories when we arrive at the planet? How easy it would be for them to stop pumping the vanilla mint oxygen and to start pumping in poison gas. Or to just stop pumping anything. Either way. Both as effective.

In the middle of the night, an insidious thought takes over my thoughts and travels to the anxious part of my soul to wreak havoc: I'm in SPACE. *Space. Utter darkness. Trapped by weightlessness. No oxygen. If I breach the fishbowl, oblivion.*

My stomach sours, so I sit on the futuristic toilet of enlightened shit inside the PSF. I try to slow down my breathing by counting. I don't have any pills left to handle the meltdown inside me.

If one thing goes wrong with this ship . . .

BOOM—floating, belly up, dead in space.

Just. Like. That.

What if Beruk had blown through the gate that keeps us from traveling, and instead blown a hole in the side of the ship? He could've killed us all.

Even worse, what if my bird theory had led to a ship explosion? Fire on spaceships can't be good. Fire + oxygen = BOOM. I could've killed everyone.

As my body breaks into a blinding hot sweat, I strip off my clothes and turn on the PSF. This time, though, it doesn't work as well because my skin just gets hotter and hotter, the room begins to spin, welts appear on my stomach. I try to breathe and count like I'm supposed to.

I Just.

Can't find.

The.

Oxygen.

Don't get tricked by a thought.

But when I had a thought about a bird being a programmed hologram, I was right. *My anxiety was right.*

It could be right again.

And I could be dying for real this time.

IKNOWIMDYINGIMDYINGIMDYINGIMDYING.

I flee the PSF to find air, running out of my LU half-naked, tossing my uniform shirt over my head, jumping into a maglift, and traveling down to the Hub. It's late, so not many people are around, but some are. It doesn't matter. I just need to cool down and escape the heat.

I douse my face and then thrust my whole head into the cold stream, soaking my hair, begging for relief and escape. It helps a little, yet it's impossible to escape the thought of my body as a floating space corpse.

As the water runs over my hair, I wonder if it's even real. *How will I ever know what's real again? Will it eventually not matter?*

And then, while the top half of my body is still in the water, branches of electricity surge up from the ground and bite at my legs. SIDEKICK materializes next to me. "The BME has been automatically activated. Please remain calm and orderly as we deal with the infraction."

My body convulses before hitting the ground. The sign on the fountain reads:

`For personal hydration only. Storing or cleaning with water is forbidden.`

The transparency pins me underneath for everyone to witness. Inside the BME punishment chamber, colored lasers poke through me in rotating sequences, while vibrating sounds rattle my teeth and bones.

As night turns into day, people step over my body to get water from the fountain. No eye contact. *There it is again: small acts of self-preservation. The beginning of the end of human civilization.*

The blurry shape of Doctor A.'s salt-and-pepper beard checks on me periodically.

Another day turns into night and back again. The exhaustion from missing sleep, the hunger from missing meals, and the muscle cramping from being trapped in such a tight space creates a growing numbness that spreads throughout my body. It's a cocoon of enforced depression, zapping all motivation to care even though I'm fully aware of the destruction happening to my life.

I close my eyes to the pretty lights and vibrations. *I might as well be dead.*

DOCTOR A. CHECKS my pulse.

"Okay, move her," he says.

Benji scoops me up and cradles me in his arms. I don't have the will to fight him.

I LOOK AROUND, expecting to see the Hub. I'm in my LU. The change in location makes my insides seize in confusion.

"Where—how?" I mumble, my mouth dry and sticky.

"Lie back," Doctor A. says, holding my forehead. "You'll feel disoriented for a while. You were in the BME for almost two days, then the HME last night. The scars on your legs are healing with the help of the PSF. You had it the worst since you were in water at the time."

I can't help but look down. Covering my calves are burn marks, scars in the shape of large tongues. Thanks to the AM and PM behavioral meds the BME administered, I can't feel anything anymore.

"Benji just left. He's been checking on you all day."

I must be delusional. Benji wouldn't waste that much time on me.

THREE DAYS LATER, against Doctor A.'s orders, I leave my LU to get my mind off what happened to me and the missing time in my memory. According to my bandwidth countdown, there's only three hundred ninety-eight hours left to contribute, past the halfway point. After being medicated for days, the numbers don't register as being as threatening as they should.

I run into Kendra and Nolan, who invite me to the Holospaces. Instead, I scribble on scrap paper asking for the Umbra LU, and Kendra writes down a room number. I travel in a maglift without caring about the height.

Inside the Umbra, Katherine tinkers with small tubes and coils on a flat board. It looks like the inside of an old model computer.

"You're back in action?" Katherine asks. "Shouldn't you be in bed?"

I ignore her. I need something to distract myself. "What're you working on?"

"Makeshift radio using ration parts. It's not picking up anything, though. Frequency is all wacked. The ship must have a force field that keeps the nanoholocoms connected, but blocks other information. Trying to work around it. Course, the other ships won't know to look for a signal. Why would they?"

She keeps messing with the board anyway. I have a feeling it's just to keep her hands and her mind busy, to feel productive. We have a lot in common.

"If I can get this thing to work," Katherine asks, "who would you contact?"

"My best friend, Rita. She's my rock. We've known each other since we were little. She left Earth before I could say goodbye. And Dominick, my boyfriend."

I've been keeping them out of my thoughts to avoid an emotional meltdown. I take a moment after saying Dominick's name out loud. "I really miss him. More than I ever realized. I should've left with him. Then we'd at least be together."

"Then we wouldn't know about the comet."

"True." A part of me still would rather be with him and enjoy the time in ignorance. But that would mean condemning us all to Solbiluna-8. "My grandmother should also be around. I might have some relatives from Texas . . . not sure if they came or hid in a bunker. What about you?"

"No." She tightens a wire. "If this had happened years ago, the whole hologram invasion thing, my life would've been so different. My daughter would be here with me."

She yanks on the piece, and it falls apart in her hands.

"She was only six. Six is the perfect age. So open to experience. They'll do anything to please you." She stares at the panel. "Leukemia. I tried to raise money for treatments, and when that didn't cover expenses, I started stealing. From work. From stores. From friends. From strangers. I did what I had to do to pay the bills."

"And you got caught."

"Not then. After."

She puts down a tool, then looks at me. "When she died, I wanted vengeance. Against everything—the medical system, the insurance system, the world, God, whatever."

"What did you do?"

"What I do best. Kept stealing. People don't realize how easy some systems are to hack. I got really good at hacking websites and apps and transferring untraceable cash in seconds. Didn't get caught for a while. Racked up more money than I knew what to do with. Gave some of it to others who had sick kids."

"Like a health care Robin Hood."

"No, see, don't do that, Mississippi. Don't make a martyr outta me. I connected with the wrong people. Blew money on crap I didn't even want. Took bigger and bigger risks. I was burning on anger and that's what got me caught. Guess in some ways I wanted to get caught. I wanted out of life. Feds caught me on computer crimes, hacking, identity theft, credit card fraud, money laundering, the list goes on and on. I thought getting locked up would be an escape from life. It only trapped me with grief."

I don't know how to respond, so I don't. Sometimes people just need you to listen.

She picks the board back up and starts putting the radio together. I hand her a piece from the floor.

"This place . . ." She points to the air around us. "There's no way the vances simply decided to give everything away for free in order to form unity. The meritocracy acts like it voted for it or some shit. Nope, a lot of blood was shed for this kind of peace. That's how humans work, no matter how advanced. That's the only way they work. Nothing is free. Everything has a price."

Something in what she says reminds me of my dad. Her past anger scares me. Not because she was a prisoner, but because I can relate to it. The guilt. The desperate need for revenge. Anger as fuel. Anger that fuels you to run through a vertex. Anger that gets you caught and turns you into someone you were never meant to be.

That night I write in my journal to remember who I am again.

A WEEK LATER, with only two hundred thirty-one hours before contribution, we gather for breakfast and the Earth-mourning. It's funny how we still have these public ceremonies after seeing the spaceships, but then I remember that the majority of the people don't know about Earth yet. I wonder how many revealed lies it will take for them to wake up. How many bandwidths will glow with tainted commitments. It's so easy to fall for a compulsive liar when lies are prettier than the truth. Safer. Scarier.

My legs physically look better thanks to the PSF working its magic on the scars, but ghost electric pain shoots up from my feet every now and then. I will never stick my head under a fountain again no matter what kind of panic attack I'm having. Lesson learned. The BME is highly effective in behavioral training. Doctor A. is surprised that I'm not as emotionally affected as Nolan was given my medical history. He doesn't know the anger and desperation inside me that's blocking my depression from taking root. Both a cure and a poison.

As the Earth glows and rotates above us, I daydream about my life back on the Massachusetts coast. I just want to put my legs into the ocean and let it wash away the pain. The navy-and-green waves, the salted air blowing through my curls and changing their texture, the warm grains of sand, rocks, and slipper shells shifting under my bare feet. Dominick smiling at me from his striped blue and white towel. Oh, god, I miss him.

I miss sitting around a bonfire with Rita and Dominick, roasting marshmallows on sticks until they're almost burnt, taking a photo each year to see how much has changed and how much has stayed the same. In those moments with them I was truly alive. Who am I without them?

The holographic Earth tribute vanishes, and people begin to disassemble in the Hub. When a disembodied voice fills space and bounces off the circular inner walls, everyone stops. It's the first time the LU feels more like an arena. *Where a lion would be released and pick us off one by one.*

"Step one of integration with environment is complete. Stand by for step two. You will be transported to your new living arrangements and allowed to integrate fully into Solbiluna-8, which includes full communication and travel privileges. Please step through the vertexes one at a time."

A series of emerald vertexes appear around the perimeter of the Hub.

Here we go again. This can't be good. Why are they green?

My heart leaps for cover as my legs fire in defensive pain. I watch innocent people around me smile and scatter, probably to get their belongings. Excited while I am petrified. What else is new? *This is when it all ends. This is when everyone finds out it's a scam in some major twist of fate.*

I spot Katherine and Doctor A. huddled off to one side.

"What do we do?" I ask.

"We go," Katherine says. "Sounds like we're leaving the ship to join the planet. Can't stay behind on an empty ship."

"Or they're killing us for knowing too much."

"Doubt it," Doctor A. says. "It would be easier for them to kill us on the ship if they wanted to."

"That's reassuring," I say.

"Look on the bright side," Katherine says. "We'll have full communication and travel rights. You can see your friends."

I would do anything to see Dominick and Rita again, but stepping through another vertex is like throwing myself from a cliff. The fear makes the hairs on my arms stand on end.

"We better get going," Doctor A. says. "Looks like it might take a while."

It's the first time there's a line at the maglifts. I follow their lead because what choice do I have. I can't stay on a spaceship alone, especially since I feel trapped as it is. The longer I wait, the more time I have to think about crossing through a vertex again.

Last time adrenaline and anger got me through. This time, I'm nothing but a ball of nerve endings. I hold on to the image of a group hug with Dominick and Rita. I can do this.

Once in my LU, I grab my backpack and triple-check that I have everything. I take one last cursory look around at the fake environment I created. I'd say I'll miss it but (A) that isn't true, and (B) I can probably re-create it in two seconds. Holographic furniture has its benefits. Easy to move.

Back in the Hub, people step through the vertexes one at a time. I watch Kendra, Nolan, and his grandmother depart, followed by the mother and her reunited baby. Doctor A., Beruk, and Katherine step through. As I move closer up in line, anxiety crawls inside of me like tentacles of energy begging me to flee.

Remember to close my eyes and hold my breath.

Aaaaaaah! I can't do it again. I can't go forward. I can't go back. Not even for friends. I want to go home.

Benji and Marcus stand beside me.

"Come on," Benji says. "I'll walk with you."

I grab his hand. Sometimes that's all you need. In the future I will pretend this never happened.

"You might have to push me," I say, my chest starting to convulse.

"Anytime," he says and smirks.

"Ugh, why do you have to be so—"

—And I'm through.

CHAPTER 12

DAY 23: 229 HOURS TO DECIDE

INTEGRATION HAS BEEN SUCCESSFUL. WE THANK
EVERYONE FOR YOUR COOPERATION. HAPPY HOLODAY.

TRAVELING THROUGH THE emerald vertex is like stepping
through a cold waterfall. Not even remotely close to the torture
of the blue metallic ones.

The landscape on the other side mirrors the illusion they created for us on the spaceship. Indigo mountains piercing a bright
lavender sky. Huge, leafy green and purple-veined plants and trees
that would put Earth's rain forests to shame. Rainbow plumes of
flora. A river of scarlet water, snaking through the landscape and
pooling into a maroon lake. The smell of vanilla, mint, and florals.
Perfect weather. I am Dorothy in Oz once again.

*How do we know this is really Solbiluna-8 and not another il-
lusion, like the comet or the ship? What signifies that something is
real? Ability to handle temperature changes? Are we supposed to
keep lighting fires under things? We'll be punished in no time while
everything burns.*

Something about the planet reminds me of those shampoo
commercials for fake happiness, where a woman uses a strawberry
shampoo and she's suddenly transported into a rain forest for
an orgasmic, magical experience. Soap doesn't equal tranquility.
Neither do lies. For all we know, we are still on the spaceship with

a new program playing in the background. Like being trapped in the *Matrix*. At least they had pills.

As I pass by a shrub with pointed coral blossoms, I pluck a petal and hold it in my hand as I walk. Evidence. Small acts of defiance. Ahead, gray holograms steer people into lines that lead to two warehouse-type buildings, the same as when I first traveled through the vertex onto the ship. Where are the vances? I want to see if they will lie to our faces. The crowds are minimal; they must be disembarking the ships in intervals to avoid overcrowding.

We are given more choices. Enter one building to stay with Massachusetts people, enter the other to travel to another area. The majority of my LU community from the ship choose to stay together. I watch a few people, including the mother and her baby, go to the right, and in my stomach I know that's the last time I will see them. I hope they'll be okay.

In the past few months, the process of sorting people has triggered my anxiety, starting from the first night at the hospital with the HAZMAT team. Each sorting seems like a choice between life and death, and I'm witnessing the possible salvation or demise of others as they choose hope for survival. I search the herd of faces for Dominick and Rita, the only two people in the universe who make me feel safe enough to be me. They're the gravity in my life so I don't float away.

Inside the building is a mega holoscreen with names being posted and updated. It reminds me of the flight information screens at airport terminals. I rub my thumb and fingertips against the soft coral petal still in my palm.

A hologram near the screen states repeatedly, "Please hold your hand to the screen and state your name, age, and persons you'd like to live with or near. We will accommodate as many variables as possible."

"You're living with me and Marcus so you'll be safe," Benji says. "Katherine and the others will be there, too."

"Okay," I say. I'll finally be able to see my friends. Finally show Dominick that I kept my promise. Thank him for shielding me in the riot.

Hand to screen, as I speak into the air, I realize how foreign my life has become that I'm so ready and willing to live with Benji. "Alexandra Lucas. Age 18. Living with Benjamin Lucas-Blu and Marcus Lucas-Blu. Near Katherine Kirkwood. Near Dominick Landen. Near Rita Bernardino. Near Penelope O'Donnell."

I figure the more names I throw out there, the better. Saying my real name feels one step closer to home. I don't bother giving my code name since Katherine scrambled my bandwidth for continuous anonymity anyway. I wonder if the system will match my name to the ship's biosignature records. *Would the BME punish me for being a space stowaway?*

"Your hologuide has been provided further instructions."

My name appears on the screen in a list that is ever growing. Data collected and categorized. I am only a name and a number to them. Nothing significant.

SIDEKICK materializes next to me. "Please follow."

I wait for Benji and Marcus to give their names. Together, we share my hologuide and follow it through a series of curved white corridors and through an exit.

The world outside expands into a system of elaborate roadways glimmering with nanoholocoms. The gray walkway has the same effect but not as extreme. Across them glide silver kidney-shaped vehicles that remind me of a miniature version of the Chicago Bean, a sculpture that I remember from a project I did on Illinois in the fifth grade.

My bandwidth lights up with various colored dots.

"SIDEKICK, what's going on with my bandwidth?"

Benji and Marcus hold up their flashing bandwidths. "You've been fully integrated. You have total access to the nanoholocom network, including the global CVBE, or COM, VID, BUZ, and ED bandwidth modalities."

Be still my heart. There's more.

"You require transportation first," SIDEKICK says. "Hold your bandwidth and say *MAGPOD FOR THREE OPEN.*"

I remember copying information about magpods from the hologram Q&A website. It was the one thing that always sounded awesome.

"MAGPOD FOR THREE OPEN."

Nothing happens.

"Did I do it wrong?"

"One moment. Magpod will arrive in four seconds. Three, two, one."

A metal bean travels around the corner and pulls forward in front of us. The magpod has no wheels and hovers above the ground at knee height.

The side of the magpod slides open without a visible hinge. The metal material collapses on itself like a liquid accordion. My curiosity gets the best of me, and I don't listen to the rest of SIDEKICK's instructions. I climb into the back, tossing my backpack into the small storage area.

From outside, the magpod looked like solid metal, but the inside is transparent from chest up. Like a one-way, blue-tinted mirror all around. I expect the dashboard to be a hi-tech, complex navigation panel, cooler than even the *Starship Enterprise*, but the dashboard has only one red button. Nothing else. Beyond underwhelming. The console is more like an amusement park ride than a tricked-out vehicle from the future.

"Where's the seat belt?" I ask, searching the area to secure myself in place.

SIDEKICK has vanished, but its voice fills the vehicle. "The magpods do not require personal restraint systems."

I envision my head crashing into the blue windshield. "Why not?"

"It is not necessary."

"Where's the steering wheel?" Benji asks from the front.

"It is a self-navigating system."

Self-navigating. Code for it-can-drive-you-off-a-cliff-if-it-malfunctions. When it malfunctions.

"Where's the brake?" I ask, scooting forward to look at the floor.

"It is a self-navigating system. The override button can stop the system in an emergency. It is not recommended."

"Why not?" I ask. *Is it more like a self-destruct button?*

"The holotransport network, or HTN, allows magpods to co-ordinate with one another. Overriding disrupts nearby magpods to avoid collisions, thereby temporarily slowing the system and disrupting local transport schedules."

"How does it work?" I ask. I listen for an engine, a slight vibration, anything. "I can't hear or feel anything. Is it on?"

"It is not on until you give it a destination. The magnetic suspension and propulsion system does not require engines or fuel the way you are used to in your fossil fuel system."

For the first time, that sounded like SIDEKICK passed judgment on us mere earthlings.

"But there's no track or anything on the road," Marcus says.

"No, our HTN is far more enhanced than Earth's transportation systems. The HTN uses the nanoholocom network to navigate the magpods. A magnetic field develops as the magpod moves forward and diminishes behind it. No waste."

The science geek in me cannot handle the coolness of the supposedly real Solbiluna-8. Must not fall for the glitz of the future tech world. I need to remember what they did to us.

"You have been assigned to group LU QN25-50-8-7-27. Say *MAGPOD, GO TO LU COMMUNITY QN25-50-8.*"

Benji repeats its command. Without further warning, the magpod jets forward, gaining speed, the force pushing my body against the seat. Without a speedometer, it feels like we went from 0 to 100 in a matter of seconds. Soon, the speed evens out, and my body relaxes in the soft seat. No contact with the road means no bumps in the ride. Extremely smooth sailing. Not quite flying in the sky like we imagined in the future, but close. Even though the vehicle speeds past the scenery, there is no sound from wind resistance on the exterior.

I grip the bottom of my seat with both hands to stop myself from pressing the red button. The coral flower petal crushes in my hand.

"SIDEKICK, how fast are we going?"

"Approaching four hundred eighty-two kilometers, or three hundred miles per hour."

And I thought maglifts were bad. I imagine what would happen if the magpod hijacked itself due to a small technical error. *One tiny glitch, sending me toward the wrong location at top speed. Faster. And faster. With no seat belts. Why are there no seat belts? People screaming and jumping out of my path. Some too late. Blood splattering across the blue-tinted windshield.*

Sweat pools on my hairline and the back of my neck.

"Can I put the windows down?" I ask.

"These are viewshields, not windows. Magpods conduct energy. You do not want to interrupt that magnetic field."

I imagine touching a moving magpod and my skin boiling on

the metal exterior. *Human frying pan.* I make a mental rule never to touch a magpod.

Colors of the foreign scenery blur past the viewshields. Other magpods pass us, but I can't tell if they're occupied by humans since they are completely encased in metal. Cold. Inhuman. Trapped.

I tap my hands back and forth on each thigh. It doesn't work. Impossible to focus in a flying magpod of death. *Crashing into a tree, a wall, and still not stopping. Never stopping. Bouncing off the tree and barreling toward a cliff. Flipping over in midair, smashing into rock, and plummeting to the bottom of a ravine. Trapped inside with Benji and Marcus, bleeding to death in an overturned magpod. With an activated, holographic intelligence that, instead of saving us, might decide to put us out of our misery based on an algorithm doubting our chances of survival.*

"SIDEKICK, does this thing have music?" I ask, glancing at the blank dashboard, desperate for a distraction. "I don't see a radio or anything."

"Music is stored in your bandwidth. Say *MUSIC OPEN.*"

"MUSIC OPEN."

"Please no pop music," Benji says.

"I make no promises."

It takes me a few minutes to search through Earth songs from the past. As the rhythm begins and U2 sings the opening lyrics of "With or Without You," my anxiety transforms into choking sobs. This is my parents' favorite song. I remember catching them slow dancing to it in the kitchen one morning. They looked so in love that day. I rub the wilted flower petal in my hand. The problem with real things is they don't last, either.

Benji and Marcus stay silent.

"Do you require assistance?" SIDEKICK asks.

"No, I'm fine." I need to remember them. Grieving is stronger than fear.

A gigantic community of circular, glass structures shines in the distance as the magpod approaches at top speed. Instead of one circular structure, there are neighborhoods of interlocking links laid out in an endless field in a pattern like crop circles. My hand itches to hit the red button. I focus on the music playing, the vivid landscape so cheerful the colors mock and mask the motive behind it all.

Why are we here? Is it all about contribution? There has to be more to it. As the magpod slows down, a transparent shield activates and pins my body in place. Like a ghost airbag, simultaneous terror and protection, included for our safety. The magpod parks itself in front of one cluster of buildings. The buildings are similar to the structure set up on the spaceship except on an enormous scale. From this angle, I count five buildings lined up in a V formation with a taller one in the center, but I can't see if there are other buildings behind them. A field of blue-green vegetation separates the neighbors, and then another cluster of domed glass buildings begins. There are so many LU communities interconnected to one another, I can't count them.

The clear shield releases, my body able to move once again, and SIDEKICK's voice prompts, "Say *MAGPOD EXIT.*"

"Gladly. MAGPOD EXIT."

The sides of the vehicle automatically fold into themselves, freeing me from my metallic prison. I exit the music program on my bandwidth, grab my backpack, and plant my feet back on solid ground. My first few steps are so wobbly, Marcus holds me steady.

"You okay?"

"Yeah, just need a sec."

"Take your time. That ride was surreal."

The magpod doors close before the empty vehicle speeds

away. I wonder how it doesn't run down pedestrians. Then again, I don't see any people walking near the roads.

SIDEKICK rematerializes next to me to lead us toward the closest LU community. "Please follow."

Benji and Marcus walk with SIDEKICK. I lean over and try not to vomit before the next phase of the journey. *Deep breath, hold it, release.* I let go of the dying petal and watch it drift to the ground.

"We don't have all the time in the world," Benji says. "I have work to do." He walks ahead with SIDEKICK while Marcus and I straggle behind him. Doesn't he ever think to slow down? I don't know how Marcus can stand him.

I didn't think this through. I volunteered to live with Benji without our parents? Are you kidding me? This will be like medieval torture: the sibling device. I came all this way to save human beings from holographic time traveling kidnappers, not to live with my strict brother. And Marcus is nice, but living with a former teacher is super awkward. Plus, with the Umbra to reorganize, Benji'll be more stressed out. And when Benji's stressed out, he takes it out on me. Come to think of it, maybe Benji has his own stress disorder. It runs in the family.

The new Hub is much larger than the last Hub, probably half a football field in length, with two food and ration platforms on either end. I scan it from end to end for the vances. Nothing. Only Earth humans. *At least, they look like Earth humans.* I want to break everything apart like Nolan tried to do and make the planet crumble like on the ship. But this world is real. *Supposedly.*

Paranoid much?

Watching other people smile, hug, and celebrate in the Hub strikes me in an envious place at my core. Life as leisure. I've never experienced that kind of relaxation. Not temporary or fleeting, but like an eternal vacation. The sense of just being in time without worry about what comes next. An escape from feeling responsible for everything. A small nagging part of me wants to relax into it, to finally tame the shaky feeling inside of me and tell myself to just let go of my agenda. But underneath their smiles and hugs, I know they have hard truths they can't escape, either. No one is immune. Even though my anxiety keeps me from feeling settled, it also keeps me searching for more.

It's time for me to find Dominick and Rita.

SIDEKICK SHOWS US to our new LU on the seventh floor. It's three times larger than my solitary one on the ship, empty except for a huge scenic window and a PSF. Benji and Marcus can design the LU however they want as long as I get a hammock.

"I'll be back later," I say. "Gonna try to find people." I step into the hallway before Benji can argue with me. SIDEKICK follows.

"How do I find people?"

"Hold your bandwidth and say *SEARCH PEOPLE*. Then state name and age."

I follow its directions. A holoscreen appears with the words SEARCH and PEOPLE.

"Dominick Landen. Age 18."

A list of three Dominick Landens fills the display, but only one is 18. I touch the name, and a picture of him appears. *Oh, my god, it's him.* My eyes blur with emotion.

Three choices float before me: COM, VID, or LOCATE.

I choose LOCATE since I need talk to Dominick in person. I can't tell him that the comet was a fake over the nanoholocom network. *For all I know, it might start a massive sweep of FBI vance agents who consider me a space enemy.*

A holographic map of the region opens in front of me with a blinking light and QN25-50-22 under it.

"How do I get there?" I ask SIDEKICK and point to the spot on the translucent map.

"You may walk or travel by magpod."

No, not another magpod. The day has been so overwhelming, my body feels sore with exhaustion. But I will walk until my legs fall off if it will bring me to Dominick.

I check the network for Rita. She doesn't exist. I even check again using her full name, Margarita Bernardino, and still nothing. Did she use an alias like me in case her parents came looking for her? But they would never come looking for her. Too religious and anti-vertex. *So where the hell is she? Did she not make it through? Did her parents catch her leaving and lock her in the basement? Did I abandon her?*

In a panic, I look up my grandmother, Penelope. Also missing. *What's going on? Do the vances collect women? Is this some sort of* Handmaid's Tale *situation? Am I next to be captured and impregnated, to give birth to a future alien species?*

"SIDEKICK, how come some people aren't coming up in the search?"

"All humans in the nanoholocom network are included in search feature."

"Well, that didn't answer my question. HOLOGUIDE EXIT."

It bows. "May your contribution lead to freedom."

I take a few deep breaths to shake the negative possibilities out of my head and try to focus my energy on Dominick for now. My black uniform needs an upgrade for a happy reunion, so I holofy the top to a deep cranberry and smooth my curly hair the best I can with my fingers into a ponytail. Following my bandwidth like a personal GPS system, I take the maglift back to the Hub and exit my new LU community. As I walk past other LU communities to the blinking light next to Dominick's name on the holomap, I notice the design of the communities is not what

I initially thought. Nine huge, circular LUs form each community, lined up in an X formation, not a V, with the building in the center taller and windowless. I hope that's not a new punishment tower.

I wonder how many of these linked housing systems are needed to house everyone who traveled through a vertex. Bigger question is still why. As I walk past, I swear some of the outside walls of certain LU buildings shift ever so slightly clockwise, like a flower following the sunlight. I pull off a yellow leaf from a nearby bush and carry it with me. I never know what will disappear anymore.

Dominick's LU community is identical to mine, Hub and all. My heart flutters with first-date jitters even though I could probably map every freckle and scar on his body. Traveling through space and time to save someone you love really increases the pressure of the reunion. I just need to hold him again and never let go. The bright lavender sky shines through the prism dome and breaks into cascades of rainbows. As I walk through the Hub of strangers, all seemingly from Earth, two familiar faces in the lounging crowd catch my eye. Dominick's little brother, Austin, taps on a holoscreen floating over his bandwidth, and Dominick's mother watches nearby. My heart stumbles at the hope of seeing Dominick, but he's nowhere in sight.

"Ms. Landen?"

"Alexandra?" She stands up from the ground and hugs me. "Oh, my god, you made it. Dominick has been worried sick. Austin, look who's here!"

"Hi, Dominick's girlfriend," Austin says. He swipes his bandwidth's holoscreen, barely making eye contact.

"Hi, Austin."

"Alex, my hologuide is a Pokémon."

"You can modify your hologuide into a Pokémon?"

"You can do anything here." He taps and tosses forward from

his bandwidth's holoscreen, and a miniature holographic Pokémon character emerges in the grass. Austin takes off running after it. I wonder what will happen to Earth children here if we don't get them home soon.

I turn my attention back to Dominick's mother. "Where's Dominick?"

"He's in the Holospaces with Rita. He'll be thrilled to see you."

"Rita's here? I couldn't find her in the nanoholocom network."

"Really? That's odd. They should be in there." She points to the huge tower. "The Holospaces are not in the LU buildings any-more. The center building in every LU community is dedicated to Holospaces."

So entertainment buildings, not punishment towers. And Rita's here, so I don't have to track her down. Two birds, one stone. Isn't that what they say?

"Thanks."

Walking to the Holospace building, I imagine kissing Dominick again, feeling his lips on mine, spinning with my feet in the air as he swings me around. Then bear hugging Rita and telling her everything that happened after she left. *I wonder how long it took for them to find each other. Without me.* There are more than thirty Holospace rooms per floor, each with a holoscreen on a white door with a list of occupants.

They probably think I'm dead. Dominick probably thinks I be-trayed him and didn't keep my word. So they probably got together to reminisce about our good times, turned to one another during a time of loss . . .

I'm being silly. They're my best friends.

I walk faster and faster down each hallway, touching and scanning each list for their names, my excitement to see my best friends again bursting inside me. By the time I find the right door, I'm on the third floor and out of breath. `Dominick Landen` and R. Bern. is listed on the outside. *Is that supposed to be Rita?* I push open the door without tapping the screen to see an image of inside.

Dominick.

With Rita.

Playing a holographic board game, side by side.

Backs to me.

Sitting. Touching. Her head on his shoulder. Him stroking her hair.

Together. With her sweeping dark hair and big boobs.

Like two lovebirds. Happy.

Me, long dead and forgotten.

I drop the yellow leaf.

Rita glances over her shoulder first and makes eye contact with me. She taps his shoulder, and he turns to look at me.

The guilt spreads across their faces as their smiles melt into shock.

Oh, yeah, I'd like one stone, please. A heavy one.

CHAPTER 13

DAY 23: 226 HOURS TO DECIDE

SOLBILUNA—8 GLOBAL HAPPINESS HAS INCREASED BY 19%

HOLOSPACE USE IS UP 42%

I'M SEETHING IN the hallway area, staring at the holoscreen on the door and trying not to hyperventilate. Dominick and Rita head toward the door, all smiles again. I can't talk to them. Not in my current mental state. The BME would zap and shellac me again for sure.

I race from the Holospace building and through the adjacent Hub at top speed, avoiding Dominick's mother and brother. I need to hide in my LU and lock myself away from my universal mistake of thinking I was special to someone. I came all the way here to tell people the truth, especially Dominick and Rita, and especially Dominick since I promised him. I promised him I would come here, and we had wonderful, lovely, sheet-flouncing, bodies-floating sex in the bedroom by the ocean, and here he is mucking it up with my best friend.

And her! How could she do this to me? I'm like her *hermana*. We've known each other since we were little. She knows how I feel about Dominick, how he's supposed to feel about me. How he said he felt about me.

Big picture. Focus on what's important. I came through the vertex to spread the truth. Get us to fight back. Get us back to Earth if that's possible.

Were they flirting back on Earth? Did I miss something? A soft touch, a white lie, a subtle smile?

My insides cannot handle the cosmic meltdown. There's nothing to extinguish the horrible fire that is shame.

My mission is stupid. Heroes aren't supposed to care about themselves. Who am I kidding? I'm not a girl who came to save her world. I'm a girl who came to keep a promise to a boy. A boy who has forgotten about her.

Being forgotten is a terrible, terrible ache at the core, tearing at the worthy parts of you and testing their strength. I am my worst nightmare. A girl unglued by a boy. I knew this would happen. That's why I didn't want to follow him to Boston for college. And instead I followed him to another galaxy. *I am a cosmic idiot.*

Fleeing through the Hub, I avoid walking through a garden area and instead smack into a group of strangers.

"Hey, hottie."

Four of them in their early twenties, maybe younger. Shirtless. Confident nipples and abs on display. Bored. *Boredom is a dangerous thing.*

"I haven't seen you in this LU before. I'd remember that ass. Where you heading, cutie?"

"Home," I say, but the irony of that word hits me like an arrow through the chest.

"How 'bout you stick around here for a while. We have some homemade stuff stashed. Little party time?"

"No, thanks." I move off the glittering walkway to avoid them and crush soft grass under my boots. They follow.

"Aw, come on. What else do you have to do? This place is paradise."

One of them grabs my shoulder. His touch makes me completely short-circuit. I spin around and push him.

"Let go of me!"

"Chill, he didn't mean nothing," another says, touching my back.

"Don't touch me!"

"Girl, relax. You really need something to get you on a perpetual vay-cay."

That's when I explode.

"This place isn't a vacation. It's a trap. Get away from me!"

Other people gather closer at my outburst.

An older man comes running first and asks, "Are you okay?"

"No, I'm not okay." I start sobbing. I give up. "They lied and kidnapped us and brought us here and I don't know why."

"Who? These boys?" the man asks and points in their direction.

I shake my head no and catch my breath. Dominick's mother and Austin run over. Having them as witnesses won't stop me. Nothing can stop me. I know it's the wrong time, but there will never be a right time anyway. I don't care if the BME gets me. I have nothing left to lose. Dominick and Rita are no longer mine to hold on to.

"The comet was a hologram. Do you hear me? It never crashed. The Earth is fine. The comet was a hologram! The comet was a hologram!"

The four shirtless guys look at me like I've become the crazy lady. Maybe I have. Between their bare shoulders I spot Dominick and Rita racing toward me through the Hub.

Traitors.

Dominick's mother speaks. "Alexandra, I think you might be stressed out. Confused."

I avoid looking at my former best friends. "No, I'm not. The comet wasn't real. The holograms lied."

"Honey, scientists confirmed it. Remember? We all came before the comet crashed. That's how you survived. That's how we all survived." She places her hand gently on the back of my neck.

I flinch from her touch. "It's not like that."

"Yeah, don't touch her. She gets all feisty," one shirtless guy says.

"Why don't you sit down?" Dominick's mother offers. "Maybe we should call the HME."

"I'm fine. I don't want to sit down."

The crowd begins to disperse at the lack of drama. The shirtless group shoulder-bump each other as they leave.

I let the truth out, and it didn't set me free. It didn't set anyone free. Not a blip on their radar. No one cares. No one believes me. Not even a little. Not even a slight doubt. Even the BME didn't activate and put me out of my misery.

And my best friends are boinking each other.

"Alex!" Dominick lifts me off my feet and presses my body to his like a drowning person to a life preserver. "You made it. Oh, my god, you made it." His eyes water as he smiles and keeps hugging me, patting me, touching me to make sure I'm real.

Relief at his touch warms the muscles in my back, but the anger and fear and hurt and confusion remain.

"So you made it with your parents?" he asks.

I nod and try not to cry. I can't tell him that I abandoned them for him. He doesn't deserve it. "I see you found Rita."

"Yes, well, she found me."

Rita grins. "I'm so happy you're here!" She reaches out to hug me. I'd like to knock her teeth out of her head.

"Aw, isn't that nice? You two, finding each other."

Their expressions change as they look at one another and then back at me. *Ha, caught ya!*

"I've been searching the nanoholocom network since I got here a week ago," Dominick says. "I thought you didn't make it."

Yeah, didn't make it, so you two got chummy. That was fast. I stall, then whisper, "I just got here. You wouldn't be able to find me anyway since my bandwidth doesn't know my real name."

"Why? And why are you whispering?" Rita asks.

I shrug.

"What name did you give them?" Dominick asks. I can't explain Katherine and my tampered bandwidth and the Umbra organization right now. "I . . . er . . . River."

His familiar dimples return. I forgot how deep they go.

"River, huh?" he says and grins more. "Like the 'Spoilers' River from *Doctor Who?* Or the *Firefly* 'I can kill you with my brain' River?"

"Does it matter?" I say, annoyed.

"Yes. Yes, it does." He laughs, and Rita laughs, even though I know she doesn't get the references.

I let out a harsh, manic chuckle. *What, I'm either the kick-ass love of his life or a psycho? Sums up our whole relationship.*

"I tried to search for you, Rita, but you weren't in the nano-holocom network, either."

"I'm with the Geotroupes. Off the grid. I'll introduce you. I was hoping you had joined with the Geos, too, since we couldn't find you. Didn't know you were hiding under an alias as a top secret sci-fi agent."

Didn't know you were a boyfriend stealer.

"Yeah, what was that all about?" Dominick asks. "The comet being fake?"

It's now or never. I told the truth and no one cared. No penalty box.

"The comet was a hologram. Earth is still there."

They look at one another and then back at me. *I imagine them feeding each other strawberries, naked.*

"Alex, you sound kind of paranoid," Dominick says.

I am dumbfounded. My Dominick, my science fiction,

conspiracy theory, science and math freak cheating boyfriend, won't believe me.

"I am not paranoid. I saw it with my own eyes. The comet wasn't real."

Rita holds me by both shoulders. "You think you saw it crash. It might be your brain not wanting to deal with . . . with . . . This may be your way of coping."

"No, it's not like that."

Dominick embraces me and whispers into my hair. "We're here for you. Things will get better with time."

I push him off me. "You're not listening to me. It was a hoax!"

"Alex, that doesn't make sense. Why would they make such an elaborate plan? If they wanted us, they have the power to just collect us. Look around. They are way more advanced than we are."

I turn to Rita. My former best friend. Surely *she* will believe me even if he doesn't. Instead, she turns to him, and he to her, and they exchange a knowing glance between each other. Of pity. For me.

"You two are screwing each other."

"What?" Rita says, her mouth agape.

"You heard me. It's like a bad cliché. You thought I died, so you two got together. Admit it."

"Alex, we would never do that," Dominick says.

"I saw you. In the Holospaces." I wipe my face on my uniform sleeve, then point at Dominick. "I ran through to keep my promise to you. I should've stayed with my parents on Earth. Where it was safe."

"God, you really have lost it." Rita flips her long hair to one side. I want to yank it from its roots and run with the strands to see if she's really my friend or if she's a figment of some alternative nightmare.

Dominick sticks his hands into his pockets, and that's when I see it. His bandwidth glows gold around his wrist.

He contributed.

I've lost the two greatest allies of my life.

I give up. As I bolt to escape their betrayal, I overhear Rita mumble to Dominick, "Just let her go."

CHAPTER 14

DAY 23: 225 HOURS TO DECIDE

THE NANOHOLOCOM NETWORK DOES NOT EXTEND OUTSIDE
THE ESTABLISHED BOUNDARY ZONES. ENTER AT YOUR OWN
RISK.

THANKFULLY, BENJI AND Marcus are not in our new LU
when I get back, and they've already modified the place. I hate
it, but I don't care enough to change it. I scribble in my journal
to get my emotions out of me and onto paper; then I soak in the
comfort of the PSF to see if it can erase heartbreak.

*How can they do this to me? And on top of that, how can they
not believe me?* I thought Dominick and I had something real, not
something he'd give up on so easily. *Something timeless and able
to withstand a holographic, apocalyptic, time traveling, fraudulent
kidnapping scheme. Like all teenage love stories.*

Can I really stay mad at him? He thought I was dead. *Yes, damn
it. I deserve at least a year of mourning before he gets to date again.
At least. He didn't even last a month!*

A month. Over a month.

I never got my period.

My brain goes into a tailspin.

*I am pregnant. With Dominick's baby. Who is now boning my
best friend. I'm going to give birth alone, on another planet, in another time, without my parents to help or yell at me. Benji's gonna
kill me.* I already feel like throwing up.

Wait, if I have the baby here, then is it considered an alien baby? Am I going to give birth to an extraterrestrial life-form?

But we used protection every time, and condoms are 98% effective. I read it on the box.

I'm the two percent.

I leave the PSF and hold my bandwidth. "HME OPEN."

"Please state your medical needs."

"Am I . . . pregnant?"

"Scanning. One moment. No."

"Oh, thank god." A wave of relief passes over me. "Then why didn't I get my period? From stress?"

"All Earth travelers were temporarily sterilized upon arrival during the first HME. Females will not menstruate. You cannot get pregnant."

Sterilized? Excuse me? "So we can't have children?"

"You must petition the meritocracy for permission to have a child. Once granted, the sterilization will be reversed."

"So it's like mandatory birth control."

"Mandatory population control. Solbiluna-8 is about balance."

Solbiluna-8 is more about total control with a smile.

HOURS LATER, THE LU door beeps while I'm in the PSF. I want it to be Dominick and Rita even though I'm pissed at them. As the cycle completes, the PSF door clicks open, and I see Benji in the LU.

"Your skin's gonna fall off if you keep using that thing."

"Whatever. Wait, can it do that?"

"Guess you'll find out." He rummages through his bag of belongings.

I step out of the PSF and plop onto my holobed.

"I thought you'd be looking for your friends."

The image of Dominick and Rita making out and laughing at me pops into my mind. "Friends are overrated. Hey, did you know we were all sterilized when we first got here as a form of birth control?"

He pulls out a few items from his bag, pockets one, then sits on the fake holosofa and rubs his face with his hands.

"Doctor A. gave me a full report of their medical system and ideology."

"You knew? Why aren't we up in arms?" My voice cracks.

"We need time to gain power. How many times do I have to tell people that?" He sighs, and I realize it isn't about me since he covers his face with his hands.

"What's up?"

"Umbra stuff. We've joined forces with other established Umbra groups. It's hard to manage all the personalities and agendas."

"Can you talk about that in here?" I whisper.

"Katherine took care of our LU. No BME. We're in constant sleep mode." He stands and looks out the huge windows at the navy mountains in the distance. "Sometimes I wonder . . ."

I sit up. "Wonder what?"

"If coming out and marrying Marcus was the right thing to do."

"What? Where did that come from?"

"I don't know. If there hadn't been a looming crisis, I would've waited. There was more pressure to rush. My life is so much more complicated."

"But aren't you happier not living with that secret? And you love Marcus."

"Yes. It changed things, though. The military didn't know before. It's hard to maintain the same level of respect. The same authority. Even people in the Umbra make small gestures, comments. Heard another one just now."

I join him near the window. "Benji, you are one of the toughest people I've ever known. I think you're even tougher than Dad. You're the same person you were before you came out. Don't back down with the Umbra. It's who you are and why you are good at your job. Give them hell."

"I never thought you'd be the one telling me to toughen up."

I smile. "Me, either. So what's the latest plan with the Umbra?"

"Secure a headquarters in the QN25 region. Share information with other Umbra groups. Find the location of the vances and the meritocracy. Return home."

Home. The word reverberates inside of me like a tuning fork.

He shakes his head. "Convincing the other Umbra leaders on the planet to believe in the word of one teenage girl that the apocalypse on Earth never took place without hard evidence is not an easy feat, let me tell you. I'm taking a lot of heat."

"I need to tell you something," I say and pick at my thumbnail.

"Shoot."

"I, uh, sorta told a group of people that the comet was fake and the Earth is fine."

"You what? Alex, what did I—"

I flop on the holobed. "It didn't matter. No one believed me, and the BME system didn't care."

"What were you thinking?" he yells.

"I wasn't thinking. I'm an idiot."

"Well, at least we agree on something. You could've compromised the Umbra's mission."

"I know. That's why I'm telling you. All this time we've been holding back the truth, and it didn't even matter. How's the mission going to work if no one believes what happened?"

"Interesting that the system didn't react. If the BME had subdued you, it might make your claim more valid. No reaction creates the assumption that what you're saying is not dangerous or true, and you look like a fool."

"I feel like a fool."

"Good. Don't do it again."

A tiny beep echoes from Benji's waist. He picks up a square metal device, the size of a paper clip, and squeezes it.

"Duty calls."

"What's that thing?"

"Going back to a kind of beeper technology. If it beeps, Jackson, Beruk, Katherine, Marcus, or you needs me." He reaches into his pocket and throws one at me. "A different Umbra group created them. They made them as soon as the communication field opened up. Piggybacked the signal onto it to avoid detection." He holds up his bandwidth. "Don't trust the CVBE COM or VID for Umbra business."

I nod and clip it onto my uniform shirt.

"What the hell are you doing? We're a secret organization. Clip it somewhere less conspicuous."

I clip it to the back pocket of my uniform. "Better?"

"I suppose. Yours only beeps me. I'll come when I can. Don't click it during one of your panic attacks, either. Only use it in real emergencies."

Part of me understands what he's saying. Part of me wants to shove the clip down his throat.

THE NEXT MORNING, too early for typical humans, Benji and Marcus are already up. Through the space in the holographic room dividers, I see them dressed in their holofied uniforms, Benji in full dark blue with white edging, Marcus in a rich plum top with gray pants.

"Where are you going?" I groan, rubbing my eyes.

"Meeting Katherine. They found the Umbra a QN25 head-quarters. Get out of bed and come check it out."

I'm not used to Benji being nice to me. I climb out of the holobed.

"Might as well," I mumble.

It's not like I have a best friend or a boyfriend to look forward to anymore.

After breakfast in an empty Hub, Benji, Marcus, and I meet Katherine outside our LU community. I expect another magpod ride, which I don't think I'll ever adjust to, but instead Katherine sets us out on foot. The sun rises between two sharp mountains, bringing light and color to an otherwise dark landscape. We pass by other neighboring communities. Dominick's LU is on the other side of the ringed compound, so I don't have to worry about running into the two lovebirds. Part of me wants to run into them again, though. I'm not done screaming at them.

By the time we hit the perimeter of the entire LU linked region, the sun has reached civilization. We face a line of short, gnarled trees with limbs extending outward in haphazard directions. *Don't people read enough fairy tales or watch enough horror movies to know never to go into the forest?*

Apparently not.

Without questioning her sanity, Katherine leads the group through the terrain. Along each limb, I search for signs of alien life-forms. *Killer monkeys, two-headed bears, vampires? Something must lurk in every shadow.* The only animals I spot are more dinochicken birds. They don't seem to squawk in any kind of sequence, so they seem real enough, I guess. I pull off leaves as I go to check for realness. It also gives me something to keep my hands busy. As my heartbeat drowns out other sounds, I follow my counselor's advice and separate possibilities from probabilities. *The chances of getting attacked and eaten alive and our bones being picked over by scavengers—is it possible? Yes. Probable? YES. Rita and Dominick will probably be happy to find out I'm dead. Let them off the hook.*

I can't figure out how Katherine is navigating through the area since everything looks the same to me. I want to leave some kind of trail to make sure we can find our way back. We're lost enough for a human lifetime.

A glowing insect flies near my head. It's the first bug I've seen since I left Earth, and instead of being afraid and swatting at it, I find myself fascinated by it. *What if it bites? Will I develop alien Lyme disease?* Upon further quick inspection, though, I realize it's not an insect at all. It's a tiny robot.

"Did you see these robot bugs?"

"Yes, they pollinate the area," Benji says. "According to my hologuide, bees went extinct here a long time ago and they had to compensate. Don't worry, they're not drones spying on you."

"How do you know?"

"I pulled one apart," Katherine says.

As we travel deeper into the forest, the trees change from separate, spread-out knotted trunks to huge, pale trees with tiny red leaves that tower over us. The tall skeleton trees support dark, eggplant-colored foliage that snakes up the trunks to form a luxurious canopy above us. Up close, the huge leaves have soft, downy hairs covering their surface. I pull one off and can't stop touching it until I wonder if it's an alien form of poison ivy.

The four CVBE lights on my bandwidth go out, and our uniforms revert to their initial iridescent color. We must be out of the nanoholocom network. It's like leaving Oz and returning to Kansas. I break into a sweat, and right when I'm about to quit, we reach a clearing.

A dark, decomposing city spreads before us. The dilapidated structures don't glitter like the rest of Solbiluna-8. The circular structures are much taller and wooden, like buildings made of hollowed-out sequoias cut and roofed. Branches of skeleton trees have grown through the missing roofs, and a chartreuse moss blankets the outer walls. Some windows are intact, but others don't show any sign they ever had glass.

"Welcome to the waste land," Katherine says, "our local Umbra headquarters."

"Waste land?" Benji asks. "Is that from Stephen King?"

"Poem by T. S. Eliot. I memorized some of his work in prison."

My chest caves in. The thing I've been trying to avoid takes hold of my mind. Crazy lady spewing random lines of T. S. Eliot's "The Hollow Men" in the hospital and on the news. *In the past.* My mind cannot handle the paradox. *Don't think. Don't think. Don't think.*

Katherine cracks her knuckles one finger at a time. "Some weird shit in that writer's brain about people and the world."

Oh, Katherine, you have no idea.

"So what is this place?" Benji asks.

"Discarded territory. No nanoholocoms. From what Professor Marciani can surmise, when Solbiluna-8 transitioned into nano-holocom technology, it was probably cheaper to create new structures with embedded technology than to add the technology to old buildings. The newer glass buildings are made of clear solar panels to collect extra energy to run the nanoholocoms."

Katherine points and continues. "We've claimed the medium-sized building on the right as Umbra headquarters. Setting up camp now. Some of the smaller structures are already claimed by squatters. They call themselves the Geotroupes. Religious granolas. Harmless."

Rita mentioned being part of that group. *Why does she live here? I'm surprised she and Dominick don't live shacked up together in their own LU.*

Benji pats Katherine on the shoulder. "Looks promising. Let's head over." They set off together with Marcus and me behind them.

"Did Beruk do a security check?" Benji asks.

"His team swept the entire area. Completely abandoned. By the looks of it, it's been a long freaking time."

Marcus says to me, "It's like walking into another culture's history."

"That's because we are."

"I'm waiting for a T-rex to jump out from behind a building and snack on us."

"Right?" I laugh, a mask for my fear.

Professor Marciani meets us outside the new headquarters. He smiles like a kid with a new video game system.

"So, Professor, does it meet your standards?" Benji asks.

"Yes, especially under these circumstances. Time is crucial."

"How do we know this place isn't another hologram?" I ask. "Another trap?"

"Good question," the professor says. "We tested it by fluctuating the temperature, and nothing happened to the structures. I did several other more complicated tests as well. It's as real as you and I. Beruk and his team did not detect any nanoholocom network signals running through the region."

I place my hand on the surface of the building. The bright moss and thick wood brim with an energy that I haven't felt in a while. A sense of strength and stability. A sense of being alive. A sense of being connected to something greater. Maybe it's all in my head. Even though the professor said they checked for holograms, as the others step inside the building, I peel off a bit of moss to double-check.

The maglifts inside the building don't work. Katherine leads us to a hidden staircase behind a sliding panel. I wonder if there are hidden sections in our LUs. As we walk upstairs, the moss sits idle in my hand. Safe so far. I can't help but also double-tap my bandwidth for SIDEKICK. Nothing happens. We're in a safe zone from all things holographic. I click my beeper clip. Benji's waistband beeps.

"Sorry, just testing."

"Don't use that unless it's an emergency," Benji says. "You'll waste our time."

"Benji," Marcus says, "you're being a bit harsh."

"Please, when you've lived with her longer, you'll see."

Marcus goes silent. I don't like it.

"How come the clickers work, but the bandwidths don't? Don't they use the same network?" I ask.

"The clickers, as you call them, are on a lower radio frequency, so they carry farther and wider than higher frequency signals, even through this area," Katherine says, and then changes the subject to address Benji. "We've established the fourth floor as home base. The other floors can be used as needed."

"Why not the top floor?" Benji asks.

"Too hard to walk up constantly. Fourth floor is convenient and safe enough."

"Safe from what?" I ask.

"The first few floors are always the most vulnerable. Vulnerable to attacks, flooding, *et cetera*. We could probably sleep on the fifth floor."

"Wait, we're moving here? I don't have my bag. And what about the PSF? And food?" My stomach fires on all cylinders, and I wonder if the toilets here work.

"Marcus and I will crash here most nights rather than travel back and forth from the LU," Benji says. "You don't have to stay here."

Before we reach the fourth floor, I hear voices rise in argument.

At every step, the voices intensify. Benji quickens his pace, and we follow.

The fourth floor is an open, gutted space with no interior walls. Like living inside a horizontal wooden wheel. A group of people shout at each other—Jackson and members of the Umbra, and some people I don't recognize.

"What's the problem?" Benji's voice echoes through the empty space.

"We were here first," a woman says. "The Geotroupes claimed the wooden territory when we found it months ago."

"This building wasn't claimed," Jackson says. "It was empty. From the intelligence we've gathered, you have only enough people to fill two of these buildings. There are hundreds of buildings here."

Another man steps forward. "We expect our numbers to flourish with more people arriving."

"We already have the numbers," Katherine says.

"Describe your group to me," Jackson interrupts. "Maybe we can come to an agreement."

"I don't have to explain anything to you," the woman says. "This is our territory."

I back up to create distance between me and a growing mob. Been there, done that. As I move, I feel a breeze blowing through the area. I think nothing of it until Marcus yells, "Alex! Look out!"

I stop and spin around, teetering on the edge of a missing window. Fourth floor and inches away from plummeting to my death. My stomach drops as if I'm on a roller coaster, and goosebumps rush down my spine and limbs. Marcus grabs the back of my uniform and pulls me to safety.

I flee back down the stairs as quickly as my feet can carry me, skipping steps along the way. *I will never stay here. Never. No, thank you.* I never thought I'd prefer the LU holotech world to a broken, natural world, but all I want is to hide forever in the PSF.

Outside, I take deep breaths, count like I've been trained, and let them out slowly. I repeat and repeat to try to slow the spiraling energy inside me. I look up and see the open spaces where windows should be, the distance my body would've fallen. I sit on the safety of the ground, as low as possible. The reddish-brown soil is damp, which doesn't make sense to me since it never rains.

Doctor A. finds me. He doesn't ask questions, just sits with me and then walks me back to the LU community. As soon as we move from the skeleton forest to the wider, shorter treescape, my uniform returns from translucent to cranberry, which reminds me why I changed it in the first place. Doctor A.'s changes to a crisp white business suit. Once we get to the Hub, I stop at the platform to get my second food ration of the day to settle my stomach, and then head up to my LU. Too exhausted to argue, I allow Doctor A. to lead me into the maglift instead of searching for a hidden emergency staircase.

All I want to do is cry and escape my life in the PSF.

Waiting at my LU door is Dominick. I want to run and hug him and scream in his face for abandoning me.

Doctor A. looks from me to Dominick and back again. "It seems you have company. How are you feeling, Alex?"

"Better," I say, lying. Seeing Dominick is making my emotions go haywire. "The food and walk helped."

"Glad to hear it. I don't think we've met." Doctor A. extends his hand, and Dominick shakes it. "Dr. Aiyegbeni."

"Dominick. Sorry, I missed your name. Doctor who?" Dominick asks, then catches himself and grins. I can't help but crack up laughing even though I'm pissed off. There's a reason we liked each other. *Loved each other.*

Doctor A. nods in my direction when I laugh, and his eyes light up. He returns his gaze to Dominick. "Ah, no TARDIS here, I'm afraid. Dr. Aiyegbeni. Call me Doctor A."

Major nerd points to Doctor A.

"Nice to meet you," Dominick says.

Don't let those dimples fool you, Doctor. He's a traitor.

"You seem to have a positive effect on this young lady. I'll leave you two to your business. Very nice to meet you, young man. Take care, Alex."

"Thanks for walking me back."

"Anytime, my dear."

Once Doctor A. disappears into the maglift, I turn on Dominick.

"Where's Rita? Aren't you two joined at the hip now? My two best friends have to hook up immediately as soon as they think I'm dead—"

Dominick pushes his body toward me, wordlessly, throwing me off guard. I was ready for a full-on verbal argument.

"Please shut up," he whispers into my face. His voice runs over my skin like warm water. His body pins mine against the LU door. He lets his lips speak for him, softly at first, then more forcefully. His hands hold my face as if it's made of glass. We make up for lost time. I can't stop myself. I can't get enough.

When we come up for air, I say, "Did you just tell me to shut up?"

His dimples do me in. "I waited long enough for you."

"So you and Rita?" I whisper into his face. I miss his glasses.

"Are friends. Your friends. Like always."

"It looked like you were together. In the Holospaces."

"Alex, I've been a mess without you." He presses me against the wall again and kisses me harder. I stop asking stupid questions and let myself melt into him.

CHAPTER 15

DAY 24: 203 HOURS TO DECIDE

AS OF TODAY, 52% OF EARTH REFUGEES HAVE
CONTRIBUTED.

THE OFFICIAL EARTH-MOURNING CEREMONIES WILL END.

DOMINICK AND I somehow make it into my LU.

"I've been waiting for you here all morning," Dominick says. "It wasn't easy to track you down. I had to ask people. You really aren't in the system."

"No, I'm not." I move my backpack out of his way so he has room to sit on my holobed.

"Can you believe this place? Pretty much like they said it would be. Better now that you're here."

I fake a smile. "Have you noticed any problems?"

"Only with our people not used to the system. Wanting extra rations. One guy is trying to create a monetary system using rocks. It's not working, though. I mean, everything is free, and ... they're rocks."

I smile again. It's amazing to see him after all this time, but it's so hard to talk to someone who hasn't experienced the world the way you have. "Did you see anyone get punished by the BME?"

"Yeah, one guy punched another and got surrounded. Pretty effective."

I lift up the pant leg of my uniform to show him one of my fading scars.

"What the hell? What happened?"

"I stuck my head in the water fountain."

He tries not to laugh, and it makes me laugh.

As he slides closer to me and puts his arms around me, his bandwidth glows on my shoulder. A reminder of what he could become. A reminder that I found him too late.

I cover my leg. "Did you know we were on a spaceship?"

He looks at me like I've grown five heads. "No, when?"

"Before we arrived here. We were on a spaceship the whole time we were out of communication range."

"We came here through vertexes in our old Hub."

"That was really a spaceship. I guess your deck didn't see the windows. Wait, you've been here over a week? So we weren't on the same ship."

"I wasn't on a spaceship. I was in a whole LU community. Sun, stars, and moons . . ."

"Dominick, it was a spaceship. My ship took down the illusion. It was all holographic. Everyone in my LU community saw it. Ask them. The meritocracy even admitted they used the illusion to avoid upsetting us during the integration process. Seamless integration."

He stands from the holobed and looks out my window wall. "Have you seen the future humans?"

"You mean the vances? No."

"Vances?"

"For advanced humans."

"Oh. I hadn't heard that one." He sticks his hands in the pockets of his uniform. "Alex, the stuff you said about the comet not being real . . ."

"All true."

He rubs the back of his neck with one hand. "It can't be true. There's no way. It's too incredible and terrible."

"You need to meet the Umbra."

"No, not another group like Rita's. What I need . . ." He sits closer to me and kisses me again. It's already not the same since he's not listening. I want to let him in, but how can I when he doesn't even believe the truth? When he doesn't believe in me? I break away.

"Are you afraid your parents will come back and catch us? Did the HME fix your father's health? They healed my eye and arm, and I don't need my glasses anymore. Although," he reaches into his uniform back pocket and places his black-rimmed glasses on his face, "I popped out the glass and kept the frames."

I walk over to the PSF and lean against the cool, blackened surface. My mouth doesn't want to form the words.

"Alex?"

"My parents didn't make it through the vertex. They're back on Earth."

His mouth hangs open, silent. He knows what it's like to lose a parent since he lost his father. "God, I'm so sorry."

"Don't be sorry. They're the safe ones. Hopefully. We're the ones who are screwed." The memory of my parents stranded in the middle of a cold Boston road, Dad in a wheelchair, Mom screaming my name, returns to haunt me.

Before Dominick can respond, a beeping sound echoes through the room. At first I think it might be the clip Benji gave me, but it's followed by a calm, monotone voice: "Please access the CVBE for an important BUZ message from the meritocracy." The third tiny, colored light on my bandwidth blinks. Through the golden hue, Dominick's blinks as well.

"Probably about to tell us another lie," I say.

"It's probably to allow us more access," Dominick says.

Before I get a chance to hold my bandwidth and open a

holoscreen, Dominick taps his and throws an imaginary object at the wall. The entire wall turns into a holoscreen.

The same leader who spoke on the spaceship, with graying hair, white robe, and silver necklace ending with a gemstone, emerges on the screen. The rest of the meritocracy sit behind him.

Dominick squeezes my hand, and we sit on the holobed to watch. His eyes sparkle in excitement. He doesn't see our saviors as our conquerors yet. I click my clip over and over again. Benji needs to see this, and he's out of range.

"Greetings. We are the meritocracy, the ruling body of 2359. My name is Keron. I serve as the voice of the meritocracy. Welcome to the final stage of integration. We hope you will enjoy acclimating to Solbiluna-8 and explore the full benefits of our world. Feel free to travel our planet using magpods or vertexes, and use your bandwidths to access the CVBE features. The Holospaces are always available for recreation, education, and group worship, and the Skylucent will continue each night.

"We must remind you that our world can survive only if we balance our leisure time with the greater good. Solbiluna-8 is built upon the belief that humans were made to thrive, not toil away precious time. We wish you to think, explore, create, enjoy. By providing freedom from commerce, we provide freedom from work. In order to continue this luxury for future generations, however, we need your contribution in death. As of today, 52% of Earth refugees have contributed. We believe that with everything our world has to offer, that number should be 100%."

I click and click my stupid clip. Where's my brother when I need him?

"As we explained before, our nanoholocom network only works with the vast pathways of the human brain. Rest assured, only your thoughts and neural matrix will be integrated with our systems. As a biohologram, you will no longer have physical and emotional needs. In this holographic state, you will be able to work for our society, assuring that future generations will enjoy the same luxury of leisure during their life spans that you did.

"While contribution is not mandatory, in fairness, those who do not wish to become bioholograms will be put to work and have less time to enjoy our luxuries. The choice is yours. Once you decide, please let your hologuide know. Your hologuide is also available to answer any questions. You have two hundred and three hours remaining to decide. May your contribution lead to freedom."

"100%? Can you believe this?" I say. "Who are they kidding? I can't believe they got 52%."

"I contributed," he says, letting go of my hand and holding up his bandwidth.

"I noticed. I can't believe you volunteered to upload yourself. Come on, it's wicked creepy. The vances keep pretending they are here to give us what we want, but all they really want is to enslave us." My mind races with worries and possibilities, including a vision of him dying and turning into an emotionless hologram. "Did Rita contribute?"

"No. She said it was for religious reasons." He goes quiet.

I use that line of thinking. "What about the idea of an afterlife? The soul? What if your soul gets trapped in technology? Then you'd live for another, what'd they say—another fifty years—with an enslaved soul?"

Where's Rita when I need her? This is getting way too deep. I don't know if I believe in souls and an afterlife. I just can't let him sacrifice himself to a culture based on fabricating sophisticated lies.

Dominick stays quiet. I sit next to him and rub his arm.

"What you said about souls doesn't bother me," he says. "I'm an atheist. I actually like the idea of becoming a biohologram.

Giving myself to science. People donate organs all the time. So I don't really have a problem with that part. But you made me think about my father. I'm wondering how I would feel if my father were a biohologram. Would I like seeing him again, knowing he didn't care? It wouldn't really be him, but he could remember me. Or would it bother me more, seeing a hollow version of what he used to be . . . like a ghost?"

I hadn't thought of that. I don't know what I'd want in that case, either.

Dominick tucks one hand in his pocket and offers me the other one. I don't know what this means. "It's pointless arguing about it, anyway," he adds. "When I contributed, my hologuide said you can never take it back. Can't have people contribute, skip out on years of work, and then try to take it back before they die. Once you contribute, it's permanent."

The information etches itself on my heart like marking his gravestone. I don't know what to say.

BENJI, KATHERINE, AND Beruk call an emergency Umbra meeting. I find myself dragging Dominick to the Umbra head-quarters even though I just told myself in the morning that I'd never return. But someone has to talk some sense into him. I use the bandwidth COM and call "R. Bern" to invite Rita so I can apologize, but the COM fails. She must be with the Geotroupes off the grid and out of range.

As Dominick and I walk through the forest with Doctor A. and Marcus, Dominick says, "The Umbra is like Rita's group, isn't it? Same trail."

"Her group lives in a different section of the abandoned area. Katherine says they're like hippies. The Umbra is far from that."

"Who's Katherine?"

Loaded question. It's not the time to discuss crazy lady and time travel paradoxes. It'll just confirm that I'm the one who's crazy. Not that he doesn't already think that.

"She's one of the leaders and a technology genius. Really down-to-earth." Something in the phrase strikes me as odd and meaningless while on a foreign planet. "You'll love her and Professor Marciani from MIT."

His eyes brighten, and I know he's curious.

The Umbra headquarters remains an open floor plan, with ashen furniture added for comfort. I'm not sure where the furniture came from until Katherine asks me if I will give up one of my daily supply rations to print nails and screws for building with the pale wood from the forest. Everything around us must be hand-built. Impressive. I didn't realize how talented people are.

Thankfully, someone boarded up the gaping window area. It reminds me of home when I helped Dad board up our windows after looters ransacked our food supply. I thought he was losing it. Maybe he was stronger than I gave him credit for. Maybe not.

I introduce Dominick to as many people in the Umbra as possible so he can get a feel for the scope of the project, including Kendra and Nolan. At least a third of the group are new. Benji finishes talking to Jackson and comes over to us.

"Dominick, it's good to see you here. Maybe you'll think about joining us. Marcus speaks highly of you."

"Thanks," Dominick says and shakes Benji's hand. I notice Dominick's bandwidth is deactivated here, no longer a beacon of light reminding me of his possible death.

"Why didn't you come when I clicked the clip thing?" I ask Benji.

"Too busy. I figured it was about the new meritocracy message. We got word."

"I thought something might've happened to you."

"Sometimes you remind me of Mom."

I can't tell if that's a compliment or an insult. Since it's coming from Benji, I assume it's the latter.

When Jackson calls the meeting to order, everyone gathers in one area. Dominick and I end up several rows back. Even though the Umbra joined forces with local established groups, it looks like Jackson's still in charge. He asks Beruk to speak first.

Beruk updates everyone on the security of the headquarters and how they've reached out to other Umbra groups to spread the word about the comet hoax and the state of Earth. He discusses a wide sweep of the area to investigate how the landmass functions since the nanoholocom network won't provide complete global maps that include abandoned and natural regions. Their primary goal is to pinpoint the location of the meritocracy and the vances in order to infiltrate when the time is right. Dominick's shoulders broaden as he listens to him speak.

Professor Marciani takes the floor next. "Unfortunately, the DQD, our first cryowave-particle weapon, exploded during testing. We believe the next model will be viable. We have not been able to create a stable vertex on our own. Now that we have travel privileges, I sent a team to the closest vertex guidepost to see if we can reverse engineer them."

The professor nods to Benji, and my brother addresses the group.

"Some of us need to offer to contribute. Otherwise, we'll have to work, giving us less time to build Umbra intelligence and plan a rebellion. If all goes well, we'll be in control before it matters."

I interrupt. "You seriously want us to contribute our deaths? Are you nuts? It matters. It's permanent." I try not to make eye contact with Dominick.

"If we don't, I have a feeling we'll be targeted. You heard what the meritocracy said; they expect 100% participation. If none of us contribute, it might raise suspicion."

"That's like mandatory volunteerism," Doctor A. says from the opposite corner of the open space, near the boarded-up window. My stomach drops, my limbs getting pins and needles at the memory of almost falling.

A twenty-something guy I've never seen before speaks up. "He's just telling you like it is. If you support the Umbra cause, you might also have to save face and pretend to support theirs."

"But the whole point of life is to contribute when you're alive. To make meaning through work," Doctor A. says. "Do the vances expect us to just sit around all day and play? It's so hedonistic."

"I think you'll be surprised how lazy people can be," Benji says. "The concept appeals to people. They are tired of struggling."

Dominick clears his throat and rubs my back. I can't believe he already contributed.

Doctor A. adds, "People leading frivolous lives is just as dangerous as people leading menial ones."

"We'll see," Benji says. "I think you underestimate the human capacity for leisure. If the vances don't get 100% participation, I'm afraid there might be consequences."

Doctor A. holds his beard. I can't believe they're not listening to him. I clear my throat. "But what about the consequences of contributing. Maybe that's why they lied about the comet. To turn us all into hologram slaves."

A slow murmur spreads through the group of Umbra members.

Someone snickers and mutters, "Oh, she's the one."

Benji mouths "Not now" to me.

Another stranger says, "Earth is gone, kid."

I look around the room at new Umbra members, their eyes full of pity. The old Umbra members won't look at me.

Jackson steps in. "We aren't here to discuss that today."

"Why not?" Kendra asks her grandfather. "Isn't that our main goal? To get back to Earth?"

At least I have one ally in the room.

"Not at this time," Jackson says. "Our priority is to secure the Umbra foothold in this region and on this planet."

Kendra folds her arms over her chest. I grit my teeth together. Dominick whispers to me, "I thought they were on your side."

"They were."

AFTER THE UMBRA meeting, Dominick and I walk back to the LU community before it gets dark. On the way, we talk about the food in the LUs, the PSF, anything and everything other than the meeting.

Finally, I blurt out, "I can't believe the new members don't believe me. Do you believe me? About Earth?"

He takes a few steps in silence before responding. "It was a lot to take in. Give me time."

I can accept that. Sort of. "How much time? Like an hour?"

"Stop it," he laughs, and then he stops short. "Wait, let me get something straight. If it's true, and the comet was a hologram, why did you run through the vertex?"

"What?" I stall.

"Why did you run through? Didn't you think if the whole thing was a setup, it could lead to instant death?"

"No, I knew it didn't. And you needed to know the truth."

"How could you know?" His voice cracks.

I know it's going to mess up the truth and make me look insane, but I have to tell someone the whole story. I take a deep breath, and in the middle of a strange forest, on another planet, in the year 2359, I let it all out.

"Do you remember the crazy lady from the hospital? From

the news? The day you left, I ran into her at the vertex. She was on the ground, dying, and she handed me a note, something I had written in my journal about heroes. It was bizarre."

"What does that have to do with the vertex?"

I lean against a pale tree trunk. "When the fake comet disintegrated, I realized in that moment that there was no way she could have known about it, unless maybe I had given it to her. In the future."

"That's impossible."

"It is, but it's true. Katherine is the crazy lady. Only here she's coherent, and she doesn't know anything about it."

As the words flow from my mouth to his ears, his face looks like Han Solo frozen in carbonite. Maybe telling him was a bad idea.

"Say something." I prod him with my hand.

"What can I say? That's ridiculous." His eyes shine with curiosity, so I know his statement is not a criticism.

"Right?"

"And she doesn't know anything about it?"

"Katherine, you mean? No, and I don't want her to know. I don't want to her to travel back in time and end up dying. I'm here, so that's all that matters."

"That's not how time travel through parallel universes works. I read about it back on Earth on the hologram Q&A website, if you trust anything they say. If she was in the past, then she leaves in the future. It's a closed circuit. Done deal."

"No, I don't believe that. I can stop her. She doesn't have to know."

"Alex, I hate to tell you this, but you have no power to stop this."

"Why not? If the holograms can time travel, so can we. Go back like she did and stop people from coming."

"That's not how they explained it. It's like . . . you know, in quantum physics, how a photon can act as either a particle or a wave, but once it's observed, its actions remain consistent?"

"You lost me."

"Schrödinger's Cat?"

"The cat in the box thing? Not getting how that connects to time travel."

We continue to walk through the forest, and I collect a skeleton tree twig from the ground.

"Basically, it means if you were successful at going into the past to stop everything, you'd automatically be part of that past and present and it would've happened already. The event is observed, so it remains a constant. So if you weren't there, it didn't happen. It's like when people ask, 'What came first, the chicken or the egg?' In terms of time travel, it would be both. They both exist simultaneously. Classic paradox. She was there, so it did happen, and it will happen. Am I making sense?"

Dominick's words cement something that I was trying to avoid. I refuse to believe that I can't stop her. That she has no freedom to choose not to go.

"I'm going by what the holograms said, so I could be wrong." He shrugs. "I still can't believe you came all the way here if the Earth was safe. That was reckless. Selfless, but reckless."

"Oh, and laying your body over mine during the riot at Stop & Shop wasn't?"

"Who told you that?"

"My dad. He said to thank you for protecting me."

He kicks at a fallen branch in the dark. "You're welcome. But it wasn't close to traveling through space and time to find me."

"Let's call it even." I pull him close to me and kiss him as the sun sets in the distance.

"I have a feeling we will never be even." He tickles me on my side, reducing me to tears of laughter despite the circumstances. Only the best people have that power.

By the time Dominick and I return to my LU community, the Skylucent flashes in the sky. We decide to stay and watch it. He knows I need a distraction after the Rita showdown.

The shifting stars fade as the holographic show steals the sky. Tonight's feature is *Beauty and the Beast*. More Earth films to make us feel at home. I wonder when they will shift to future films displaying their holoculture instead of ours. I wonder if the changeover will be so seamless we won't notice the difference. The golden glow of contributed bandwidths around us looks like candles for lost souls at a memorial. Almost like the death of humanity gone to a type of fake heaven. I will not be joining them, no matter what the Umbra says. I know what I saw.

Even so, I can feel myself slipping into complacency. My muscles beg permission to relax after being stressed out for so long. There's no real stress here other than the stress I'm giving myself. I wouldn't need to keep throwing myself in the PSF if I wasn't thinking about the holograms and what they've done. If Rita didn't hate me and my parents were here and we hadn't been tricked to leave Earth, this place would seriously be paradise. That's how other people are seeing it.

"Why is Rita living with the Geotroupes anyway?" I whisper to Dominick as the movie plays above us.

"Dobby was confiscated."

I prop up on my elbows in the soft grass. "What happened to him?"

"The holograms wouldn't tell her. They kept repeating that no pets are allowed. Perfect storm for Rita. She loved that damn cat. The Geotroupes were forming an anti-tech, open religion, naturalist group, and even with her religious hang-ups, the group appealed to her after Dobby was taken."

I try not to imagine Dobby being cremated alive by holograms, his fur singeing in a horrific ball of flame. Don't get tricked by a thought. Don't get tricked by a thought.

"The Geotroupes sound like a cult," I say to trick my mind to drop the image.

"Nah, I thought the same thing, so I checked them out. They're harmless. It's like summer camp."

I stare up at the Skylucent, and Dobby's burnt body interrupts my thoughts. I try to focus on home.

"Remember going to Sea Lab during the summers in middle school?" I ask.

"How could I forget? You and Rita crashed the sailboat into the jetty."

"We told the instructor the rocks were close. He kept ignoring us with his back turned."

"Those were fun times. You two were always together."

"Yeah." I attempt to chip at my nail polish in the dark, forgetting that my nails no longer have polish.

"She'll be back."

"How do you know?"

"Because you're family. Chosen family. Even stronger than biological."

I choke back the feelings of tears in my throat and stare up at the remarkable sky. *Chosen family. How many movies have Rita and I watched together in our lifetimes so far? How many text messages gossiping over nonsense? How many times will I reminisce about my life before the holograms came and stole my world? If I stop reminiscing, is that when I'm truly defeated? When I can't remember how good and simple it was because the new world has taken over my consciousness?*

Watching the holographic display above us, I lay my head on

Dominick's chest in the dark. He wraps his arms around me. If I could freeze time, I would.

I look up at his face. "Benji and Marcus are sleeping at Umbra Headquarters." It takes a moment for my statement to sink in. His dimples show through the darkness.

"Was that a sleepover invitation?"

"Maybe. Do you believe that the Earth still exists and the comet was a holographic hoax?"

"Maybe."

"Then I guess we're at a stalemate."

"I think I can be convinced," Dominick says, still grinning.

"I knew I liked you."

DESPITE THE CIRCUMSTANCES, Dominick and I reconnect like we were before everything changed. In that moment I am home again, back on Earth, back with him, back as me.

"Do you have a condom?" he asks from my holobed. "I didn't think to bring any."

"Not necessary. The HME sterilized everyone during processing."

"What?" He sits up.

"Yep. Supposedly, it's reversible. When you want a kid, you ask the meritocracy for approval. Doctor A. is looking into it."

"So they control procreation to control population with forced medical procedures? That's a quick way to destroy the natural biology of a species. If something goes wrong with their procedure, complete extinction of our people. And do they not have STDs here?"

"You're catching on. I told you we can't trust them."

He takes a minute to process the information. "I believe you. Umbra all the way."

"That's the sexiest thing you've ever said to me."

"Stop it. I can do better than that."

We make up for lost time, lost worlds. Being with him makes me forget the holoworld of fantasy and remember what it's like to love and be loved.

Afterward, Dominick sleeps while I lie next to him. I try to clear my mind, but I can't stop thinking about my parents, and Earth, and everything that has gone wrong. The tremendous guilt that follows overwhelms my reason. *How can I have sex when my parents are technically in a dead past? How can I have sex when we are on the brink of war with the future?*

Dominick wakes and kisses me again in the darkness, and I learn to forget. Just for a few minutes. Just for the night. Maybe even in times of great stress and despair, we need a break to remember our humanity. Remember why love is worth running through vertexes for. Remember to hold on to what's real in our lives.

CHAPTER 16
DAY 24: 196 HOURS TO DECIDE

THE THREE-YEAR MERITOCRACY CYCLE ENDS IN 4,320 HOURS. TESTING FOR EACH OF THE 1,001 VOTING SEATS WILL BEGIN IN 2,160 HOURS.

EQUAL ACCOMMODATIONS WILL BE PROVIDED TO ALL, REGARDLESS OF LIFE STATUS ON EARTH.

AS OF TODAY, 76% OF EARTH REFUGEES HAVE CONTRIBUTED.

I DREAM ABOUT my parents.

Mom holds a shovel with both hands. She's digging a hole in the backyard near her garden. Dominick and I sit on the warped tan-and-peach-striped patio furniture, watching her.

The hole breaks into a chasm, then ignites into a technological, electric, metallic-blue cavity.

A vertex.

She cries and pulls at something on the ground, dragging it forward. Right as she's about to pitch it into the hole, the automatic light in the yard catches her movements. I recognize the shape.

It's my dad.

She throws his body into the vertex and begins shoveling dirt into the space. Her face contorts with emotion and slowly becomes unrecognizable. As she works and weeps, her features continue to morph until she becomes someone else.

Crazy lady.

I wake up sweating. I can sense it coming on in my bowels and fluttering in my chest.

Full-blown mode.

No pills.

And Dominick sleeping beside me.

I let myself relax for the night and I didn't write in my journal to decompress and now I'm getting penalized. I try to fight it, pretend I'm not about to look like a psychopath in front of him. He's never seen me have a full panic attack, and now is not a good time to start.

No, no, no, I beg.

Oh, yes. You are not in control. My body keeps performing inner gymnastics on my heart, lungs, stomach, and muscles. I'd rather be shot in front of him than temporarily lose control of my mind and body. It would be easier for him to understand, and I wouldn't have to live with the knowledge that he's seen me at my absolute worst.

But here she comes, and I can't stop her. I run to the PSF. The light and humming noise wakes him. He talks to me through the darkness like I'm listening, and I murmur back "Uh huh" like I can focus on what he's saying. All I can focus on is my full physical and emotional demise about to unfold before him.

Don't do it. Don't do it.

I have to do it. It's like a scuba diving tank running out of oxygen. You must swim wildly to the surface. Survival instinct.

I must fight to the surface. I must lose myself to save myself. I exit the PSF since it's making me overheat, and plop cross-legged onto the floor. Me, naked, rocking and shaking, holding my head and stomach. *Don't run to the water fountain. Don't run to the water fountain.*

He says nothing at first, or nothing that I can make out. He crouches down beside me.

"Are you okay?"

"Just go."

"Did I say something wrong? Wait—why is your skin all red? You're breaking out in hives."

It's as if he's suddenly realized I'm a reptile after shedding my old skin, and we are different species who don't belong together. Despite the heat, I throw on my uniform shirt to hide.

"Is this your anxiety? Oh, man, it is, isn't it? Just try to calm down."

He backs up when I look at him. Shooting daggers at him isn't even close. More like a blow torch. I can't find the words to explain. I rock and rock. If Rita were here, she would understand. *Don't tell me what to do. Don't tell me how to feel. Just wait. Distract me. Give me a whole lot of fucking space. Don't breathe my oxygen. Don't stare at me like I'm ill.*

"I had no idea it was this bad. Should I call the HME?"

"No, get Doctor A."

He nods and runs for help.

He runs. That was my biggest worry. That when he saw the truth, how bad it can be, he would run. He could've easily used his bandwidth and stayed with me.

I wanted him to see me as Alexandra Lucas, kick-ass future defense lawyer. Girl of the Galaxy. Not Anxiety Girl. Never Anxiety Girl. And now he knows that we don't match. He can fly. I'm stuck on the ground, never able to quite pull myself together.

It's not fair. No matter how hard I try, it will always be there, ready to pounce, from everyday stress, from losing my parents, from being taken from Earth, and even after the best night I've had in a long time.

Minutes later, Doctor A. finds me back in the PSF in the fetal position. Dominick stands in the doorway, keeping his distance. It's just what I need and not what I want.

Doctor A. takes one look at me and says, "It's time to call the HME. It's okay to get help."

I hug my knees, and every ounce of my soul fights to stay in place. Like any movement will destroy the little sanity I have left. But somehow, looking into Doctor A.'s kind face, I know he's right. I agree to HME treatment.

SIDEKICK AUTOMATICALLY MATERIALIZES next to me when the HME system activates. A light travels over my body, and I agree to transport myself to the HME facility fully conscious. My bandwidth flashes bright blue. Doctor A. and Dominick travel with me in a medical magpod to the nearest HME facility, a sparkling, square building taller and larger than any LU community. They are not allowed inside. Patients only.

Once admitted, SIDEKICK walks me to my private room the size of a pantry. There is no door. Once I lie on a platform in the blank room, more light runs up and down my body, but no audio assessment is given this time. Maybe it knows I'm too exhausted to listen. Maybe because this time I'm compliant.

Through the doorway I can see other human patients, unconscious, in nearby rooms. One patient, however, is a basic, gray-clad hologram. Its image fades in and out of existence as light surrounds it. I didn't realize the HME serviced holograms as well. *Must be malfunctioning.*

SIDEKICK stares down at me from my bedside. Why the

vances thought having your hologuide with you in a medical situation would be a comfort is beyond me.

The AM and PM meds wash over me, and holographic visuals of close-up textures and calm sceneries float above me. The table hums with a low vibration. The multisensory experience encompasses my total mind and body. It's almost impossible to focus on anything else.

From the other room, the gray hologram yells nonsense at the HME light. I've never heard a hologram raise its voice before. "Earth water and metals. Earth water and metals. The river will save you! The river will save you!"

It reminds me of when crazy lady kept yelling random lines at the hospital HAZMAT team back on Earth. I close my eyes to remember what life was like then, before I knew the truth, before I became the girl no one wants to believe.

An ear-piercing scream from the other room brings my anxiety back to full throttle. The gray hologram flails about on the table before shouting, "I will—"

The HME stabilizes its fluctuations, and its face loses all traces of emotion.

Something is very, very wrong. SIDEKICK has even turned its attention to witness the commotion.

I keep quiet and pretend to be too weak to understand the implications.

HOURS LATER, THE HME releases me to my LU after one anxiety treatment. It's not a permanent solution unless I return throughout the next week. Doctor A. arrives and places a heavy, cooling gel blanket over me, an invention he made with his rations. Shivers pass through me, and I almost tell him to take it off, but after the goose bumps, my body temperature starts to reset itself, and I stay calm.

"Was my attack from medicine withdrawal?" I ask him.

"Could be. No way to tell."

"I woke up to it. I had a nightmare, but I was feeling okay about that. I hate when it happens when nothing seems to cause it."

He touches my forehead to check my temperature. "Sometimes there are delayed responses. It could be the stress of something that happened a day ago and stuck in your subconscious. Like an echo of stress coming back. I had one once."

"After something bad happened?" No wonder he's so patient with me.

He nods, then changes the subject. "Sometimes it can even happen after an overwhelmingly good event. Do you know how many weddings start or end with panic attacks? And these people are happy with their spouses. You're living on another planet with conniving vances and holographic technology that makes you question reality. You aren't my only patient having trouble adjusting."

My body brims with a calming coolness. I pull the blanket off me.

"Keep it," he says.

"I can't—" I hand it to him, my fist not wanting to let it go. But I can't have him spend his rations on me.

"Knowing I made something here, something good, even if it's small, gives me hope that I can still help people. I can make more. A warm version as well for other types of trauma."

He hands the blanket back, and I hug it, the cold against my forehead. He has to be the nicest doctor in existence.

"Doctor A., there was a hologram getting medical treatment at the HME."

He rubs his dark hand across his smooth, bald head. "That's unusual. Could you tell what was wrong?"

"It faded in and out and kept screaming stuff. It looked like it was in pain."

His eyes search the air for answers and then return to my face. "Let me worry about it. I'll do some detective work."

Someone knocks on my LU door, and my bandwidth nano-holocom screen lights up. Doctor A. and I see Dominick on the screen.

"That's my cue. He's been checking on you all morning."

"Thank you," I say as he turns to leave.

He nods. "My pleasure."

Dominick passes Doctor A. in the doorway, and they exchange a few words that I can't hear. Dominick sits next to me on my holobed.

"How're you?" he asks. His eyes are bloodshot.

"Much better."

"Seeing you like that—" He bites his lip.

"Freaked you out."

"Yes. No. I—"

"Ruined the romance. I knew it would be too much to handle. It's so embarrassing."

He holds me gently by both shoulders. "Would you let me finish?"

I stop talking.

"I finally saw you," he says.

"Yeah, weak. In the fetal position. That's sexy."

"I never knew anxiety was so physical. It reminded me of my father before he died. Seeing you go through that only made me love you more. I had no idea it was that bad."

"Can we not talk about this?"

"Why not? You shouldn't be ashamed of it."

"It's not that. Talking about my anxiety can cause anxiety."

"Oh, geez. Sorry. I didn't know." He sticks his hands in his pockets when they should be around me. "Changing the subject, then. Any chance you'll be feeling up to going to the Holospaces for some downtime tonight?"

"I don't know." It'd be good to take my mind off myself and relax, but at the same time I'm not sure if I have the energy to stand. Even with the HME treatment, my mind swarms with unanswered questions and unsure alliances.

I SPEND TIME alone to destress and write in my journal. I tap and toss the latest BUZ on the CVBE onto the wall so I can have my hands free to copy notes. Three reminders from the meritocracy catch my eye.

First, the three-year testing and replacement cycle is coming up in a few months. I'm surprised that's not something else they lied about. I copy down the areas for testing that I can recognize: nanoholocom and bandwidth technology, biohologram upgrades, environmental controls, HDP, BME, PSF, and HME engineering, vertex pathways, CVBE specialties, Holospace programming, space aviation. All super hi-tech stuff. Guess I won't ever have a chance to be part of the meritocracy.

The next message states all people are equal on Solbiluna-8. It's an odd statement for them to clarify, so I check the CVBE to see if anyone has further information about it.

Through personal VIDs, apparently famous people, rich people, and politically powerful people from Earth are not happy with the "equal" LU conditions. Some are being "stalked, harassed, and ridiculed" by people who used to have little personal access to them. They formed an "elite special status committee" and have requested that the meritocracy consider them for "special treatment" and separate LU communities to "reestablish their status and safety" on the new planet. The meritocracy hasn't responded to their demands. It's the only time I semi-respect them.

Finally, the current contribution total has risen to 76%, already up from when the meritocracy spoke yesterday. Benji is more right than I realized. Those of us not contributing will stick out as rebels. What else is new? I always feel like I stick out, anyway. I don't even fit in with the Umbra anymore.

The fake holowindow display that Benji and Marcus modified on the wall switches to a rainstorm. Droplets of water hit the false glass and create a familiar plink plink in the background. My clear bandwidth rubs against the fabric of my cranberry uniform, and I use the COM to try to contact Rita. She's still unavailable. I need to apologize to her. Even with Dominick around, I feel lost without her.

I spin my bandwidth in a tight circle around my wrist, then double-tap it for my hologuide.

"River Picard, please state your needs."

"SIDEKICK, if people don't contribute, what jobs do they have to do?"

"One moment. Work requirements will be determined once numbers are finalized."

I copy the answer into my journal, my pen tip almost ripping through the paper. "How are we supposed to decide without the details?"

"Unable to comply." I notice it blinks even though it's unnecessary. An added human trait to make us feel safe.

"Are you a just a hologuide or a biohologram?"

"We are both. All hologuides are both."

I write into my journal. "So do you have memories?"

SIDEKICK doesn't fidget like a human would. "Yes, data storage and uplink with the nanoholocom network."

"No, human memories. From your life."

"Yes."

Its answer surprises me. "Who were you?"

"Female. One offspring. No spouse."

"Does it bother you?"

It blinks. "We do not understand."

"Do you have emotions connected to your memories?"

"Bioholograms do not have human emotions, only human intelligence combined with nanoholocom technology."

"Is contribution painful? Do you ever feel pain?"

"No. No."

I copy its answers and put down my pen. "Then what happened at the HME to that hologram? I saw you watching."

"Unable to compute."

"Figures." I lay in my holobed, place my journal on my chest, and listen to the plink plink of fake rain. "Do you ever wonder what's the point of life?"

"Are you referring to philosophies of existence?" It says it so robotically that it's almost comical.

"You actually have programming on that?"

"Philosophy is stored under religion and history with other obsolete knowledge."

"Whoa, I thought you holograms were supposed to be all evolved and open."

"We are highly evolved and open to different views. Scientifically, existence is a causal, temporary, fluctuating state depending on definition. Those files are rarely accessed."

"Did you enjoy your life?"

"We do not understand."

"Do you mind being a biohologram? Are you happy?"

"I . . . We do not understand."

I've never heard SIDEKICK make a mistake before. "What was that?"

"Request unclear. Please ask again."

"Did you just say, 'I'?" The biohologram did the same thing in the HME when it was freaking out. I examine SIDEKICK for any other signs of meltdown.

"Please finish your statement." It blinks obliviously.

"Ugh, never mind." I lift my curly hair from my neck and fan it out across the pillow. "HOLOGUIDE EXIT."

"May your contribution lead to freedom."

"Wait, one more thing."

"River Picard, please state your needs."

I toss my journal onto the floor near my backpack. "Can you stop saying that phrase?"

"Which phrase would you like to delete from programming?"

"Can you stop saying 'May your contribution lead to freedom'?"

"No, that cannot be modified."

I watch the fake rain hit the fake glass of the fake window. "Can you at least call me Alexandra Lucas?"

"Alexandra Lucas. Saved."

I wish it were that easy.

When I exit SIDEKICK's program, I get a sick feeling inside my stomach that I've trapped an old, human soul in a technological dimension. Waiting at my beck and call for me to need her again. It's a new form of slavery, and I know from history how history can easily repeat itself regardless of the means or technology or the planet.

But if I could somehow free her from the program, she'd be dead.

THAT NIGHT, DOMINICK meets me back in my LU to see if I want to chill in the Holospaces. I convince him to bring me to the Geotroupes instead so I can find Rita and apologize.

As we step off the maglift and into the Hub, we run into Benji and Doctor A.

"Your brother and I were coming to check on you," Doctor A. says. "Good to see you out and about."

"How're you feeling?" Benji asks. His concern for my mental health throws me off guard. What did Doctor A. tell him?

"Better. Dominick and I are going to see Rita."

"Rita's here?" Benji asks.

"She's with the Geotroupes," Dominick says.

Benji takes a moment. I notice his bandwidth gleams with soft golden light. I can't believe he did it. I guess he'd be a hypocrite not to since he's asking others to do it. Doctor A.'s bandwidth is still clear.

"We were hoping to form an alliance with them since they know the land masses better than anyone here, but they're impossible."

"I've been providing medical services to the Geotroupes," Doctor A. says. "They'd be excellent allies. They have a ton of knowledge, and they refuse to contribute as well. They cook their own food from LU leftover ingredients and live off the land. We'd stop wasting time bringing food back and forth from the Hub platforms to headquarters if we learned to cook."

"Except we are fighting technology with technology," Benji says. "They hate everything we stand for. It'll be a tough sell. But Rita's there?"

Dominick nods.

"Interesting." I can sense his mind turning with plans and possibilities. He can't stand Rita, but he knows that she can be pretty persuasive and popular. I need to fight to get her back in my life. "With Doctor A.'s connections and Rita there too, it might give us the in we need. Let's go."

"You're coming with us?" I ask.

Benji charges ahead, not bothering to see if we're following him. Of course, we are following him. He didn't give us a choice.

CHAPTER 17

DAY 25: 172 HOURS TO DECIDE

KILLING ANIMALS FOR FOOD OR CLOTHING IS ILLEGAL
UNLESS SANCTIONED BY THE MERITOCRACY FOR HDP
SUPPLY INGREDIENTS.

THE MERITOCRACY URGES EVERYONE TO COMPLY WITH
WATER REGULATIONS.

THE WALK TO the Geotroupes' territory is shorter than I need
it to be. Doctor A. and Benji use their bandwidths as flashlights.
I didn't realize that even out of the nanoholocom network range,
the device still has some local capabilities.

I really can't handle a fight with Rita in front of Benji. What
was I thinking?

"Why didn't you tell me Rita was there before?" Benji asks.

"You never asked." *Oh, god, I sound like SIDEKICK.*

"Does she know the leaders well?"

"She said they treat her like family," Dominick says.

Benji grumbles in the dark and keeps charging forward. At
times like this, he reminds me of Dad. It makes my heart hurt for
too many reasons.

"Benji, what's up with the new Umbra members? They don't
believe Earth survived?"

"Not without hard evidence. It's not an easy sell."

"But how will we get home if it's not part of the Umbra agenda?"

"I'm on it. Give it time. Keep yourself healthy, for starters. It's hard for people to believe a girl who's been admitted to the hospital for mental issues."

My body fumes. "I . . . that's not fair."

"Take a number."

As we approach the campsite area, Benji slows down his pace. "Let me and Doctor A. talk to them."

"Whatever," I say. "Not like we have much of a choice."

Even though the Geotroupes' housing is in the waste land area like the Umbra headquarters, their living conditions resemble an Earth campsite. Most of the activities take place outside, other than sleeping. Children color with chalk on rocks. A fire pit with a turquoise flame and the smell of home-cooked food. Crafts. Candles. Books. The smell of hearty food and fire bathes my nostrils. While everyone has basic iridescent uniforms, the Geotroupes have ripped and repurposed them to suit their personalities. They spot Benji coming. Some run inside. I don't blame them. I'd hide from him, too.

An older woman with cropped blond hair steps forward, the same woman I saw arguing at Umbra headquarters about territory. Those who fled come running back out to watch the showdown. *Why do I suddenly feel like we're in the Wild West and they're about to spin guns and shoot?*

"We told you this is our area," the woman says. "We don't want you to meddle in our group."

Benji holds his hands up. "I'm here to make an alliance between the Umbra and the Geotroupes."

"Bull," an old man says and spits. "You know what happened on Earth when people with different visions made alliances? One vision was always destroyed."

Doctor A. nods in solidarity with the old man. Rita comes out of a nearby building with a girl with long, blond hair, both wearing layers of handmade string necklaces draped over their chests.

"Who's that?" I ask Dominick.

"Hannah. You'll like her."

Doubt it.

Rita and Hannah join the other side in the gathering crowd. I should be standing next to her.

Benji keeps his hands raised. "The meritocracy will target our groups once the contribution period ends. We should support each other as dissenters."

"The meritocracy are peaceful," the woman says. "We are happy and peaceful here. Your group will bring only violence and distrust."

You're not totally wrong there, lady.

Benji stops inching forward. "You have knowledge of this area that we desperately need if we are going to return to Earth."

"Earth?" the woman asks. "What about Earth?"

"Earth was not destroyed. We can explain—"

"Why should we trust you?" the woman asks.

It's the same question I asked the first hologram on Earth. Its answer was that we had no other options.

Benji goes silent. "I don't know why you should trust us. But she knows us well." He points to Rita. "And Doctor A. has been helping you. He's with us."

A silence ensues. Rita's front and center, and I know she hates me and might use it against us. Using my telepathic-best-friend-superpowers, I beg Rita to step in and help.

Rita clears her throat and says, "I'll vouch for them."

"So will I," Doctor A. says.

The Geotroupes immediately argue among themselves.

The old man says to the older blond woman, "Marie, we don't need no outsiders here. Eugene, am I right?"

The cook, with matted blond hair and holding an iron skillet, says, "I heard they're hi-tech over there. Their group's getting larger by the minute. I can't feed those kind of numbers."

"Our number one rule is no tech," a younger voice says.

Benji's face drops, and he turns back to us.

"I don't know what else to say," he says. "Maybe we should head back and think of a different strategy."

I look around. As more people voice their concerns, no one is paying attention to us anymore. Rita and I make eye contact over the fighting. Her eyes look vacant, void of her usual peppiness. I just spread problems wherever I go.

A familiar voice rings through the Geotroupes' camp. "I can vouch for them." Penelope, my grandmother, has stepped out from a building. "They're family."

The rest of the Geotroupes wait and watch the interaction between us. The old man balks and retreats into a building.

"Ignore him," Marie says. "Any family of Penelope is a friend here. If you'll respect our rules here, no tech, I'll agree to initial talks."

"Agreed," Benji says.

I run forward and embrace my grandmother. It feels so good to hold a piece of Earth and family in my arms again.

"Marie, this is my favorite granddaughter, Alexandra. Well, so she's my only granddaughter, but still." I shake hands with the woman who's been the most vocal. "This is her significant other, Dominick, right?" Penelope asks.

Dominick smiles. "Yes, ma'am."

"And my favorite grandson, Benjamin. Where's your cute new hubby?"

Benji shirks her question and shakes Marie's hand.

"This is Marie, one of the founders of the Geotroupes in this area, and a dear friend I worked with years ago at a non-profit."

"Welcome to our space," Marie says. "Please join us for dinner. It should be ready soon. That will give us more time to speak."

"Rumor has it you actually cook here," Benji says.

She shakes her head. "Yes. We gather and cook food the old-fashioned way. Fire and wood, and thankfully a few chefs brought some cast-iron pans and supplies with them when they crossed over. Even though this is a tech-free zone, I admit we sometimes use HDP leftovers to supplement missing ingredients."

"We'd love to stay."

For once, my brother and I are on the same page. I cannot wait for actual cooked food.

Marie gives us the full tour of the Geotroupes' camp. "We gather around the fire pit for meals. Everyone must clean their supplies afterward."

"How do you have water?" Benji asks.

"It wasn't easy. We built an old-fashioned filtration system using rocks, evaporation, condensation, you know, nature's way of filtering." She points to their water supply. "Takes time but gives us drinkable water. Not enough to bathe with, though. There's something else I want to show you. I'd like your take on it."

She leads us to the back area of the camp, hardly lit, and a small part of me worries that we're about to be ambushed. We step over fallen skeleton tree limbs and overgrowth along the path. The waste land region extends beyond my initial impression. It's more than a few communities of buildings.

"Over here," Marie says. "Have you seen anything like this?"

It looks like an old train station, an open area of tunnels overrun with yellow-green moss. A series of strange stone doorways line the area like a future Stonehenge.

"Cool," Dominick says.

I touch the cold surface of the smooth stone. The moss crumbles beneath my hand, and a multi-legged insect the size of a praying mantis scatters into the brush.

"It has a similar layout to the vertex guidepost stations," Benji says. "The Umbra has used newer ones to travel around Solbiluna-8. This one looks ancient, though." He kicks some moss on the ground with his boot. "Yep, control panel. Old school, not holographic."

"Good to know. If it's a vertex site, we don't want any part of it."

Same. This place gives me the creeps.

"Would you mind if I sent a team out here to research this area?"

"Feel free. It's not an official part of our camp since we weren't sure what it was."

We finish the tour and head back for dinner.

Penelope gives Dominick and me some supplies, real bowls, spoons, and cups, and I want to cry. The fire pit burns an incredible bright turquoise instead of the orange flame of Earth. They scoop a rich stew into my bowl. It tastes like home.

"Why is the flame blue?" Dominick asks the cook. "Is there copper or gas in it?"

The cook replies, "Not gas. We burn wood. Copper could be in the soil. I just know it burns hotter than usual. Gotta keep the pan moving, pulling it on and off."

We sit on a hewed log to eat.

"Where are your parents?" Penelope asks.

I never realized that leaving through the vertex would carry so much burden with it. Like a sword of truth that I must carry and hurt people with, twisting to make sure the depth of the wound is felt.

"They, er, didn't make it."

The look on her face could silence a packed auditorium. I'm not sure where to start. "I . . ."

She holds up her hand. "Don't. Don't make excuses for that stubborn bastard."

"It wasn't like that."

"I don't want to hear it. I'm just glad you were brave enough to break away from him. Braver than your mother."

I open my mouth to defend my mother's decisions, but Penelope's wrinkles shift from bitterness to a deep sadness. She thinks her daughter is dead. Lost in a comet. Here we go again. *Alexandra Lucas, breaker of souls, killer of last hope.*

She steps aside, and I let her grieve. What choice do I have? These people don't know the truth yet. These things take time to learn. Time to process. They need to trust us before we shatter their world. Much like the holograms did.

Dominick and I eat in silence until Rita and Hannah walk over to join us.

"Hi," I say. My voice barely registers.

Rita waves, dismissively. "Hannah, Alex."

"Ooh, Alex. I've heard a lot about you," Hannah says.

"Hannah and I've become good friends. We have *a lot* in common."

If she told me that to hurt my feelings, it worked. I shove more stew into my mouth.

"Looks like you two are back in business," Rita says.

Dominick coughs on his food and stands. "I'm going to check out the filtration system."

"Me, too," Hannah says.

I scoop more stew into my mouth to keep from begging them to stay.

"He talked about you all the time," Rita says. "I was worried he was getting depressed."

"Rita, I'm really sorry. You know me—"

Rita rakes her fingers through her long, dark hair. "Exactly. And you know me. I cannot believe you actually thought I would do that to you. After all we've been through. No, I'm pissed. I thought we were more evolved than that. You reduced our friendship to fighting over a boy—Dominick no less."

"I know," I say, my voice rising an octave. "I'm so sorry. I just saw you two happy together without me—"

Rita cuts me off. "And you jumped to a conclusion as always, letting your imagination run wild, thinking the worst. Whatever. I'll get over it. Life's too short. You know?"

"You're lying. I can tell you're still upset. I'm really sorry. I think I got so mad and desperate because I've missed you both so much."

She sits next to me and begins to cry. I know my best friend. This is different.

I rub her back. "Are you okay?"

She shakes her head no. "I know all I did was complain about my parents, but I thought they would give in in the end, come and join us here. Choose me over the church. But they didn't, and I miss them. I miss their stupid rules. I even kind of miss the church." She wipes her tears on her basic uniform sleeve. "I didn't even say goodbye. Then I thought they burned with the comet when the time ran out. And if I hadn't left, that I'd be dead with them. Then you said the holograms lied, and I just don't know how to feel."

There are no words to comfort her. I hug her and absorb her pain, the pain of a child who loves her family despite their issues, and it mingles with my own. The hard truth is this: Even though our parents survived the comet hoax, they still might be dead if Earth decided to rebel or collapse under the weight of the lie. The longer we stay here, the more likely they perish.

"I'm here for you," is all I manage to say.

"Thank god, you bitch," she laughs through tears.

We laugh together, and the laughter cements our friendship back where it should be. It's easy to forget what it's like to have a true friend.

"How did you end up with the Geotroupes? I thought organized religious groups were not your thing."

"So did I. They're not really a religious group. They believe in reconnecting to ourselves and others and learning to respect, nurture, and interact with the natural environment. My parents would have believed in all of their values, except they would've added a bunch of extra rules and Bible passages. They've been like a family to me. Marie and Eugene run it." She points across the area at Marie, Penelope, and Benji laughing near the cook, the long-haired man wearing cutoff iridescent uniform shorts, serving food at the fire pit. Even from a distance, I can tell how much they both love life by the light in their eyes.

A flash of sadness spreads across Rita's face again, but it's interrupted by an announcement that the food is ready.

"I thought we just ate."

"Dessert." She grins. "We always have dessert."

"No wonder you joined. Brainwashed by sweets."

"Is there any other way?"

Back around the campfire, people pull a chunk from a huge loaf coated with a sticky substance and pass the rest around. It tastes like a warm, glazed donut.

"This is delicious. How did they make it?"

"Eugene works miracles."

As I chew, we find a seat on a cut-down log with legs attached to raise its height. Dominick joins us.

"It's peaceful here," I admit.

"We're all about getting away from technology and connecting with nature," Rita says. "It's comforting, actually. You'd be surprised how much stress being hooked on gadgets has added to our lives. No wonder people were always so miserable."

Hannah comes over with her hands full of dough. "I convinced Marie to give us extra." She breaks off hunks for each of us.

"Awesome," Dominick says, and he takes a huge bite.

Through the trees in the far distance, a flash of colors bend and shift in the night sky. Like an intense Aurora Borealis.

"Hey, what's that?" I ask, pointing.

"It happens every night. It's the distorted light traveling from all the Skylucents playing in different LU communities."

We sit and enjoy the night. It would almost feel like the three of us were back home at our annual summer beach bonfire if it weren't for the moving images in the sky, the inactive bandwidths on our wrists, and the turquoise flame in the fire pit. A terrible feeling builds in my gut that it might be the last peace we see in our lifetimes.

CHAPTER 18
DAY 29: 94 HOURS TO DECIDE

THE MERITOCRACY COUNCIL MEETINGS ARE HELD AT TRICENTERS NEAR EVERY MAJOR LU PROVINCE EACH MIDDAY. WE CANNOT BE EVERYWHERE AT ONCE, SO WE SEND HOLOGRAPHIC REPRESENTATIONS OF OUR IMAGES FOR MEETINGS ACROSS SOLBILUNA-8. YOU MAY ATTEND OR VIEW ON THE CVBE. THE NANOHOLOCOM NETWORK WELCOMES FEEDBACK AT ANY TIME.

I TRY TO sleep alone in my LU and wonder if I should move into Umbra headquarters or join Rita with the Geotroupes. Despite the alliance, over the last few days the Geotroupes and Umbra haven't seen eye to eye on the need to contribute some of their deaths to make sure the vances don't target both groups. Some of the Umbra have decided to do it, to throw the numbers off and to have more time to gather intelligence instead of being put to work. The Geotroupes plan to stay out of range, never contribute, and never report to work. Sometimes pacifists are more rebellious than people give them credit for.

When the contribution countdown clock on my bandwidth hits double digits, the PSF calls to me. I resign myself to the fact that maybe being a loner in the future has its perks. Deciding whether or not to contribute my death to Solbiluna-8 is another mental conundrum I don't feel equipped to answer, especially without knowing why the vances brought us here, whether or not we will return to Earth, and whether or not I will be punished for refusing to contribute.

I write in my journal:

> *Worst-case scenario #1: I don't contribute, and I must work while everyone else lives a life of leisure. That seems unfair, to watch everyone else enjoy life while I'm stuck in work mode. Not much different from some people's lives on Earth, actually.*

> *Worst-case scenario #2: We stay here forever, and I become a biohologram slave after I die but get to live a life of leisure. If that's even the truth. I mean, when did life become about work and stress and buying and looks and less and less about how we feel and think? At least the vances got that right. No need for material items, no shopping till you drop, no money or work necessary.*

Maybe I should just give in. So what if they kidnapped us? Maybe it was for our own good. Maybe I'm losing my mind. Maybe I'm finally making sense.

The peer pressure is palpable. *No, no, not like this. Never like this.* I want to connect with people in a real way and make a difference. Like Doctor A. said at the Umbra meeting, I want to contribute for real, when I'm alive, to something bigger. I want my life to mean something to someone before I die. This is insanity.

IN THE MORNING, after little sleep, I lie in my new modified hammock and flip through my journal, reading all of the promises the holograms made to us on Earth. So far every detail is accurate other than the most important questions we never thought to ask.

The door beeps, and Dominick's face appears on the screen. Punctual as usual.

I open the door and give him a quick peck. He pulls me back for a longer kiss.

"Rita should be here in a few minutes," I say, breaking away. "I was thinking we could hang out in the Hub, maybe search the forest area."

"I thought we were going to hang in one of the Holospaces. Someone made a replica of Hogwarts."

How can I talk him out of that? "Maybe you and Rita should just go."

"What did I miss? Are you jealous again?"

"No, I swear. I just don't like the Holospaces."

"Why? It's amazing."

"No, it's another trap. They took away all the freedom and luxuries we had, gave us food, shelter, and medical, and they gave us a fake existence to play in. In exchange, we basically give them all of our creative ideas for free for people to access and receive basic needs in return. There's a big difference between sharing and exploiting. Something about it doesn't seem right. Fake things feel dead to me. I want real life back on Earth. I want to pet an actual cat, climb an actual mountain, swim in the actual salty rich ocean. I miss the quiet realness of it all."

He grins. "Great speech."

I put on my boots. "Thanks. I bet there's something else we can do for fun." I double-tap my bandwidth.

SIDEKICK appears, and I ask her for recreation ideas. Everything she lists connects to the Holospaces or the Skylucent later tonight unless we travel.

"Well, she was no help," I mutter after closing her program. "I don't want to use a magpod, either."

"I love how your hologuide is dressed like a superhero," Dominick says from the hammock.

"What's wrong with that? Let me guess: your hologuide looks like Albert Einstein."

He avoids eye contact. "No, but that's a good idea."

"You're hiding something."

"No, I'm not."

"Yes, you are. Show me your hologuide, then. You're making fun of my choices; let's see this awesome hologuide of yours."

"No, I . . . Hologuide files are personal."

I ambush him in the hammock and try to double-tap his bandwidth. He evades my swipes at his wrist even when I tickle him.

"Show me, and I'll go to the Holospaces."

"Fine," he concedes, holding his hand up in defeat. He double-taps his bandwidth, and his hologuide materializes.

It's an exact replica of me, down to the freckle on my chin. Its long curls look salon-perfect, though, and it has on a super tight *Star Trek* uniform. I might as well be Seven of Nine.

"Dominick Landen, please state your needs."

My brain doesn't know how to process the image in front of me. I should be flattered. It's wonderful. It's sad. It's the most incredible thing he could've done.

It's also wicked creepy. *Please state your needs. Please stab my eyes out.*

I hold my face in my hands. "Why?"

Dominick climbs off the hammock. "I missed you. I wasn't sure if you were ever coming back. I wanted to see you again."

I walk around his hologuide to see myself from different angles. It's a sliver taller than I am, and I swear its boobs seem larger. "But it's not me."

Dominick sticks his hands in his pockets. "I know that."

I point at him. "Wait, did you try to kiss it and stuff?"

"No. Well, once."

"Dominick!"

He shakes his head. "I'm trying to be honest with you!"

"Dominick Landen, please state your needs," his hologuide repeats.

If I could punch the image of myself begging to service him, I would. "Change it. Change it now."

"I can't delete her," he says. "She's you."

"She's not me! I give you permission to delete her."

"I don't need your permission. She's my hologuide."

"She's me!"

The door beeps, and Rita's face appears on the screen. I let her into the room before Dominick has a chance to exit the program. Her uniform shirt has been holofied into tiny, fluorescent polka dots that shift colors and size every second. It's nice to see her back in fashion.

She giggles hysterically. "Oh, man. Sex hologram if I ever saw one."

I wave my hands in front of me. "Ugh, gross!"

"It's not like that," Dominick says.

"Do you require additional time?"

"Hold on—" I say and grab Dominick's bandwidth. I find MODIFY HOLOGUIDE and the DELETE CLOTHING option.

I am mortified at the result.

He frantically adds clothing back onto the holo-me. "I never did that. I swear."

"Swear on your father."

Silence.

"I knew it! Change it!"

"I will. Promise."

Rita pulls us into a group hug. "I really missed you two."

SINCE I PROMISED Dominick that I'd go with him and Rita to the Holospaces if he showed me his hologuide, we spend the day playing live Hogwarts fanfic and space invader games in one of the Holospaces, lounging in a pool on a Mars colony, and running through obstacle courses in floating tree houses. Exploring without danger or limits should be invigorating for me, but even still my anxiety spikes. I repeat *Don't get tricked by a thought. The danger is fake.* And I fall back into the fun. Living here is like being high. It calls to me like a drug, and I can feel myself easily being addicted to it if I let it in. There is peace here, an addicting, satisfying peace. It's almost good practice in dismissing irrational thoughts. I allow myself to get lost from reality, for just a little while.

Exhausted, we return in time for dinner in the Hub.

"I still don't understand how we can touch holograms," Rita says. "It's bizarre."

"That's because of how you perceive solids," I say.

"Exactly," Dominick says.

Rita raises her eyebrows. "Sometimes you two scare me with how you communicate."

"It's like this." I hold out my edible plate. "There are a certain number of molecules in the plate and in my hand. At some point, those molecules intersect and my brain gets a signal that I'm touching something. Touch is just molecules from different areas interacting. You don't need physical objects for this to work. If you lie in the sun, you can feel the rays, right?"

"I guess," Rita says. "It's weird, though. Holograms are just light."

We find an open table and bench to sit. I didn't realize how much of a workout I had gotten in the Holospaces until I rest my body. My legs are killing me.

"I don't understand that level of quantum mechanics, either,"

Dominick says. "From what I've learned using the CVBD's ED program, the vances discovered that at the quantum level, electromagnetic forces can build between protons, and when they force complex entanglement to occur under the right conditions, a solid can form. I never thought that was possible. They use the nanoholocoms—"

"Blah, blah, blah, science jargon overload," Rita says. "Too bad in reality the consequences are cool and terrifying." She takes a moment to eat and think. "Ever think the nanoholocoms are like a giant, invisible net and we're the fish?"

Her thought lingers in my mind, and I can picture my body being wrapped in holographic ropes. Gives a whole new meaning to my hammock. Might have to delete it.

"Isn't this against the Geotroupes' rules?" I ask. "Interacting with technology? Going to the Holospaces? Eating food from the platform?"

"Rules? Don't you know me at all?" Rita says.

Dominick clears his throat. "What if this whole planet is an illusion, some programmer's sick joke to make our lives nothing but entertainment for another population?"

"Thanks a lot," I moan. "And I thought I was the paranoid one."

"You two," Rita says. "Perfect couple."

After dinner, people gather in the grass for a proper view of the Skylucent. My friends and I join in, and I realize I haven't felt this good in a lifetime. The collective bandwidths around us shine like stars through the darkness, lights that signify the beauty of death. Maybe there comes a point when truth is irrelevant, when history is in the past, when you simply live for the present and move on and let go. Maybe at some point you stop struggling because you realize that, like the Borg said, it's futile. If you just relax, blend in, life will be okay, even if you have to ignore a gnawing at your gut. *Why fight it?*

This is why I didn't want to return to the Holospaces. It's addicting and dangerous for me. *For all of us.*

DOMINICK RETURNS TO his family for the night, and Rita decides to sleep over in my LU. Inside, Rita and I find Marcus on his holobed.

"Do you mind if Rita stays here tonight?" I ask.

"Of course not. Sorry if I'm in the way. I needed a break from the Umbra. Bad headache."

"You're not in the way. We're just here to crash." I plop onto my holobed and design a spare for Rita to materialize nearby. She sits with me as we wait for hers to entangle and solidify.

"How's it been going?" Rita asks Marcus through the holographic room divider. "With the new alliance, I mean."

"Okay, I guess. A little boring. The Geotroupes provided lots of information about the local landscape. I've been working with Professor Marciani and Katherine over at the old vertex site. I need a break from it all—my head's been pounding. Too many math calculations. I'm reaching my limit." He chuckles. "That was a bad math teacher joke."

"Yes, it was," Rita says, shaking her head. "How's the research going?"

"Awesome. We've learned a lot quickly."

"How's Benji been?" I ask.

"Distant. He's always distant, but I was so busy with teaching before that I hadn't fully realized."

Distant. Not a word I'd ever use to describe my brother. He's usually too in my face.

The door beeps, and I expect it to be Dominick or Benji. It's Doctor A.

"I came to check on Marcus. See if there's anything I can do."

"You didn't have to come all the way here from headquarters," Marcus says from his side of the LU. "I'm fine. Just need some sleep."

Doctor A. takes his temperature and listens to his chest. Rita checks on her holobed. I pull up my holographic blanket and stretch my sore legs underneath the supple fabric.

"You had enough to eat today?" Doctor A. asks.

"Yes, I'm fine," I hear Marcus say. "I just—"

His voice trails off awkwardly, and I hear a weird shaking sound. Rita and I rush over to the room divider. Marcus's body flails about in his holobed. Doctor A. rolls him to one side and holds him steady so he doesn't fall out of bed and injure himself. He's having a seizure like crazy lady did before she died.

I hold my bandwidth, and my mind goes blank. "What the heck is the code for medical?"

Rita yells, "HME OPEN. Emergency."

Marcus's hologuide appears beside him, an unmodified, androgynous form in a gray uniform. A voice states: "Please step away from the patient, Marcus Lucas-Blu."

His hologuide reaches its hand out and covers Marcus's forehead. A violet light comes out of its hand and surrounds Marcus's head. His body stops jerking.

"Are you directly administering medical care?" Doctor A. asks the hologuide.

"Yes. We administer treatment if necessary to stabilize patients for transport."

The HME voice fills the room. "Patient will be admitted to HME facility to be monitored for further evaluation and treatment."

Within seconds, a holographic platform materializes underneath Marcus's body. Once it entangles, his holobed vanishes, leaving Marcus floating in midair on the thin platform. A clear structure closes over the top. It looks like a clear, flying coffin.

His hologuide leads it out of the room. I use my private clicker to alert Benji. Doctor A. pulls on his beard several times in a row and stares at the empty space where the holobed used to be. His eyes water.

"I guess I'm done here," he mumbles. "Excuse me." He exits the room before I can respond.

I sit back on my holobed, and Rita joins me. "What just happened?"

"I don't know. I think he had a seizure. Doctor A. seemed shaken up, and he usually keeps his cool."

Rita nods, then glances at the door. "That wasn't good. I've never seen Doctor A. act like that before."

"I don't think he ever felt replaced before." The thought lingers in my mind long into the night and mixes with fears about what happens to humans when they are no longer able to contribute in a real way.

AS THE COUNTDOWN hours reach single digits in the middle of the night, curiosity brings people to gather in the Hub regardless of their bandwidth status. It's natural to huddle in groups when a planetary deadline comes to a close. I stand with Rita, Dominick, Kendra, Nolan, and some new members of the Umbra. Last time a countdown ended, I faced a holographic comet hoax. *What is the consequence for my inaction this time?*

"We can refuse to go," Rita says to me. "Who says we have to choose? They can't force us into physical labor."

When our bandwidths light up with a CVBE announcement, several people around the large space tap and toss holoscreens into the air for group viewing. Keron fills the screen in full array.

"The initial contribution period has ended. Thank you for contributing your death to the welfare of future generations. In the act of fairness and equality, anyone who has not contributed to our society at this time will be immediately contacted by the Contribution Assignment Centers in the morning. You will have the opportunity each day to reevaluate your decision.

"The meritocracy values all members of Solbiluna-8 and hopes to inspire everyone to dream rather than work. May your contribution lead to freedom."

As soon as the announcement ends, my bandwidth releases a low-tone signal several times and changes from a clear, lighted band to cloudy, steel gray. Rita, Kendra, and Nolan check their bandwidths. Steel gray. Dominick's remains golden.

A tall woman with bright red hair and a glowing bandwidth whispers to us, "Why didn't you just contribute? Why complicate things? He's the smart one." She points to Dominick's bandwidth.

Rita and Kendra roll their eyes in unison. Nolan chuckles.

"Not this time," Dominick mutters.

"We don't have to cooperate," Rita says. "They can't make us work."

She's naive if she thinks that's how the vances operate.

We agree to meet back in the Hub for breakfast. I get very little sleep throughout the night despite an exhaustion that makes me light-headed. I'm the first person in the Hub at the platform. More and more people arrive, the same look of dread on their faces if their bandwidths are clouded, smiles if their bandwidths shine with glory. Rita, Kendra, and Nolan arrive. Dominick decided to stay at Umbra QN25 headquarters to see if he could pitch in with the research.

"Where's Hannah?" Kendra asks Rita.

"She's staying off grid since she didn't contribute. We can always make a run for it ourselves."

I'm too afraid to disobey. Like Benji said, we don't know the consequences of not contributing.

Our bandwidths flash, and holomaps appear above them, each with a blinking light over a different location marked with CONTRIBUTION ASSIGNMENT.

"We can just stay here," Rita says. "What are they gonna do?"

"Rita, I don't think—"

"They're all about keeping peace. They won't hurt us."

She's wrong, and I know she's wrong. I stay with her anyway.

"Travel to your contribution assignment immediately," an emotionless voice announces from each holomap.

"See? They can't even get angry," Rita mocks. She tries to close the holomap, but it's frozen above her wrist.

The lack of emotion is exactly what terrifies me. "Maybe we should go to our assignments. Benji wouldn't want me to make waves for the Umbra."

"Since when do you listen to Benji?"

"Good point. But have you ever been cocooned by the BME? I have." I lift up my uniform pant leg. The scars are faint but visible.

"Oh, my god, Alex. That looks painful."

"Come on; we can do this. Day 1. Think of it as a rebellious sacrifice."

She agrees, and together we each head to our assignments.

"I'll meet you tonight at . . ." I glance at the nanoholocoms and back at her, "you know where."

Each of us takes a separate magpod to follow the spot on our holomaps. Ten minutes later, I arrive at an HME facility. I follow the holomap to the outside doors before the map closes on its own, and the first CVBE light on my bandwidth turns on. I hold for the COM audio message.

"Welcome to your Contribution Assignment. Only patients are allowed inside the HME facility. Please remain standing at the entrance and check for blue bandwidths. If unauthorized guests enter the building, the BME will be activated for all parties, including you."

Seems easy enough, although I'm not used to working under threat. The first few hours are mindless. I pace around to keep my legs moving. Patients come and go, some voluntary, some unconscious on holocots, with their hologuides alongside them. Even though the hologuides have different modifications, I can spot them from their blank expressions.

I am allowed two five-minute bathroom breaks, but there are no breaks for meals. My stomach growls, and my legs get sore from standing for so long. After several hours and several close calls, all I want to do is go back to my LU and let the PSF massage my aching muscles.

It gets hectic at one point when too many patients arrive at once, but I manage. I think I have things under control until a husband argues with me about going inside with his wife.

"Let go of me," he says and twists his body to escape my grip. "My wife's in there. She needs me."

"Please, sir, you have to obey the rules. We'll get punished by the BME."

His holofied uniform sweater slips from my fingers, and he runs through the doors.

The BME zaps my legs, and I collapse to the ground. Through the clear doors, I see the husband get punished. It's a mild zap, and no cocoon follows. Except afterward, the husband stands and takes another step forward into the HME. Another jolt for both of us.

"Sir, please," I beg from the ground. "Stop."

He crawls back outside, and we sit together to recover.

It's just enough to make me want to contribute after a futile day of meaningless work.

CHAPTER 19

DAY 33

THE INITIAL CONTRIBUTION PERIOD HAS ENDED. AS OF
TODAY, 82% OF EARTH REFUGEES HAVE CONTRIBUTED.

AS SOON AS I leave my work assignment, I head to the
Geotroupes' camp to find Rita and Dominick and complain.
Hannah is alone with a group of children, craft materials spread
among them. I see Dominick's little brother there.

"Have you seen Rita and Dominick?" I ask Hannah.

"Rita hasn't come back yet. Dominick went with the team to
the old vertex site."

"Thanks."

"How did it go?" she asks.

"Mindless."

"I guess that's not so bad."

I shrug. Despite my concerns about the contribution period
ending, it wasn't that terrible. I imagined much worse. Maybe the
vances aren't as bad as they seem, other than the tricking us into
leaving Earth part. Maybe they've only just started.

The old vertex site opens before me. Like stepping through a
time machine and landing in a Celtic folktale. Stone doorways in
a semicircle, a blanket of bright moss covering them. I hear voices
in one of the short tunnels radiating from the center.

I find Dominick with Katherine and Professor Marciani among

a team of other scientists, wearing goggles and deep into what looks like an experiment near a control panel.

Dominick comes up behind me and puts his hand on my shoulder. "How was it?"

"Long."

"I take it you all contributed," I say.

"Our work is here," the professor answers. "Put these on." He hands me goggles, and I slide the strap under my ponytail and secure them in place.

"Mississippi, you're just in time."

"In time for what?"

Professor Marciani's eyes light up. "Our first makeshift vertex attempt maintained integrity for two seconds before it collapsed. We've recalibrated to form another portal. Our second attempt should be fruitful."

"I thought it would take a while to make a vertex."

"It can't actually be used yet, but this old site is an amazing find," Katherine says.

Visions of Earth's green grass and blue sky cloud my vision. "So we can go back home."

"Eventually, perhaps," says one of the scientists. "If we can figure out how to set coordinates and connect to our present-day Earth. Right now, controlling it is a guessing game."

"Ha, so you admit that Earth is still there."

"Don't get ahead of yourself," Professor Marciani says. "But yes, eventually, this vertex could provide proof once we test out coordinates."

Another scientist announces, "Stand back. In five, four, three, two, one . . ."

And there, in full glory, is a magenta, metallic, swirling vertex among the moss and overgrown stone tunnels. Technology alive again among ruins. I've never been so happy to see one.

"Why is it purple?" Dominick asks. "I thought it would be blue."

"Not sure how the colors work," Professor Marciani admits. "Need to work on that."

"So we could technically just go back and stop people from ever coming here," I say. "And then none of this would've ever happened." I think of all the time travel films where they go back and rewrite history.

The other scientists chuckle under their breaths as they jot down information.

"I told you, we can't go back in time," Dominick says. "It doesn't work that way."

I refuse to believe that. Crazy lady did it, and she's standing right next to me in the future. "Why not?"

Professor Marciani steps in. "Maybe I can be of help here. After studying vertex technology on Earth and what I'm allowed to access at the hololibrary here, according to the vances we cannot and have not traveled in time. We can only travel successfully to another universe's present. Parallel universes are each in their own stream of time. Those streams are not equal. Some universes are further along their stream than others. One universe may be ahead of another in technological or cultural advancement, so going to their present will feel like time travel to the future. Some streams do not develop as rapidly; traveling to their present will feel like traveling to the past.

"It's why we are having so much trouble learning to control the navigation of the vertexes. To attempt travel to a universe's past, to a time stream that has already begun degrading, would have dire results. I'd imagine we would experience the past as it collapses around us. We would lose coherent chronobonding. We'd die a horrible death. I believe it's how the universe protects itself from chronotampering."

That's what happened to Katherine. She did it, got me to come here, and it scrambled her brain and killed her. The magenta vertex twists and pulls at the air around us, and I still believe there has to be another way. As Katherine takes a reading, it crackles and folds into itself. A sense of déjà vu washes over me as I see Katherine stand in the fading magenta haze.

"Let's call it a day," Professor Marciani says. "Good work."

Dominick and I remove our goggles and help gather tools to return to headquarters. We make the trek to the Geotroupes' camp first to grab dinner. As we walk through the ancient city, I wonder if Doctor A. ever looked into what happened to the hologram in the HME.

"Katherine, did Doctor A. tell you that I witnessed a biohologram having a nervous breakdown?"

Katherine wipes the sweat from her forehead, her goggles around her neck. "He mentioned something about it."

Another scientist asks for details, so I tell the group everything I saw and heard.

"Earth water and metals," Professor Marciani repeats. "Nanoholocom units require precious metals to function. Perhaps . . ." He twists his knobby hair in deep thought.

Another scientist jumps in. "Perhaps the river is a safe passage to somewhere. We haven't even researched the water supply."

As Professor Marciani and the scientists continue their debate, I pull Katherine and Dominick aside.

"There's something else. It's minor."

"Shoot."

"It said, 'I.'"

"And?"

"And they usually say 'we.'"

She thinks it over. "Probably another glitch in the human/hologram upload, however it works. It sounds like its emotional memory surfaced. Minor compared to what you've told us about it exhibiting pain."

"Yes, but the same thing happened once to SIDEKICK, my hologuide."

"Actually, that happened to mine a couple times," Dominick says. "I thought she had just . . ." His face turns red when I elbow him for the reminder of his holo-version of me.

Katherine's eyes move back and forth, comparing, calculating. "After the Umbra meeting tonight, let's meet at your LU. I'd like to run a few tests on your hologuide."

THE COMBINED UMBRA and Geotroupes meeting outside QN25 headquarters is rowdy. I pull a thick blade of plum green grass from the ground and flip it in my fingers.

Dominick mumbles, "May your contribution lead to freedom."

"Or your lack of contribution lead to chaos," Rita says.

I watch as more and more people gather around us. Without looking at their bandwidths, I can tell who contributed and who had to work based on the exhausted and angry looks on some faces.

"I'm not going back tomorrow, and I'm never contributing," Rita says. "I'm officially a Geotroupe and off the network so they can't force me to work."

"I don't want to contribute, but I don't know how long I can take it. My mind will start spiraling at some point, and then what?"

"Hide out with me," Rita says.

"I dunno. I'm afraid of the consequences if our bandwidths are accidentally reactivated."

"I wish I hadn't contributed," Dominick says. "It doesn't seem right that the two of you have to deal with this while I sit here, eat, and play games."

"Can't argue with that," Rita says. "It isn't right. But you didn't create the system."

"No, but I'm benefiting from it while you're getting punished by it. I can't just sit here and do nothing."

"We need to find a loophole," I say. "A real way out of the situation. One they can't punish us for. I'd much rather stay here and help than stand around like an idiot while the hours of my life tick away."

Katherine approaches us. "Mississippi, have you seen your brother?"

"I think he's still with Marcus."

"He's supposed to be here, to convince people to contribute. Never mind; I'll have to run the meeting with Jackson, Beruk, and George Rogers."

"The astronaut?" Rita asks. "I love him!"

We watch Beruk step up onto a raised stone area near the front of the building and hold up his hand to quiet the crowd. Jackson emerges from inside headquarters with George Rogers, and Katherine takes off to meet them.

"It's him," Rita says. "I can't believe he's here. Why does Katherine call you Mississippi?"

"Remember my fake name?"

"Ha, River." Dominick cracks up laughing.

The crowd settles in. Hannah joins Rita's side, and Kendra and Nolan stand next to me. Marie and Eugene join the Umbra leaders on the raised area as a show of Geotroupe support. I don't see Doctor A. He really was shaken up after Marcus went to the HME facility. I hope he's okay.

Jackson speaks first, using a rolled piece of white bark as a handmade megaphone to carry his voice over the crowd. "We are here to ask everyone to consider contributing your death to help our cause. We all have questions, and we want answers. Help us expose the truth about Solbiluna-8."

The crowd isn't having it, especially the Geotroupes. Even I'm not having it. I don't want to contribute even though the alternative tasks they assign are the most mindless, muscle-draining, waste-of-my-only-life chores.

George Rogers intervenes, his voice loud and proud. "I've been sent here by the United States Secretary of State from the SN10 region headquarters to reassure you that your efforts and information have been vital to the Umbra cause. You don't have to worry. If we confirm that Earth still exists, we will take over the meritocracy and return home before your contribution will even matter."

That doesn't work. We know true freedom. We don't like being told what to do, even politely, even by an American hero. We like choices that are real, not illusions. People shout back at them in protest.

"You sound like the meritocracy," someone yells. "More promises that I don't trust."

"Please," Katherine says and holds out her hands. "We need your cooperation. It's the only way to buy enough time without the vances seeing us as a target."

How else can we stall?

I flip through my mind for something to use against the vances. Something from my journal . . .

Meritocracy meetings . . .

Meritocracy testing . . .

Doctor A. being obsolete in the future . . .

Knowledge being obsolete in the future . . .

Two thoughts merge in my mind, and something clicks.

I try to run through the crowd, and Dominick immediately follows me.

"I almost lost you once. I don't plan on doing it again."

"But I have an idea. I have an idea," I yell louder than before. The crowd is so loud, no one hears me.

Rita whistles a high-pitched, ear-smashing sound. Everyone turns in our direction. I drown in a sea of eyes.

"You have the floor," she whispers.

Too many angry heads and faces stare at me at once. My throat betrays me. "There's an alternative," I mumble.

"I can't hear you," a woman off to one side complains.

Dominick nudges my shoulder. "I . . . uh . . . there's an alternative."

"You already said that," a voice behind me taunts.

I face Rita and Dominick to pretend they're the only two people I'm addressing. I take a deep breath and let my voice carry through the crowd.

"You know how the meritocracy is all about being fair. Well, remember how they said every three years there's testing for new council members? And that anyone can enter? And only the best in each field become part of the meritocracy?"

Jackson interrupts me. "Are you saying we should infiltrate by passing their tests and getting on their council?"

"No, I . . ."

"The next testing cycle is months away. We don't have that kind of time," Beruk says.

The crowd gets impatient and starts murmuring. Aggravation takes over my fear. "No, listen! You don't get it. We need to protest."

"Protest what?" Rita asks, perking up.

"The unfair testing requirements. The tests are based on 2359 knowledge in all specialty areas. There is no way for people from Earth to catch up with their knowledge in our lifetimes. It's systematically rigged. We will never have ruling power even though they claim it's fair. We need to refuse to contribute our deaths to their system until they change the testing requirements. That should buy us time."

This time, no one speaks. Katherine breaks the silence. "I will take it from your silence that Alex's plan sounds more appealing."

The crowd cheers. I think that's the first time she's ever called me Alex.

George Rogers speaks. "Let's try it. I'll contact the Secretary of State and spread word to other groups."

Dominick puts his hand on my lower back. "You're a genius."

I want to hide from the attention.

When the meeting ends, Dominick and I walk back to the LU community so I can meet Katherine. Once she arrives, he takes off to spend time with his mom and brother.

I open SIDEKICK's program for Katherine, and she pulls up several holoscreens at once.

"How did you come up with the testing idea?" she asks.

"It popped into my head because I had written about the meritocracy's testing requirements in my journal." As soon as the word *journal* slips from my mouth, I want to retrieve it. "Even Doctor A. wouldn't pass their light- and sound-based medical tests, and he's the best doctor I know from Earth."

Katherine swipes and taps like a conductor in an orchestra. "Humm, this is interesting."

"What is?"

"Nothing. Just an idea of my own. Not sure if it will work."

The first two CVBE lights on my bandwidth go off. Jackson and George Rogers are on my COM and VID. Katherine stops working so I can exit SIDEKICK's program and answer the call.

"Alex," Jackson says on my holoscreen, "glad we caught you. George Rogers has a message for you. George?"

"Alex, it's a pleasure to meet you," George Rogers says and

waves. "I just spoke with the Secretary of State, and he'll be sending a short speech for you to deliver to the meritocracy."

He must mean Katherine. He's looking straight at me.

"Me? Hell, no!"

Katherine chuckles.

"Who else, young lady? It's your idea, and we've agreed that you won't come across like a powerful rebel. The meritocracy won't see you as a threat. You're still a kid."

"I can't give a speech to the meritocracy. I can't even give a speech in front of my English class."

"You just did," Jackson says. "This is non-negotiable. The Secretary of State is the head of the entire Umbra operation."

"Katherine can do it."

George Rogers points at me through the VID. "I witnessed you turn the crowd when I couldn't do it. I understand you are the girl who flew through a vertex to tell us the truth. They need to learn to trust you. It's a win-win. You will be the messenger."

CHAPTER 20

DAY 37

WORK UNITS HAVE BEEN SCHEDULED FROM SUNRISE TO SUNFALL FOR THIRTY CONSECUTIVE HOURS. CONTACT YOUR HOLOGUIDE FOR ADDITIONAL INFORMATION AND ACCOMMODATIONS.

MY MIDDLE FINGERNAIL bleeds as I pick at it. I suck the blood, hoping I will wake up and realize it's all been one sick dream. The taste of iron coats my tongue, and the reality of the situation seeps under my skin.

I hide under the cooling blanket Doctor A. gave me. The past few days have been spent with me doing tedious contribution assignment tasks. Yesterday, I was sent to patrol the closest vertex guidepost. I had to stand the whole time and direct people to the correct tunnel using a holographic grid. If I didn't find the region quickly enough, the BME let me know it.

Earth refugees with gold bandwidths traveled in packs throughout the day. Several laughed at me and my job. They found it even funnier when I got zapped for being slow. I swear sometimes the transport system sabotaged me on purpose. Again, just enough ridicule to make me want to contribute.

Today, I've been chosen to speak at the meritocracy council meeting. How ironic that it took a holographic alien invasion and me jumping three hundred years into a parallel future to realize that my dream of becoming a defense lawyer and speaking on people's behalf is actually one of my worst nightmares. How did I become the speaker for two fringe groups on another planet? Is it too much to ask for a girl just to want to talk in a courtroom? I should've kept my mouth shut. Contribution is looking better and better. A light lobotomy is sounding better and better.

The door beeps, and I escape the cool blanket and let Rita inside.

"You ready?" she asks.

"No." I crawl back under the gel blanket.

"Come on, Alex. You've been imagining this forever. Arguing your point in front of a courtroom. You can do it. You were made for this. You just have to get into the zone. You must hope for the best instead of expecting the worst."

Hope is not a word I understand anymore. Maybe ever. To hope is to fear.

"Besides, I heard Benji telling Katherine that you can't handle it."

"He said that?"

"Yep."

I can't tell if she's lying, but it works anyway. Part of me wants to shove my success in Benji's face. *But how can I show up and push through all that initial fear, the pounding heartbeat, the shallow breaths, the sweat, the heat, the silent opinions of the audience coming at me like a dense fog that my pores suck in and analyze and reevaluate, condemning me to failure and negativity?*

"But what if I freeze?"

"I've seen you tear people apart on the debate team," Rita says. "We just have to light a fire under you. You can't be so afraid of failure and embarrassment that it controls you from taking any action. Especially action that could save us all."

"Wow, no pressure there."

"Or that makes Benji look like an idiot."

"Good point. That's better."

DOMINICK, RITA, BENJI, and Beruk escort me in a mag-pod to the closest vertex guidepost. It's the fastest way to get to the closest TriCenter where the meritocracy council meeting will be held. Dominick and Rita practice the speech from the Secretary of State over and over with me. My hands shake as I read it off the paper from my journal. I have it memorized, but having the paper makes me feel safer.

The modern vertex guidepost mirrors the one behind the Geotroupes' camp. It looks like a hi-tech train station with door-ways in sequence around a stone perimeter, except this one buzzes with electric energy. Holograms usher people into proper lines to travel to various locations across Solbiluna-8. When I see the swirling green vertexes, I'm grateful it's not a blue one.

We travel through a vertex to the TriCenter, a gorgeous tri-angular glass building, similar to the Louvre museum in Paris that I saw in a magazine once. It makes me want to throw rocks and demolish it. Around the TriCenter is a depressed city where concrete buildings with no windows populate the area. Beruk points out that those buildings hold the province's HDP food and supply rations. Those buildings pale in comparison to the majestic TriCenter.

Dominick, Rita, and Benji escort me inside while Beruk ex-plores the area. Inside, everything is transparent. Even the walls. I'm not sure what the walls are for then, since the weather is always perfect. What exactly are they walling out? Or walling in? Probably used to create a false sense of trust, keeping everything transparent while the truth is kept obscure. A live waterfall feature embellishes the lobby, a cascade of water across an entire wall, splashing over amber stones in a basin. I snag a polished stone and hold it as I walk forward to the meeting. It vanishes before I get there, just like I knew it would. They are way too picky about their water supply to waste it on decorations.

The center of the TriCenter is dug into the ground, creating a concave middle with circular bench seating all around and a tiny middle stage. Reminds me of an underground colosseum. Or layers of Dante's *Inferno*. It's empty other than people like me and my friends standing idle, waiting for the meeting.

"Where's the meritocracy?" Dominick asks.

"They'll be here," Benji says. "Alex, how are you feeling about this?"

"Like I might vomit."

"If you can't go through with it, I've been authorized to step in for you."

"She's got this," Rita says.

Dominick kisses the side of my forehead. "She's a fighter."

At the sound of a loud chime, like the one used during the Earth-mourning sessions, the meeting begins. Holographic versions of every meritocracy member materialize in their seats wearing robes and glowing orb necklaces.

Even if we wanted to attack them, we still can't reach them. Tight holographic security using technological doppelgangers. For the one thousand and one elite, tested and chosen.

The holographic meritocracy stands, bows, and recites the chant that I've grown to hate.

"May your contribution lead to freedom."

Keron, the leader who spoke to us from the screen on the ship and in the LUs, spouts ration numbers, positive statistics, successful integrations, contribution goals, and new technological advances that I can't come close to understanding, never mind repeat. The statistics enter the nanoholocom network for CVBE bandwidth access. He clasps his fingers together like a yin-yang symbol in front of his stomach the whole time he speaks. My hands shake.

What will happen if there is an actual revolution here? How will we fight the invisible? Will we just turn on each other?

"We will now hear from the floor."

The wait for my turn is endless. Person after person from Earth speaks. One asks for more Holospace time and another offers Earth food recipes for the HDP. I don't see any vances at the meeting, either. *Where are they?*

My heart pounds as I move up in line. I hand Rita my journal to hold, the speech crumpled in my sweaty palm. When I am waved forward, I step down into the dead center, with the meritocracy circled above me, to speak. It's like standing in a bull's-eye. Dominick and Rita wait in the lower audience with the other guests. Dominick touches his tongue to his nostril, and Rita smiles and thumps him in the arm with my journal. Benji stands with his arms crossed across his chest.

I gather my thoughts, the ink on my notes smudged in sections. The Umbra and Geotroupes have ensured the meeting will play in every Hub they manage to notify in time. They are afraid the meritocracy might delete the recording from the CVBE history. We need people from Earth to witness whatever happens live. My throat swells with fear.

Don't pass out. Don't pass out.

Can you die of nervousness?

The meritocracy waits.

"Uh, my name is Alexandra Lucas. I have a complaint." My voice echoes up through the circular seating, catching me off guard.

"Voice it," says a young boy wearing a kelly green stone. I wonder what his talent is that got him a political seat.

"You asked us to contribute our deaths to Solbiluna-8 so that generations can experience leisure."

Keron smiles with a perfect set of huge white teeth. "Yes, we value contribution over currency, dreams over work."

"Uh, that would be a fair trade," I say, "if we were all considered equal here."

"We are equal. Everyone's needs are met, and if you choose not to contribute, you can serve in other ways."

He interrupts again, and it throws me off since I practiced the speech all at once. The next line of my practiced speech won't work. I skip a few lines mentally to find a line that will work. "But . . . but no one from Earth serves on your meritocracy."

The child lowers his eyes, then stares back at the screen. "Predecided. The next round of tests are open to integrated Earth humans." He sweeps his hand to dismiss me.

"Wait, I know that," I say, my voice shaking. I drop my paper and scurry to the floor to pick it up. My face burns with frustration and the room spins.

The holographic meritocracy shifts impatiently above me. As if their fake bodies actually need adjusting.

I stand, flustered, trying to remember what came next. Benji uncrosses his arms and straightens his uniform shirt to ready himself to step in for me. Dominick nods with encouragement. Rita holds up a closed fist.

I close my hands into fists and ball up the speech. *Remember what they did to us. They fucking stole us from our planet. From my home. From my parents.*

I spin my lit-up clouded bandwidth, hoping the BME doesn't suddenly electrocute me as I say what I'm about to say.

"The problem is there's no way Earth refugees can compete

with you. Our people are three hundred years behind yours in all areas of knowledge and skill. Our best knowledge is obsolete here. We demand new tests be created which measure our talents equally with yours. To make things fair. I know how much you value fairness."

I smirk. I can't help it. Keron unclasps his peacekeeping hands. All fidgeting stops.

"We will not contribute our deaths to your world until such tests are made. Any contributed Earth deaths prior to this announcement are automatically rescinded as is only fair until this matter is resolved. We are so very grateful to be here." I try not to vomit in my mouth. "We don't want to abuse our welcome, but we need our cultures to merge without unfair practices. Otherwise, it'll seem like you brought us here to fail. It'll seem like you brought us here to use us. The choice is yours."

Keron stands. "We will take your concern under advisement and respond through the CVBE. Thank you for bringing this issue to light."

As I leave the floor, all hell breaks loose in the meritocracy as they scramble to find a fast solution to a problem that will take time to solve. They naturally wanted us to adapt to their specifications, lure us with luxuries, and make us forget about leadership. They don't want to have to change. But they know I'm right, and if they don't address my issue, they will be admitting to unfair practices in setting up terms in our new world. And they believe in maintaining a public sense of false equality.

Small acts of rebellion. This is how we win.

Every utopia has a breaking point.

CHAPTER 21
DAY 37

THE MERITOCRACY WILL RECONSIDER THE EARTH REFUGEE
TESTING REQUIREMENTS. ALL CONTRIBUTIONS HAVE
BEEN REVOKED. ALL CONTRIBUTION ASSIGNMENTS ARE
POSTPONED UNTIL FURTHER NOTICE.

THE CVBE REPORTS that the contributions are "revoked" and
work "postponed" indefinitely while the meritocracy designs new
tests. All our bandwidths change to clear. Dominick and Benji are
free from their death pledge. Checkmate holosuckers.

When we get back to headquarters, people congratulate me.
I've never had so many people waiting for me. Staring at me.
Patting my shoulders. I want to hide in a PSF.

Marcus greets us. It's great to see him back in action. The
HME works magic.

"Excellent speech, Alex," Marcus says.

"Thanks. You look better than the last time I saw you."

"Feeling much better, thanks. I haven't had a seizure since I
was a kid. Stress must've triggered it."

I wait for Benji's criticism.

"You did good," Benji says, "aside from dropping the paper."

I smile through the silent screaming in my brain. "Yeah, well,
we can't all be perfect like you." Dominick and Rita nudge me
from either side.

Penelope interrupts our conversation and hugs me. "Alex, I'm so proud of you. My grandchild sticking it to the man."

I stare at Benji over her shoulder until he turns and leaves with Marcus.

"How did it feel," Penelope asks, "being up there to represent Earth?"

Earth? I was focused more on my family and friends. If I had realized that I was representing Earth, I would've crumbled.

"Er, terrifying?"

"You didn't look it. You have never looked more beautiful."

Beautiful? I haven't brushed my nest of hair in forever. It might be untamable at this point.

"Let me ask the three of you something. Do you know that man?" She points across the outdoor area. "The one sitting near the new fire pit?"

I trace her line of view and see Doctor A. He stares off into the trees, lost in thought. He's never looked so unfocused.

"That's Dr. Aiyegbeni. He goes by Doctor A. He was a pediatric surgeon at Boston Children's Hospital." I cringe at the word *was*. He always says it in present tense.

Penelope runs her fingers through her skunk-colored hair. "He can be my doctor anytime."

"Grandma, eww!"

"Oh, stop grandma-ing me. You know I hate that. Come introduce us."

"Eww times a thousand," I say.

"Oh, grow up, Alexandra," Penelope says. "A woman needs to have a little fun at any age."

Dominick rubs his eyes. As if her words are making his corneas dirty.

"I'll do it," Rita says, grinning widely. "I love a good romance."

Rita and Penelope lock arms, and she escorts her over to

Doctor A. Dominick and I watch from a distance as Rita plays matchmaker. Doctor A. perks up like a dehydrated plant given water.

BACK AT THE Hub, Dominick, Rita, and I enjoy the Skylucent as celebration. Rita holofies her uniform to all black with soundless fireworks that fly up from her boots and explode over her chest. She's already breaking her rule about staying out of bandwidth nanoholocom range to join us. Guess without mandatory work, it doesn't matter anymore. Around us, the golden hue from all bandwidths has gone dormant. I did that. I freed them from making a terrible, irrevocable decision. Despite the Skylucent feature above us, my thoughts return again and again to the vertex and the possibility of going home to my parents. So close and yet so far.

It's funny how much change can make us realize the things we should have valued when we were taking them for granted. All I know is that the people who are always there for me, who care about me the most, I need to fight to keep them a part of my life. I used to think I needed to push them away or break away completely in order to function. With Dad, I need to focus on the good and separate when it's bad. I'm not responsible for the bad. My mother was good at that. I didn't get that then.

When the Skylucent goes dark and people sit up from the soft grass to leave, a beeping sound stops everyone in their tracks. Our bandwidths flash with a new CVBE meritocracy update. Several people tap and toss screens for public viewing.

On the screen is Keron, the speaker of the meritocracy, with other members in the background. My heart thuds in my chest, my palms itch with pins and needles. A biological red flag.

"Good evening. We would like to extend our apologies for not recognizing the meritocracy testing problem sooner, and we thank Alexandra Lucas for bringing it to our attention. We request your assistance in solving the issue. We would like help in the creation of new testing programs in the Holospaces that reflect Earth expertise. Please input possible test subjects and sample questions into the nanoholocom network to compile."

Dominick touches my shoulder in the dark, either to make sure I'm okay or to congratulate me once again. I can't tell the difference.

Keron smiles and clasps his hands. "In the meantime, in all fairness while we are creating these new testing programs, ration amounts must be lowered to counterbalance the lack of contributions and working humans. Our system works on give-and-take. We cannot have only take without a natural consequence. We hope you will understand. Lower rations are only temporary until we figure out a more viable solution.

"May your contribution lead to freedom."

It's the first time that their statement feels like a punch in the gut.

The screen vanishes.

In the dark, voices grumble and mix and turn on me.

"You. You're that girl." A lanky woman points her finger at me, her long nails like talons capable of decapitation. "I watched the VID. You are the one who complained about the tests. Why are you messing with them?"

"Me? I, er . . ." As I look around for allies, the crowd encircles my friends.

"Look around. Everyone's happy. Well fed. No violence. Why are you messing with a good thing?"

I touch a pebble in my pocket and rub my thumb against its smooth surface. "'Cause it's not fair."

She gets in my face. "Oh, and Earth was fair?"

Rita pulls me back and pipes in. "You don't even have the whole story."

"Which is?" a father asks from the side, his young daughter under his wing.

They still don't know about the comet, and I don't know if it's the right time to tell them. The anger building on their faces targets me as the enemy. It reminds me of when the looters turned their anger on my dad.

"People like you, you're never satisfied," the woman with the long nails says. "Can't leave well enough alone. Have to ruin it for the rest of us."

"Screw this. I'm contributing again right now," someone says.

"No, please," I say. "You don't understand."

"Oh, we understand," a teenager pipes in. "We understand you don't care if we eat."

Someone bumps into me, and Dominick pushes back.

"Wait, don't! The vances scammed us," Rita blurts out. "The Earth is fine. The comet was a hologram the whole time. Do you understand? It wasn't real. The whole damn thing was a trap. We don't know why yet, but we shouldn't be contributing anything to them. They stole us."

Their faces change and twist as their minds fight the truth and grapple with fear. My mouth drops. Not because Rita blurted out the truth, but because she's willing to stand up for me, share my story, without evidence.

"We want to help get everyone home. Back to Earth," Dominick says.

Laughter erupts from one section. "You're crazy. Earth blew up."

A teenage guy gets loud. "Alright, fine. Let's pretend what firecracker here said is true even though it makes no sense. Why the hell would we want to go back?"

Rita steps in his face. "Because this place is built on a lie. We will never know who or what to trust. With holograms, everything can be an illusion. Most of the stuff here is fake."

"Honey, we were already living in a fake world," an older woman in a bright floral uniform says. "Why not live in a better fake world?"

"You can't mean that," Rita says.

"The hell I can't. This place is paradise. I don't care how we got here. We're here. Why would we go back? Here we get food, shelter, fun, and we don't have to work until our minds go numb. Being here is the first vacation I've had in fifteen years."

"But don't you think the future should be earned instead of handed to you?" I ask. "If you don't earn it, it becomes meaningless."

"No, the future happens regardless of effort," the teenager says. "Good, bad, miserable—it all just happens. If I can skip all that for this, I'll take it. Why wait? You're an idiot if you think life is still about working hard for your future. That shit's broken. It's about taking advantage when the opportunity arises. It's a rich-eat-poor world. At least on Earth. I'd take this place any day."

My brain hits frustration levels. Waiting is the absolute worst, but sometimes, waiting is necessary. As corny as it sounds, waiting builds character. And God knows the world could use a little more patience.

I squeeze the pebble in my hand.

Images of science fiction flash through my head. "So you're willing to contribute yourself at death? Haven't you ever heard of the Borg? The Cybermen? Doesn't that scare you? Do you really think the vances want to give us all this," I point at the LU building, "because they simply care? Come on, no one is that nice."

A twenty-something girl flips her long ponytail and rolls her eyes. "It's just our minds. It's not like it's our bodies."

I want to smack some sense into her. "Can you imagine how

the people on Earth are feeling? They think we've been kidnapped." The words stick to my ribs as I imagine my parents suffering.

"Oh, please," the girl says. "Like you can fake a comet."

The crowd chuckles at us. We are outnumbered.

The woman in floral speaks again. "If Earth is still there, so what. They'll figure it out and move on and we can chill in paradise."

"Are you willing to give up your freedom?" Dominick asks.

"Yes. Absolutely," the woman in floral answers. "Let the vances rule. They're smarter than we are anyway. I don't want to take any tests. I just wanna live my life in peace." Others shout in agreement with her.

"It's pointless," Rita says to me and Dominick. "They're not listening to reason. They barely flinched when I told them about the comet."

The truth hits me. This was the vances' plan all along. *Entrance. Evade. Entrap. Evolve.* They knew we would accept it once we were here because that is our nature. Path of least resistance. *Consider. Contribute. Converge. Control.* Again and again we've been warned by philosophers and writers against combining technology with the human body. We just assumed it meant we'd be fighting against enforced assimilation. But we are not fighting an external war; we are fighting our own eventual willingness to become Cybermen, to assimilate, become technology, to upgrade and forget what it means to be human. What it means to be real. What it means to want to be real.

My hands won't stop shaking. I don't know what this emotion is, but it's not anxiety. I think it's hopelessness. *How do you help people who won't listen to reason? Who crave what will destroy?*

Someone in the crowd pushes me from behind. A teenage boy pummels me on the side of my face. My eyes blur with pain and tears. The BME takes him down before Dominick gets a chance.

Another man hits Dominick, and someone pushes me into Rita. More BME intervention.

Hologuides appear and chant in unison, "The BME has been automatically activated. Please remain calm and orderly as we deal with the infraction."

The rest of the crowd slowly backs away. Cocooned around us are those who tried to harm us. We are linked to the BME consequences, linked to negativity, linked to their oppression. I am the enemy of the people, the source of their new hunger, the catalyst of the problem, the thing holding them back from utopia. And I brought my friends with me.

CHAPTER 22

DAY 39

GLOBAL HAPPINESS DECREASES BY 71% AFTER RATION
RESTRICTIONS

THE MERITOCRACY IS WORKING HARD TO DESIGN NEW
TESTS THAT SUIT ALL MEMBERS OF SOLBILUNA-8.
WE REQUIRE INPUT FROM EARTH REFUGEES FOR THE
CREATION OF RELEVANT TOPICS AND QUESTIONS. WHILE
WE APPRECIATE THE FLOOD OF RECENT CONTRIBUTIONS,
WE CANNOT GRANT ADDITIONAL RATIONS AND HOLOSPACE
TIME UNTIL A FAIR, PLANETARY COMPROMISE CAN BE
MADE REGARDING THIS ISSUE.

PEOPLE GROW IMPATIENT and angrier at one meal and one
material ration a day, and less Holospace time. The Umbra and
Geotroupes try to convince them that I am not the cause of their
distress. That the holograms caused all of it on Earth. They aren't
listening. Many of them recontributed in defiance only to have
the meritocracy deny the return of their rations and Holospace
time until we compromise.

Benji puts me on lockdown on the sixth floor of Umbra headquarters for my safety. Rita, Dominick, his mother, and his little
brother also join us for protection. Just in case.

No more PSF for me. No more Skylucent. *How did I become
the face of the enemy?*

I risked everything and came here to deliver the truth. No one even cares. *What kind of world is that? What does that say about us, that we can abandon a planet through kidnapping and not even bat an eyelash in complaint?*

I don't want to do this anymore.

In the middle of another sleepless night, I write in my journal.

> *We are taught by philosophers that truth is universal. Truth as fact. Can't be questioned because it simply is, like part of existence. But truths become subjective. One person's truth isn't another's. I never understood this before.*
>
> *My truth is that I came here for selfish reasons. I wanted my friends back. I couldn't let the holograms win.*
>
> *The truth is that doesn't matter.*
>
> *My truth is that humans should want to return to Earth, to their home.*
>
> *The truth is that many humans don't want to return to Earth, even after learning the truth about the comet hoax.*
>
> *My truth is that humans should be wary about contributing their deaths to an unknown world.*
>
> *The truth is that many humans are willing to contribute if they get to live a carefree life, regardless of unseen consequences.*

The opposing views pull at my insides like teetering scales of justice.

At least I have Dominick and Rita with me. I spend the day with them, and with Katherine tinkering with SIDEKICK's program, then write in my journal at night. It's boring being a captive in your own rebellion. I leave my cot and wander around headquarters at night wearing the gel blanket that Doctor A. created to cool my body. My body sweats constantly from too much anxiety. I'm probably dehydrated from the lack of water. I pretend not to notice the odorous cloud rising from my body until Penelope hands me some futurist stone that stops armpit odor for days when you rub it against your skin. Strangely enough, it works.

Dominick and I attend Umbra meetings, we listen in on their research, and I record data. Using the same technology the clickers use to locate each other, Beruk was able to trace and locate a signal from a possible area where the vances are being secretly housed. It appears to be a cliff, but on further inspection scientists think they have a holographic cloak disguising them, like when the holographic tree was a cover for the spaceship. They want to reveal their location, hack into their mainframe, and get some answers.

"We need to cut the power to the area," Benji says. "Simple and effective."

"The problem is the nanoholocoms are embedded into everything without wiring," Katherine says. "The sheer numbers alone are impossible to disable. We've only been able to disable rooms so far. Nothing large-scale."

Beruk steps in. "According to the SN10 Umbra intelligence reports, the environmental controls are located on several space stations in orbit. The Umbra also has a few vance ships in our possession, but they can't figure out how to fly them."

"DOT could fly the ships," Professor Marciani says.

"What's DOT?" I ask.

"You mean, who is DOT," Katherine says, grinning. "DOT is the secret weapon I've been working on."

She gestures to the hologuide next to her. A generic kind. Gray uniform. I'm not impressed.

"I thought this region had no holographic technology," Dominick says.

"It doesn't. DOT is a rogue biohologram." She points to a device strapped to its leg. "See this box? It contains her own nanoholocom mini-system that I developed. It lets her travel anywhere after she uploads in the nanoholocom region. I've been reprogramming her."

"To be what? A mobile, hologram-killing machine?" *Why is it that inventors always create the thing that will destroy them?*

"No, a spy for us. She can access information from the nanoholocom network without it knowing. And she would know how to fly a ship."

"So it's a hack?" Dominick asks.

"Precisely. It's working, too. Talk to her."

"Hello, DOT. My name is Dominick."

"Hello, Dominick. My name is DOT."

"DOT could serve several purposes. Just give us a little more time. We may also be able to send her through our experimental vertex as a test. She could potentially let Earth know we are safe and attempting to return."

"That is," Professor Marciani adds, "if we can establish and navigate into the proper parallel time stream."

Maybe my parents might at least get to hear we're safe. Well, as safe as can be right now. *If they're safe.*

I watch DOT blink obliviously. She might be the ultimate hologram since she's not tethered to the network or another human. I worry about how she views human life.

Beruk pushes up his sleeves and exposes his hairy arms. "I say we plan a coordinated attack. Have the other Umbra use DOT to fly the ships and temporarily disable the environmental controls over that region. We wait at the signal area that I pinpointed, and when the time is right, we go in."

"Wait," I say. "If you bring down the HDP system, that region won't have access to food."

"That's what the Geotroupes are for," Benji says. "They can provide temporary food."

"What about the HME? Won't that go offline, too?" I ask.

"Yes, but we have people like the doctor around for medical needs. We can do this. We lived on Earth without a massive safe-guard to our every move. It's the same thing."

"I guess. Won't the BME electrocute us for rebelling?"

"When we are offline, it won't work either."

"Wait, but that means weapons and explosions will work?"

"That's the plan. If we take away all the holographic contain-ment fields in that area, we'll gain the advantage."

Destroy a society for a cause. But how do you know if you are fighting on the right side of justice? Doesn't everyone think their side is the right side? What if your contribution is just reinforcing corruption?

When the others disperse, Katherine lingers, tinkering with DOT's programming on a holoscreen above the box on its leg.

"I'm sorry, but it's creepy," I blurt out.

"What if I work on her programming? Give her more person-ality. Would that help?"

This is like when Data on *Star Trek* gets a personality and feelings chip. No, thank you. Which reminds me . . .

"It would help more knowing that she had a STOP button. Like a giant override, delete program, or autodestruct." *In case she's secretly a double agent.*

"Like Data's off button?" Dominick says.

"You read my mind."

"Good idea," Katherine says. "Why didn't I think of that?"

You fight invisibility with a sword of words and code. And

always make sure your hologram allies have safeguards so they can't turn on you.

MY IDEA WORKED better than I imagined. The meritocracy struggles with the testing plans. Without bandwidth CVBE access, I have to get information secondhand, which is driving me crazy. From what I gather, Earth refugees and meritocracy members keep arguing on the CVBE about the philosophy behind having a ruling meritocracy on Solbiluna-8. They believe the brightest minds in the one thousand and one areas should rule. If they create new testing subjects for us, it will technically dumb down their society since they are more advanced, no question, thus they would no longer technically be considered a meritocracy. And yet, if they don't comply, they will admit that, on a fundamental level, the entire planet is based on an unfair government policy that puts us as the inferior group for an obscene number of generations. Even more, if they agree and gather new testing material, won't the test makers have an advantage once again?

Welcome to Earth.

THE NEXT NIGHT, Benji allows me to attend a fire pit party in the Geotroupes' camp to celebrate Rita's birthday. It's weird needing my brother's permission to go. Rita makes a bad joke that she doesn't expect presents, only our presence.

Everyone's there, gathered around the turquoise fire for Eugene's latest dessert. It's like a miracle that they can concoct such amazing pastries using an open flame and few ingredients. Kendra and Nolan talk around the fire pit while Nolan's grandmother helps Penelope and Marie serve food.

"I swear this is the best party I've ever had," Rita says. "Remember my lame parties at my family restaurant?"

"Remember when Tyson kissed you on the cheek and your parents sent him home?"

"Oh, my god, that was so embarrassing! Hey, where's Hannah?"

"She stayed at headquarters. She wasn't feeling well. Doctor A. said he'd check on her again later. Eugene went to bring her food."

I watch Penelope join Doctor A. to eat. She straightens the top of his iridescent uniform for him, reminding me of Mom and Dad.

"Check out the lovebirds," Rita says.

"Stop, no. Not even funny. That's my grandmother."

"Age is only a number."

Off to the side, I see Marcus and Benji talking and laughing. It's about time my brother relaxes. Benji puts his arm on his back and they kiss. It's nice to see them have couple time. Seeing couples together makes me miss time with Dominick. We haven't been alone together since we moved into headquarters under strict watch. Like being a prisoner in my own life. My body feels stir-crazy.

When Rita starts a conversation with Kendra and Nolan, I walk over to Dominick and whisper in his ear, "Follow me."

He doesn't ask questions.

We steal away from the party and sneak into the dark woods behind the camp. I draw him to me slowly, backing myself into a tall pale tree trunk that reminds me of a gigantic stalk of cauliflower. My back presses against the flaking trunk as he kisses me hard. I return the favor and reach my hand down for more.

"Here?" he asks.

"We have no privacy anywhere else."

Even in the darkness, Dominick's eyes catch the light, and his curiosity and hesitancy make me want him even more. I kiss him back to show him I mean it, to show him I mean everything.

I try not to think about the possible wild animals, hidden fungus, or tiny foreign mites that could crawl into crevices and put up camp.

Time floats away from us, and we forget where we are and how we got here. We become one with nature. We lie on the soft bed of the forest floor, the vast stars above dancing along with our movement, the heady floral and moss fragrance better than man-made perfume.

"I missed you," I whisper.

"I missed you, too." He brushes one of my loose curls behind my ear.

I fix my basic uniform. "Not knowing if I'd see you again, it changed me."

"Changed you how?"

"I'm in this with you," I say. "For the long haul. In good times and bad. If that's okay."

"It's more than okay." He pokes me in the stomach. "It's about time."

I dust off any remaining debris from my clothes. Something snaps and breaks in the woods behind us.

"Did you hear something?" I ask.

"Like what?"

"I don't know," I say and glance behind me at the dark woods. "I thought I—"

A man steps from behind a tree and yanks a handful of my hair. My scalp burns. I flail and fight for freedom.

"Ow, let go of me! Help!" I scream into the forest.

He presses a sharp object against my neck. "Don't make another sound or we'll slit your throats."

Two other men have grabbed Dominick. As he struggles to fight them, they punch him in the stomach and bind his hands behind his back.

My hands are bound so tightly, they go numb. I watch Dominick being blindfolded. *Not by holograms. Not by the vances. By Earth humans.* As they cover his eyes, he gives me one final look, worse than when he was in the hospital after the riot on Earth. His eyes convey the fragility of love and the terror of mortality. My heart sinks into the darkness of my own blindfold and gag.

"Move."

A hand on my shoulder and a sharp object pointed on my back. I hear breathing, heavy and shallow. It doesn't match my own rhythm. I wonder if it's Dominick. As long as I can hear that breathing, I know he's still alive.

We're like animals about to be slaughtered by the humans from Earth I came to save. I focus on Dominick's breathing to keep from panicking. *He cannot die. He cannot die.*

I use my clicker to alert Benji. Please let him trust me this time.

Can't make a run for it or fight blindfolded and bound. Can't argue my way out of a situation when I've been silenced. What would Dad do? Find an escape route or fight. Two options. I try not to allow my mind to focus on the third possibility. *Dominick and me dismembered, stuffed into body bags, and buried in the skeleton forest until alien maggots eat us.*

I count footsteps and try to mentally map out the direction they are taking us. Dominick's breathing gets louder. I hope he's doing that on purpose so I can hear him. I don't want him that scared.

Time becomes measured by footsteps. *Twenty. Thirty. Fifty. Eighty.* It would be much easier if I could see a landmark. Anything. I stumble over what must be a fallen branch, and the brush in the area gets thicker against my calves the farther we travel. *Ninety. One hundred.* I listen to Dominick's heavy breathing and focus my energy on checking to see if he sounds okay. *If he's okay, I'm okay. If he's okay, I'm okay.* The slope of the ground changes to an incline. I don't remember the forest landscape having hills. My boots pull against the ground and stick in the wetter soil. *What if they walk us off a cliff?* Every step brings the possibility of falling to my death. If I could move the blindfold just a little . . .

I make slight sobbing noises and rub my nose with my shoulder to push up against the blindfold. It doesn't move. I try again and manage to create a tiny sliver of light under one eye. It's something.

"Knock it off."

That's what I'm trying to do. I quickly use the other shoulder to wipe the other eye, creating a small space at the bottom.

The forest floor doesn't give me any clues to our location, but from the distant sounds of Skylucents on my left side, I think we're walking parallel to the LU communities. They must be avoiding the BME and bandwidths to escape punishment.

The floral and moss smells are replaced by the smell of a campfire. We come to a full stop.

Stopping freaks me out. Traveling meant we were still safe.

I see the edges of brown tarps flapping in the slight wind. Makeshift tents. Iridescent boots on the ground. We're still out of range.

"We got her." Male voice. Deep, raspy tone.

"You sure?" Male voice, higher pitched.

"Yeah, positive. Told ya we'd get her."

"Who's that?" Female voice. Ironically sounds like my mom.

"The boyfriend. I've seen them together."

My gag is removed.

"Are you Alexandra Lucas?" the female asks.

I don't respond. A hard object slams into the side of my head. Sharp pain shoots across my forehead. My nose drips uncontrollably. More scuffling, movement of boots. A thud. I can make out the shape of Dominick's body when he hits the ground. They kick him repeatedly.

"Stop! I'll do whatever you want."

"Whatever, huh?" the higher pitched male voice says off to one side.

"Just let him go."

"No, he's useful. Get him off the ground and bring them to the main tent," the female says as she replaces my gag. "Stand guard. Don't let them out of your sight. And if she gives you trouble, kill the other one."

CHAPTER 23
DAY 42

THE GUARD ORDERS Dominick to sit in one corner of the tent, me on the opposite side. It's not like in the movies where they sit us back to back so we can untie each other. Even though the side of my forehead throbs, I know it's not as bad as what happened to Dominick. Panic rises in me, a tide coming in during a hurricane. He needs Doctor A. or the HME. I remember Mom pushing me in a wheelchair to visit Dominick after the food riot on Earth. At the time, I didn't know he took the brunt of the pain so I wouldn't get trampled. I thought that was the worst day of my life.

This is worse.

I rock back and forth. *We're going to die like this. I'll never see my parents again. Never see Earth again. Never enjoy life as an adult.* I click and click and click for Benji. Tears soak my blindfold.

"Cut the crying," the guard says, "or he'll get it."

It's like asking someone with broken legs to run a marathon. *Oh, god, I wanted to help save Dominick, and instead I'm going to be the one who kills him.*

My mind snowballs into an avalanche of worries. My body shakes in convulsions, my heart rate and breath in a duel for my soul, my stomach a raging river. I puke all over the inside of the tent.

"Shit. I thought you were supposed to be tough," the guard says. He yells to the outside, "Someone bring me a shovel and some red sand to soak up vomit."

"Sure thing."

I know that voice. We've been infiltrated. We are screwed.

"Move over." The guard pulls me up from the ground and pushes me down elsewhere. One step closer to Dominick. Maybe I should keep puking.

"Here," Hannah's voice returns. Rita's friend from the Geotroupes. I knew I didn't like her.

"Great. Do you mind cleaning that?"

"Sure." Her voice wavers slightly. "What's wrong with that one?"

He laughs. "They kicked the crap out of him."

"Figures," she says.

If my hands weren't bound, I'd strangle her with her beaded necklaces. The sound of scraping and patting as she shovels. *How can she be so two-faced?*

"What do we have here?" a husky voice asks. "Leave us."

"Sure thing, Eugene," Hannah says. "Do you want me to bring dinner?"

It can't be Eugene, the cook from the Geotroupes? He could've been poisoning us for weeks.

"I'm good," says the guard.

"I already ate," Eugene says, "The prisoners can eat later if they behave. I'll let you know."

Footsteps slowly approach me. "Hello, Alex. Sorry we have to formally meet like this."

I don't respond. My nostrils burn with the acidity of vomit.

He rips off my gag and blindfold. It takes a moment for my eyesight to adjust to the light. Dominick lies across from me. I stare at his chest and see it trembling up and down. Eugene still wears cutoff uniform pants. He has blond, shaggy hair that's tied back and matted on one side, and he's wielding a butcher knife.

He always seemed so carefree at the Geotroupes' camp. The guard stands at the entrance with his back to us.

"You are going to set things right. Undo the damage you caused and let people live out their lives here in peace."

He walks over to Dominick and lifts him by the arm. Dominick winces in pain. He places the blade on his cheek, looking at me.

"I expect your full cooperation."

I nod in agreement, unable to hold back the emotion on my face. He smiles a sadistic, toothy grin.

"You will record a new message that we will send to the CVBE. We want our rations reinstated. You will take back everything you said about testing. Say you realize that the testing has nothing to do with contributing. Then you will contribute yourself live as a show of good faith."

"Alex, don't," Dominick says.

Eugene slides the blade along Dominick's bicep, a clean, shallow cut. Dominick cries out in pain.

"Stop!" I yell. "I'll do it if you leave him alone. But it doesn't mean the meritocracy will listen."

"Oh, they'll listen. It was their idea."

THE GUARD COMES back inside the tent and replaces my blindfold.

"Choice is a funny thing, isn't it?" the guard says. "You can get people to do almost anything under the right circumstances."

He fits right into the culture on Solbiluna-8 and how the vances operate. There's no freedom here.

Hannah's voice interrupts. "Eugene said to bring them food. Said you can go on a bathroom break."

Someone coughs and hacks up a ball of phlegm. "For flavor," the guard says.

"That's disgusting," she says and laughs.

His footsteps leave and her footsteps approach me.

I click and click for Benji and try to back away from her.

She lifts my blindfold and whispers. "Alex, no, it's not like that. My family volunteered as spies for the Umbra. Jackson got word this group was forming, and some of us were recruited. Don't talk to people you recognize from the Geotroupes. Some of them are actual traitors, including Eugene, not recruited like my family. We sent word back to the Umbra that you were both taken." She glances over at Dominick. "He doesn't look so good. Hang on."

Hannah tends to Dominick, ripping a piece of her uniform and wrapping his bleeding arm. Then she comes back to me. My body trembles with distrust.

"I'd feed you, but he spit in it. Alex, I don't want to freak you out, but they plan to stage an accident that will kill you. They want to force your contribution to activate. They figure if people see that you've become a biohologram, they'll give up questioning . . . and you won't become a martyr for our cause, either. We can't let that happen."

I clear my throat, and she loosens my gag. "They'll hurt Dominick if I refuse."

More coughing and hacking. "Damn. The guard's coming." She readjusts my blindfold, and I'm left in the dark. "I'll come back if I get more information."

I HAVE NO idea how long Dominick and I remain under guard, but I keep clicking for Benji. Night must have turned into day, because Hannah returns with breakfast and a bucket for bathroom privileges. *Where is Benji? I've cried wolf too many times. I wonder if Hannah actually sent word, or if she's really a traitor?*

Once the guard steps outside, she warns us. "They're moving you to one of the LU communities."

She scoops watery grains into my mouth. I swallow and cough at the texture. "Why?"

"They want you within CVBE bandwidth range when they release your contribution statement. Rumor has it they plan to push you over the edge of the Hub. Make it look accidental, and then your contribution will activate."

My stomach plummets at the thought of splattering inside a Hub across an HDP platform. *Waking up a biohologram.* I wave off the food, and she moves to Dominick. I'm sure my hands would be shaking uncontrollably if they weren't tied behind my back. I'm as defenseless as an ant stuck on a mountain of concrete, a giant sole about to crush me. No one cares about one ant.

"Where's the Umbra?" Dominick asks as Hannah attempts to feed him.

"I don't know. I thought they'd have come by now."

I don't tell her about my private clicker connection with Benji. Just in case.

"We can't let them move our location," Dominick says.

"I can try to set up a diversion with some of the others," Hannah says, thinking quickly. "Like a fire. It might blow our cover, but we have to try something to get you out of here."

"Do it." Dominick then focuses on me. "You okay?"

"I love you," I answer. The words come from a desperate place. Time is short. Just in case.

"Don't," he says. He knows me well.

"Say it."

"I don't have to say it. You know. When we get out of here, and we're safe, I'll say it again."

The guard returns moments later, and all conversation ceases as blindfolds and gags return.

HANNAH KEEPS TRUE to her word. Hours later, loud voices echo, "Fire! Fire!" in the distance.

"Shit," the guard mutters.

The sound of footsteps and voices shouting at each other retreat into the distance. Footsteps run toward the tent and inside.

"Get ready to run once they give the signal," Hannah says. She uses a knife to free my hands, and I pull off my blindfold and gag. I use the clicker one last time to signal Benji. Nolan is in the corner, cutting Dominick loose.

"Thanks, kid," Dominick says. "Didn't know you were here."

"Don't mention it," Nolan says, and his voice wavers. "Just don't tell my grandmother."

AS WE WAIT for the signal to escape, the commotion outside stirs up my stomach. I hate waiting. Dominick's face looks paler by the minute.

Hannah peeps her head out of the tent one last time. Someone whistles.

"That's it. Let's go," she says.

I watch Dominick rise slowly to his feet and then grab his stomach and wince.

"Go without me," Dominick says. "I think I might have a broken rib or something."

I grab his arm. "Not gonna happen."

Nolan helps Dominick on his other side. Hannah peeks out of the tent to double-check. "It's clear. Come on."

We step outside. Tents alight in the distance, and the smell of wood burning fills the air as we run in the opposite direction. Dominick struggles to breathe, and it reminds me of my dad after he regained consciousness in the hospital. We run and run, clearing the front of the encampment.

"I . . . can't . . ." Dominick wheezes.

"Head to those bushes to hide," I say. "He needs to catch his breath."

Footsteps run at us from another direction. I turn in hopes of seeing Benji. But it's Eugene, along with several other guards.

He yanks me by my hair. "Did you really think you'd get away that easily? I have plans for you today. As for your friends here, they are expendable. Maybe next time you'll listen to me. Kill them."

"No, wait," I beg. The guards ignore me and snatch Nolan, Dominick, and Hannah as they struggle to get away. "I'll throw myself into the Hub. You won't have to stage it. Just let them go."

Eugene grins. "Heard the plan, huh? Doesn't matter. Baby, I don't think you understand. You're going regardless."

A popping sound, and white, thick smoke fills the area. It becomes impossible to see, like walking through clouds.

Eugene's voice yells, "Ambush!"

I twist my body and manage to knee him. It must have landed somewhere crucial because he lets me go. I turn and lose my sense of direction. "Dominick? Hannah? Nolan?" I manage to say before I cough and gag on the smoke.

Someone grabs me from behind, and I swing wildly in the fog.

"Ow, Alex, it's me," Benji says.

"Sorry—"

"No time. Let's go." He's wearing a thin mask over his mouth, carrying a knife, and has odd canisters attached to his vest. "Put this on." He covers my mouth with a similar mask.

"Where are the others?"

He pushes me forward without a response. I push back. "No, we can't leave them."

"Trust me. I have people on it. You're my priority." His voice changes, and he sounds a little like Dad. He grabs my forearm, and I run with him into the woods.

The farther we go away from the chaos, the louder my heart beats. My body tears itself in half, one side desperate for my own safety, the other desperate to save Dominick and the others.

Katherine and other Umbra wait in the wings. Doctor A. takes my pulse and reminds me to breathe slowly so I don't hyperventilate. "Dominick's hurt," I tell him and look back at the smoke for signs of him. There's no movement.

"Where are they?" I ask Benji. "You said they'd be okay."

Benji sighs. "Stay here."

He races back into the rising fog, knife in hand.

Minutes tick by, and I beg God, if he or she exists, to intervene. I made Dominick come with me to the woods. It cannot end like this.

Through the fog, Hannah runs forward with other Umbra soldiers, wearing masks.

My body convulses, and I puke near a pale tree trunk. Katherine rubs my back.

"Alex," Hannah says, and I look up. Beruk emerges from the smoke, carrying Nolan's body. "Is he okay?" she asks.

He places Nolan's body on the ground. Blood seeps and spreads onto his uniform in several spots on his chest. Beruk's uniform is also stained. Doctor A. checks his vitals and shakes his head. Hannah falls to the ground and sobs across Nolan's body. I hug her from behind as she cries for him, for us, for everything.

"Where's Benji and Dominick?" I ask Beruk.

"They aren't here? You were Benji's target."

"He went back in," I say. An intense burn travels from my lower stomach to my heart. *They have to be okay. They have to be okay.*

Just when the forest starts to spin around me, Benji emerges from behind several bushes far north of our location. He's carrying Dominick.

I race to them. "Oh, my god, Dominick?"

"Alex?" Dominick asks. Hearing his voice makes my heart beat again.

"Right here," I say.

"I love you," he manages to say before his head drops and he loses consciousness.

A GROUP OF Umbra rush Dominick back toward headquarters. Doctor A. says he lost a lot of blood.

Some stay behind to deal with the traitors.

The rest of the team returns together through the forest. Benji and Katherine walk next to me and Hannah.

My love for Dominick almost got him killed. *I'm not okay if he's not okay.*

Benji's voice rings through the woods. "What were you thinking, leaving the party? Do you not understand that the majority of people are angry at you? You are their reason that rations have been cut. You are a target, Alexandra. You can't just go off gallivanting."

"I—" My hands shake from the experience, from almost losing everything. "Not now."

Hannah moves ahead of us to avoid the conversation.

"Bullshit, not now." Benji grabs me by the crook of my arm. "I had to waste an entire Umbra special force team to retrieve you."

I pull back. "You're not Dad. I don't have to listen to you."

Benji's eyes fire up, and he addresses Katherine. "Will you talk some sense into her?"

"I agree. She shouldn't have wandered off. But do you realize how much stress she must be under? Give the girl a break."

"A break? Marcus and I have had no time together either. This isn't break time, it's war time."

"And you're losing him because of it. He's not happy with your shit, either."

I storm past him without speaking.

"Hey! We aren't done," Benji says.

"Yes, we are. Did you forget you're my brother? You're not my parent. We're equals."

"If you want me to treat you like an adult, act like an adult. Don't run off when you have Umbra members trying to keep you safe. Don't assume your needs are more important than the group."

"I don't!" I refuse to cry in front of them.

I flee through the woods back to camp with Hannah. By the time I reach Umbra headquarters, we both can't hold back the damage.

CHAPTER 24
DAY 43

I AM NOT there when Doctor A. delivers the news to Nolan's grandmother, but I overhear him tell Marcus he's worried she may have a stroke. Kendra and Hannah hold a memorial that night for Nolan around the Geotroupes' fire pit. I can handle it for only a short time before I return to Dominick's bedside.

On a handmade cot of cloth and wood in my guarded floor space of Umbra headquarters, I sit and watch Dominick sleep. My mind replays the kidnapping over and over again, with different endings, each more dire and gruesome. In every scenario, Dominick dies. I write in my journal.

I force myself to think of something else to stop the terrible loop, and my mind drifts to my fight with Benji. *He's right. He's so right. I screwed up and almost got us killed. I screw up everything I touch. This is why Dominick and I should not be together. I'm going to be his downfall.*

I watch Dominick's chest rise and fall and remember Dad in the hospital on the ventilator. My parents must be just as worried that Benji and I didn't survive. *Dad and Mom making a homemade shrine to me and Benji in the living room. Dad pulling the boards off the windows with one hand, beer in the other. If there is beer. Maybe there's still a shortage of alcohol, and he's left with no way to hide from the memories. Maybe the economy can't recover fast enough with so many workers gone, and no food shipments arrive. Maybe my parents don't even exist anymore. Maybe no one will survive this.*

I jump off the cot, kiss Dominick's forehead, hang on to my journal, and leave the room to escape the images. Talking to someone will help distract me. I find Katherine tinkering with DOT.

"What are you doing up?" she asks.

"I could ask you the same question." I sit near her with my journal on my lap and watch her work.

"I heard Dominick will be fine," Katherine says without looking at me.

I nod but say nothing.

"DOT is almost ready. Working out a few kinks and trying something else." She swipes her hand rapidly across a holoscreen above the black box on DOT's leg. "I left you a surprise, by the way."

My curiosity mixes with anxiousness. "What? Where?"

"Not telling."

In that moment, she reminds me of Benji driving me nuts with half-answered statements. Well, if he were nice.

"Consider it my gratitude," Katherine says.

"What did I do?"

She turns from DOT's program and faces me. "Told the truth. At the old vertex site, the focal point of the vertex parabola locked onto Earth's physical location."

I blink. "What?"

"Professor Marciani confirmed the Earth wasn't destroyed."

"Seriously?" Relief spreads through me that something is finally going right. "So we can go back?"

"Not through the vertex. We can't maintain navigation yet. The vertexes still appear magenta and lose structural integrity. But the confirmation changes everything. The Umbra has switched tactics into battle mode."

I swallow and fidget with the wooden and metal tools on the table. It's what I've been waiting for, but as I think of Dominick in recovery, I know battles come with human cost.

"Imagine if we had never met," Katherine says and gestures for me to hand her a sharp tool. "If you had never been brave enough to trust me. All these people not knowing what happened. Being abducted from Earth and not knowing. You did this, you know. You even changed me. You gave my life purpose again. I haven't had that for a long time." Her smile holds pain behind it, pain for the loss of her daughter.

I shrug. "That's not true. The Umbra was already established by the government. They gave you a purpose."

"We wouldn't have known the whole truth, never tried to get back to Earth. You gave us our real mission. And I wouldn't have developed DOT if you hadn't told me about SIDEKICK and the biohologram you saw. You had guts coming through that vertex."

"Sometimes I don't know why I did it." I go back to that moment in my mind. *Was I being selfless or selfish?*

"Wow, your bravado is killer. Really. Take a compliment."

She doesn't realize that I don't feel proud of it. Not really. It's not as if I had a hero-complex moment. *Like, was I so full of myself that I really thought little me was going to change the world? I wanted my friends back. I wanted to keep a promise to my boyfriend. A boyfriend that I put in danger. Another boy who has died.*

As I'm lost in thought, Katherine smiles at me and says, "Mississippi, it doesn't matter why you did it. It only matters that you did, and it made a difference to a lot of people."

I can't let her think it was all me. She pushed me to come here. "You helped." The words fly out of my mouth before I can clamp my teeth over them.

"Me?"

"You told me I could be a hero. Sort of."

"Mississippi, I have a good memory. I never said that."

"Trust me. You made the difference." She doesn't understand, and I will never explain it to her.

I came because of her. She pushed me in with that note. It was the last piece to the puzzle, the only thing that let me know something was definitely waiting on the other side. I knew there was someone to rescue. Someone to tell. I wouldn't have jumped through without that inkling of hope. I wasn't looking for a suicide mission. I was looking for survival.

"The only thing I was ever proud of before was my daughter. I also helped a driver during a minor rebellion on a prison bus on the way to the vertex," she says. "The other prisoners were ready to kill the guard and run for it. Funny that I stopped a rebellion only to join a different one."

"Wait, that was you?" I flip through my journal. "I saw that report on the news. Look, I wrote about it. The guard said you saved her life. Called you a hero."

"Wow, you write down everything. Yeah, it's all about perspective and context, isn't it? One person's felon is another person's hero."

"Wow. Your bravado is killer. Take a compliment."

BENJI DEMANDS THAT Rita and I go with him in disguise to the Holospaces later that week. He doesn't give details. It must be important if he wants to take the risk and put my life on the line. I'm still public enemy number one. Rita, of course, is more than willing to oblige. Dominick's been cleared by Doctor A. but has been told to take it easy. He refuses to stay put and decides to come with us. I should be more anxious about leaving, but I've been cooped up so long it will feel good to get out. Plus, and I'd never admit it to him, Benji makes me feel safe.

Once our bandwidths activate in the forest, we alter our uniforms to include hoods. I miss hooded sweatshirts. As we enter the LU community, people walk past us, smiles on their faces, bellies full. Bandwidths glow once more. I take a deep breath and hope they don't recognize me.

Benji brings us to the next available Holospace, a large empty blank canvas waiting for programming.

He stands with his chest out, his face stoic.

"None of you have official clearance to do this. I'm going out on a limb here. You have to listen carefully to all my instructions and take this seriously."

We nod automatically and ask no questions. He can be intimidating when he pulls that military tone. I find myself caring about my posture, standing a little taller. He moves to a side panel and messes with the nanoholocoms in the area.

"Okay, the room isn't being monitored, so we can talk freely. Give me a sec to start the program."

We stand idle as he activates his bandwidth and initiates a program titled BenTarg and then inputs four participants into the filter. I close my eyes to avoid the bright flash as the program loads. When I open my eyes, we are in a field of grass. It looks like any scene from Earth, except that at each of our feet is a huge, double-chambered object.

"These are holographic versions of the DQDs that the Umbra have developed. Highly intense weapons. They look nothing like these blocks. Didn't want to give the specs to the nanoholocom network when we made this program, but they will simulate the experience of shooting them."

The cubed chambers are stacked on top of each other, almost seven inches thick. It's the boxiest, ugliest weapon I've ever seen. Dad would love it.

"What does DQD stand for?" Rita asks.

"Dual Quantum Detangler."

"Sounds like something I'd use in my hair," Rita says.

Rita and I laugh. Benji and Dominick don't find it funny.

"I want the three of you to practice hitting moving objects. Alex, I know you've practiced with Dad, but those were stationary targets and different ammo. The two of you ever shoot?"

Rita and Dominick shake their heads no.

"Why do we need to practice?" I ask. "We aren't in the Umbra fighting forces. We can't go into battle."

"No, I wouldn't ever send you into battle," Benji says. "However, the three of you are clearly targets, as recent events proved. Not only did Earth refugees and some of our own allies get involved, but the meritocracy put a hit out on you. We can keep you safe for only so long. I don't want what happened to Nolan to happen to any of you. The best thing I can do is prepare you to defend yourselves just in case. Not everyone in the Umbra agrees with me since these weapons are highly dangerous. Rita, I know using technology is against Geotroupes' rules. If you want out, say the word."

"I'm down." Rita picks up the weapon to her waist, then lowers it back on the ground. "Damn, that thing weighs a ton."

"Exactly. There's a lot to get used to. Put the strap around your head and across your body for support. The DQD is a heavy weapon, and it's not easy to aim and time. Dominick, I'm not sure if your body can handle this yet, so you can sit and watch for now."

I put the strap around my head, feel the weight around my neck, and remember that night in the attic when Dad choked me during one of his flashbacks. I immediately take it back off.

"Alex, please," Benji says.

"I'll just hold it."

"It's gonna mess you up."

He picks up a weapon, throws the strap over his body, and demonstrates. "You hold it with two hands, one in the front here near the first trigger, and one back here near the second. Keep the gun at waist level on the side of your body. It's the only way you'll be able to handle the weight and fire properly. It'll be harder to aim, but you'll adjust.

"The DQDs are designed to destroy holograms in case they turn on us. You pull the first trigger, count to three, then pull the second trigger in the back. The first shot is a cryowave. It basically forces a hologram to freeze in a solid, intransitive state so it can't convert back into a transitive state. Takes three seconds to work. The second trigger is a wave particle beam that will blow the suckers up on a quantum level where they will be unable to rematerialize. You have to time the three seconds yourself. Too soon and the wave particle beam will pass through them. It's the best we could do."

"What happens if it hits a person?" I ask.

"You don't want to know." He shakes his head. "It will be highly effective."

I hold the DQD in my hands. I am enamored by its weight and petrified by its potential.

"Let's practice." He swipes on his bandwidth, and deer pop out of the grass and charge toward us from a distance, unafraid.

"No humanoid holograms?" Dominick asks.

"Don't want the nanoholocom network to catch on. Take it seriously even though it's a simulation. It's designed to help with wielding the gun, targeting, and reaction time."

Benji takes the first shot from his hip, one foot in front of the other to brace himself, hitting a deer. The sound is remarkably soothing, like the hum of a microwave. The deer freezes in place. "One Mississippi, two Mississippi, three Mississippi." It's weird to hear Katherine's nickname for me being used by Benji as a counting device. He pulls the second trigger, and a booming crack like a lightning strike physically startles the three of us. The deer vanishes.

"I can't sit out. I have to try this," Dominick says. When he lifts the heavy strap onto his body, he winces. He misses the deer at first, aims again, and after a successful first hit, pulls the second trigger and misses again.

"You need to put more weight on your back leg before you release the second trigger, and lean forward a little. Once you get used to the weight of the weapon, you'll get it."

My turn. On the second pull, the gun's vibrations surprise me, and I let go. Without the strap on my shoulder, it drops out of my hands, and the dying beam hits me as it falls.

"And you're dead." Benji grabs my weapon from the ground and hands it back to me. "That's what the strap is for."

"I can't use it."

"At least put it around your body. I know you can do this."

"My turn," Rita says. She aims, shoots, and freezes a deer immediately. "One Mississippi, two Mississippi, three Mississippi." She fires, and the deer vanishes. "Oh, yeah! Did you see that? In your faces!"

"Nice work," Benji says.

"Oh, it's on," Dominick says. "Best out of ten."

"You can't beat me. I'm a natural."

I hold the strap of the weapon in my hands and realize that the past can affect our future in so many small ways that add up over time. Dad would be disappointed in me for still being afraid and not protecting myself. I want to do it. I want them to be proud of me. I want to protect the people I love.

My hands shake. I wrap the strap around my waist. It's the best I can do.

"It's a start," Benji says and pats me on the shoulder. "Now let's see what you can do."

CHAPTER 25

DAY 55

THE FIRST ROUND OF PRACTICE TESTS WILL BEGIN
IN THE HOLOSPACES. PLEASE REGISTER ON YOUR
BANDWIDTHS.

A WEEK LATER, the meritocracy announces the existence
of practice tests. Since they are using biosignatures to register
and record testing results, anyone with an altered bandwidth
signature, including me and the top leaders and scientists in the
Umbra, cannot register. Dominick and his family are also staying
put, as well as all the Geotroupes.

At dinner, we find out additional news from SN10 headquarters. The major Umbra plan is a go. All factions on board. DOT
has been sent orders to fly a spaceship and temporarily disable
a space station that controls the environment where Beruk discovered the vances' signal. Late tonight, facades should fall. Our
alliances will hopefully infiltrate the exposed vance territory and
take them hostage.

We will finally meet these vances and demand answers. I
should be excited. I lose my appetite.

THE UMBRA AND Geotroupes position themselves in locations
around the region, including the area where Beruk believes the

vances are hiding. They are ready to attack and capture the vances as soon as DOT brings down the power.

Dominick, Rita, and I beg Katherine to let us tag along with the last group to watch. There is no way I can sit in headquarters under guard, worrying about what's happening.

"Fine, but stay out of the way. Your brother will kill me if you get hurt."

We gather into various-sized magpods—us three friends behind Katherine and Doctor A.—and set travel to the vertex guidepost.

Another magpod. *What has happened to me? When did I decide that it would be a good idea for me to fly in a magpod following a convict who's part of an alliance with my brother and a rogue hologram?*

"Is it bad that this is fun?" Dominick asks.

"Yes," I say, half-joking.

"No, it's true. It's so exciting. I feel like Indiana Jones," Rita says. Dominick and I laugh.

"What?" Rita asks.

"Nothing. I'd just go with a more hi-tech analogy," I say.

"Like we're taking out the Death Star," Dominick says.

"You forget I live with the Geotroupes. I'm old-school and proud of it." Her eyes change, and I know she's thinking about her parents. Then she smiles through the sadness. "Except I'm fashion-forward. Well, only when I'm on the network." She pulls up on the high, stiff peacock collar of her uniform, and the feather images align like cobalt eyeballs around her neck.

Our magpod whooshes past other LU communities glowing in the darkness. I remember first hating the sensation of magpod travel, being driven instead of driving, floating with magnetic forces over paved nanoholocoms. Tonight, it's slightly comforting to have something powerful lead the way.

Ours is the last group of magpods to arrive. We gather near the closest vertex guidepost and exit the vehicles.

"What are you doing here?" Benji shouts in the dark. "You three should be back at headquarters."

"I need to see it for myself. I want to see the meritocracy fall apart. If I started it, I want to see it end."

"You're a liability."

"I let them come," Katherine says. "She's the face of the rebellion, for God's sake."

"If she freaks out, she's your problem."

"I'm not going to freak out," I say, immediately worrying that I just might. Doctor A. nods at me, and I try to take in his confidence.

One by one, we step through green vertexes and walk to the established Umbra meeting point.

Beruk announces to the group, "This is the lookout and medical team location area. Troops head to the signal spot and wait for the holographic cloak to drop to attack."

Benji points to us. "You three stay here. Katherine, they're all yours."

We watch from a shadowy field outside the city as our special forces creep in the darkness toward a cliff. *What if DOT turns on us and warns the meritocracy that we're coming? What if Katherine is secretly a double agent sent by the meritocracy to infiltrate the Umbra and lead us to our demise? What if Beruk is a double agent and plans to push Benji off the cliff?*

Don't get tricked by a thought. Don't get tricked by a thought. Don't prove Benji right.

Oh, that one worked. New mantra. Highly effective.

"This is a letdown," Rita says and sits on the ground. "I can barely see anything from here."

I join her side. Dominick stands behind us.

"I want to fight with them," he says.

"Over my dead body," I say.

"That's not funny," Dominick says. "But Rita's right. This sucks."

Katherine joins us. "You heard your brother."

We wait in the stillness. Endless time passes.

"Anyone else need to pee?" Rita asks.

"Me," I say. "We'll be right back."

Rita and I find a private spot in nature and take turns. "Benji would hate me if he knew this is what I was doing while waiting for a battle to begin."

"Nature calls," Rita jokes. "Especially in girl world."

By the time we return to the lookout area, Katherine's pacing back and forth. Doctor A. talks with a group of medical trainees. I notice Dominick is with them.

"Is something wrong?" I ask Katherine.

"DOT should've executed by now, and we lost verbal contact with the troops."

I squint my eyes to will them to see through the darkness. In the far distance, human shadows huddle and move near the signal area.

"They seem okay," I say.

"Maybe you miscalculated," Rita says.

Our outfits revert to basic uniform mode, and our bandwidths go dormant. DOT must've reached the target. We wait for the holographic cloak to fall. I want to look the captured vances in the eye, shake out the whole truth.

A screech pierces the night sky, an instant blaze and thunderous sound.

"Run!" someone from the medical team screams.

From the sky above, the fireball grows in intensity. Rita, Katherine, and I flee the area alongside the other lookouts.

We can barely get traction and distance before a ship barrels toward us and crashes, pieces scattering in all directions.

The ground shakes and knocks me off my feet. Rita helps me up as we scramble to escape the cloud of debris and smoke.

"Are you two okay?" Katherine asks.

Rita and I nod. I cough as the dust surrounds us. "Do you see Dominick?"

"No," Rita says. "I can't see anything near the crash site."

The Umbra troops move out of the shadows and pull people to safety. Benji races toward us.

"Are you hurt?" Benji asks.

"No. I . . . my ankle's sore, but I can walk on it."

"Move," he commands. "This place could blow. Get back to the vertex guidepost. Now. Katherine, Jackson wants answers."

Katherine's eyes go wide and intense. She follows orders and herds people away from the area.

"Wait!" I grab Benji's arm. "Doctor A.'s medical team was sitting where the ship crashed."

"I'll have the team look for them. Go."

"I can't just go. Dominick was with them." I remember Nolan's body being carried toward us. "I can't lose him."

He grimaces. "Alex, I promise to find him for you, but I need to know you're safe. Deal?"

I nod, tears on the brink. Rita and I join Katherine and race as far from the crash site as possible. Out of breath, we regroup with others and look back at the disaster.

Where are they? I search for them in the shadows and the chaos of bodies. I can't even fathom the possibilities.

Rita hugs me, and I lay my head on her shoulder. She's crying. I can't cry yet. I'm still waiting.

Waiting for the inevitable. There are always casualties.

"Alex!" Dominick comes running forward and hugs me and

Rita. Doctor A. is behind him. Their faces and clothes are covered with ash.

"Thank god," I say.

"It's bad over there," Doctor A. says and nurses a wound on his leg.

"Benji pulled us free," Dominick says. "We were pinned under rubble. He was right behind us . . ."

I scan the crash site for signs of movement. "Where is he?"

"He might need help," Dominick says.

We race to the disaster, my uniform pulled over my mouth to help filter the smoke. My ankle throbs, so I limp some of the way. Katherine and Doctor A. scour the area to the left, so I take the right. Rita follows me, and Dominick stays in the center. He climbs over a metal panel, and I try lifting one away, but the heat of the metal burns my hand.

"Something smells toxic," Rita says with her hand over her mouth.

A familiar dread crawls under my skin. "How could you not notice he was missing?" I ask Dominick, frantic.

"He's Benji. When does he ever need help?"

If he's not okay, it'll never be okay. He's the glue that holds our family together. He's held me together. We will never be okay.

"Way over there," Rita says. "His foot looks wedged."

I spot Benji among the debris. His foot is stuck between two pieces of the ship. He pulls and pulls on his leg and it eventually releases.

Relief runs through my veins as I run forward to help him. To thank him for saving Dominick. To apologize for . . . holding so much against him, being difficult, being such a basket case—I'm not even sure.

He raises a hand to say something—

A tremendous fireball knocks us off our feet as the entire

shipwreck explodes. I'm thrown backward and land hard, pain shooting up my spine. Benji's body disappears in the flames.

"Oh, god. Benji!" I scramble to my feet and ignore the pain in my leg and shoulder. Rita holds me back. A group of Umbra rush in to help.

All we see is dark smoke and bluish-orange flames.

"HME OPEN!" I scream. Nothing happens. The damn thing's offline.

Katherine and Doctor A. remain on the scene while Umbra members force Dominick, Rita, and me to retreat to a safer distance with them. Dominick and Rita hold on to me as I fight to run, fight to stand. Rita hides her face in her hands.

Minutes later, Doctor A. returns. "I'm so sorry, Alex."

CHAPTER 26
DAY 55

KATHERINE RETURNS FROM the scene of the explosion, tears streaked across her face in the dark.

"We need to move." Her strong voice betrays the worry on her face. "Let's go. The magpods are offline. Everything is offline."

There are so many feelings racing through me I cannot process them. My body goes numb.

My brother's dead. I should've let everything be.

I came here to bring the truth. My brother, who drove me nuts most of my life, finally believed in me. Now he's dead. *It's all my fault.*

"Alex, we have to leave." Dominick pulls me to join the retreating Umbra.

My feet won't listen to my brain. I'm short-circuiting in a brand new way. Dad's way. The way only war can.

Rita shakes me. "Alex, we have to go back. Let the special troops handle the rest."

Katherine intervenes. "The impact of the crash temporarily brought down the vances' barrier. Beruk will rally the troops to attack while they have the opportunity."

Waiting for Benji's instructions.

"Benji's death won't be in vain. I won't let it be in vain. It's my fault. I don't know what happened with DOT . . . We can do this, Alex. We have a chance to bring everyone home."

Everyone but my brother. Home. Oh, god, my parents . . .

I think I'm crying. It's hard to tell. Dominick holds my body tight. It's the only thing keeping me up.

"Alex, listen to me," Katherine says. "The greatest sacrifice always comes at the expense of self. Your brother knew this. That's why he was military. I have to follow his lead and make it count. Let's make it count together."

Make it count. Her words allow me to temporarily ignore the truth, ignore the painful tide rising inside to drown me. She thinks Benji did it for the Umbra, did it for the cause. Did it to save them. *But he did it for me. I know he did it for me.*

If the Umbra and Geotroupes are ready for attack, I'm going with them. I am done being their victim. I want revenge. Rage is power.

Together, we head back on foot to destroy the meritocracy, my grief a quick fuel that will burn until I realize that I'm empty.

THE CROWD REMINDS me once again of the Stop & Shop riot back on Earth, and all those old feelings come rushing back inside me. But grief is stronger than anxiety, and right now I couldn't care less about my safety. Fear has its limits. Grief is fathomless.

"As far as we can tell," Beruk says, "the vances inhabit that LU community. The area appeared to be a canyon before, but when the barrier crashed, the scenery changed." He looks at me. "I'm sorry for your loss. He was a good man."

The Umbra have explosives strapped to their bodies, DQDs drawn in front of them. I thought those were only for holograms. In the darkness, Jackson leads the way. We storm down the hill in the darkness and enter the LU. My ankle hurts as I run, but my heart is broken. As soon as we reach the first Hub, I know something is terribly wrong.

The vances are waiting for us. They wear robes, not uniforms, but other than that they look similar to Earth refugees. They stand with their hands in the air, weaponless. It's too easy.

Is it an ambush? Did they know we were coming? Did DOT really turn on us?

"You're surrounded!" Beruk yells. "Surrender!"

The Umbra and Geotroupes send up a mutual cheer.

I don't join in. The enemies, they don't feel right. There's so much confusion in their silence. Confusion in the noise. Questions upon questions upon questions in jumbled sounds. The language filters are offline with the power down. We can't understand each other.

It's in their eyes, on their faces. They are heartbroken. They aren't even trying to fight. *Like they've already been defeated.*

The hairs on my arms raise. Like truth molecules hitting each skin pore.

One vance moves forward too quickly, and a young Umbra soldier turns to fire.

"Hold your fire!" Jackson yells.

The Umbra soldier freaks and misfires, and the first cryowave misses its target and hits an LU solar window. The panel freezes on contact and then shatters. The sounds ricochet through their Hub. Another vance steps forward and holds his arm up, his bandwidth smashed and clouded inside. He places his other hand on his chest. Like pledging a courtroom oath with the heart in place of the book. Like holding up a Vulcan peace sign.

No one moves. Another repeats the action. The tension in the air shifts slowly from one of anger and attack to one of peace, and then shifts once more to far deeper acknowledgment as we see the growing crowd holding up smashed bandwidths and hands over their hearts.

It takes a few seconds for the whole truth to sink in: they

destroyed their bandwidths in rebellion since they couldn't remove them.

We were naive to believe we were the only victims.

How many others are there? It's impossible to know how many others are hidden behind veiled walls of oppression. Collected from parallel universes. Nothing can be done to stop it.

Motives don't even matter anymore.

We are as insignificant in the universe as a grain of pollen on a windshield. I mean viewshield.

And we still don't know where the meritocracy is hiding.

One of the vances shifts focus and points at Katherine. Others follow, and soon the entire front group is pointing at her, saying something we can't understand.

"What's going on?" Katherine asks. "Am I a target?"

"Don't know," Beruk responds, DQD raised and ready. Another vance mumbles something and extends his hand out for Katherine to hold.

"I think he wants you to go with them," Rita says.

"Like hell," Katherine says.

The rest of the vances sink to one knee.

"Let's go," Jackson says to Katherine. "We need to find out what they want."

The team follows the vances down through their region, similar to our LU communities but with an unkempt, much older design. Much of their daily life seems to take place outside instead of inside based on the amount of items strewn in the walkways. The Geotroupes would get along with them.

"Get ready for anything," Beruk warns. "It could be an ambush."

Without a weapon in my hands, my adrenaline goes into hypervigilance mode.

"There are nanoholocoms here," Katherine says, "but none of them are active. It looks like it's been that way for a long time."

Dominick and Rita are silent. They know I can't handle reality right now.

We travel into a much larger expanse with a huge statue in the center. The area looks like a homemade marketplace with items littered in rows for barter. *Is this where we are headed if our rebellion fails and we don't make it back to Earth?*

As we get closer to the middle, the vances talk more often, full of guttural sounds and clicks of their tongues. I've never heard a language like it. Like mixing German and dolphin. Without the language filters on, we have no way to communicate. They point toward the statue, and it takes a few seconds for the truth to sink in.

The statue is a monument.

The rusted and decayed surface doesn't hide the fact that it's clearly a statue of Katherine.

"What the hell?" Katherine spins around to face us. "How ... ?"

"There's an engraving at the bottom," the professor says. "I can't decipher it without the bandwidth's instant translator."

I reach out and touch the dull metal surface. We are only a tiny piece to a very large puzzle, and without the outer edges, nothing makes sense. *Nothing can be done to stop it. Their motive doesn't even matter anymore.*

I look around at the faces of my allies, the faces of the vances, new friends and old enemies, and all I see are families just trying to survive.

My mind caves in.

I give up.

I surrender.

My brother is dead.

PART 3

"Our truest life is when we are in
dreams awake."
—*Henry David Thoreau*

CHAPTER 27

DAY 55

WE INVESTIGATED A RECENT EXPLOSION AND DEATH.
REST ASSURED THIS WAS AN EXTREMELY RARE ACCIDENT.
ALL PERSONS INVOLVED WILL BE SUBJECT TO
INVESTIGATION. THE MERITOCRACY WILL NOT PROVIDE
FUTURE UPDATES UNTIL THE ISSUES HAVE RESOLVED.

DOCTOR A. TELLS Marcus the news that Benji is dead. It must be hard to deliver news that will shatter people. I watch Marcus to know how to react. To kill the numbness. To find the pain.

His face changes in stages. It morphs from frozen and open to wrinkled and pained. To fury. To devastation. Like a universe just collapsed before his eyes, and he alone survived.

The past ruined.

The present destroyed.

The future erased.

My pain follows. T. S. Eliot was wrong; worlds don't end with a bang or a whimper. They're not exclusive. One always follows the other.

WHEN I WAS eleven, Dad woke me and Benji in the middle of the night for a road trip. He wouldn't tell us where we were going, just that it was a surprise.

"What about Mom?" I asked in the car.

"She wouldn't understand," Dad said.

When we hit the New Hampshire border, I knew something was wrong. The silence in the car between Benji and me spoke volumes. For some reason, when a parent acts truly crazy, the children go silent. Not sure if it's a genetic thing, a self-preservation thing, or a self-destructive thing. But you separate yourself in the moment, denying any relationship to avoid injury.

Benji and I held our tongues and didn't ask questions as Dad drove us farther and farther away from Mom. No one expects their own parent to kidnap them. I thought I would never see my home, my room, or my friends again.

Dad checked us into a log cabin in the middle of nowhere. No phones. After many more hard drinks, he passed out cold.

"Grab his feet," Benji said.

I listened. Together, we struggled to drag Dad back into the car. Benji drove us home before dawn. He didn't even have his license yet, and he swerved a few times over the highway lines. I remember worrying we would crash but being more scared of never seeing home again. At least the highway was empty. I knew deep down that Benji would never put me in danger. He was always like that. Reliable. Predictable. He did what he said. Period.

Dad woke up the next morning and acted as if nothing had happened. I actually don't think he remembered.

I never thanked Benji for not freaking out. For bringing me home.

For being my brother.

THE NANOHOLOCOM NETWORK mends itself, coming back online in the region within days. I stay in bed in Umbra headquarters. People come and go. Dominick, Rita, and Doctor A. take shifts, bringing me food from the Geotroupes' camp, talking at me. It doesn't matter. Nothing matters.

Katherine pokes me awake. "You didn't show up at the big meeting. Didn't Dominick tell you I needed to talk to you?"

I turn in my cot to face the wall. "Benji's dead, and we're so over our heads outsmarted, why fight it? More people might die. We can just live here in luxury instead. It's what the majority wants, anyway. Be lazy. Chill in technoworld. Everything's back online like nothing ever happened. They can all go play in the Holospaces and eat until they contribute. I'm done."

Katherine grabs my arm and rolls me to face her.

"Ouch!" I rub my arm where she pulled me.

"We deciphered the engraving on the statue. Someone named the Navigator, a person who looks exactly like me, visited them one hundred years ago and delivered a message."

I sit forward. I don't want to hear this and yet I know. *The inevitable is coming.* "What was the message?"

"The river will save you."

My mind recalls the same message by the biohologram at the HME. "So do the vances think that water is the answer?"

She stares into my face. "Mississippi, if I'm the Navigator, you are the River."

My heartbeat fights to escape. "What? That's impossible. Did the vances say that?"

"No, they thought the actual river would save them from the meritocracy's rule, so out of spite the meritocracy tainted all natural water sources in the region to stop the rebellion. It only made it worse, and they've been waiting since. For a generation."

The two of us sit in silence. I will myself not to let her in. *Not telling her will save her. It has to save her.*

"What I don't understand is how this can be true. How can I

be a figure from their past? How did I refer to you in a message to them when we met here? Was it a hologram of me?"

"Maybe," I say, picking at my nails.

She starts pacing the room, cracking her knuckles. "You said I told you to be a hero. You never said when. Maybe I time traveled through a vertex and warned them. To help our cause unite. To get you to bring the truth."

"Time travel isn't real," I blurt out and jump off the holobed. "It doesn't work. We traveled from one parallel universe's present to another. They were just more advanced so it seems like we time traveled. Actual time travel would rattle your brain as old history unraveled around you."

"So you do know something."

"Er ... Dominick and the professor asked the holograms about it."

"What did they ask?"

"How time travel worked. To see if we could just all go back in time and fix everything. Remember?"

She stares at me. "Bullshit. I can see it on your face. Tell me why there's a freaking statue of me with a prophecy about you on it if time travel doesn't exist."

I clam up. She can't make me tell her.

She comes closer to me and points in my face. "This isn't about you anymore. Or me. This is bigger than us. We affected history somehow. From the first day I met you, something has been off. Tell me what you know."

"I can't." I wipe away tears and think about Benji and Nolan and everything that has already gone wrong. "I saw you die."

"What are you talking about?" Katherine spins around. "I'm right here."

I hold my head in my hands. "I met you on Earth, sort of, but you were ... different." There's no way I'm telling her she was a crazy lady spewing poetry. "I don't know anything about the statue."

She paces back and forth again, thinking. "We never met on Earth. We met here."

"We met on Earth. And I saw you die there."

"Maybe it wasn't me. Maybe that was a hologram of me."

"You *died*," I stress. "Holograms don't die. You gave me a note and died. And . . ." the truth bubbles up inside me, "the only way you could've written that note was if it came from the future. That's why I ran through the vertex at the last minute."

"What the hell did the note say?"

I try not to look at my backpack leaning against the wall where my journal is safely stored. I shake my head. "Too personal." I refuse to give her more details that will kill her.

"How did I write you a personal note if I don't even remember meeting you? How did we meet if I was in prison?"

More time passes between us. The past mingles with the future.

"You can't do it," I say. "You die. I saw you die."

"If I go back to Earth, I go back to jail. The future isn't etched in stone," Katherine mumbles.

"That statue says the opposite."

"Fine," Katherine says, "I'll come up with something else."

"Promise?"

"Yes." She stands. "I promised the vances they could meet you as River. Ever since they smashed their bandwidths in protest, they've been trapped behind the veil without the technology to escape. The meritocracy destroyed their planet before they ever got to return home."

I take a moment with this new information. "Their planet is gone?"

"They told us the meritocracy empties planets to create future bioholograms. It requires full cooperation to ensure the bioup-loads aren't rejected, so they create a massive ruse to encourage submission. Forcing contributions creates rebellious tendencies, probably what you witnessed at the HME facility. Then they de-plete the planet of precious metals to build nanoholocom units."

"So Earth is in danger?" I imagine my parents on a dying world.

"According to the vances, yes, but we have a window of time before the damage is irreversible. They ran out of time."

"And you think," I lie back down, "that we can defeat the mer-itocracy when people who have been living here for centuries were abandoned after their rebellion? The same thing's going to happen to us."

"We have a new plan, but it won't work without you. The troops need a rallying cry. You are that cry. Our troops are hurting." She doesn't mention Benji's name, but I know what she means.

"You're there. You do it."

"Their morale is too low. I don't have the crowd. You do. They know how far you've come for the truth. How much you've lost. You are the uniting force with the vances, and the other Earth refugees have come around now that they've heard what the vances have gone through. If you believe, they'll believe."

"You don't get it. I don't believe in anything."

"You have to. You're the prophecy."

KNOWING THAT I'M no longer a target of the masses and the nanoholocom network is fully functional, I move back into the LU that Benji, Marcus, and I shared so I can escape the Umbra and Geotroupes nonsense in the soothing PSF.

My bandwidth COM lights up. It's Rita.

"Heads up. Dominick hasn't been sleeping or eating. He's spending all his rations in the Holospaces."

My stomach sinks. "Why?"

"Benji's program. You need to talk to him. He won't listen to me."

I end the call with Rita and fix my hair for human interaction. Using my bandwidth, I track down Dominick in the Holospaces. On the way there, I pull a leaf off a bush and hold it in my hand. A new habit. Trying to see how long I can hold on to things before they disappear.

His name is on the door's holoscreen, but when I try to enter, I am refused access. My old paranoia rises again, and I use my bandwidth COM to talk to him.

"Dominick, it's Alex. I'm outside the Holospaces. Can I come in?"

After a few moments of silence, the door slides open. He's standing in a field of grass, grizzly bears charging toward us. He doesn't say hello, just turns and shoots. His body shifts, waits, and shoots again in a three-second timed rhythm. Bear after bear freezes and then disappears. I block my ears from the constant humming and crackling sounds, a terrible choir of violence. He's so good, it terrifies me.

"Dominick, stop." I pull his arm holding the simulated DQD. He ignores me, so I pull harder. The gun fires right through my body, harmless in these circumstances, but it's enough to get his attention.

"Alex, what the hell. Don't ever do that." He brushes me off his arm and pauses the program with his bandwidth. "Do you want to join in? I can set the filter to two players."

"I know what you're doing," I say. "Rita said you're in here all the time, using up most of your rations. Skipping meals."

He un-pauses the game to resume action.

As he shoots, a sadness builds inside of me for what we've become. *This is what they did to us. Always remember.*

"Okay, two players. Set me up. One hour, then you need to take a break."

He agrees and activates my role. I pick up the DQD and think about that day in the attic with my dad. I take a deep breath and put the strap around my head and across my body. Benji would want me to prove him wrong.

EVEN THOUGH IT'S not necessary, I strip off my clothes and let the PSF clean them separately while I allow the white light and waves to penetrate my skin. My shoulder aches from the weight of the DQD. At least I helped Dominick and got him to eat.

I want to feel alive again, but I don't know how. A childhood memory of Benji and me playing in the snow circles in my mind, and I break down. Nothing will ever be the same.

SIDEKICK suddenly opens without my prompting.

"Alexandra Lucas, please state your needs."

I grab for the clothes and cover my body. "Hello? Privacy! Did the HME activate?"

"Privacy? We are a hologram."

"I don't care what you are. Get out! HOLOGUIDE EXIT." SIDEKICK remains staring at me. It's probably worse that she's a hologram. *I bet she can memorize the vision of me naked and play it back for others. Like a Skylucent peep show of me in a PSF, on replay and in full color throughout the night sky.*

I avoid looking at SIDEKICK in embarrassment. Then I realize that she didn't even notice; she doesn't recognize embarrassment as a human emotion. They don't care about most human feelings. Not in a real way. Only if it seems like a medical issue. The thought scares me beyond belief.

"Is something wrong with your programming? I want to EXIT program." I double-tap my bandwidth.

"Diagnosing my programming. No errors."

Maybe it's my bandwidth. I'll have to ask Katherine to look at it. "Turn around."

SIDEKICK spins in a circle.

"No, I mean turn and look at the wall until I tell you. I need to get dressed."

SIDEKICK follows my orders. Once dressed, I tap my bandwidth COM and ask for Katherine. Across the screen it reads COMMUNICATION FAILED. I try Rita. Same. Both off grid.

SIDEKICK still stares at the wall.

Dominick answers instantly when I call. "Alex? You okay?"

"Where are you?"

"In my old LU to get away. You?"

"Same. Have you seen Katherine around? I can't reach her on her bandwidth. My hologuide is acting funny. Won't shut off." I watch as SIDEKICK reaches under Benji's holobed and retrieves a small black box. She straps it to her ankle.

"No, last I saw her was at headquarters earlier in the day. She was arguing with Professor Marciani. Something about the makeshift vertex . . ."

My backpack lies zipped on the floor. *It can't be. It can't be.* I rush over and pull out my journal, frantically flipping for the right page. The page where the quote should be. My quote.

The page has been torn out.

The page after it says the following:

> *Mississippi—*
>
> *Destiny calls so that others can follow.*
>
> *—Katherine*

I drop my journal and flee from the LU to the old vertex guide-post station behind the Geotroupes' camp.

I run

and run

and run.

SIDEKICK runs beside me, a holographic reminder that I can't escape.

I can't erase the past.

Katherine's actions now cause what already happened then. Cosmic effect and cause time reversal.

If I'm the River, she's the Navigator. If she's the Navigator, I'm the River. One cannot exist without the other. Chicken and egg. Closed circuit.

But I run anyway, and I try to stop it anyway.

Because that is what we do.

We try to prevent the inevitable even when we are powerless to change it.

I reach the ancient stone tunnels and open doorways lined in a circular formation. Scientists tinker in each corner. A magenta swirling vertex calls to me from the center. I watch the electric patterns crack and turn before me. I never had a chance. Professor Marciani stands beside me.

He twists one of his curls and won't look at me.

"We couldn't stop her. I don't know what she was thinking. Maybe the pressure became too much for her. I'm not sure what happened to her. The vertex isn't calibrated properly for travel."

MY JOURNAL IS splayed open on the floor where I dropped it. Katherine's note back to me serves as evidence. I tear every single page out of it, ripping and shredding and cursing the universe while SIDEKICK watches. If I had destroyed it sooner, Katherine would never have been able to copy the lines and give it to me in the past. *Right? Isn't that how time travel and paradoxes work? Or*

would the time-space connection have crumbled and spun us all
back to the dinosaurs?
    If the future can affect the past,
and the past can affect the future,
can the future affect the past and change the same future,
therefore destroying the past and the present?
Or once something is the past, it is the future. Locked in stone.

My mind swims with logic and nonsense, and I continue destroying all evidence from the past so it can never be used against me again.

My counselor was wrong. Words do have power. Tremendous power. The power to change, the power to mend, and the power to corrupt.

I gather the pieces and run out of my LU, tossing them over the edge. They flutter down through the circular open air and onto the Hub below. I continue until nothing is left.

CHAPTER 28

DAY 59

RITA AND DOMINICK listen as I explain what happened. "I shouldn't have told her about the past. The vertex scrambled her thoughts. All she could do was repeat that T. S. Eliot poem." I pace around my LU, SIDEKICK still activated. "Nolan is gone. Benji is gone. Katherine is gone. And I'm supposed to be the River and save everyone. Who are we kidding? We can't win. I can't help. I didn't magically get superpowers overnight." I point at SIDEKICK. "I can't even shut this thing off!"

Rita grabs me by the shoulder. "Alex, sit."

I have no special talents, no means, no plan. I have only the truth. What good is the truth without a plan? Without action? Without people who care?

"I can't lead. I'm not a general or a politician. I don't even like politics."

"You have more political power than you think," Dominick says. "You skipped the meetings. You don't know what's been going on since—"

He stopped short. He meant to say since Benji died.

"You brought them the truth," Dominick says. "They need you to lead them into battle. They see you as the River, thanks to Katherine. And they respected and miss your brother. We all do. You've brought us hope."

But to hope is to fear. "I don't know how to rally troops for a hologram battle in a future galaxy."

Dominick cracks a smile. I almost want to crack his jaw. I stand back up and pace the room, raking my hands across my face and then shaking my fingers in front of me to stop the trembling as the two of them watch.

Rita holds me by my shoulders to keep me still and focused. "Pep talk time," she says. "Ready?"

I roll my eyes. "Go for it."

"Okay, you need to feel your own sense of power. True power is standing in your own shoes, in your own truth, and not feeling ashamed but celebrating who you've been and who you're becoming. When you speak from that place, people listen. When you listen from that place, the walls between us fall.

"That's who you need to be, Alex. You and only you. You are powerful when you use your empathy and voice for justice. That's the best thing religion ever taught me."

The lump forming in my throat is a sign that I have no choice.

"What she said," Dominick says.

SIDEKICK stands idle against the wall.

"Any advice for me, SIDEKICK?"

SIDEKICK responds, "We do not understand the question."

We laugh, and it breaks the tension in the room.

Katherine said *Make it count* when Benji died. My new mantra. I can't let both of their sacrifices go in vain. I can't live with that kind of guilt. Plus, Benji wouldn't think I could do it. I have to make it count and prove him wrong. He would want me to prove him wrong.

PROFESSOR MARCIANI KISSES me on the cheek when he sees me again. An awkward shame washes over me, like he and I somehow conspired to set Katherine's actions in motion. Dominick and Rita chat with the group of scientists. DOT,

Katherine's specialized hologuide, stands in the middle of the space with two other holograms next to her. Untethered from humans, wearing small boxes on their legs.

"Wonderful. You are here," the professor says.

"I am here." Without Katherine and Benji, headquarters does not feel the same. "I thought DOT died in the crash."

"She made herself transitive before impact. Katherine gave me strict orders to tell you and only you our plan if anything happened to her, and to allow you to explain it to others. She and I tweaked DOT's programming."

I avoid looking into his face. His bushy eyebrows express too much emotion.

"Tweaked how?"

Dominick and Rita come over to listen, and the professor stops talking.

"Do you trust them?" the professor asks.

I look at my two dearest friends and say, "With my life."

"We experimented with DOT based on something you told Katherine. About a biohologram at the HME? By my calculations, we determined that a small percentage of biohologram have the ability to reactivate their emotional pathways under the right conditions, but it's impossible for us to locate them. DOT has been programmed to seek them out and tamper with the program that keeps the hippocampus and amygdala from being stimulated. Remember, bioholograms still utilize the neuropathways of the contributed human brain, so if we can manipulate the programming to produce the proper neurotransmitters, we can get them to join our troops."

"So they'll create sort of hologram zombies?" I ask. "But with feelings?"

"Yes, so to speak. Who will fight for us."

How do you fight holograms? With more holograms.

"How can you be so sure that they won't attack us?" Dominick asks.

"Part of the programming. They will been given orders to seek out the meritocracy members and alert us of their whereabouts. Since most of the last generation of holograms were former vances, they should want revenge once they understand what happened to their families."

"How long will it take?" I ask.

"Not long. We tested our theory on a small scale and already had success stories. Of those, we programmed three additional bioholograms to seek out recruits. Once we release it on a wide scale, it should take only days before we see results and hopefully have enough holographic allies to form a holographic army."

He holds out his arm in a gallant show.

"You've met DOT. Meet PIXEL and GALILEO."

"Where's the fourth one?" I ask.

"She said that one was a gift. For you."

SIDEKICK. Dominick, Rita, and I glance over at my rogue, clueless hologuide.

"I highly doubt SIDEKICK's going to be a soldier," Rita says. "She just stands there."

"Do Jackson and Beruk know about the plan?" I ask.

"They already authorized it. We need your help to fully implement it. The public isn't going to like it."

"Because instead of contributing to their society, we are basically corrupting it to get home."

"Precisely."

The thought bothers me. *And if we can't get home? Why does it seem like the only avenue to freedom is destruction?*

THE NEXT MEETING of the Umbra and Geotroupes is held in the field outside the LU community near where Benji died. The turnout is tremendous. People I recognize from the Hub, and people I don't recognize from other communities who weren't part of either group, have joined the ranks. I was asked to make a speech, but I refused. The last time I made a speech for the Umbra, it almost cost me my life.

The Umbra thought of having the rally near headquarters, but the group decided to use the nanoholocom network to send our message to others through bandwidths using DOT's stealth connection. Ironic that we are using the network we are about to corrupt.

There's a palpable, somber silence. *How does an eighteen-year-old girl like me become one of the leaders of a planetary rebellion?*

Would you rather contribute to society or destroy it?

Am I starting a war I won't be able to stop? Where's the OFF button?

Think about Earth. Think about your parents. Think about Nolan and Benji and Katherine. But the holograms didn't kill them. I did. It was my fault.

Beruk has asked me to stay out of sight. He's worried about my safety. Dominick, Rita, and I watch the crowd using Rita's bandwidth VID tossed on my LU wall. SIDEKICK stands fully activated beside me, a shadow that I can't escape.

"So when this starts, don't hate us," Rita says, handing me food.

"It was important," Dominick says.

"What are you two talking about?" I ask. "Ooh, it's about to start."

The rally begins, and an exact replica of me steps up on a high platform in front of the crowd.

"What the hell?"

Rita hides inside her skyscape shirt and ocean pants. A shark swims past.

The hologram of me smiles, exhibits facial expressions, and even clears her throat. Then she gives the speech of a lifetime. My voice carries wide and echoes through the field, through each person's bandwidth. The vances stand next to Earth refugees to listen since their bandwidths don't work.

"I'm here because of my brother Benjamin Lucas Jr. and my friend Katherine Kirkwood. Someone said to me that a soldier's death cannot be in vain. They were honorable people, trying to do the right thing. Trying to get us back home. We have to make it count."

My real throat constricts, and I choke on tears. I lose it, and panic surges with emotion. The VID scans the audience, and I see Marcus crying on camera. I can't. I can't. My brother is dead, Katherine is gone. It's personal. Private. Not revolutionary.

I half-listen to the rest of my speech. It seems to be familiar to me. "I swear I actually said some of this recently."

"SIDEKICK recorded you," Dominick says. "We were told to ask you the right questions to get you to say certain things."

My mouth hangs open. "SIDEKICK, is that true?"

SIDEKICK blinks. "Yes, we recorded your conversations with friends and Umbra leaders and designed the perfect speech using your language and a holographic image."

I cannot believe they tricked me. I should be angrier, but I'm relieved to not have to make the speech myself.

"And gee, I wonder where they got the holographic image of me from? Dominick, any idea?"

He chuckles and shrugs. Rita cracks up laughing.

"Payback's coming," I say to them. "You, too, SIDEKICK."

"We do not understand."

On the VID, Doctor A. speaks next, and I wonder if it's him

or a hologram of him. "It worries me that a president could be assassinated and replaced with a hologram and we'd be none the wiser. Or that an artist or actor could live on agelessly into infinity. Where does that leave future generations? What role will they fill if generations past live on through holograms? A life of leisure without meaningful work is no life at all. They are taking away our right to live and our right to die, our right to matter. Life isn't as glorious and precious once it can be artificially replicated. We cannot let them continue to destroy human cultures throughout time to support their own ideology. It's wrong."

He nods to Professor Marciani, who then speaks into his bandwidth. "The only way to stop them is to create a holographic force against them. We've discovered a way to unlock the stored emotions of some bioholograms and allow them to join us in the fight against the meritocracy. They've been asleep for far too long, dealing with a century of servitude, unaware that their sacrifice was in vain, their people forgotten. With their united tech power along with all of you behind the alliance, the meritocracy will crumble. And we will be able to return to Earth."

Hannah raises her hand in the front, reminding me of me when I spoke to the holograms on Earth near the train. How time changes things.

"How can we help?" she asks.

Beruk answers her.

"When the hologuides gain emotions, they are not the enemy. They are not the ones who brought us here. We need to fight the source, and they will be our new allies. Remember that they were humans once, too, who for the first time will find out that they were not rescued from their own dying planets, but were victims like us, their Earths destroyed. We have to work with them in order to return to Earth. We need you to extend your trust to them to make the plan work. We need as many troops as possible."

The hologram of her lifts my bandwidth into the air, making a fist. "Make it count."

The crowd responds, bandwidth arms in the air, fists ready to fight for freedom.

I glance at my two best friends sitting with me in an LU during the beginning of a rebellion.

Books and movies always make it seem as if there's one hero during revolutions. Like out of everyone out there, one special person makes the difference. It's not true. It may start with one person's action, but out of that one moment, many heroes are born.

DAYS PASS. SLOWLY, people report biohologuides getting emotional and angry at the truth, and joining the Umbra. SIDEKICK doesn't seem to be experiencing the same emotional breakdown as everyone else. Perhaps Katherine and the professor designed the four main carriers to exhibit more control over their emotions. Seems odd to me. At least Benji died before his mind could be uploaded as a biohologram. Since his contribution was rescinded, he wasn't tethered to this horrible world. *Will my parents be proud, or will they wish they could at least have a hologram of him?*

Dominick, Rita, and I sit by a fire pit in the Geotroupes' camp, admiring the Skylucent light show from a distance. SIDEKICK stands like an idle, hi-tech lamppost off to the side.

"What do you think happens next?" Rita asks.

"Beruk is prepping a special ops team for battle with the meritocracy, hologuides included," Dominick says.

"I heard a group of Umbra testing the real DQDs. Sounded intense all at once," Rita says.

"You're stressing me out," I say. "All I want to do is stare at the moving stars and dream of home."

Dominick moves closer to me and wraps his arms around me. "Done."

The three of us watch the fire and the sky, and I hope for the best.

"When we get back to Earth," he asks, "what's the first thing you are going to do?"

"I like this game," I say. "Eat a giant bowl of ice cream."

He laughs. "I figured you'd want to walk the beach."

"Ooh, that too. Rita?"

"Not sure. Depends if my parents let me off my leash after leaving them."

"I want to go to college," Dominick says. "Well, after I finish senior year."

"Are you still on that again? College? After all we've been through?" I ask.

"I decided that I want to go to college for premed. I want to be a doctor. Doctor A. said he'd help me make connections in Boston."

"Here I am picking ice cream, and you want to be a doctor. Way to upstage me."

He tickles the sides of my stomach, and my legs flail in response.

"Doctor, huh? I can see that," Rita says.

"Thanks." He stops tickling me, and I catch my breath. "So what's your plan?" he asks me.

"If I can follow you to another planet, I guess I can move to Boston."

"Deal." He kisses me under a canopy of foreign stars, and I almost feel like myself again.

A strange, piercing beep comes from SIDEKICK. *Great, she's malfunctioning even more than before. Now she's a fire alarm with a dying battery.*

I break away from the kiss. "SIDEKICK, do you mind?"

"You might have the most annoying hologuide ever," Rita says. "What is with that sound?"

My bandwidth suddenly lights up, and my uniform holofies.

SIDEKICK moves to my side and yanks me up by the arm. "Run, Alexandra Lucas."

"What? Why?"

"They're coming."

"Who's coming?" Rita asks.

Dominick stands. "How is my bandwidth activated?"

"And our outfits?" Rita points to her holofied, leopard print uniform, complete with miniature leopards leaping out from behind the spots.

SIDEKICK doesn't respond. Within seconds, Kendra and Hannah come running. "The Umbra headquarters has been attacked. By holograms."

"But there are no nanoholocoms at headquarters," Rita says. "Did the rogue ones turn on us?"

"Were my mom and Austin there?" Dominick asks.

"Run, Alexandra Lucas," SIDEKICK repeats.

It's question overload. I look into SIDEKICK's blank stare and know something is terribly wrong.

A high swooshing sound overhead makes my ears pop. Dark, dart-shaped shadows loom high in the clouds over us.

I know that shape.

Spaceships.

And if they can make a fake comet on Earth, they can create holograms anywhere.

Even a holographic army.

Before we get a chance to run, a generic hologram in a gray uniform materializes in front of us.

It reaches out and grabs Rita, its hand passing through her skin and into her body. Her face turns purple, and my throat caves in.

I look around for something, anything to help. I grab one of the Geotroupes' cast iron pans near the fire pit and throw it. It passes right through the hologram's body.

"Go," she manages to whisper. *Nolan, Benji, and Katherine. I can't lose her, too.*

Dominick lights a stick in the turquoise fire. He runs it through the back of the hologram. Nothing happens at first. Then the hologram turns into balls of light and dissipates.

Rita collapses to the ground.

"Are you okay?" I ask.

She nods, but I see the tears. I know that fear.

Five more holograms materialize, including one in the same spot where Dominick melted one.

"Run, Alexandra Lucas," SIDEKICK repeats once again.

Dominick and I pull Rita to her feet. We scramble out of the area along with Hannah, Kendra, and other Geotroupes, who are grabbing whatever supplies they can salvage. Marie, their leader, yells at them to grab food supplies. I glance behind us and see a hologram use the flame from the fire pit to set the Geotroupes' camp ablaze. There isn't time. I hear the screams of people engulfed in flames, and I watch as the hologram destroys itself in the fire.

They don't experience self-preservation. They are expendable and replaceable.

They can touch us when they want, but we can't touch them when we want. We can't stop them. We can't fight them.

We flee through the forest area, each pounding footstep

matching the rhythm in my chest as my body remembers the fear of being blindfolded in the same area. My hearing dulls as more holograms appear in the distance before us. They line the forest around us. SIDEKICK remains at my side. I check to see if she's joined the hologram army and turned traitor.

In the distance, I watch as another hologram breaks someone's neck.

"SIDEKICK, how do we escape?" I ask.

"Computing. There is no mathematical escape."

"Sorry I asked."

Some people climb the pale trees to hide under the huge leaves. I almost follow until I see holograms defy gravity, walk up the trees horizontally, and pull them off the limbs. I turn away before the first person hits the ground, but the sound punches my heart.

"Alex." I hear the tone in Dominick's voice. I turn to see him on the ground, holding Rita in his arms. Her eyes stare blankly into the sky.

NO.

I collapse on the ground beside her and check her pulse, her breath. I tap her bandwidth. "HME!"

No response. The lights blink aimlessly.

I start doing chest compressions and breathing into her mouth. Dominick takes over the compressions.

"Alex, they're coming," Marie says. "We have to get out of here."

"I'm not leaving her!" I scream. Dominick rechecks her vitals. Nothing.

I start the process again.

"I think the hologram damaged her organs," Dominick whispers.

I stop and stare at her perfect, lifeless body. My best friend in the universe. My *hermana*.

"Run, Alexandra Lucas," SIDEKICK repeats at my side, clueless and emotionless.

I want to shake SIDEKICK to wake her up and realize the threat is real and she was real once and now she's nothing.

I was real once. But grieving isn't something you do, it's something you become.

"Stay here," Marie says.

Marie moves forward with other Geotroupe members. They create a wide circle around us, a sea of human bodies for the holograms to plow down first.

No, no, I can't stay back and have them die for me.

But when I struggle to run forward, to die fighting, people pull me back, lining up in front of me, and it grows dark as they camouflage us with the forest floor.

I lie on the ground holding on to Dominick and Rita's body and wait for the inevitable. The holograms must have a way to seek us out, detect our heartbeats or heat. *This isn't going to work.*

I think about my parents, Benji, Katherine, Nolan, Earth. Singing in my backyard with Rita, and listening to her beautiful voice hit notes I could never reach.

The crunch of footsteps gets louder, the symmetry like rhythmic poetry. Our deaths should be more than huddling in a circle.

An eerie metallic scraping echoes through the woods, and a louder explosion in the sky rocks the area and hurts my eardrums and chest.

"A ship went down," Dominick says. "Look."

Smoke fills in the skyline, the stars an afterthought.

Then familiar sounds, like the hum of a microwave, followed by crackling explosions. *The Umbra DQD weapons.*

We watch as the Umbra troops fire and fall to protect us. They tap their bandwidths and activate the rogue holograms. I recognize DOT, PIXEL, and GALILEO among them. They even have weapons ready and race to the front lines to protect the Umbra. SIDEKICK shadows me, useless.

Dominick races to his feet and runs forward with the Umbra before I can stop him. He grabs a discarded DQD from the ground from a wounded Umbra soldier. He ducks behind a tree for cover.

I don't want to leave Rita, but I have to help Dominick and the others. I run toward him, and on the way I see another hologram send its fist through an Umbra soldier and back out again. The Umbra member drops to the ground, lifeless.

The hologram turns to me next, but Dominick fires on it twice. I kneel beside the fallen soldier. He reminds me of Benji. I put his DQD strap around my head before pulling him by his feet behind a tree. The DQD fire around me turns the noise into muffled, slow-motion actions.

A hologram appears behind Dominick. I fire twice automatically in a three-second interval, the way we were trained. *Benji is with me, encouraging me inside my head to take this seriously, holding me to high standards.* My hands shake against the heavy double trigger.

I see Dominick's hands shake too as we stand back-to-back with weapons ready.

We were not made for this. We are lovers, pacifists, not fighters. *They did this to us. Always remember that they did this to us.*

The never-ending battle ensues, and I am someone I never wanted to be.

I am my father's daughter. My brother's sister. I understand war and its ugly truth. I understand their pain and their pride. I understand the human cost of freedom.

Rita will be another casualty among casualties, a number among numbers. To me, they will never be casualties. They will always be family. Friends. Neighbors. Allies. My people.

Suddenly, dead silence. Their holographic forces vanish simultaneously.

Dominick and I creep forward, along with the remaining Umbra and Geotroupes. The silence of the DQD double fire is like the death of sound itself. The troops fall back.

"Did they surrender?" Jackson asks. Some of the group raises their weapons above their heads in victory. I clutch my DQD close to my hip.

"We need teams to spread out and survey the damage," Beruk commands. "Has anyone seen Doctor A.?"

"He and Penelope stayed at Umbra headquarters," Kendra says. She takes one look at me and says, "They were safe when I left them."

Beruk uses the COM on his bandwidth, and Doctor A.'s answers. He's alive, Penelope's alive. Dominick's mom and brother are alive. Doctor A. promises to arrive soon to help the injured and collect the dead.

Collect the dead.

I walk over and sit on the ground near Rita's body where the Geotroupes moved her. I remove the DQD strap from my body, place the gun next to me. Tears fall, and I feel like a shell of a person. I rake my fingers through her swirling, dark, silky hair, pulling leaves and twigs out of it. I straighten her moving leopard print uniform top, a leopard leaping across it every few minutes, and notice her flashing bandwidth.

Wait a minute, why are our uniforms still activated? Why are our bandwidths still functioning?

I jump up from the ground, throw my weapon back on. "It's not over. The ships are still over us somewhere." I point to my bandwidth. "Still activated."

Everyone goes back into battle mode, gearing up and waiting for the next wave of attack.

Time passes and nothing.

"Maybe they forgot to turn off the signal—"

Right then, another horde of holograms appear, with DQD weapons of their own. They target and fire on the rogue holograms immediately. Our holographic forces vanish in quick, devastating numbers.

"Run!" Beruk yells.

I flee even though I know there's no way we can win if the holograms use our weapons against us. It's over, and I know it's over, but I run anyway, because that is what we do. I think about my parents and know that I will see them soon. And Rita and Benji and Katherine.

As the rogue holograms' numbers dwindle, more Umbra troops die fighting to save us. More than I can count. I have to step over some as I run and shoot, and the human part of me that wants to stay and help them fights with my fading will to survive.

As my lungs begin to heave, I can't stop my body from surrendering to the moment. I slow down. Everything slows down. It's like running to the vertex to bring the truth, but this time there's nowhere to go.

Dominick takes my hand.

We say nothing. We already know.

CHAPTER 29
DAY 64

IS SURVIVING WORTH losing your identity? Your dignity?
Perhaps. I'm not sure anymore.
Rita would know the answer.
I am not proud of who I am.
I wonder where she is in the universe now. Is she with the stars? In heaven with God? She believed in those things.
She even believed in me. She had faith like that. She believed my voice could help the greater good.
I stop running. I cannot watch more people die. I know what will stop the violence. I hit the CVBE on my bandwidth and publicly record a call to the meritocracy so everyone can witness it.
"I am Alexandra Lucas, also known as the River to the vances. I want to contribute live for the planet to watch. Solbiluna-8 has so much to offer us, and we should all contribute as a sign of respect and gratitude for saving us. Please accept this truce."
Silence. They know where to find me now even though Katherine scrambled my identity.
The gray hologram army ceases fire. Dominick puts his arms around me. There are no longer words. I'll take defeat and sacrifice over watching the slaughter any further.
Bandwidths light up with meritocracy approval. My CVBE message repeats on everyone's wrists.
A green vertex materializes before me. It has always been about my sacrifice. Sometimes it's the only way.

I kiss Dominick one last time. As I say goodbye to others around me, I whisper something quickly to Beruk. He nods.

As I step through the vertex, I take one last look behind me. Dominick runs forward and tries to follow, but Beruk holds him back for me.

We have to separate in order for him to stay whole.

IN THE NEXT second, I come through the other side of the vertex.

In the center of the room is a huge holoscreen made up of mini-holoscreens. Gray holograms swipe and tap and modify midair data streams from the nanoholocom network. Beyond them, a floor-to-ceiling window, and Solbiluna-8 sparkles far below us. I'm in space again. This is how they watch over the planet, a sort of control center.

Behind me, beeping. Whooshing. Human brains attached to spinal columns float in liquid, tubes and technology blinking and calculating. Half of the liquid columns have gone dark and inert. Biohologram soldiers cut down by us.

A generic hologram touches a cold device to my forehead to treat me with AM and PM to be more compliant. SIDEKICK still stands idle like a doormat. I'm going to die with the idiotic thing blinking at me.

Members of the meritocracy materialize one by one, their eyes on their bandwidths, and gather in a far corner near the windows. After all this, I can't believe they sent holographic versions of themselves. They still can't even show their real faces to watch my demise live for the planet. Unless . . .

Do they not actually exist? Are they, like, elite bioholograms? But they say "I" and show emotion. They can't be . . .

Keron swoops in. His white robe billows behind him as he

graces me with his presence. I wish I could get close enough to his robe to rip a piece off and see what he's made of.

"Alexandra Lucas," he says, "or should I say River?"

His voice is low, deep, captivating as it echoes throughout the area. It shakes inside of me like a death rattle. "We are sorry we had to resort to violence. We are not a society that believes in or condones violence. However, the meritocracy's mission is to continue Solbiluna-8 at any cost. I am glad you realized that your contribution is essential to our continued values. Essential to save your people.

"We recognized long ago that humans are never kind to outsiders. The best way to convince them is not by force, but by creating want and necessity. We allow them to contribute to a solution, and we are rewarded with gratitude and compliance. It is our greatest achievement. It is a universal construct. It works to manipulate any culture. The only reason you have suffered is because you resisted what we clearly laid out for you."

Keron unclasps his hands to swipe on a nearby holoscreen. "Without us, humans throughout time will never become the force for good that they claim to be. We decided we would fix it. Make a human utopia. Most Earths have a system of work and a system of rest. Your planet called it retirement. Over time the system becomes impossible to maintain when technology reaches a threshold, people unwilling to work during youth to fulfill their dying years, technology calling them to play. Wars begin. Earths end. We watched it happen in so many timelines.

"When our nanoholocom and biohologram programs reached capable limits, we reversed the system. It solved the problem of paying workers. No compensation necessary. There was less pollution, less waste with holographic and printable goods. Yes, we must deplete planets to build and update the nanoholocoms. It is the cost of evolution. A small price."

I try to stall, get SIDEKICK's attention, plan some attempt at survival. SIDEKICK doesn't move. Keron swipes more on a screen and whispers something to his colleagues. "Why do you even need people to contribute?" I interrupt. "Why not just create holographic programming?"

"Early holographic workers could not handle problem solving tasks in the same way as sentient forms. We needed sentient intelligence as a template."

"Why not just create drone copies of the same hologram? Using one human?"

"We did. It couldn't handle highly nuanced, complex tasks. Variety is necessary in science, much like a gene pool. When creating a holographic world with holographic beings, the differences create strengths in programming, problem solving, processing data, and understanding the finesse of human work, cultures, and language. Even then, the programming eroded at a faster rate than people die or reproduce in a modern world of leisure. The solution, every few generations, was to bring others willingly to Solbiluna-8 to replenish the system and reset the perfect system we created."

"Your world is not a utopia. It's all about lights, sounds, and technology and nothing of substance. You're not even real, are you?"

Even his smile is fake. "Solbiluna-8 is the greatest thing that will ever happen to the human race. And you will contribute to it as promised. Do you concur?"

I swallow. "Yes. As a truce."

Keron taps his bandwidth, and a holoscreen appears.

"Greetings," he declares to the screen. "Alexandra Lucas, whom many of you regard as the River, is here with members of the meritocracy, to demonstrate her trust and faith in Solbiluna-8, and to contribute as a show of her change of heart. Alex?"

He flips the holoscreen so it focuses on me. I can see my reflection, see SIDEKICK next to me, and I fidget with my bandwidth. I have to do this. *Become what I was never meant to be.*

I tap my bandwidth to officially record my decision. "My name is Alexandra Lucas. And I contribute my death to Solbiluna-8." My bandwidth beeps, and SIDEKICK automatically says, "Thank you. May your contribution lead to freedom."

The screen vanishes on Keron's orders. Members of the meritocracy debate on the other side of the room.

I know what's coming next. My contribution and then my death. I'll be subverted into a hero for their world instead of becoming a martyr for mine.

"We are mapping out your fate. We need to do this properly. Effectively."

"Are you going to kill me?"

"Yes, when the time is right. We have no reason to stop fighting, nor do we believe that your death alone will stop the rebellion."

"You promised."

"That is the thing about promises. Once we get what we want, we no longer need to compromise. You are powerless. The sooner you accept that, the better your life will be."

A high-pitch and continuous beep comes from SIDEKICK. Keron scowls and taps on a screen. The longer time passes, the swifter his tapping movements.

"No . . ." He races to the wall of windows. Other meritocracy members follow his lead.

"Brace yourself, Alexandra Lucas," SIDEKICK says.

The floors and walls tremble, knocking me off my feet. A fleet of their dart ships fire on us.

"Eliminate that hologuide program," Keron commands. "It's corroding the system and broadcasting our location."

The holograms quickly tap on all screens. SIDEKICK stands emotionless as always, unaware of its technological mortality.

"Not possible," a hologram says. "The two are locked. Program cannot be shut down unless Alexandra Lucas is eliminated."

Keron takes a moment. Another round of weapons from the ships shakes the walls, but this time I maintain my footing.

I can't die now. It solves nothing. I was doing this for Benji. For Rita. For Nolan. For Katherine. The rebels will still be under attack, outnumbered and outgunned. And Dominick . . . I've already lost so many people I love.

"There has to be another way," I say to stall, my hands shaking, my heart freezing.

Keron smiles. "Thank you for your contribution. I will personally make sure you are part of our holographic forces against the rebels you helped to create. Perhaps we will even model the hologram in your likeness." He taps and swipes on a screen, and an armed hologram appears in front of me.

I brace myself. There's nowhere to run. Nowhere to hide. A picture of my parents flashes through my mind. Dominick. Rita. Benji. Marcus. Penelope. Doctor A. Katherine. Everyone I've met. Everyone I've loved.

It can't end like this.

We can't stay in this world. We have to make it home to Earth.

"Please don't," I say, and my whole body trembles like a child afraid of the dark.

"We gave you the greatest opportunity available to humankind, freedom, and you tried to destroy us," Keron says. "Eliminate her."

The hologram shoots. A blast of white electric energy heads toward me.

SIDEKICK instantly reacts and steps between me and the

light and reflects it. The beam hits Keron and freezes him on the spot. Other members step back in horror.

"Your self-righteousness will be the downfall of the entire human species," Keron says, coming apart at the seams. He evaporates into molecules of light.

I am so grateful that I haven't died that it takes me a few minutes to catch my breath over my pounding heart before I realize what just happened. SIDEKICK grabs hold of the weapon from the hologram and slides it toward me. I fumble to hold it. Without a weapon, the hologram loses its mission and joins the others at the control unit.

Some of the meritocracy kneel before me for mercy. Others flee from the area. The holograms controlling the nanoholocom network continue their work, unconcerned. SIDEKICK takes over one of the holoscreens and clicks and swipes faster than my eyes can follow. The ships outside the station cease fire.

"SIDEKICK, you saved my life."

"Yes. We overrode the system. It was an emergency."

"Wait, *we* overrode the system, or *you, SIDEKICK,* overrode the system?"

"We. SIDEKICK."

I laugh. "You can do that?"

"New protocols established."

"I think you just like me," I joke, "since I'm your only friend."

"We do not understand."

"That's okay, you don't need to. Thanks."

"You are welcome, Mississippi."

Something Katherine said tugs at my memory. *I left you a present.*

"What did you say?"

"You are welcome, Mississippi."

CHAPTER 30
DAY 66

AFTER THE UMBRA rounds up the remaining members of the
meritocracy, the QN25 Umbra group, along with the Geotroupes,
travel to meet with the United States Secretary of State at SN10
Umbra headquarters to talk terms. SIDEKICK has to come, too,
since I still can't shut her off.

Before the general meeting, the Secretary of State shakes my
hand and thanks me for my sacrifice. He ignores SIDEKICK. I
doubt he personally knows anyone who died on Solbiluna-8. His
smile doesn't leave his face.

We gather in a nearby TriCenter to plan our exit strategy. Since
not everyone can fit inside the building, some Umbra members
are given special access to a CVBE bandwidth feed of the meeting.
I don't see why they don't broadcast it to the whole planet since
it affects everyone. I pick up another stone from the standard
waterfall feature and watch it slip away. The last time I was here,
I thought I was helping my allies, and instead I created more
enemies.

The Secretary of State conducts the meeting. Jackson and
Professor Marciani are the only QN25 members invited to sit on
the head panel. I sit with Dominick, Marcus, Penelope, Doctor
A., Beruk, Marie, Kendra, Hannah, Nolan's grandmother, and
SIDEKICK, of course. I just want to go home.

"Let's begin," the Secretary says. "The good news. We've

taken all one thousand and one members of the meritocracy into custody."

He waits for our applause, and we give it to him.

"However, during this process, we discovered that the entire meritocracy was made up of bioholograms the whole time, the oldest programs in the nanoholocom network. They were set on an original, outdated mission to continue Solbiluna-8 indefinitely regardless of cost. We have destroyed their programs so they will not repeat the same crimes in any more parallel worlds."

I lean forward from the curved stone bench and hug my legs. At least it's over. They're gone.

"We are here to weigh our options and vote," the Secretary says. "This will not be an easy decision, so please listen carefully."

I fidget in my seat, my stomach on high alert. *What won't be an easy decision?*

"It is our recommendation that the entire planet of Solbiluna-8 be destroyed."

I swear the entire room stops breathing for a few seconds. To save a world, we must destroy another. We knew this all along.

"It is also our recommendation that all bioholograms also be destroyed."

I glance at SIDEKICK. She blinks, emotionless. They were people, though. People who sacrificed themselves for the greater good. Or so they thought. *Isn't that killing them? When is enough death enough?*

The Secretary continues. "It is my understanding that some of the vances and Earth refugees would like to remain on Solbiluna-8. The problem is the planet only works if the nanoholocom network and the bioholograms are intact. Despite this opposition, the Umbra firmly agrees that the only way we can have reassurance that this crime will never happen again is if we destroy Solbiluna-8 and all bioholograms."

A woman on the panel with a shaved head speaks next. "This decision will not be popular with everyone and will affect life back on Earth. If we destroy Solbiluna-8, the vances have requested asylum on our Earth since theirs will be destroyed."

I can feel the change in the audience around me.

Penelope whispers, "I don't trust bringing them to our planet, but I don't trust leaving them here, either."

"They're victims like we were," Doctor A. says.

She touches his knee. "You're such a bleeding heart."

Jackson has the floor. "Before we vote, Professor Marciani and I spoke to the Secretary of State about a possible compromise to help assuage the situation. We want our return to Earth to go as smoothly as possible, and we understand many would rather enjoy the luxuries here. What if we promise to bring some of those luxuries to Earth? Professor Marciani?"

He twists his hair. "As a scientist, it is my recommendation to bring nanoholocom and vertex technology with us. The possibilities are too great to ignore. If this prevents a planetary outcry, even better."

The Secretary of State holds up his hand. "It is time to vote on the three issues. First, the resolution to destroy Solbiluna-8 and all bioholograms. Second, to allow asylum to the vances on Earth. And third, to bring some of the nanoholocom and vertex technology home with us. All in favor, vote using your bandwidth."

I hold my bandwidth, and a special ballot appears. My pointer finger shakes above each option. I can't do it. I close the program.

The votes are tallied, and all resolutions pass. War has complicated alliances, consequences, and agendas that you never see coming until it's too late. Once we step through the final vertexes, the remaining Umbra on spaceships will destroy the empty planet and any people, vances or Earth refugees, who refuse to leave.

Destroy one planet to save an infinite number of universes. No more choices. *New rebels wiped out in the process. Bioholograms destroyed. The moral answer. But still a type of genocide.* SIDEKICK doesn't notice as I pull a hair from the back of her head and hold on to it to prepare.

AFTER ONE LAST time in the PSF, I collect my thoughts for the journey home. SIDEKICK still stares at me.

"SIDEKICK, I'm grateful for your help, but this is ridiculous. Katherine had to give you an OFF button."

SIDEKICK blinks at me. "She did."

"She did? Why didn't you tell me?"

"You did not ask."

I shake my head and chuckle. "What's the OFF button?"

She removes the portable, black nanoholocom unit from her leg.

"We can turn off now. Mississippi is saved."

I can't tell where Katherine ends and her programming begins. I zip up my backpack.

"SIDEKICK, how do you feel about the Umbra destroying your program?"

"We have been dead a long time."

I sling my backpack onto my shoulder. "I guess this is goodbye. HOLOGUIDE, EXIT."

SIDEKICK bows. "May your contribution lead to freedom."

As soon as SIDEKICK vanishes, I miss her. She was my last tie to Katherine, one crazy and remarkable lady. I reopen my backpack and place the portable black box inside. Something to remember them by.

MY NEW AND old friends gather together in the Hub to pass through the vertexes. We must first get HME clearance, undo the sterilization process, and remove all bandwidths before departure. My naked wrist doesn't feel like my own.

"Ready?" Dominick says. "I'm nervous."

"Same. I can't wait to see my parents." The statement hangs there, full of guilt that I survived and Benji died. *What if Dad won't forgive me and Mom falls apart? What if they're not even alive after everything we've gone through? What if Earth isn't the place we left it?*

"I can't wait to take a shower," Dominick says. "I miss feeling water."

"Right?"

We laugh. It feels wrong to laugh without Rita.

I grab his hand and squeeze.

And one by one, we step through for the solo journey back home.

CHAPTER 31

DAY 71

EPILOGUE

BIG BUSINESS HAS INVESTED IN NANOHOLOCOM STOCKS

NANOHOLOCOMS WILL PROMOTE GREENER LIVING, ENVIRONMENTALISTS AGREE

UNITED NATIONS ACCEPTS NANOHOLOCOM RESEARCH PROPOSALS DESPITE LOCAL OPPOSITION

NANOHOLOCOMS WILL REVOLUTIONIZE HOW WE LIVE AND INTERACT

NANOHOLOCOMS WILL PAVE OUR FUTURE

CONVICTED FELONS MUST REPORT TO JAILS TO FINISH SENTENCES OR FACE SERIOUS PENALTIES

GRIEVING IS LIKE being trapped in an alternative world and slowly realizing there is no going home.

Mom and Dad survived a broken Earth. They made it back to our house with the help of Dad's Boston military friends. Soldiers have memories and bonds civilians do not understand. Mom had buried plastic bins of nonperishables in her garden as a backup plan after our house was ransacked, and they lived off the food. Dad posted a handwritten cardboard sign in front of our boarded-up windows that reads HAVE GUN. WILL USE.

President Lee called them before I arrived. I couldn't have

told them the news myself. Yesterday, the world attended Benji's funeral. My parents allowed live media coverage for the ceremony at the Massachusetts National Cemetery. Dad said it would help our nation heal. The military presented Marcus with the folded American flag, and Marcus gave the flag to my dad. I thought Dad was going to collapse. He told Marcus he'll always be part of our family.

People came and went from our house to offer condolences. I caught my reflection, in a black dress instead of a holofied uniform, in the parlor window, and for a long moment I wondered if the shell of the person staring at me was actually a hologram. I had to cut off one of my curls in the bathroom and leave it behind to believe again.

Last night, I slept with Mom in the room she set up for Benji when he came back to guard the vertexes, on the same quilt I wanted to inherit. I've taken a lot of showers. Benji and Rita should be here. Not me.

We have electricity only for half days, and food is being rationed until the economy recovers. President Lee has reassured everyone it's temporary. She stated that we "cannot allow what they stole from us to be our defining moment." She promised we should have things back to "business as usual" in no time. I doubt we'll ever see normal again.

In a later news brief, she mentioned the government will study the nanoholocom program "to provide innovation and freedom in our lives." Then she said that if we would like "to gain a free world of integrated holotechnology with less focus on commerce and menial work, we must be willing to lose some independence to make fundamental choices about global connectivity." Dad and I agreed that the government basically wants to replicate Solbiluna-8. Mom said we're being paranoid.

Tonight, Dominick and I held our annual beach bonfire

—without Rita. It wasn't the same, but it's all we have. He gave me a new black leather journal that I'm writing in now. At first I was afraid to write in it, afraid that it would cost more people their lives. Dominick convinced me that writing will help me recover, make sense of the insanity. We spent most of the night in silence, survivors who know the risks, sacrifices, and losses we've endured. Maybe someday it will feel worth it.

I think about the untold stories of Benji, Rita, Nolan, Katherine, and the others who contributed to our cause and lost their lives. No one even knows about Katherine Kirkwood and her sacrifice, or has mourned her death. She's somewhere lost in time. I will remember her, remember them, write about them in my journal. When the world is ready, they will hear their stories. They will hear what happened to us. We can't repeat the same mistakes.

We need to make it count.

ACKNOWLEDGMENTS

WRITING *CONTRIBUTE* WAS not the journey I expected. It's as if I stepped through a vertex into the brave new world of publishing. I want to express my gratitude to online bloggers, my local community, and early fans for their support of *CONSIDER* and anticipation of *CONTRIBUTE*. Your continued excitement and kindness got me through many ups and downs in the last year.

First, I'd like to thank Mari Kesselring and Megan Naidl from North Star Editions for their reassurance after the sale of Jolly Fish Press. To my new agent, Kathleen Rushall, for stepping in when I needed help even though you were in the middle of vacation. To my editor, TJ da Roza, for your commitment and protection of the series. I will always value our friendship.

To the Sweet Sixteen authors, thank you for sharing a fabulous debut year with me. You are all such amazing people.

To the Philip K. Dick award committee, I still can't believe it.

To Michelle Cusolito, for sending your feedback all the way from Ireland.

To Elyse Baggen and Laura LaTour, for being my local cheerleaders.

To Kristine Asselin and Erin Bow, you know what you did.

To Kylee and Dan, for your quick feedback and answers to strange questions.

To Trish and Carolyn, for listening, laughing, and keeping me real.

And of course, to my husband, Eladio, and daughters, Kylee and Chloe, for your love and patience as I run through to discover what's on the other side.

KRISTY ACEVEDO is a YA writer, high school English teacher, and huge *Star Trek*, *Doctor Who*, and *Harry Potter* fan. When she was a child, her "big sister" from the Big Brothers Big Sisters Program fostered her love of books by bringing her to the public library every Wednesday for seven years.

A member of SCBWI, she has her M.A.T. in English and graduated summa cum laude from Bridgewater State University. *CONSIDER*, her debut novel, won the 2015 PEN New England Susan P. Bloom Children's Book Discovery Award and was a finalist for the 2017 Philip K. Dick Award for Science Fiction. She lives in Massachusetts with her husband, two daughters, and two cats.

Follow her on Twitter at @kristyace

Visit her online at kristyacevedo.com